LYNCHS ROAD

by **D.D. Armstrong**

SMASH & GRAB

A complete catalogue record for this book can be
obtained from the British Library on request

ISBN 9781844266760

The right of D.D. Armstrong to be identified as the
Author of this work has been asserted by him in accordance
With Copyright Designs, and Patents Act 1988

Copyright ©2009 D.D. Armstrong

The Characters and events in this book are fictious
any similiarity to real persons dead or alive is coincidental
and not intended by the author

All rights are reserved. No parts of this book may be reproduced,
stored in a retrieval system or transmitted in any form or by
any means electronic, mechanical, photocopying, recording
or otherwise, without the prior permission of the publisher.

This book is sold subject to the condition that it shall not, by way of
trade or otherwise, be lent, re-sold, hired out or otherwise circulated
without the publishers prior consent in any form of binding or cover
other than that in which it is publisher and without a similar condition
including this condition being imposed on the subsequent purchaser.

First Published by Smash & Grab Books
www.smashandgrabbooks.com

D.D. Armstrong has asked that the Arts Council's logo
be added to this book to recognise their help and
support of his writing career.

FOREWORD BY
NOEL CLARKE

On February the 8th 2009 in front of a packed audience of celebrities and industry peers which included the likes of Brad Pitt, Angelina Jolie, Danny Boyle, and Kate Winslett, I became the first Black actor to ever receive a BAFTA award in the history of the ceremony (later that night I was joined by Steven McQueen, director of Hunger). As I held the coveted mask in my hand, I delivered my acceptance speech. It was a brief thank you to my wife, friends, family and all those who supported my career. Smiling I looked at the award and ended my speech with three words *'Yes we can.'* Who was I addressing this statement to? A swell of new up and coming British talent and the likes of D.D. Armstrong.

So who is D.D. Armstrong? Like myself he is a fellow West Londoner and author of the book you are about to read. I first met him over ten years ago, before my own career had started. Back then he was sixteen, and a close friend of my younger cousin. I don't actually remember our first meeting, but I do remember when he and my cousin later attended the same college. He was the smallest of his group and very quick tempered. To say he was a troublemaker would be unfair, but to say he invited trouble would be spot on. I recall on a number of occasions, he would turn up late to college and on asking of his whereabouts he would reply, 'I just got back from court' or 'I had to go probation.' His blasé and cavalier approach to his arrests were amusing and jokes of him getting locked up were frequent. He would often return the banter by warning everyone, 'if I get locked up I'm gonna come out hench, and bang you all over one-by-one,' before trying to wrestle everyone. He was definitely a character, and one I later honoured in my film *'Adulthood'* (D-dee appeared and was played by Fraser Ayres in a prison scene).

As I moved into acting and my career started to take off, I would see D.D. on my way to auditions or filming. He would always wish me luck or congratulate me on a new role, expressing his excitement at seeing me on television. When I'd ask him what he was up to, a broad grin would cross his face and he'd say, "You know me, the same old, same olds. The usual innit." Eventually the same old, same olds and the usual led D.D. to serving time in both Wandsworth and Bellmarsh maximum security prison.

When my cousin told me D.D. was inside I'd like to say it saddened or shocked me, but it didn't. Like a lot of young black men, D.D. was fulfilling the only role in society he knew and as he will readily tell you, it didn't surprise anyone when he went jail. Fast-forward a few years to 2006 my career was flourishing. I'd been in a number of stage productions and notable prime time television programmes including Doctor Who, and I was preparing to premiere my first feature *'Kidulthood'*. It was then after a screening and Q&A session in Battersea that I bumped into D. I hadn't seen him in ages (he hadn't got hench) and he came strutting over smiling to congratulate me. He's exact words were 'That films' a good look brother. It's gonna be big. It's good to see you doing your ting.' It was a phrase that I would later become accustomed to hearing.

As the success and popularity of *'Kidulthood'* grew to cult status, I realised it was people like D.D. that I was representing in my movies. Me *'doing my thing'* as he would later tell me meant *'doing your thing for us.'* It is the sole reason why *'Adulthood'* went to UK Box office number one in the summer of '08, because there is an audience that want their story told. This put me in a position of great responsibility. Primarily I am an actor, but after *Kidulthood*, I knew that I wanted to write a sequel that addressed the consequence of the behaviour and mentality displayed in the film. Immediately I realized that this could only be achieved by using Sam as the lead. At the end of *'Kidulthood'* Sam the film's antagonist provided the biggest character arc, with the catalyst for change stemming from his future time in jail. It was this factor that gave me the opportunity to reconnect with D.D.

After writing the first drafts of *'Adulthood'* I met with D.D. in the late summer of 2007. I invited him for brunch at Balans restaurant in Kensington on a warm Sunday morning. To my surprise when I got there D.D. was early. He sat outside waiting for me quietly reading a book. As we entered I told him to order what he wanted, he declined informing me that he was fasting. We got down to business and discussed in depth the psyche of men whom frequently went in and out of jail. We also looked at key points and various scenarios that could push a character into different directions. As we conversed I noticed for the first time D.D.'s new demeanour. He had changed. He was a lot calmer and placid and for the first time he showed me another side to his character. By the end of the meeting one thing that struck me about D.D. was his ability to recount and articulate his experiences with an amazing detail and I decided to bring him on board the film as a consultant.

As he told me story after story, I shook my head in disbelief. I looked at him and told him he needed to write a book. Grinning he told me 'I've already written two.' The First *'Lynch's Road'* as you will discover, is phenomenal, not only in its style, but in its ambition and scope. The book has two timelines. One set in the late nineties, telling the exploits of Gilyan Gates a young drug dealer and the second set in the present. The second timeline shows three characters reading Gilyan's autobiography and is used as a device to illustrate today's attitude towards social problems. The books complexity make it an interesting and timely piece of writing given Britain's current issues of drugs and gun crime. It's a unique book that takes the reader on a conscious journey and rollercoaster ride of emotions. It cleverly explores the ongoing psyche of not only young black men, but historical attitudes towards them. It is brutally honest and unashamedly violent. In this book D.D. depicts a world that show little compassion for its shortcomings while allowing you to comprehend why? Like *Kidulthood* and *Adulthood* it is set in the backdrop of West London and reflects London's segregation between social classes (rather than colour) permitting us to witness how the worlds of the 'have's' and 'have-nots' only collide during acts of crime. The books opening line *"Boo-who, boo-who, pour me another one. So what if he's black, so what if he comes from some shoddy council estate, why should we care?"* is genius. It questions the level of responsibility we all have on society and our actions. For me *'Lynch's Road'* may truly be one of the most important pieces of writing in Black British literature and sets a new precedent.

The night I accepted my BAFTA, I expressed to the world that with hard work and determination you could do anything. The next morning when my head cleared, I looked through the numerous texts on my mobile phone. One of the first texts was from D.D., it read – Brap I told u bruv well done G. Yes we can...yes u did...gwan... bless Dd. So in the completion and publication of *'Lynch's Road'* I'd like to return the sentiment to my dear friend and say
        'Yes we can...Yes u did... Gwan D,'

        Bless Clarkey

ACKNOWLEDGEMENTS

First and foremost I would like to thank Allah the most merciful and beneficial for whom nothing is possible. I'd like to thank determination and perseverance that saved me from myself. My mother and family for constantly making me the black sheep (note the price of black wool just went up). To my older brother Troy for every beat down he ever gave me. To my enemies that thought they could destroy me (you should've realised it's not that easy). To every punter I ever sold to. To Marley and my cousin Nas for teaching me everything they knew. To my Uber and Czar Fam I don't need to mention your names you know who you are. To my partners in crime, love you for life, Lapz, Big Ty, Robo, Sawnoff, Scarface Sean and Monte. To all my eleven brothers and sisters I got love for you all no matter what, especially Baby Bros Day-Day & Marc'os, my twin Deek'os, Crazy Nat, Naf and the feral kids. To Graham Langley and all the other heads I was locked up with. To my brother Liban Ali aka Miserable. To my bredrin Yardie Gary and Big Ewing T it hurt me the day they freed me and lifed you off. All My Brothers in Jail keep your heads up. Big Shout to my lil cuz Stevie-O and Le Cha for all the help. Big shout to Muriel too. Thanks to my cousin Carla and her big mouth. Everyone I ever did a move with or ever worked with. To my whole Sugakane fam Alaye and Big Money Beth C. *'Plutz'* I don't know where this road is gonna lead, but as long as it goes somewhere lets do our ting. Des had to squeeze you in. To all those who passed before their time Jay-Jay, Havoc and Jam I'll never forget you save a place for me upstairs. To my Granny who always keeps it raw, whether it was with a belt or slipper, love you loads Mrs Roach. To everyone that I forget to mention you know me, there's always love. Last shout to the everyday unsung heroes and those who will read and understand what I'm putting out.

Peace and one love D-Dee

This book is dedicated to my **Superboy** *son* **Niran**
and the Power of Knowledge & Dreams

CHAPTER: 1

"Boo-who, boo-who, pour me another one. So what if he's black, so what if he comes from some shoddy council estate, why should we care?" The words boomed across the crowded room and received a number of looks. "The problem with society nowadays, is everyone wants to put some sort of spin on wrongdoing."

"I'm not trying to spin anything. Nor am I asking you to care. I'm asking Claire to take his situation into account." The second statement rung out just as loud and TV executive Claire Bareham tried to settle her two colleagues as people began to stare. She looked up at the stained glass window and asked the smiling Michelin man who rode his bicycle and smoked his cigar not to let them spoil her meal. The Michelin man grinned and used his coloured glass to cast a number of blue and yellow patterns on the table, but it didn't help. Dinning in the plush Bibendum restaurant in South Kensington, Claire was joined by producer Anna Allender and director Libby Proudfoot from her production company *Nedu Associates*. Her two friends were famous for their heated debates and today's riveting topic was the departure of Marcel a young production runner. Listening Claire sliced her roast quail and wiped the meat in the armagnac and thyme dressing.

"Why? How's his situation relevant?" Libby quizzed. She poured another glass of red Bordeaux and gulped half.

"Because," Anna huffed, "he's the only black member of personnel in a staff of 20-30, and he's the only person accused of stealing."

"Because he's the only person been caught stealing." Libby slammed down her fork and sat back. She covered her mouth as she spoke with her mouth full. "He's a bloody thief."

"And you're flipping slanderous."

"Okay, that's enough." Claire stopped the two executives from bickering. "Libby, Marcel was not caught stealing."

"Okay then," Libby swallowed the rest of her wine. "What do you call it when somebody's caught dipping into petty cash without permission?"

"A misunderstanding," Claire answered.

"Of course it is, Claire." Libby scoffed. "A bit like when Geoff was caught sleeping with his secretary; he didn't *mean* to fuck her, it was just a misunderstanding."

"That's below the belt," Claire pointed her knife. The subject of her recent divorce was still a touchy one. "I suggest you make your point or move on."

"Well I'm sorry," Libby threw her hands in the air. "Sometimes certain things need to be said. Especially if people like Marcel are going to call the race card. I think you've been way too soft on him. If it were me, I would have had him arrested."

"On what grounds?" Anna protested. "The poor boy said he was asked to get a black cab for a client."

"So," Libby shrugged her shoulders before filling her mouth.

"Claire," Anna pled. "Please tell her again what happened."

"Libby you really haven't been listening," Claire sighed. "Marcel explained he had been asked by, Barnaby Routh to get a black cab for one of the corporate clients. He reasoned that in his experience, black cabs didn't stop for black men, unless they're waving money. He said he didn't have any notes on him so he went to get some from the petty cash."

"And that's when he was caught stealing?" Libby twisted Claire's words.

"No you stupid cow," Anna dropped her cutlery. "That's when Sean Moore-Tearing accused him of stealing."

"So why did Claire fire him for calling the race card?"

"Libby." Claire gestured to Libby to lower voice. "No one ever said he called the race card?"

"Of course he did." Libby insisted. "He practically marched into your office waving it."

"That's it, I'm finished," Anna crossed her arms and pushed her plate away. "She's completely ruined my meal."

"Look," Claire gave Anna a consoling pat on the arm. "Let me reiterate the story again so everyone's got it correct, then that's it."

"Fine," Libby rolled her eyes and zipped her mouth. "If it pleases some."

Claire tried again. "When Sean told me about the incident he said that all cash must be signed out by accounts using the right procedures, blah, blah, blah and advised me that Marcel should be fired for gross misconduct."

"I can't flipping stand that Sean Moore-Tearing," Anna interrupted. "He's such a jumped up little Hitler."

"Hold on a minute, let me finish." Claire hushed Anna politely. "Now Marcel argues that there wasn't enough time to find someone from accounts, and that's why he was in the cash box. Now I wasn't going to fire him over that. So in light of the situation I decided to give him a written warning."

"Good." Libby said raising her glass. She ignored the indignant stare Anna shot her way. She wiped her mouth with the napkin. "What happened next?"

"Well Marcel refused to accept it. He said that he thought we embraced the idea of cultural differences, but as soon as something goes wrong we used those same differences to alienate him into a stereotype. He said that he was only being accused of theft because he was black, and accepting any warning only justified the accusation."

"So that's when the big fat race-card came out?" Libby hurled more wine in her glass before sipping.

"Look can you stop saying that." Anna snapped. She snatched the bottle from Libby and placed it on the other side of the table. "I really can't believe you're attitude towards this situation. If it happened in another office you'd be saying lets make a documentary about it exposing the underlining racism in the industry."

"Bullshit." Libby said pulling her face in disdain.

"Pardon."

"I said, bullshit." Libby repeated herself. She wasn't the type to entertain any nonsense. "This is the industry he chose. It's not Claire's fault that he feels alienated. If someone chooses to be a minority at work, then they can't sit around complaining about it. "

"That's easy for you to say." Anna argued. "But he's a young black man in a not only predominately white industry, but a middle class industry that must seem like miles away from the environment he's use to."

"And that's our problem, how?" Libby brushed the matter to the side. She refused to conceive any reason why Marcel should be treated differently. "Our problem is to act professionally in the work environment and produce quality programmes. Marcel's a bloody runner for Christ sake, he's suppose to do as he's told. I mean bloody hell, Anna, anybody would think you were shagging him the way you leap to his defence."

"How dare you insult my integrity like that." Anna seethed. "We don't all drop our knickers at the first guy that walks by like you."

"Maybe you should," Libby raised an eyebrow. "Maybe Marcels exactly the runner you need, all that energy; and he's black." Libby smiled at Claire as Anna's mouth gaped open. "Have you been with a black guy before, Anna?" She began to tease. "I once went with a black guy. You know what they say don't you? Well this one had the biggest..."

"Libby!" Claire stepped in. "May I please continue, before you say anything else that's deemed inappropriate."

"Claire, please do," Anna insisted. "Somebody's obviously drunk too much."

"What?" Libby frowned. She wiped the lipstick smear off her glass. "I was only going to talk about his feet. Size 14 they were."

Claire laughed and signalled to the waiter that they were finished. "Anyway, whether Marcel is a runner or not," Claire continued. "I admire his stance. Foolish as it was, he demanded that Sean apologised to him or he'd resign."

"Are you serious?!" Anna's eye's lit up.

"Deadly." Claire grinned. She leaned back, as the waiter cleared her plate and passed the desert menus. Looking on the menu she ordered the chocolate truffles with vanilla ice cream, thinking her *Atkin's diet* could wait a day. "Marcel apologised to me and said, he couldn't work in an environment where the company culture worked against him."

"Good for Marcel!" Anna beamed. "That Sean's a bloody troublemaker. He's always got some bee in his bonnet." She said refilling her glass for the first time.

"Well." Libby said in a condescending tone. "I don't see what he accomplished by throwing away a perfectly good job. For all we know that could be his way of covering up his act of stealing."

"I suppose you know all about stealing?" Anna sneered. "You threw that U shaped astray in your handbag as soon as we got through the door."

"Ha!" Libby scoffed. "For your information I haven't stolen anything. The ashtrays are a signature piece of the restaurant; they expect us to take it. The cost is covered by our mandatory 15% service charge, I doubt Marcel can say the same."

"Oh, Libby behave." Claire weighed in as referee. "You know Marcel's not a thief. He's a very nice guy and a hard worker. As a matter of fact he gave me this book when he came by the office to pick up his P45 today."

Claire reached into her bag and handed Anna a paperback book.

"The Journey Of A Slave, what's it about?"

"I have no idea." Claire said flicking a small piece of cress off the table. "Marcel said it was a thank you present for all the help."

"Hmm, a thank you present," Libby looked at the book. "Too bad he didn't give one to Anna. Then maybe we'd have a great topic for a documentary. 'How do men with big feet's, girth ratio match to the diameter of horny middle class female producers' vaginas."

"Libby!" Claire laughed as Anna kicked Libby under the table.

They continued to converse about office antics until it was time to leave. The three women left the restaurant in giggles and laughter feeling like they were in a scene from *'Sex and the City'*. Kissing her friends, Claire said goodbye and headed to her BMW X5 parked around the corner. Climbing into the luxury 4x4 Claire glanced at the time on her Patek Philippe. The time was twenty past nine. The thought of a nice warm comforting bath distracted Claire as she pulled out almost clipping a blue Vauxhall Corsa.

*

The traffic was light as Claire hastily made her way to her semi-detached house in Chiswick. Immediately kicking off her shoes she made her way straight up the stairs and into the bathroom. Lighting the aromatherapy candles Feng-shui around the mint green suite, Claire ran the taps and poured in a healthy potion of bath salts into the kidney shaped tub. It was time for relaxing. Fiddling with her Bang and Olfusen sound system she selected a CD and strip-teased to the sounds of Prince. Throwing her clothes into a pile on the bedroom floor, she grabbed a towel and her silk robe. Testing the scented water Claire smiled and hurried to retrieve her handbag. She pulled out the book Marcel had given her. Tying her hair in a bundle Claire slipped out her robe and climbed into the tub. Slowly she submerged her body beneath the warm bubbles and h_2o. Claire hadn't a clue why Marcel chose to give her the autobiography of a drug dealer, but with an open mind she began to read.

THE JOURNEY OF A SLAVE

By Gilyan Gates

CHAPTER 1: CROSSROADS   *The Journey of a Slave.*

They say that life is a constant journey from the moment of birth, to your final breath. But have you ever asked yourself what is this journey, and where exactly is it taking you? Are there any tour guides, maps, crossroads, trains, planes or automobiles that will make the journey any easier? Perhaps you asked, who else is on this journey and do we choose our companions upon the way? Is this journey what I really want, and ultimately will I be happy when the journey is over? Of course you have, because you are only human. But what and where are the answers to assist you on this mystical and often mythical journey. Some may tell you it lies in religion. But with so many contradicting, conflicting and all too often confusing religions, with hierarchies, dogma, sacred scrolls, scriptures, and new age life energy answers how do you make the right choice?

There are those who will say that it is buried in the histories past. But if history is quoted "*doomed to always repeat itself*" where, oh where does that leave the likes of you and me? You see there are some questions that you can't answer, and I try to say this without being patronising. It's like when a child asks a question for example "why is the sky blue daddy?" And you reply because God made it that way (that's if you are amongst those who have chosen a specific religion to guide your journey). Now the child with all their innocents and zest for life continues "But why did he choose blue, Daddy? Why not red or green?" In reality no matter what you tell your child at this point to supplement their newly found thirst for knowledge is irrelevant. Because just like that child you don't know the answer. So what do you do when looking for answers? – Me? I deal with the questions that I can answer.

It was a cold autumn night as I headed to Darren and Jane's flat. They lived in a quiet council estate at the back of Fulham, behind the South Park. The estate was always deserted at night, which is how I usually preferred it. I rode my bike past the shops at the front of the estate and towards the block that Darren lived in. Reaching into my pocket I read the time on my mobile phone. It was approximately 3:40am as the ring tone broke the eerie silence.

"Hello, Janey," I said. "Where are you at the phone box? Okay, luv, meet me upstairs... Yeah, that's right, sweetheart I'm just outside the block".

Looking at the last number I knew Jane was on the other side of the estate, probably racing to me. When shottin', juggling, or running gear (whichever you prefer to call it) you become accustomed to recognising the numbers of the local phone boxes. It helps you get an idea of who was going to be on the end of the line asking for what and how far you were from them. Amused I smiled realizing I had finally perfected my wide-boy accent. For some reason the punters seemed to respond better to the Jack-the-lad voice. It knocked the edge off the reality of what we were doing. It was as if they preferred giving their money to a cheeky toe-rag than a predatory drug dealer. It made the impersonal, personal and placed us all in the same boat. Thinking of the punters and me in the same boat, my smile quickly disappeared and I let out a sigh. *Whatever...*

At the block I rang the intercom. Darren, Jane's husband answered the buzzer. " Who is it? " he said in a strong Irish accent.

"It's me, Gil."

"Oh come up, mate, come up," Darren said buzzing me into the block.

I rolled my bike into the tiny lift and pressed the button for the second floor. Reading the graffiti on the walls I thought to myself, *'Yeah I like Darren and Jane, they're good punters always got the right money, no complaints, no short change'*. It was how you wanted all your customers to be hassle free.

As the lift opened, Jane came running up the stairs. "You alright, Gil luv," she said. "Sorry to call you out so late."

"Its alright, darling." I said propping my bike up to hold the lift door. "I'd rather you phone me then someone else."

"No, no, Gil," Jane said opening the front door. She ushered me in. "I always phone you and Mel first. You're the best out of all the lads round here. You always come nice and quick. Some of these other guys tell you they're gonna be five minutes and they take all of half an hour. I don't understand why they can't be like you, Gil? Either they've got it or they haven't."

"Well that's the problem right there, Janey," I grinned and tugged on my coat. "Not many of them got it like me."

"That is so true" Jane smiled with her black mouth. Her thin lips caused her oily face to wrinkle. "Darren!" She called inside. "Gil's here!"

"Ahhh you alright, Gil." Darren said coming out the living room. He was about 5'10 with greyish brown hair. He walked with a slight hunch and a heavy limp, which made him struggle with every step.

"I'm cool, bruv. How's the leg?"

"Ah it's still bad," Darren said pulling up his trouser leg. His pink ankle had swollen to the size of a small melon and showed signs of bruising. "The swelling hasn't gone down. It's gone all hard round here." He prodded at his leg. "I think it might be infected."

"Oooww," I said pulling my face. "Daz, mate you wanna go to the hospital and get that sorted out. That, don't look right brother. How long 'as it been like that?"

"Almost six weeks now. It weren't so bad at first, but now I tell you, Gil my man, I just want to chop it off."

"Oh put you leg away, Darren," Jane said slapping Darren's back. "Gil doesn't want to see that. I told you not to go and buy from Inches, now look at you."

"Well how was I suppose to know he mixes his shit with fucking brick dust?" Darren waved his fist.

"I Flipping told you!" Jane slapped him again. "You never listen. Just shut up and give Gil the money so he can get out of here. He doesn't want to stand around all night listening to you."

Darren rolled his eyes and smiled. "Sorry, Gil."

"It's alright mate," I said spitting out the contents of my mouth into my hand. "What did you want?"

"Ah can I get two and two, Gil my man?"

Using my jumper I quickly wiped the saliva off the wraps. I picked out two red and two blue. I always wrapped my work in different colour bags so I could automatically identify which was brown and which was yeng. I exchanged them with Darren for £80 in crisp notes. As I counted my money, Darren squeezed the two blue heroin wraps to see how much was product and how much was wrapping. He handed the two red wraps to Jane. Quickly she disappeared into the living room as Val stepped into the passageway, followed by her gormless boyfriend Rufus.

"You alright Gil?" She said preparing to soften me up. "Listen, luv, true we all just brought those off you." Val indicated to the wraps in Darren's hand. "Could you throw in another rock to buff up the pot?" She said giving me a quick wink and a nudge.

Repulsed, I looked at the sloppy white woman in her early forties who tried to fit into a pink velour tracksuit, two sizes too small. Her love handles hung out with huge stretch marks on display. Disgusted I watched as she plucked at a discoloured thong from between her buttocks.

"No." I said, keeping it plain and simple.

Throwing back her mousy brown hair, Val clapped her hands together as though praying. "Please, Gil. You know we're gonna phone you again tomorra. Go on, luv."

"Yeah," Rufus added to her plea. "Come nah, Gil."

"No" I said unmoved.

You see if Darren and Jane were the type of punters you wanted then, Val and Rufus were the type you didn't. I could see their play instantly. Somehow Val and Rufus had managed to meet up with Darren and Jane, just as they got some money. They'd probably helped Darren and Jane sell some goods or something. Now because they helped Darren and Jane sell the goods, they claim they're owed a smoke. Jane then calls me to come round, and after Darren makes a purchase, Val then asks for an extra stone, claiming that the purchase was for all of them. If I then gave them the stone, that's Val and Rufus's free smoke, plus anything they take from Darren and Jane.

Right, this is where a hustler distinguishes between a punter and a cat. The punter is that sweet customer that gives no problems. All they want is their wraps, good gear, a quick service and they're happy. The cat on the other hand is just like that annoying house cat that's always there when you want to eat, always begging, always whining and always moaning. A cat is always scheming on a free stone or bag. Always got a story why they're short with money and always wants some tick or credit, which they'll pay back tomorrow or at the end of the week. This is why they're called cats because all their whining sounds like cat meows. That persistent meow, that makes you want to kick them. Now you see I have a lot of time for punters, but little time for cats. If they didn't make me so much money I'd put them in a bag and drown 'em.

"Oh come nah, Gil," Rufus said placing his hand on my shoulder. Then he quickly decided to move it. "Listen, Gil, me get paid at de en' of de week man. Don't worry, me mek sure me pay you back."

Rufus was a dark skinned Jamaican with short fat dreadlocks that stopped just short of his shoulders. He covered them at all times with a black woolly hat with an embroidery cannabis leaf. His big hands were forever dry and hard from labouring on the building sites.

Val and Rufus were a right pair. They suited each other. He was the so-called breadwinner, but Val called all the shots. There was something about them that irritated me. It was as though they thought they were smarter than you, like they constantly planned to get one over on you. They'd give you every excuse and try every trick and when you didn't budge they tried to make you feel guilty. In my early days some of their tricks worked, but by now I was a seasoned vet, and the same gags didn't cut it in tonight's show.

"Nope, can't do it, mate," I said moving to the door.

"Come nah, Gil man, me giv' you on Friday." Rufus said desperately.

"Nope."

I guess it wasn't the fact that I didn't believe I'd get my money on Friday. I was growing accustomed to hating cats like Val and Rufus that couldn't take no for an answer. They'd abused the trade relationship we had in the past and I didn't see why I should compromise now. It was strictly Sparks' rules now; NO Tick, NO Change, NO Shorts.

"Please, Gil, me begging you." Rufus said blocking my exit. "Friday, me pay you back Friday."

"Nope," there was almost a smile on my face. "When you can go in Sainsbury's, pick up whatever you like, and tell them I'll pay you back on

Friday, den come back and we'll talk. Otherwise I think you need to phone Inches. I hear he's got some good brick dust."

Rufus held his arms wide in surrender. "Gil, why you gwanin like dat?"

Smirking, I shrugged my shoulders opening the door. Rufus continued to beg.

"Oh leave him, Rufus!" Val yelled in frustration. They were still behind me. "He's a tight bastard anyway." I wasn't going to reply to her insult, but she persisted.

"Are you listening, you tight bastard!? I hope your mother's proud of you! She probably charged you when you was born, for climbing out her cunt!"

In an instant I answered Val's question. I was listening. I hit her twice in the mouth with the butt of my phone. As she crashed to her knees, I followed through with a kick to the mid-section and a blow to the temple. Rufus jumped in to save her, but as I turned on him, he backed up. The slamming of Darren and Jane's door quickly brought me to my senses. I grabbed my bike and hurried down the stairs. I looked at my hand. My knuckle had already begun to swell. As I rode out of the estate, I could see Val banging on Darren and Jane's door. I knew they weren't going to open that door anytime soon. Val stood outside, mouth bleeding and dazed. Good I thought. I hope I knocked out a tooth.

I started peddling faster as Rufus chased behind me shouting, "Yo, Gil, comeback man! You must hav'fe tick me till tomorrow for that star. You can't just beat up my woman like so. Come man, sort me out!"

Fleeing the estate, I hadn't noticed the Patrol car approaching on the opposite side. My heartbeat rose, and my eyes met with the officer in the passenger seat. His blue eyes scrutinized me as we drew level. I watched them dart from me, to the wretched crackhead, running up the street calling my name. Instinctively my legs began pumping rapidly. I didn't need to look back to know they were going to give chase. I heard the change in gears and rise in revs. Immediately I formed a plan. Cutting down a side road, I tried doubling back on myself and headed towards South Park. The gates were locked, but I managed to throw my bike over. Climbing over, I heard the sound of a reversing car speeding towards me. Peddling I sped across the desolate park. From the darkness behind me, a white shirt clambered over the gate. As I reached the far side my bicycle chain came off. I threw the ridgeback to the floor. Scaling the spiked fence I jumped down. The sound of sirens was in the air. I could hear *'blue eyes'* calling. "Stop! Stop!" He cried.

I bolted to the top of the street and across the Wandsworth Bridge road. I looked at the looming towerblock in front of me. I didn't want to run inside and be trapped, but without my bike I would never make it home. Luckily I knew the intercom was bust. I ran in and up to the first floor. I made sure *'blue eyes'* was giving chase. I could hear his heavy shoes slapping against the stairs. Jumping off the balcony, I looked up while *'blue eyes'* stared down. He was out of breath and I smiled.

"Stop!" He shouted, but I was on my toes, as I saw the patrol car shoot past.

I headed for Townmead Road and the back of Sainsbury's supermarket. I could hear the sirens closing in on me. Running out of steam, I refused to be caught. Reaching the back of Sainsbury's, I climbed into one of the large disposal bins and hid.

Sitting in a pile of waste and rubbish, I tried to catch my breath. My chest heaved up and down. I tried to control my lungs, but the smell of rotten eggs was suffocating. For the next hour, I sat in the rancid spot thinking of three things. One I wasn't getting arrested tonight, two I was gonna kill Val and Rufus, and three - it was amazing what I would do for a little money and the thought that was living.

The next morning I began dwelling on the night's events. It would be one of the many times when I would look at my life and query what was I doing? Where was I going in life? I had too. Gradually I realized if this was living - then it wasn't living right. I wondered whether this was all that was out here for me? How the hell did I get here, and was this what I truly wanted from life? In truth compared to some of the things I've seen and done, the event was - *minor*. Yet it still marked a point in my life, a point in my journey where I was met with a turning point or a crossroad.

You see if there are crossroads and turning points in your life. Then it truly seems as though we are on a journey. Faced with this fact, does it mean that your journey or my journey can be determined by other factors in place before we are born? The answer must be yes. If you agree then would it be fair to say that a whole generation, or number of generations, or even a race maybe placed on the same journey. While on my journey I stumbled upon factors, which were installed centuries ago that would mean the misguidance of many black brothers and sisters that are still relevant today in the 21st century. Like my ancestors that walked in shackles and chains before me, my peers that walk in present day Nike Air's, and for my successors that will walk in the footwear of tomorrow. This is my journey, a journey of enlightenment, a journey of conscious awaking, and a journey of realisation. *This is my story* 'THE JOURNEY OF A SLAVE.'

Finishing the first chapter Claire was fascinated by the authors introduction. She wondered where the book was heading. Engrossed by the theme, Claire thought it might make a good documentary. She flipped to the front pages to read the author's brief.

Gilyan Gates was born in West London. ***'Journey of a Slave'*** *is his real life account, detailing his escape from the lure of the drug dealers and criminals that plagued his area.*

Sighing, the passage made Claire think of Marcel. She pondered whether he'd been exposed to similar scenes detailed in the first chapter. Running the hot water Claire posed what would happen to Marcel now he'd left Nedu Associates. *Marcel wouldn't sell drugs* she concluded *he's not the type.* Reaching for the soap Claire paused. She thought she heard someone coming up the stairs. Then dismissed it, remembering she still needed to feed her cat Thompson.

***

CHAPTER: 2
WE WERE AT THE BIBENDUM TOO.

Mark and Roland drove down Brompton road in silence. They hadn't been scanning the West End for long before they saw her. She came out of that fancy restaurant in South Kensington, the one with the stained glass Michelin man. (If you ask Mark he'll tell you all about it). She looked as though she had money. Mark was sure of it. The couture of her jacket, the style of her Manolo Blahnik straps, the small flash of ice from her bracelet; they all stood out like a sign saying rob me.

Mark enjoyed studying womens' and fashion magazines. They were like case studies detailing what the rich and famous wore, where they ate, and how much they were spending. Research was imperative in his profession. Knowing the latest fashion trends enabled Mark to select who was the most profitable to rob.

His eyes homed in on her, the one in the Cavalleli raincoat. She had left the restaurant with two others, but she seemed to standout. There was a confidence in her stride. Something that equalled money, Mark could sense it. Pointing her out, he told Roland to follow her slowly in the car.

A few years ago they would have pounced on her as she turned the corner. Like a pair of hyenas, they would've clamped her and savagely ripped the *kettle* (watch) off her arm. The bracelet would've gone too. Now things were different. Now Mark needed to capitalise on his prey. His environment was forever changing. Street robbery drew too much attention, too many witnesses, too many have-a-go heroes, too many cameras; they all amounted to too many ways to go back to jail. No nowadays Mark followed his targets to their homes. As the woman turned the corner Roland almost lost her.

"Where's she gone!" Roland shouted frantically scratching his neck and turning the steering wheel.

"There!" Mark yelled. "She's there, getting into the X5."

Mark's eye was like an eagle's, watching and waiting for the right moment. "Turn around," he ordered Roland, pulling at the steering wheel. "Quick, quick, man, I don't wanna lose her." He slammed his fist on the dashboard.

The side road was narrow. Luxury cars were parked either side. Roland was forced to drive past the silver BMW before he could turn round. Suddenly the woman pulled her X5 out wildly causing Roland to swerve the blue Corsa out off the way. Furious, he made a three point turn on the narrow street and followed the woman.

"Not so close, Rolly," Mark warned. "I don't want her clocking the car!" He told Roland to fall back a few cars.

Rubbing his clammy palms in his trouser leg, Mark could feel his nerves tingling. It was the beginning of an adrenaline rush. It always happened whenever he followed behind them.

"Don't lose her, don't lose her." He whispered to himself. *"Just let her get back to her crib and we're live. I'm sure of it, she's the one."*

Mark's nerves danced a mumbo until they reached their destination. But his instincts were right. He smiled as he watched the silver X5 pulling into the driveway of the prestige Chiswick house. They parked their car a little further down, so they could observe the house without being seen. Together they sat in silence and waited.

The road remained quiet and empty. Not a single car had driven down the road in over 15 minutes and Mark assured himself it was time. They'd been outside for almost half an hour. All the downstairs lights, bar one, were still off and there didn't seem to be a sign of anyone else returning. Thinking, Mark thumped Roland in his chest. "Stop that man! What's wrong with you?" Roland's constant fidgeting and scratching had become irritating. "Why don't you try taking a bath?"

"I ain't got time for no bath." Roland said digging away at his neck back. "I need a smoke man, what's going on?" He said picking the black dirt from beneath his nail. "Are we going to do this or not?"

Mark looked at the clock on the dashboard. It read ten past ten. He couldn't wait, it was now or never. He picked up his gloves and balaclava. "Alright come we go."

They moved in the dark shadows like phantoms. Even when they were under the streetlight they were unseen. As they ran up the driveway like two ninjas, the stones from the pebbled drive made a light crushing noise.

Mark moved swiftly to the side of the house ignoring the front door. Hugging the side of the wall he pulled Roland by the collar. "Check to see if there's any dogs," he said pushing Roland forward.

"That's fuckery, blood. Why me? Why can't you go?"

"Cos I said you," Mark slapped Roland round the ear. "Stop moaning and fucking hurry up."

Roland trotted round the other side of the wall and out of sight. Mark waited and scoped his surroundings. The high garden fencing and shrubbery would screen them from nosy neighbours. Looking up, there was a light on upstairs. *She must be in her bedroom or something* he thought. Roland returned signalling for Mark to come. "There's no dog," Roland said. "But there is a cat flap on the back door. We might have to boot off the front door."

"Don't be so stupid." Mark whispered. He pulled out a set of Jimmy-keys he'd recently stolen from a Locksmith's van. Fiddling with the lock Mark prised open the door. "That's the bang-bang baby we're in. Come we go."

"Could you be the most beautiful girl in the world? Plain to see, you're the reason why God made a girl," Claire sang along to her Prince CD as she dried herself off and wrapped her towel around her wet body. Taking a minute to feel her breast for any lumps, she thought, *I wish Prince was here to feel my breast. He could feel them and a whole lot more.* Picking up the book she'd been reading, she headed to the bedroom, imagining a night alone with Prince. Suddenly a white light flashed before Claire, as her legs gave way and her body crashed to the floor. Her nose began to bleed and a sharp pain began to flood in. A hand grabbed her by the hair and draped her off the floor.

Oh my god I'm being robbed, I'm being robbed, ran through Claire's mind at a hundred miles an hour. Her first instinct was to scream, scream loud, somebody would hear her. Maybe Mrs Johnson next door would hear. Yes she would hear her screaming and call the police. Yet her scream couldn't come. It was too late. He pinned her against the wall and covered her mouth. His firm hand clenched her jaw.

"If you make a noise, I'll hurt you, do you unnerstan'?"
Shivering trying to hold onto her towel, Claire looked into his yellow eyes. The dark pupils sat in the middle. It was the only thing she could see. Her heart began to race, as he pressed harder on her mouth.

"Do you unnerstan', yes or no?"

Claire answered with a petrified nod. His body was pressing against hers. She could feel he was becoming aroused. His body odour was strong. No, intense. It burnt away at Claire's nostrils. His body weight crushed Claire against the wall. Leaning closer, he sniffed her like an animal smelling another's scent. Suddenly, Claire was thrown into a deeper panic as he began to stroke the wet hair from her face. She could only see his eyes between the holes in the balaclava, but she could tell he was smiling. She didn't know where to look. He looked her up and down, all the time grinning underneath the mask. Running a leathered gloved finger across her body he stared. *Do something*, Claire thought, *he's going to rape you*. The two self-defence lessons Claire attended were worthless as she stood against the wall, paralysed with fear.

"Who else is in the house?"

"Nobody, please don't hurt me please..."

"Be quiet!" The man cut her off. "Where's your husband?"

"I, I don't have one, please."

"You, bes' not be lying," the man pointed his finger in her face.

"No," Claire flinched. "It's just me."

Roland could tell she wasn't lying. The terror in her face lay as proof. The thought that this woman would now do exactly what he said amused him. Grabbing her arm Roland dragged her towards the bedroom.

"Noooo please!" Claire screamed falling to the floor. "Please don't hurt me please. Take whatever you want. I won't call the police. Please, please I'm begging you, don't hurt me."

It was useless. Roland picked her up and tossed her into the room.

"What the fucks wrong with you?" Mark yelled at the sight of the screaming woman. "Where's her clothes?"

"She ain't got none," Roland said pushing Claire into the corner. "She was coming out the bath, when I grabbed her. She says she's the only one in here. She ain't got no husband or nothing like that."

"Okay fucking shut her up and find her something to put on."

Mark moved around the room frantically in a blur of chaos. To the untrained eye it looked as though he was ransacking the room. Mark knew exactly what he was doing. Every draw and cupboard was emptied out one by one. Always on the bed and then anything of worth went into a pillowcase. Everything else was thrown in one corner.

Wiping the blood from Claire's nose with a towel, Roland gave her a woollen jumper "Here lady put this on."

Mark was emptying out the fitted wardrobe. There were boxes and boxes of shoes. He didn't have time to go through them all. He started knocking them on the floor. They were hiding something they had to be. He'd already searched the other draws and cabinets in the master bedroom, there was no jewellery. Then, as he got to the last top cupboard he found it

"Yes! The bitch has a safe."

It was a small dark grey safe slightly larger than the ones in hotel room. It had a digital panel and was bolted to the wall.

"What's the number?" Mark shouted.

Claire looked at him and then at Roland. The both began barking at her like two wild dogs "What's the number lady! What's the number?"

"Its 2,9,0,6,7,8."

It wasn't Aladdin's cave, but it was a score and a half Mark thought as he opened the safe. He grabbed two necklace cases and looked at them before shoving them into the pillowcase. There was an 18ct divers, (Rolex men's oyster submariner), plus a woman's platinum ins and outs (Rolex with diamonds on the face and bezel) with *Date-Just*. There was also a women's 18ct pasha Cartier and a pearl necklaces. Mark couldn't believe it; his head was rushing. All the certificates of purchase were also in the safe as was the spare key, and registration documents for the X5. Everything went in the pillowcase. Then he saw a passport. Opening it he looked at her name. Mrs Claire Louisa Bareham.

"Go and check the rest of the house." Mark said.

"Why?" Roland asked.

"She lying," Mark said jumping down off the stool. "She's got a husband."

Both men stepped closer to Claire. "No, no, no! Please, I already told you I don't," Claire pleaded. "Please, just take what you want and go."

"You're fucking lying! Who's men's watch is this?" Mark held up the Rolex. "Why you got men's clothes in the wardrobe?"

"They belong to my ex, we're divorced."

"You're lying." Mark didn't believe her. He ordered Roland to check the rest of the house. Immediately Roland searched the two upstairs rooms first. They were empty. Downstairs also seemed quiet enough, but he wasn't taking any chances. Creeping through the hallway he went to the kitchen. He half expected someone to jump out and wrestle him to the floor, or to see a carving knife missing from the knife rack, but there was no sign of movement. The dinning room was empty too. A pile of letters and papers in the corner marked where Mark had already been.

Mark's tripping, Roland thought, *there ain't nobody here*. Feeling hot under his balaclava he decided to remove it. He wiped his forehead and went to the fridge. Opening the large American style door, he studied the contents. Everything was from Mark's and Spencer or Waitrose.

Mmm, Roland thought, *there's no budget shit in here*. He opened a carton of Tropicana and took a couple refreshing gulps. In the centre shelf sat a sandwich from Bluebirds Café. Opening the paper bag Roland took a bite out of the ciabatta roast beef and salad roll. Wiping the flour from his mouth he walked through to the dinning room. Walking around the house in the darkness, he began to appreciate the size of the Semi-detached house. He walked through to the reception room wishing he could live in a house like this. The truth was burglary was the closest he'd every get to such property. He picked up a picture of Claire and some friends on a skiing trip. He studied their bright coloured jumpsuits and smiles thinking, *it's a good thing black man don't ski.* Then, turning around, something caught his eye on top of the mahogany display cabinet. Two shinning orbs gleamed in the darkness. They were like golden eyes staring at him. Squinting Roland stepped forward to examine the orbs. In an instant they darted towards him and the screech of a cat was heard. Thompson Claire's black cat, clawed away at the face of the intruder drawing blood. "AAARRGGHH!" Dropping his sandwich and Tropicana, Roland held his face in anguish. Thompson stood a couple feet away from him hissing, claws retracted ready to pounce again. Furious, Roland chased the cat into the hallway as it darted out of sight. "I fucking hate cats."

Looking at his bleeding face in the large hanging mirror in the hallway, Roland thought it better he cover up. Putting his balaclava back on he ran upstairs.

Seconds felt like minutes to Mark. What was Roland doing downstairs? He looked at Claire sat in the corner of the room, still holding the towel in her hand like it was a shield of great protection. Claire Bareham was her name he thought. He shouldn't of read the name on the passport yet he should have waited. No one really wants to know the name of their victims. It didn't matter now anyway, two more minutes and they were out of this house and on their way to having a good smoke. Mark knew he'd spend a couple grand on the pipe tonight, but he didn't care. Some people might have called him a crackhead, Mark thought different. *Crackhead, crackhead,* he thought, *no way, I'm a heavyweight smoker, I smoke boulders not rocks.* Finally Roland came back. "Its all clear. There's no sign of anybody else living here." Watching Claire cowering on the floor Roland asked,
"Should we tie her up?"

"Forget that shit," Mark said wanting to deal more important matters. "Listen to me. I'm gonna leave now, take the X5 and the goods to the safe place. Either you tie her up good and proper, or you make sure you give me a 15 minute head start, okay?"

"Okay." Roland nodded.

Tossing the Corsa keys at Roland, Mark ran down the stairs heading for the back door. Halfway down, it hit him, Claire was in the bath. He quickly rummaged through the pillowcase then ran upstairs into the bathroom. He looked around, the lit candles, the silk robe on the floor and then the sink. On the sink sat a diamond bracelet, and a leather strap Patek Philippe watch. Mark grabbed the bracelet and watch shoving them in his jacket pocket. As he was leaving he tripped over a book. He picked it up looking at the title, *The Journey of A Slave by Gilyan Gates*. He knew that name from somewhere, but couldn't remember. Ignoring the noise coming from the next room he thought, *it's Jade's birthday soon she likes to read* and grabbed the book.

When the second man finally left, Claire let out a deafening scream of horror and pain. Terrorised in her own house she felt violated. The tears rolled down her face as she screamed louder and louder. Cutting through the silence, Claire wanted somebody to hear her. She wanted somebody to come to her rescue. Her screams went unheard and she lay on the floor motionless. She cursed God for abandoning her. What had she done to deserve this *"Oh lord why, why me?"*

CHAPTER: 3
THE 28 BUS TO WORK

Jade rode the number 28 bus to work everyday from Wandsworth to High Street Kensington. She would find a seat at the back of the bus and read her book. Between working, studying, and looking after Jayvan, Jade didn't get much time to read. As a young girl she loved to read, it was her private escape route from the outside world. They transported her into realms of fantasy and romance, danger and mystery. Now as a single mother, student, and grown woman, escaping the outer world was becoming a task. Jayvan was at that *'terrible two'* stage and was destroying everything in his path including Jade's patience. Had it not been for the support of her mother and older sister Anita, Jade figured it would have been impossible to achieve her goals. They hadn't always been supportive though. When Jade first told her family of her pregnancy they had been dead set against it. Her mother said nothing at first other than "Ya sure, Jade." Anita screamed, "No, Jade he's a bum! I don't want you to have it. Not for that, dutty lil deggae, deggae boy. He's a criminal! He's just trying to drag you down, while he runs around doing bare foolishness." It wasn't the type of reaction Jade was hoping for. "You're going places, Jade. You're going to go Uni." Anita pleaded. "Think about it. He's gonna be locked up in jail, and your gonna be on your own. Is that what you want?"

Jade remembered how vex she had been with her sister. "How can you say that?" she asked.

"I'm only speaking the truth," Anita insisted. "That boy is nothing, but trouble."

Nevertheless Jade ignored her older sister and was determined to have her baby despite what her family thought. The only person who was supportive was her older brother Mark. They shared a special bond. He always brought her things, told her what he was up to, advised her to watch out for certain guys, don't be loose, men will respect you more. He always supported Jade and told her 'do whatever you think is best for you.' Jade sighed. She hadn't seen Mark properly for awhile, although he did stop at the house briefly for her birthday. Jade's mum and Anita had thrown her a surprise party at the family house for her twenty-third. Mark said he didn't want to make a scene or be anywhere where he wasn't wanted, so he'll wait outside in the car. He beeped the horn as Jade came out.

"Woo, new car, Mr. Godfrey,'" Jade said looking at the Golf GTI. "What happened to the Corsa?" she said jumping in the passenger's seat.

"I gave it to Rolly."

"Why!" Jade yelled. "You know I need a car. Why didn't you let me buy it off you?"

"Rah," Mark said, with exaggerated surprise. "You never said you were looking for a car,"

"Come on, Mr. Godfrey, don't lie now," Jade slapped him. "You know I told you to look out for something for me."

"Nah, sis," Mark grinned. "I swear. You never told me."

"Mark Godfrey!" Jade looked at him. "Are you really going to lie to me?"

"I swear, sis. You never said nothing to me."

"Mark, James, Almont, Godfrey!" Jade banged each syllable on Mark's dashboard. "Are you going to lie to me?"

"Nah, hold on, hold on a minute," Mark said getting flustered. He pushed her hands away. " Why you using my whole name?

"Why you lying?"

"I ain't lying," Mark said getting vex. "If you asked me, then you asked me, but I don't remember, innit. Just let me speak to Rolly and I'll see what he says. And then after that, you better not come bothering me."

"Thank you." Jade kissed her brother on the cheek.

"Don't thank me yet." Mark insisted. "I want a good P on that car. Don't think you're getting it for free."

"Of course not." Jade tried to hug him.

"Move!" Mark tried to shake loose. "How's my little Nephew?"

"Oww," Jade put her hands together in pray. "He's trouble, Mark. It's takes all I can do from smacking him every minute."

"Smack who?" Mark said. "I'll smack you, if you touch him. That's my little soldier." He leaned back and drew a bag from the back. He passed the Nike town bag to Jade. "Here. I brought him a couple of tracksuits and ting. Let me know if they fit."

"Thanks Marky," Jade said looking inside. "Don't you wanna come inside and see your little soldier? Perhaps you could give him some manners, instead of spoiling him."

Mark looked towards the house. "Nah I'm cool. I'll come round next week or something."

Jade knew Mark wouldn't go in while Anita was there, but she tried anyway.

"There's a present in there for you," Mark said. "So, don't say I never get you anything." He smiled as she began rummaging through the bag. "Hol' on Jade" He said stopping her. "Take time, open it inside."

"No. I wanna open it now," Jade said getting excited.

Mark shook his head "Open it inside."

Giving her brother a kiss goodbye, Jade ran inside.

Once Jade opened her present, she knew exactly why Mark had told her to open it inside. There was a ring of heads gazing at the diamond bracelet.

"Wow!" Jade's best friend Tania drooled. "That's why I love your brother, you know, Jade. He always spoils you."

"Please, Tania," Anita huffed. "There's nothing to love about Mark. He probably stole it."

"Why you got to say that!" Jade snapped.

"Because it's the truth."

"What and the book too, Anita?"

"Probably." Anita picked up the book. "What's Mark know about books?"

"Why don't you leave Mark alone for once?" Jade snatched back the book. "You're the reason why he doesn't want to come in and say hello to his own family."

"What family?" Anita fumed. "Mark hasn't got no family in here no more."

Jade didn't bother to argue, Anita and Mark had too many issues to deal with. It felt like they'd been arguing all their lives.

Sitting on the bus Jade opened her book. The last book Mark had given Jade was *Green Eggs and Ham* by *Dr Seuss*, when she was four. "Read it to me, Mark, please. Read it," she would beg.

"Jade, you got to learn to read it yourself," Mark would say. Now Jade did read for herself and the book was *The Journey of a Slave*. She tried to ignore the school kids at the back, and began reading.

KINGS & QUEENS I   *The Journey of a Slave.*

The heavy bass line pumped from the speaker box as the melodic beats of Dr Dre's *Still D.R.E.* blared out of the car stereo. It signalled our arrival into the estate. The day was bright and the last rays of summer sun graced us. As Mel jumped out of the car and ran up the stairs of his block of flats, I seized the chance to throw in one of my old skool soul tapes. *Aaaaahhhh* that's what I wanted to hear, an old skool classic, something that everyone could appreciate. *The classics never get old* I thought; *they just remain timeless.*

I felt blessed as the velvet voice of, Mr. Marvin Gaye caressed the airwaves, cutting through the hustle and constant grind of city life. Sitting in the comfortable leather interior of Mel's 3 series Beemer, I let the music engulf me. The strings from the song subdued my mind and relaxed my soul. The music supplied a natural high, and instinctively I felt the urge to sing aloud as Marvin posed the question *"What's Goin on?"* It was a good question and always relevant.

Peering into the rear view mirror, I checked to see where my partner was when I noticed a familiar figure lurking near the stairwell. The dry face was hard to make out as the figure wiped the tangled hair from her face. Thick and untamed, it was like the mane of a lion. Again the breeze blew strands across her face as she lazily wiped them away. I began to eye the way she moved and anxiously fidgeted. Her restlessness was an obvious indication - *she was a cat.* Yet it wasn't this that aroused my curiosity.

Intrigued I studied her for some clue. She wore a faded grey Versace t-shirt, probably some rip off from a market stall, a gold chain that hung from around her neck, and a pair of black Levi jeans. On her feet she wore a pair of Nike Air Rifts that were in fair condition.

There was nothing extraordinary about her. On an ordinary day, I wouldn't look twice. I'd tell Mel, *'give her the ting and come we go'*. Yet something bugged me about this girl. It was her physique, her frame. It was as though I had studied it many times before, but hadn't. It was the type of feeling you had when you entered a room and you knew something was missing, but couldn't put your finger on what it was.

My brow frowned as Mel Jolted down the stairs and into view. Quickly he shoved something into her hand. The exchange of money was done so swift, that I almost missed it. Tilting the mirror to get a better look, I noticed Mel point over to the car. He was telling her something. Then, as she peered over, it hit me. It struck hard, like an overhand right from Mike Tyson. It was the eyes. They were the final clue needed.

Although they still had the sleepy matter around them, the beautiful brown eyes and slender eyelids spoke volumes. *Alicia* they said in a low whisper; *it's me Alicia.* Despite the fact she'd lost weight and her face looked gaunt with her delicate cheekbones, it was still definitely Alicia.

Alicia had been one of those girls from back in the day. The ones that I'd always labelled 'out of my reach'. She was like a queen in my eyes, high maintenance. There was a time when I would've done anything to get into her draws. I'd sit and think about how long I could last before I burst. Two minutes, four minutes, no maybe one. And when I couldn't count the minutes, I'd calculate the strokes and pumps. But it wasn't just sex. No, it was more than that, I wanted her to be mine, I wanted her to want me.

Alicia had that aura, that little extra something that brought her to everyone's attention. She studied dance and performing arts in college and had the thighs and body to match. When she walked through the cold grey hallways of college, you could feel the male approval of her presence. It was like a crowd turning out to watch the warm colours of the carnival floats go by. You never forget that euphoria. She was a mix of natural beauties and heavenly goddesses rolled into one. Beyonce, Halle Berry, J.lo, Venus, Aphrodite, Nefertiti, you name it she was it. Yet such beauty is never easily obtained.

Alicia never went out with anyone in our age group. She opted for older men, as most attractive girls usually did. But she wasn't the type of girl that thought she was too nice. She was cool with it, which added to her appeal. There were moments when my world would slow down, and seconds would become minutes as I watched her walk by. A slight wave and smile and off she'd go. This was one of those moments. Yet the intense emotions I felt were not the same. Not the feelings of boyish lust and wonderment; but sorrow, pain and bewilderment.

What had happened to my queen, the giver of fantasy and want? Her eyes looked vacant as she tossed her head back and put the wraps in her mouth. Stunned by her transformation, I remained speechless. I wanted to say hi, how you doing? What you up to? Where've you been? How's life been treating you? I wanted to say something, anything to acknowledge her, but I couldn't. I could only mime the words of the ballad and ask myself, *What's goin on?*

When Mel returned to the car I was still in a daze. My world had slowed down one last time for Alicia.

"You and your old 70's music," Mel said climbing in and starting the engine. "You think you're some ol'pimp innit."

"Boy, what you know 'bout this here music? This is grown folks music." I teased. Laughing we pulled out of the estate and headed towards Shepherds Bush for some West Indian takeaway.

Weaving through the traffic, I thought to myself how had my queen got into such a state? Why was she out here smoking work, looking like any other cat? This wasn't Alicia, not my Alicia. What had happened to reduce her to this?

Growing up, I often heard people say, 'you know us black people use to be Kings and Queens'. We use to have great empires, you only have to look at the Pyramids and Egypt to see that, but when ever I asked so 'why were we like this now?' The same people never had an answer. I'd ask, 'why are we no longer kings and queens with great empires?' Gradually it dawned upon me, slavery.

My people, Alicia, Mel, my mother, sister, friends, family, and even me, we were never Kings and Queens. We were slaves and descendants of slaves. We had been sold as slaves by Europeans and by our own people. Our bloodlines, links, and ties to the great kings and queens had been destroyed by slavery. All my people knew was slavery and oppression. It was something that had been passed down generation to generation. My people were from the Caribbean not Africa. Our heritage as handed down by tradition, were the traits of slaves, not those of warrior and kings.

I wondered, did this make us inferior? NO! Of course not, but the realisation was clear. Before we could learn how to be Kings and Queens again, we needed to learn how to stop being slaves. Black people needed to learn to stop selling our people into slavery.

It was harsh. Alicia had become a slave to drugs, and Mel and I were no better than the Africans that sold other Africans into slavery. As we reached Shepherds Bush roundabout, those deep thoughts were being whirled around my mind like a tornado and another question came to me. Howling along to Diana Ross, Mel sang the words that would remind me of the everlasting journey we undertake. "Do you know where you're going to, do you like the things that life is showing you?"

*

Jade looked up from her book as a hoard of school kids came clambering onto the bus. Pushing each other, they jumped up and down like a wild pack of animals, disturbing people then apologising. Folding the corner of the page, Jade slipped the book into her handbag.

Pressing the bell, she thought about the author's statement on drugs and slavery. She wondered if Mark ever considered himself a slave, when he went through his periods of smoking. Nothing worried her more than when she knew her brother was smoking. His weight dropped, his movement became erratic and he would give up on reasoning. He turned into a nocturnal creature with one goal. Swiftly he became untrustworthy and a liability to everyone. The end result was usually prison, but even detention had stopped being a deterrent to Mark years ago. On the only occasion Mark did ask for help, he turned to Jade with teary eyes. Crying he confessed, "Jade I can't help it. I want to stop, but I feel powerless. Help me."

The bus came to a halt. Getting off Jade debated, *lack of power*. Wasn't that the key characteristic of slavery?

***

CHAPTER 4

When Jade finished work, she caught the bus to her mother's house to pick up Jayvan. Luckily Vince, her mother's gentlemen friend, offered her a lift home. "Jade if you wait for me to finish my fish, I'll drop you home, if that's okay with your mother."

"You gon' come back." Carmen asked with her hand on her hip.

"Of course." Vince answered, pulling a fish bone out his mouth.

"Okay," Carmen waved her hand. "Gwan, go carry the children and come back, yuh hear."

Vince nodded picking at another bone.

Jade found it funny to see her mother courting again. Everything between her mother and Vince seemed so formal and regimented, yet if you asked Carmen Godfrey about their relationship she would say in a coy manner, "Mind your business, he's just a friend."

Friend or not, Jade always knew when he was coming. Her mother would buy a nice piece of fish and say, "Nobody touch de fish."

"Is Vince coming round?" Jade would ask.

"I'm not sure," her mother would reply. "He might come to see me later. So una don't boddah touch de fish."

There weren't many things that brought a smile to her mother's face, but Jade knew Vincent Gangadeen was one.

Finally reaching home, Jade put Jayvan straight to bed. After making herself a cup of peppermint tea, she made her way into the front room. She looked at her books and coursework spread out on the dinning table. She hadn't had time to clear them before she left for work and vainly hoped she would have enough energy to continue when she got back. Sighing, she blew on her tea before sipping. The coursework would have to wait. Jade decided to clear the books before Jayvan caught her off guard tomorrow morning. Packing them up, she placed them high out of reach. Crashing on the couch she picked up her reading book and tried to relax.

HOW TO MAKE A SLAVE   *The Journey of a Slave.*

The weeks and months passed, and as they did Alicia became a regular customer to a hustling dream. Some weeks I could count the grands Alicia brought in alone. She was always a good net-worker. She thought on her feet. For the most part, she kept herself tidy looking and made good money off chequebook and cards scams, which was when I saw her most. It confused me. Although she '*bun work*' on occasion you could see the old queen trying to resurface to her throne. There would be times when she would find work and frequent calls became less. Arriving smartly dressed in a prearranged spot, she'd always giggle and laugh saying, "It's Just one for recreational, G, smile, don't look so worried." I would follow her majesty's wishes with a small curve in my mouth. Other times when her weight loss and perpetual calls, were the cause of both profit and concern, I couldn't.

It was times like this when I thought of that distant moment by Mel's block, and compared her to a slave. I would never tell a soul, but secretly I hoped she would transform back to the queen she truly was. Yet selfishness, my own selfishness and greed were like a whip lashing her back to the fields of ruin. It showed. I always struggled to look Alicia in the eye. To ease my guilt, I'd throw her a freebie here and there then justify my actions with a single thought. If I didn't profit from her, someone else would. But that made me ask, who was profiting from me? Looking at the slave in Alicia only reflected the slave in myself.

It tormented me. It played with my mind like the first stage of madness. It became the torture of the subtle and mundane. The almost unnoticeable things, like a fraying piece of string on a jumper. You know pulling at it, only makes the jumper fray and unravel. The best thing to do in such situations is to cut it off, leave it alone, but here it was, the fraying piece of string that said "SLAVERY".

I asked myself, 'if there were something about me that I didn't know or understand would I want some sort of answer or explanation?' So I pulled at the string looking for clues.

Now slavery was nothing new to me, I knew about slavery didn't I? I mean I was black. It was part of my history, part of my culture. I'd studied it in Year 9 history with the rest of my classmates. I knew about the Trans-Atlantic slave trade, middle passage, Harriet Tubman, and Abolition in the U.K. and the U.S. I'd even watched Alex Hayley's Roots.

In my eyes I was already well knowledgeable and coherent about slavery. Besides if I wasn't, there were plenty black scholars in the world that were. So why was this so important? Why did I believe that it affected my peers and me still today? **WHY?**

The reality was that the education that I was supplied in school was not sufficient for black people. It was sufficient for governing boards and bodies, but for a growing generation of black youth that were to use it as a means of self-identification and self-value, it only scratched the surface. How could a topic that lasted the duration of 400 years, be spliced into one school term, become of any value, other than to say the curricula had covered black history? We spent as much time learning about the industrial revolution, which was given the same, if not more detail.

Why did this era prove to be such a consequential period? If we search through different periods in history, we see the enslavement of people from many different races. The ancient Romans had slaves, varying from Nubian, Arabian, Hebrew, and European backgrounds. The ancient Greeks and even the ancient Egyptians, all had slaves that were vital to their lifestyle and civilisations. These were great empires that ruled for centuries, creating dynasties, and legacies that have lasted the test of time. Why had these empires not crumbled at the result of any slave revolt? Other than the story of Moses in the Bible, the only other large-scale slave revolt, that I was aware of in ancient history, was that of Spartacus (and I only knew that because I'd seen Kirk Douglas in the Stanley Kubrick film). My conclusion was that it could only be within the style and form of slavery.

It is a well-known fact that the Romans styled their own civilisation, philosophy, art and culture upon those of the ancient Greeks. Historians have also proven that Egypt is the oldest documented civilisation on Earth. The first Greeks were students to the Africans of Kemet (Kemet being the ancient name for Egypt) who were the original pyramid builders. This meant the initial school of thought for all three periods began in Africa with the Kemetians, Nubians, and Egyptians.

Slavery and oppression go hand in hand like those of a married couple. In many cases the two are like different sides of the same coin. Equipped with this basic knowledge, I decided to analyse Egyptian Slavery.
My initial findings found that there seemed to be a lot of controversy on whether the Egyptians even had a real slave trade. The Egyptian slave was not like the slave of the southern states of America or the West Indian plantation. They were seen as a person with lesser rights, dedicated to a

certain task, while the plantation slaves had no rights and were at the mercy of their owners. Also the manner in how the people became slaves differed. Many of the slaves in Egypt were prisoners of war (especially during the middle kingdom) or put themselves into slavery to pay off debts. Sometimes it was deemed to be beneficial for someone to be a slave, with their masters giving them land, somewhat like the serfs of medieval times. A person might even put their children into slavery to save them from starvation. Debt slaves or prisoners of war were at times set free after serving for a certain period. On occasion slaves were set free through manumission- a practice deemed advantageous for the soul of the slave owner. This sometimes led to the slave being adopted by the family of their former master.

The most important fact I found was that the Egyptian slave filled a wide range of positions, from lowly labourers to government administrators, which is even documented in the Bible. After Joseph interprets the Pharaoh's dream, he is given his freedom and is also appointed to a high governmental position. The reason that I give for the importance of this fact is – the Egyptians were the most advance civilisation. When the Greeks first travelled to Africa, the Pyramids and the sphinx were already ancient. They had produced the world's first education system, and had the greatest architects, engineers, sculptors, chemist, astronomers, artists, mathematicians, masons you name it the Egyptians were probably the first. Because of the Egyptians success they produced the first middle class society. This middle class would have to educate the new scholars and administrate the building of new temples etc. This middle class would also have to house the inhabitants of the cities acting like civil servants.

With appointment of slaves to certain positions, the freeing and adoption of the slaves made it possible for a slave to become an accomplished man. A slave could be educated, employed, freed, and then given the opportunities to own his own property and even his own slaves with the same aspirations. This meant that a slave had the chance to ascend to the Egyptian middle class regardless of his former status, ethnic origin or other particulars. His children would then also be entitled to privileges of the middle class society.

Could you imagine the influence that such a middle class would have on their culture? Imagine if the same had been applied in America, twenty years after the first boatload of slaves arrived. Had the first slaves been set free to ascend and produce a middle class with the same education as their white peers, America would look like a very different place, along with the rest of the world. The implications on history are inconceivable. However is it an illusion that such equality could exist, because it is universal law that dictates that, "inequality is the unalterable law of human life." History tells us that the Greeks returned to conquer Egypt, destroying temples, cities libraries and claiming its riches and knowledge as their own. The Greeks became the ruling group and a ruling group is only a ruling group so long as it can nominate its successor.

With this line of thinking the maintenance of slavery is vital to the successor. The integration of slaves to a middle class could mean jeopardising future successors by the gradual removal of power from the ruling group. As the slaves or former slaves' positions get higher and higher in society; the slaves choosing their own successor threatens the ruling group's position.

If you picture the ruling group like a glass of water, it stands alone clear and transparent. Now a drop of ink represents each slave. As the slaves are freed into the society of their ruling group, i.e. the water the society changes. The water or the society of the ruling group is no longer transparent, but becomes darker like the opaque ink. The society no more represents that of the original ruling group, but a new integration of both which on appearance seems to benefit that of the former slave more. The society or water is no longer water or can be described with the same attributes. The more ink drops or slaves that are added to the water, the more it takes on the attributes of the ink until it is ink.

Ultimately the ruling group would lose its power and attributes of its society. In turn this would create the rethinking and reform of the ideology of being a slave. The slave being a person with lesser rights is now changed and he becomes a person with no rights at all. Eventually he is deemed inferior and later in history three fifths of a human being, creating the whip lashed, chained and shackled slave that we associate with the word today...

*

"Mummy."
Jade looked up from her book, to see Jayvan standing in the doorway. Tired he rubbed his eyes and pulled at his nappy. "Mummy I want bot-bot."

Jade looked at the time. It was 11:48pm. Begrudgingly she picked up her son. She wondered why Jayvan always woke up around midnight to ask for a bottle. Why couldn't he sleep right through as he did at his grandmother's house. How did he know the difference?

Giving Jayvan a quarter bottle of water, Jade went to give him a kiss when he pushed her away.

"No, Mummy 'bena." He said pointing to the Ribena syrup on the side.

"No," Jade handed him the bottle.

"No, Mummy, no, Mummy, bena," he whined.

"No." Jade said firmly. "You haven't got no slave in here. You'll drink what I give you."

"No, Mummy." Jayvan began to cry, as Jade put him back to bed.

Tucking Jayvan in, Jade gave him the bottle. He threw it across the room. Picking it up Jade asked the little boy, "Do want this or not? You're not getting no Ribena."

Cross, Jayvan looked at his mother. He was still too young to understand tantrums would get him nowhere in life. He waited for his mother's reaction. Jade could see his little mind working overtime.

"Do you want this or not?" She asked.

"Yes," Jayvan pushed up his face.

"Yes what?"

"Yes peease, Mummy."

Jade handed him his bottle thinking he's as stubborn as his father. Giving Jayvan a kiss, she turned out the light and left the door ajar. Smiling at her small victory, Jade thought, *'that little boy needs to remember who's the ruling group in this house'*.

***

CHAPTER: 5

The time read 1:06 am. Jade could feel her eyelids getting heavy. Sleep was calling. The black print on the page had started to blur, but she told herself *one more chapter, I can read one more*. She knew she had to be up early the next day, but she still convinced herself she'd be all right. The author's words were slowly absorbing her into his world, then she realized; it wasn't just his world, it was her world as well.

The drug dealers and 'shottaz' were outside on her doorstep. They roamed and shared the same streets. They profited from her brother and made him into a so-called slave. Jade knew these people by face and acquaintance. What gave them the right to claim any part of this world as theirs? Did they think they were the ruling group? Drugs and Slavery what did they have in common?

Sitting up, Jade was determined to find the answer. Her brother had given her this book for a reason. Perhaps it was a cry for help? If so, she felt it her duty to read on.

THE MISCONCEPTIONS   *The Journey of a Slave.*
OF A BUSINESS MIND

I think the biggest misconception about drug dealings is probably that most people believe that it's only the drug barons with brains within the operation. It's true to say that they must be or how else did they get to that position? But often the runner, the peddler, the street pusher, whatever you want to call him, is also just as smart and not some complete thuggish dimwits following orders.

The guys that do well are usually the guys who from the first moment perceive themselves as some sort of legitimate businessman. They believe they are providing a service to the community just as valuable as any other business. They are filling the supply for demand and apply the four Ps of Marketing; Product, Price, Promotion, and Place to achieve their goals. They deliver on time, they're customer orientated, asking about the quality of their product, giving freebies and discounts to regulars. They look to expand and update their equipment and logistics. You even hear of workers being fired, and put on warning.

You see, in my world a good street hustler is in reality another term for entrepreneur. It is the same drive and desires that spur them on. The comparisons are uncannily uncountable. They both want to succeed. They are like identical twins, split from the same embryo; they both strive for good business. Where the two actually differ is in their legality.

I remember during some months Mel and I would run a lottery on our phone line. We would let all our punters know we were giving away an eighth of white or brown to the person that phoned at the right time. We would then give it to one of our best punters, one who moved in the right circles. He/she would then certify to other custom that the lottery was real and the line would go crazy. The amount of profit accumulated compared to the loss by giving away a couple of eighths was easily overshadowed. When serving up, as I preferred to call it, you realise you need to be business minded in able to implement as many structures and policies to contain your punters and market share.

I use the word contain rather than maintain because, if you contain something you have hold of something, where as if you are maintaining you are trying to preserve something. We wanted hold of our punters and cats for the utmost reason we wanted to be the ruling group. We didn't want no competition we wanted a monopoly or at very least an oligopoly where we controlled who got what, where, when and how much.

When put like that it sounds very ruthless. Added to the moral issues that arise, it is very ruthless, but isn't this the nature of business? Ask yourself if you were in control of a multi-million pound business wouldn't you try to contain rather than maintain your business? Wouldn't you rather have the monopoly or oligopoly? Wouldn't you rather be the ruling group rather than the ruled?

It was slowly starting to dawn on me why the Trans Atlantic slave trade was still so significant to my generation and its predecessors, not just because of the centuries of oppression and slavery, not just because of the monstrosity that were carried out during the 400 years. I mean, they are never to be forgotten and no way would I try to belittle such an era in my own history, but I think like the drug dealers on the street there is one factor within slavery that maybe overlooked. Why does the drug dealer or slave trader do what they do?

We know why slaves were stolen and sold, we know the wealth and the empires that were forged, developed, and nurtured upon their backs. We know of the inhuman injustices that were carried out to preserve the order of life and the wars that were fought to bring about the emancipation of the slaves. But can we look at history the present and the unseen future and say that after so many rebellions, battles, abolition, civil right rallies, conferences, committees, and racial laws that we have achieved equality yet?

I started to comprehend the main factor that is over looked about slavery is the view of the white man, the slave owners, the slave merchants and traders. As a Black man if anyone had ever said to me "You don't know about slavery, you don't know what it was like for the white man." I guess that I would be furious, especially if I heard a white man say it. I haven't got any sympathy for the white slave owners, look what they did to my people.

Imagine what that would be like. To understand slavery, to understand your own people, to understand where you are in life, you must first understand the views of the white slaver owners. *Foolishness,* I heard myself cry at the thought of it, but hadn't I made the comparison of being like the slave master before. Wasn't it me who said I felt like the overseer, the master, or even the slave trader selling Alicia into slavery?

Maybe I never started her smoking, but I certainly never tried to stop her. Alicia and all the others were a means of money and profit. They put food on my table, clothes on my back, a roof over may head, expensive trainers on my feet, jewellery around my neck, rings on my fingers and cars beneath my bottom. They were my source of money, power, and freedom. The result of their containment brought me what I wanted, even women. The be all and end all of the matter was that to me they were my business, and I did what I needed to contain my business.

So, how did my views on street peddling contrast from the views of a white slave master, merchant or trader? They didn't. If business was business, as a good businessman and not as a black man, could I now see the views of the white slave owners as businessmen? Of course I could. When forced to look at things from this new perspective, some of the things they did didn't seem so vile. I too had seen some horrible things like mothers injecting heroin while their baby cried helplessly at their feet. Staggering around the room, they shared needles with her friends knowing the slightest prick could mean a deadly infection to their child. And all the while I stand waiting to collect my money or see how good my product is.

No, I was a businessman through and through. I could fully understand the views of the white man. The slave was his livelihood, a commodity just like my crack rock or bag of heroin. He couldn't let a thing of such value go. The slave trade meant prosperity, economic growth, and wealth. This was business just as much as any other trade market and it meant power. During the years of the Trans-Atlantic Slave trade there were many wars between the different empires and eventually against the colonies. If the slaves meant money and wealth, they meant finance for power and war. Me as a businessman and not as a black man, no sorry I wouldn't give up my slaves. Slaves could mean the defining factor in whether you were in the ruling group or ruled over. If the freeing and the education of slaves could determine whether I could nominate my own successor to my ruling group then no. The containment of slaves and the maintenance of a slave trade would have meant utmost importance to those white men who became the ruling groups. It would mean that their children and children's children would be in the prominent positions to shape the world and the future to come.

To understand the fullness of such a concept was beyond me. I never thought I could empathize with the white man's treatment to black people in slavery. It was a lie, a hideous betrayal to my own race. I was ashamed to submit to such line of thinking. Was this where my journey had brought me as a black man? This wasn't what I was searching for. I wanted answers. I wanted signs that lead to a better life. What had this brought me? It had brought me the truth and understanding. Black people were not kept in slavery just because they were black. Black people were not oppressed for centuries just because they were black, but for the mere fact that the ruling groups' desire was to continue being the ruling group. It is the same desire they had then and the same desire they have now.

Black people, my people, were enslaved, oppressed, and disillusioned by the ruling groups so that they could maintain the status quo, so they remained in power. It was straight up business and containment. It was the key then and today. If their children and their children's children held the prominent positions, shaping the world and its history, what would the children of the slaves do? If their children were the successors to the ruling group, what were the children of the slaves, successors to? If their children nominated the next successor, in which positions did that leave the children of the slaves?

My journey was beginning to take shape. I could finally detect a pattern and understand why key elements were stipulated in the roads of time. It was as though the ruling group and their successors were watching the slave travel upon his journey. The ruling group rode in a lavish horse drawn carriage and they had the slave walk barefoot behind. When the slave asked for help, they refused laughing saying 'Only if you pull my carriage.' When the slave asked for direction, they sent him in the wrong direction, giving him shortcuts that set him further back. They laughed, spat and refused to let the slave ride with them. Why did the ruling group do such things? The Ruling group liked the position they were in and did not want to share it. They knew not what was at the end of the slave's journey, but knew they must not be allowed to shift the balance of power. They must be contained in their current status and so the slaves were for the next 400 years...

*

The book finally fell from Jade's hand at 2:18am. Eyes exhausted, she laid back on the couch. *He's right* she thought. You can dispel it as bullshit, but the facts were there. Racism was just an overcoat of the truth. *Was slavery really about power and economic wealth?*

***

CHAPTER: 6

At university, Jade's book had brought up a great debate on propaganda. Sparking the fire she sat back and watched as the author's views were both attacked and defended.

"Only a sell-out would write something like that," Malachi suggested. "He ain't no, real black man."

"Why?" Obama argued. "We all know the Iraqi war is about oil, but the media and the so-called allied forces use terrorism and dictatorship to cloak their true intentions. Why can't past governments do the same with slavery? They used propaganda to say we weren't human?"

"That's true," Emma said "But the author's views rationalizes slavery and drug dealing."

"Stop." Kipling held up his hand. "Why can't slavery and drugs be a rational business? They both make money. That's the nature of all businesses."

"But that doesn't mean slavery and drugs should be rationalised, it's immoral." Emma replied.

"So, what!" Obama interjected. "Immorality doesn't mean they're not rational. Morality is a matter of ethics and emotions. I think you're missing the point."

"So what's the point then?" Malachi asked.

"The author's saying racist propaganda hid the governments' true intentions. He's not saying what's ethical or not." Obama replied.

"Exactly," Kipling agreed. "Governments only decide what's ethical, by counting the number of people who support or disagree with their propaganda."

"So, you man, agree with the author?" Malachi pointed his finger.

"Yes!" Obama and Kipling said simultaneously.

"You man are sell-outs!"

As the debate broiled into bickering and name-calling, Jade bid Emma goodbye and left the men to argue. She headed to the student library to find a nice quiet spot to read. Pulling out her book she studied the cover for the first time. She hadn't noticed there was no picture of the author. Stroking the paperback she began to wonder what Gilyan Gates looked like. It intrigued her. From his writing, she heard his voice. He was still young, past his teens, but not yet in his thirties. He spoke as if he wanted the world, but was too lazy to be bothered. Instead he stopped dreaming and conformed to his surroundings. Perhaps that's why Jade couldn't picture his face. It had become synonymous with the other black boys she'd encountered, a blank mask, an archetype with no distinguishing features. His book was like a final testimony speaking beyond the mask – *I ain't as stupid as I look.* Jade smiled shaking her head. *It's I'm not as stupid as I look.* Opening the page she began to read more.

WILLIE LYNCH RECIPE TO MAKING A NIGGER SLAVE   *The Journey of a Slave.*

When serving up it was always better to be an early starter. I always switched my phone on at 8.30 am and waited for the morning rush. However I never actually began serving up until nine o'clock. I liked to take a few orders to make sure the punters knew I was up and about. The morning rush usually consisted of the brown users with one or two requesting both. I wasn't a doctor or anything, but I knew the brown physically affected the body more than white. Some of the punters would call it their medicine, and couldn't function properly without their morning dosage. It was important for me to make sure they had what they needed, because it would enable them to go out and graft earlier. It's simple to understand. The more money a punter grafts, the more money a punter spends. You see, as a dealer there are no set guidelines. Most of them you made up as you went along, others you pinched from old gangster movies. The majority of the time, good common sense equalled good business.

Watching the office workers dressed in suits and ties darting out of the train stations, I began to think about the slave trade. The slave trade was a business like any other business. It had its stock, entry barriers, limitations, taxes, laws, import and export, but where were the business gurus?

I once pretended to study business studies at a local college. I remembered no matter which part of business it was, there seemed to be ceaseless amounts of experts who set down some sort of fundamentals. There was Maslow and his hierarchy of needs, the Boston Consultancy Group with their matrix of cash cows, problem child, stars, and dog products, but where were the slave experts? There must have been some. Were there never any lectures, conferences, or literature on the expertise of slavery? If so where was it?

I'd seen pictures of muzzles and thumb locks used to punish slaves. Were there no posters or advertisements for such items? How about articles on the best way to whip and discipline your slaves? What about lynching? Was there a special way to tie a noose? I decided that to understand the levels of containment the ruling groups used I would have to understand their methods. I would have to find one of these slave experts.

For the next few days I set up shop in the local library. While I studied, I met punters between the isles of Philosophy and Theology and passed drugs between books of Shakespeare and Keats. Quickly I established a routine. The Library had plenty blind-spots to deal from and allowed me to monitor who came in. Also the need for silence cut out any pointless chat and deterred punters from bringing large objects to sell. The irony was humorous. Here I was looking for business strategies used to enhance the slave trade and ending up enhancing my own.

Considering that lynching was the most infamous of disciplinary acts, used by slave owners and white oppressors, including the likes of the Klu Klux Klan and Black league, I began my investigation with lynching. It came as no surprise that I found the word derives from its originator Willie Lynch and means to put to death without trial. Not immediately knowing whom Willie Lynch was, I delved deeper to find Mr Lynch was *'The Man'*. I mean, he was not only a British slave owner with plantations in the West Indies, but he was the expert of all experts, the gurus' guru, the saviour of the ruling group, and a bloody slave genius. Willie Lynch was so brilliant that he travelled around the colonies like any of the modern day business gurus and gave lectures to teach his methods to slave owners in his chosen profession. He was invited to America and on the bank of the James River in the colony of Virginia in 1712 it's alleged he delivered the following speech.

GREETINGS

"Gentlemen. I greet you here on the bank of the James River in the year of our Lord one thousand seven hundred and twelve. First, I shall thank you, the gentlemen of the Colony of Virginia, for bringing me here. I am here to help you solve some of your problems with slaves. Your invitation reached me on my modest plantation in the West Indies, where I have experimented with some of the newest and still the oldest methods for control of slaves. Ancient Rome would envy us if my program is implemented.

As our boat sailed south on the James River, named for our illustrious King, whose version of the Bible we cherish, I saw enough to know that your problem is not unique. While Rome used cords of wood as crosses for standing human bodies along its highways in great numbers, you are here using the tree and the rope on occasions. I caught the whiff of a dead slave hanging from a tree, a couple miles back. You are not only losing valuable stock by hangings, you are having uprisings, slaves are running away, your crops are sometimes left in the fields too long for maximum profit, you suffer occasional fires and your animals are killed. Gentlemen, you know what your problems are; I do not need to elaborate. I am not here to enumerate your problems. I am here to introduce you to a method of solving them.

In my bag here, I have a full proof method for controlling your black slaves. I guarantee every one of you that if installed correctly, it will control the slave for at least 300 hundred years.

My method is simple. Any member of your family or your overseer can use it. I have outlined a number of differences among slaves; and I take these differences and make them bigger. I USE FEAR, DISTRUST AND ENVY FOR CONTROL PURPOSES.

These methods have worked on my modest plantation in the West Indies and it will work throughout the South. Take this simple little list of differences and think about them. On top of my list is *'Age'* but it's there only because it starts with an 'A'. The second is *'Colour'* or shade. There is Intelligence, Size, Sex, Sizes of plantations, Status on plantations, Attitude of owners, whether the slaves live in the valley, on a hill, East, West, North, South, have fine hair, course hair, or is tall or short.

Now that you have a list of differences, I shall give you an outline of action, but before that, I shall assure you that distrust is stronger than trust, and envy stronger than adulation, respect or admiration. The Black slaves after receiving this indoctrination shall carry on and will become self-refueling and self-generating for HUNDREDS of years, maybe THOUSANDS. Don't forget you must pitch the *old* black male vs. the *young* black male, and the *young* black male against the *old* black male. You must use the *dark* skin slaves vs. the *light* skin slaves, and the *light* skin slaves vs. the *dark* skin slaves. You must use the *female* vs. the *male* and the *male* vs. the *female*. You must also have your white servants and overseers distrust all blacks. But it is necessary that your slaves trust and depend on us. They must love, respect and trust only us.

Gentlemen, these kits are your keys to control. Use them. Have your wives and children use them, never miss an opportunity. *IF USED INTENSELY FOR ONE YEAR, THE SLAVES THEMSELVES WILL REMAIN PERPETUALLY DISTRUSTFUL.* Thank you gentlemen."

It was incredible on a complete platitude of different aspects. To begin it was exactly what I was searching for, a blueprint, a map, a trail that confirmed my instinct about a life journey. This speech was like a light in the dark. I was no longer fumbling around looking for a way out. I had found it, the path that my predecessors had walked. I could identify that we had been misled by others. We had been conditioned or house trained like a pet.

It was further evidence of the containment of the black man, not just physically but mentally. It illustrated the length and degrees that the ruling group took to contain another group. It focused on key elements that implemented correctly produced a success level that would probably out class any other business formula known to man. Lynch himself even forecast that his methods would last for at least three hundred years. His forecast focuses on a method that not only benefits the slave owners but their children and future generations.

He enforces his point by highlighting that his methods become self-refuelling and self-generating, creating a knock on effect that could last for thousands of years. Could you imagine the effects that would have had on the slaves and their successors? Well you don't need to because you can go outside and see for yourself. Pick up a paper, switch on the television, enter what's left of the black communities and you can see the fruits of Willie Lynch's labour.

If Lynch gave such a speech in 1712 then it doesn't take a mathematical genius to calculate that the effects of such methods would still exist to at least 2012. For the first time in my life I had received an awakening of *True Black Consciousness*. I realised you didn't need to be black to have *True Black Consciousness*, but had to be conscious of the plight of the black state of mind.

Dr. Martin Luther King, Marcus Garvey and Malcolm X were all great conscious black leaders, who were aware of the problems that faced their race. They strived to better their people and enlighten them, but this is where *True Black Consciousness* is like a double edged sword.

Willie Lynch as a ruthless and determined businessman, can also be defined as one the first men of *True Black Consciousness*. To understand the concept you must first forget what you believe you know about black consciousness. You must forget about the great black leaders and look at the word conscious. According to the Oxford dictionary the word *'Conscious'* means - 1. *Awake and aware of one's surrounding*, 2. *Knowing, or aware*, and 3. *Realized or recognized by the doer.*

Lynch was by far aware of the black or slaves' state of mind. He recognised that if it was not curtailed appropriately, it became the cause of loss profits, crops, and livestock. Lynch demonstrates that he is conscious of the Black man's condition, he knows what will elevate them, and he knows what will contain them.

Unlike Garvey, King, and X, Lynch's agenda is the complete opposite. With the awakening of his *True Black Consciousness*, he uses the concept to continue the enslavement of blacks and better his own people. He chooses to gain the upper hand on any would be uprisings, by designing methods that strip the slaves from their own black consciousness. He uses fear, distrust, and envy to control the slaves and pit them against each other.

Willie Lynch was definitely a man of *'True Black Consciousness'*, which he manipulated for the advancement of his race and ruling group. Take a minute to look at his methods that were written almost three centuries ago. Ask yourself which attributes do our society still possess. How about the Player-hater, someone who's envious of another person doing good. What about the light skin girl with her long straight hair? I remember when I was young, there were girls who always picked arguments with light skinned girls, claiming that they thought they were better than darker girls (and there were some that did). Was this not one of Lynch's methods? To pit the dark against the light? It was in Haiti, which was the first independent black nation after slave revolts that the Mulattos (mixed race people from slave owners and slaves) would sometimes deny their black heritage and pass themselves as white. They even owned their own plantations and black slaves. It was eventually a mulatto who lured General Toussaint, one of the Blacks greatest generals into a trap by Napoleon.

Ask yourself how many times have you said in jest, "where'd he get that, he probably stole it" or "ah, you know you can't trust black people for nothing."

It's statements like these and "Oh, he's late. That's just black people time," that prove that the Lynch's slave is still rife amongst our community. If this is how we see ourselves, how do you think the other races see us? The traits of the Lynch Slave is still dominant in many of us today. But if you think Lynch's genius stop here think again....

***

CHAPTER: 7

Stunned, Jade sat still. She didn't know whether to be excited or outraged by her book. She looked up and around the room to see if anybody noticed what she had just read. Ms. Matheson the old white librarian caught her eye. Checking out a book, she peered over her silver rimmed glasses at Jade. Blushing Jade looked away. For some reason she felt like saying, "What you looking at you white bitch?" Then thought about the absurdity. Making another crease in the books spine, Jade rubbed the page and read on.

*

Remember, I explained to you that Lynch was a businessman. At the heart of any businessman is the desire to make more money, diverse, and expand. Well in true guru fashion our old fiend of a friend Lynch produced a handbook. Now what would a guru be without their own manual or 'how-to-do' handbook? Could you imagine Delia smith without a book on cooking, or Alan Titchmarsh without a book on gardening? Yes, I guess in the year 1712 for a couple shillings or crown bob you could receive your very own manual on how to make the perfect slave, written by Willie Lynch himself and appropriately titled **"LET'S MAKE A SLAVE"**.

'Let's Make a Slave' is a handbook that demonstrates the practicality of Lynch and other slave owners techniques to contain their slaves. The handbook reveals a step-by-step programme of procedures and their importance. Through this handbook the reader is placed face to face with the ideology of the slave owner. It illustrates the business interests of slaveholders like Willie Lynch, and continues to highlight the fact that they were very rational and calculated about their methods. It is an insight into what were the trends and attitudes towards the cruelty of slavery. It also gives reasoning for the perpetual wrongs imposed on the slave with the accurate and premeditated thought of producing an obedient race of labourers.

LET'S MAKE A SLAVE
"The Original and Development of a Social
Being Called "The Negro."

Let us make a slave. What do we need? First of all we need a black nigger man, a pregnant nigger woman and her baby nigger boy. Second, we will use the same basic principle that we use in breaking a horse, combined with some more sustaining factors. What we do with horses is that we break them from one form of life to another, that is we reduce them from their natural state in nature. Whereas nature provides them with the natural capacity to take care of their offspring, we break that natural string of independence from them and thereby create a dependency status, so that we may be able to get from them useful production for our business and pleasure.

CARDINAL PRINCIPLES FOR MAKING A NEGRO

For fear that our future Generations may not understand the principles of breaking both of the beast together, the nigger and the horse. We understand that short range planning economics results in periodic economic chaos; so that to avoid turmoil in the economy, it requires us to have breath and depth in long range comprehensive planning, articulating both skill sharp perceptions. We lay down the following principles for long range comprehensive economic planning.
Both horse and niggers is no good to the economy in the wild or natural state.

- *Both must be BROKEN and TIED together for orderly production. For orderly future, special and particular attention must be paid to the FEMALE and the YOUNGEST offspring.*
- *Both must be CROSSBRED to produce a variety and division of labour.*
- *Both must be taught to respond to a peculiar new LANGUAGE.*

Psychological and physical instruction of CONTAINMENT must be created for both. We hold the six cardinal principles as truth to be self evident, based upon the following the discourse concerning the economics of breaking and tying the horse and the nigger together, all inclusive of the six principles laid down about.

NOTE: Neither principle alone will suffice for good economics. All principles must be employed for orderly good of the nation. Accordingly, both a wild horse and a wild or mature nigger is dangerous even if captured, for they will have the tendency to seek their customary freedom, and in doing so, might kill you in your sleep. You cannot rest. They sleep while you are awake, and are awake while you are asleep. They are DANGEROUS near the family house and it requires too much labour to watch them away from the house. Above all, you cannot get them to work in this natural state.

Hence both the horse and the nigger must be broken; that is breaking them from one form of mental life to another. KEEP THE BODY - TAKE THE MIND! In other words break the will to resist.

Now the breaking process is the same for both the horse and the nigger, only slightly varying in degrees. But as we said before, there is an art in long range economic planning. YOU MUST KEEP YOUR EYE AND THOUGHTS ON THE FEMALE and the OFFSPRING of the horse and the nigger. A brief discourse in offspring development will shed light on the key to sound economic principles. Pay little attention to the generation of original breaking, but CONCENTRATE ON FUTURE GENERATION. Therefore, if you break the FEMALE mother, she will BREAK the offspring in its early years of development and when the offspring is old enough to work, she will deliver it up to you, for her normal female protective tendencies will have been lost in the original breaking process. For example take the case of the wild stud horse, a female horse and an already infant horse and compare the breaking process with two captured nigger males in their natural state and, a pregnant nigger woman with her infant offspring. Take the stud horse, and break him for limited containment. Completely break the female horse until she becomes very gentle, to the point where you or anybody can ride her in comfort. Breed the mare and the stud until you have the desired offspring. Then you can turn the stud to freedom until you need him again. Train the female horse where by she will eat out of your hand, and she will in turn train the infant horse to eat out of your hand also. When it comes to breaking the uncivilized nigger, use the same process, but vary the degree and step up the pressure, so as to do a complete reversal of the mind. Take the meanest and most restless nigger, strip him of his clothes in front of the remaining male niggers, the female, and the nigger infant, tar and feather him, tie each leg to a different horse faced in opposite directions, set him a fire and beat both horses to pull him apart in front of the remaining nigger. The next step is to take a bullwhip and beat the remaining nigger male to the point of death, in front of the female and the infant. Don't kill him, but PUT THE FEAR OF GOD IN HIM, for he can be useful for future breeding.

THE BREAKING PROCESS OF THE AFRICAN WOMAN

Take the female and run a series of tests on her to see if she will submit to your desires willingly. Test her in every way, because she is the most important factor for good economics. If she shows any sign of resistance in submitting completely to your will, do not hesitate to use the bullwhip on her to extract that last bit of bitch out of her. Take care not to kill her, for in doing so, you spoil good economics.

When in complete submission, she will train her off springs in the early years to submit to labour when they become of age. Understanding is the best thing. Therefore, we shall go deeper into this area of the subject matter concerning what we have produced here in this breaking process of the female nigger. We have reversed the relationship in her natural uncivilized state she would have a strong dependency on the uncivilized nigger male, and she would have a limited protective tendency toward her independent male offspring and would raise male off springs to be dependent like her. Nature had provided for this type of balance. We reversed nature by burning and pulling a civilized nigger apart and bull whipping the other to the point of death, all in her presence. By her being left alone and unprotected, with the MALE IMAGE DESTROYED, the ordeal caused her to move from her psychological dependent state to a frozen independent state.

In this frozen psychological state of independence, she will raise her MALE and female offspring in reversed roles. For FEAR of the young males life she will psychologically train him to be MENTALLY WEAK and DEPENDENT, but PHYSICALLY STRONG. Because she has become psychologically independent, she will train her FEMALE off springs to be psychologically independent. What have you got? You've got the NIGGER WOMAN OUT FRONT AND THE NIGGER MAN BEHIND AND SCARED. This is a perfect situation of sound sleep and economic. Before the breaking process, we had to be alertly on guard at all times. Now we can sleep soundly, for out of frozen fear his woman stands guard for us. He cannot get past her early slave moulding process. He is a good tool, now ready to be tied to the horse at a tender age. By the time a nigger boy reaches the age of sixteen, he is soundly broken in and ready for a long life of sound and efficient work and the reproduction of a unit of good labour force. Continually through the breaking of the uncivilized savage nigger, by throwing the nigger female savage into a frozen psychological state of independence, by killing off the protective male image, and by creating a submissive dependent mind of the nigger male slave, we have created an orbiting cycle that turns on its own axis forever, unless a phenomenon occurs and re shifts the position of the male and female slaves. We show what we mean by example. Take the case of the two economic slave units and examine them close

THE NEGRO MARRIAGE UNIT

We breed two nigger males with two nigger females. Then we take the nigger male away from them and keep them moving and working. Say one nigger female bears a nigger female and the other bears a nigger male. Both nigger females being without influence of the nigger male image, frozen with an independent psychology, will raise their offspring into reverse positions. The one with the female offspring will teach her to be like herself, independent and negotiable (we manipulate her to believe she has the capacity to negotiate). The one with the nigger male offspring, she being frozen subconscious fears for his life, will raise him to be mentally dependent and weak, but physically strong, in other words, body over mind. Now in a few years when these two offspring's become fertile for early reproduction we will mate and breed them and continue the cycle. That is good, sound, and long range comprehensive planning.

*

Jade hadn't realised she was crying until a tear touched the page. Distressed she scanned the passage again mesmerised by phrases like *nigger woman, mentally weak,* and *male image destroyed.* They troubled her. Ashamed, she closed the book gripping it tightly. She could feel her body trembling and had a desire to leave. Quickly she gathered her things and headed for the bus stop.

"Jade, where you going?" Emma yelled as Jade dashed past her. "We've got a lecture in fifteen minutes."

"I've got to go home." Jade said in a hurry.

"What's wrong?"

"I can't explain!"

Sprinting Jade caught the bus at the top of the road. Taking a seat, she sat clutching the book. She wanted to read on, but was afraid. The words nigger woman frightened her and Jade knew why. Every time she read the words, she began to see her mother's face. The lone black nigger woman, removed from her spouse to raise her offspring. That was her mother, Carmen Godfrey, a nigger woman. It made Jade Angry. She couldn't stop asking herself, "How has my mother raised us?"

"The best she could," was the desired answer, but Jade's conscience told her something else.

Carmen Godfrey had done no more than Lynch's handbook required from a nigger woman. Both her daughter's were strong independent women, free from male reliance. From an early age they had been taught how to clean, how to cook, and how to budget, that things were always harder for black women and they must rise to that challenge, but what was Mark taught? He was never given the same challenges.

Anita had always accused their mother of treating Mark different, now Jade was beginning to consider the truth. Yes at 6ft 1inch Mark was physically strong, with broad shoulders and huge hands he could beat most men, but he shirked his responsibilities. He was never to blame, it was always someone else's fault. When he was wrong, his mother said 'Well they left him no choice'. It was his weakness. A weakness he had acquired from years of being shielded by his mother.

Sitting on the bus, tears ran down Jade's face as she began harbouring bitterness towards Carmen Godfrey. By the time she reached her mother's house, she could barely see through her teary eyes. She fumbled around in her handbag for her keys. Opening the door she heard the nigger woman call out. "Jade, is that you?"

Jade ignored her mother rushing into the front room. There were toys everywhere. As she picked them up, the nigger woman kept calling, "Jade! Jade!"

Each call and misplaced toy infuriated Jade. She wiped her face franticly. Finally her mother stood in the doorway.

"Jade! Wharm'? I'm calling you an' you cyan't answer?"

"What do I need to answer for," Jade snapped. "You know it's me!"

She threw the gathered toys into a box in the corner. "What the hell are all these toys doing over the place?"

"Well," Carmen sighed. She bent down to help. "Me never had time to clear them up before me tek Jayvan nursery."

"So!" Jade snatched a toy car from her mother. "What happened to Jayvan tidying up?"

"Jade," Carmen sniggered. "Jayvan is a liccle boy."

"So, I don't care!" Jade barked. "You're always making excuses for people, don't start making excuse for my son. That's all you ever do!"

Shocked Carmen looked at Jade, "Jade, it's a couple of toys, what's your problem?"

"You're my problem," Jade stood to face her mother. "Your always making excuses." She began to list them on her fingers. "You made excuses for dad, you make excuses for Mark, you make excuses for Uncle Tony, now you want to make excuses for Jayvan. Well don't do it, Mum, don't do it!"

Stunned Carmen looked at Jade's puffy eyes. She knew she should've sensed something earlier. "What's wrong, Jade, what's happened?"

"Nothing happened mum!"

"So why you crying?" Carmen grabbed her daughter by both arms "Tell me. Something's happened hasn't it, what's wrong, Jade?"

"You're what's wrong!" Jade yelled pulling away from her mother. "You're what's wrong! I don't want you making my son turn out like Mark! I don't want to be like you!"

***

CHAPTER: 8

The Godfrey house was silent. In the aftermath Jade sat in her old bedroom wallowing in guilt. After upsetting her mother, she instinctively returned there to seek solace. Reaching for an old stuffed teddy Ivan once gave her for valentines, she stroked its white fur picking out lint. Pushing her feet under the stacks of laundry and folded bed linen at the bottom of the bed, Jade bit her lip contemplating her outburst. She didn't regret her words, only expressing them aloud. She knew they were more for her benefit than her mother's

Standing up, she walked over to the mirror hanging on the back off the door and wiped the dust off. Looking at her reflection, she finally understood where her hostility came from. She looked towards the book on the bedside cabinet. Chapter by chapter it had became a mirror and her family the reflection. It pushed Jade closer to an unwanted future and Jade loathed that. Like a blemish on her face, she wanted to conceal the truth. She was no better than her mother, and Jayvan's father was no better than her own. Even more she resented the fact that she now felt powerless. Jade despised the author for making her feel so. A part of her felt lost and she did not trust Gilyan Gates as her new guide. Losing her sense of duty to Mark, Jade picked up her book and continued reading....

WARNING: POSSIBLE INTERLOPING NEGATIVES

Earlier we talked about the non-economic good of the horse and the nigger in their wild or natural state; we talked about the principle of breaking and tying them together for orderly production. Furthermore, we talked about paying particular attention to the female savage and her offspring for orderly future planning, then more recently we stated that, by reversing the positions of the male and female savages, we created an orbiting cycle that turns on its own axis forever unless a phenomenon occurs and reshifts and re-positions the male and female savages.

Our experts warned us about the possibility of this phenomenon occurring, for they say that the mind has a strong drive to correct and re-correct itself over a period of time. History advised us that the best way to deal with the phenomenon is to shave off the brute's mental history and create a multiplicity of phenomena of illusions, so that each illusion will twirl in its own orbit, something similar to floating balls in a vacuum. This creation of multiplicity of phenomena of illusions entails the principle of crossbreeding the nigger and the horse as we stated above, the purpose of which is to create a diversified division of labour thereby creating different levels of labour and different values of illusion at each connecting level of labour. The results of which is the severance of the points of original beginnings for each sphere illusion.

Since we feel that the subject matter may get more complicated as we proceed in laying down our economic plan concerning the purpose, reason and effect of crossbreeding horses and niggers, we shall lay down the following definition terms for future generations. An orbiting cycle means a thing turning in a given path. Axis means upon which or around which a body turns. Phenomenon means something beyond ordinary conception and inspires awe and wonder. Multiplicity means a great number. It means a globe. Cross breeding a horse means taking a horse and breeding it with an ass and you get a dumb backward ass long headed mule that is not reproductive nor productive by itself. Crossbreeding niggers means taking so many drops of good white blood and putting them into as many nigger women as possible, varying the drops by the various tone that you want, and then letting them breed with each other until another circle of colour appears as you desire. What this means is this; Put the niggers in a breeding pot, mix some good white blood and what do you get? You got a multiplicity of colours of ass backward, unusual niggers, running, tied to a backward ass long headed mules, the one productive of itself, the other sterile. (The one constant, the other dying, we keep the nigger constant for we may replace the mules for another tool) both mule and nigger tied to each other, neither knowing where the other came from and neither productive for itself, nor without each other.

CONTROLLING THE LANGUAGE

Crossbreeding completed, for further severance from their original beginning, WE MUST COMPLETELY ANNIHILATE THE MOTHER TONGUE of both the new nigger and the new mule and institute a new language that involves the new life's work of both. You know language is a peculiar institution. It leads to the heart of a people. The more a foreigner knows about the language of another country the more he is able to move through all levels of that society. Therefore, if the foreigner is an enemy of the country, to the extent that he knows the body of the language, to that extent is the country vulnerable to attack or invasion of a foreign culture. For example, if you take a slave, if you teach him all about your language, he will know all your secrets, and he is then no more a slave, for you can't fool him any longer, and BEING A FOOL IS ONE OF THE BASIC INGREDIENTS OF MAINTAINING THE SLAVERY SYSTEM.

For example, if you told a slave that he must perform in getting out "our crops" and he knows the language well, he would know that "our crops" didn't mean "our crops" and the slavery system would break down, for he would relate on the basis of what "our crops" really meant. So you have to be careful in setting up the new language for the slaves would soon be in your house, talking to you as "man to man" and that is death to our economic system. In addition, the definitions of words or terms are only a minute part of the process. Values are created and transported by communication through the body of the language. A total society has many interconnected value systems. All the values in the society have bridges of language to connect them for orderly working in the society. But for these language bridges, these many value systems would sharply clash and cause internal strife or civil war, the degree of the conflict being determined by the magnitude of the issues or relative opposing strength in whatever form.

For example, if you put a slave in a hog pen and train him to live there and incorporate in him to value it as a way of life completely, the biggest problem you would have out of him is that he would worry you about provisions to keep the hog pen clean. If you slip and incorporate something in his language where by he comes to value a house more than he does his hog pen, you got a problem. He will soon be in your house.

Reading over Lynch's handbook again and again, began to numb my brain. There was a pounding feeling inside my head, which kept beating away. It pounded and pounded like a drum saying wake up, understand, be aware, teach, speak, preach, communicate, don't let them be slaves. It was my conscience governing over me like Pinocchio's 'Talking Cricket'. I tried to ignore it. "Ignore", it said "Ignore the works of such a man, ignore the problems that plague your community, ignore the slave within yourself, ignore the answers to questions you sought after, ignore the journey, ignore me. You stupid boy." He was right how could I ignore such things. It would be different if I didn't fully comprehend what I had found. It would be different if I didn't want to change and make a difference in life. It would be different if my mind was closed, but it wasn't. My mind was open like a 24-hour library with knowledge at my disposal. It was my choice whether I wanted to use it. I decided I didn't want to be contained with a slave mind anymore, I didn't want my children to be contained either. No I wanted to be a King. I wanted to be in control of my destiny, to choose the path that I walked. I didn't want to be forced or pushed down the road of degradation and slavery any more as my ancestors had. Why should I, I was more than that. I was the type of nigger/slave that Willie Lynch warned about. I was the foreigner who had learned the language of the country and made it vulnerable to attack. I was the slave that had realised that he lived in a hog pen and wanted to enter the house.

Because of my will to survive and hunger to achieve, I had adapted my own thought process to deal with moral issues as strictly business. It's a thought process that throws out any other values that parents, schools, or church might teach and replaces them with one rule "it's all about the Business". If I've got to sell crack, its only business, if I've got to stab someone over my money, its only business. If I've got to lie, cheat, steal or harm anyone its only business. With such an approach to life and morality where do you draw the line? When do your actions stop being business? This was the same language that the slave owners understood. The same train of thought that Willie Lynch used when writing his handbook. The same ethics that allowed the cruelty of slavery to go unchallenged for centuries. Now I completely understood the language

I can only imagine what it is like for an explorer to discover a new world, but I reasoned it must feel like I was feeling now. Anxiety, excitement, and fear all rolled into a roller coaster of emotions. Who could I tell about my discovery? I was Einstein finding the equation to relativity only my equation was for empowerment.

(X)
Knowledge Of Slave Owner Language

$X + Y = Z$
+ *Plus*   =   *Slave Empowerment*

(Y)
Knowledge Of Methods Of Containment

With so many things to cloud young black minds, spearheaded by materialism and vanity, my people were forgetting the real struggles in life, especially my generation. Someone had thrown a sack over our heads like our ancestors and stolen us for slavery once more. We hadn't experienced hardship like our parents and grandparents. I was a third generation Black in England. We hadn't grown up in a time of visibly strong black leaders like

Malcolm X and Martin Luther King, and if we did, we certainly didn't recognise them.

We knew the legacies other leaders left behind, but we believed their fight was over. We forgot key factors in our own past and had forged no accomplishments of our own. We had become slaves again, because so easily we overlooked and disregarded our history.

If the bonds of time were to be broken, it was imperative that we were aware of this degenerate pattern in our culture. It was the refuelling and self-generating ideology that the Lynches of the past had installed and created. It was the reason for black on black crime, wide scale single parent families, the incarceration of many young black men, the mis-education of black youth and the erosion of the black family and community. It was our reason to fight for freedom once more.

My mind had begun the phenomenal process that Lynch's experts had predicted. It was correcting and re-correcting itself, breaking the doctrine and thought cycle that had been dictated to us. I was beginning to identify the slave in my people and those who carried the Lynch trait...

*

Closing her book, Jade sat up and let out a huge sigh. Saddened, she looked around her old room with its faded pink walls. It was no longer her sanctuary. Gradually it had been stripped of its previous identity and became a glorified airing cupboard for her mother's laundry and linen. It was a sign that all things change and evolve; how we label them didn't dictate their identity. Jade had to admit Gates' book was leaving her mind open.

Leaving the new laundry room, Jade went downstairs to the Kitchen. She put the kettle on and made two cups of tea. Taking out two aspirin tablets, she took a cup up to her mother. Knocking gently on her mother's door, she waited a moment before entering. Humbled Carmen lay quietly on her bed, face away from the door.

"Mum," Jade said. "I brought you a cup of tea and some aspirin."

"Thank you, Jade," Carmen said in an unusually meek voice. "Just leave them on the side."

Jade placed the tablets and the tea on the bedside cabinet and said nothing. Now wasn't the time to apologise.

***

CHAPTER: 9

Jade lay paralyzed beneath the warm duvet. Each muscle told her not to move as the morning sun shone between the gaps in her curtains. It wasn't often that she got to lie in, so from her horizontal position she decided to plan her day without Jayvan. Mentally she compiled a list of chores: washing, cleaning, ironing, coursework, and then a letter to Ivan. In between, she would cook and watch the omnibus edition of '*Hollyoaks*', but that was all after her lie in.

Hugging her pillow, Jade thanked the St Mark's Baptist Church and Saturday excursions. Guessing the time, she figured her mother and son would be climbing aboard an old stuffy coach at any moment. Their destination was Margate while hers' was tranquillity, until a loud disturbance came from next door. Through the thin walls Jade heard short bursts of Irish fury and Jamaican rants as her neighbours Shannon and Denzil waged war on each other. It was a regular occurrence. Today Jade didn't mind their arguments too much. Sometimes it was funny to hear them curse each other out. Jade just hoped it didn't end up in blows and fisticuffs for Shannon because nothing was making her get out of bed today. She gave them their complimentary five minutes before banging on the wall and the noise soon died down. Rolling over Jade went back to cuddling her pillow.

Ten minutes later the sound of sex coming through the wall ended Jade's lie in. Getting up she made a cup of tea and took her duvet into the front room. Stretching out on the couch Jade thought - *oh well, if I can't have a lie in at least I can finish my book*. She picked up her book determined to get through the remaining chapters.

I HAD A DREAM   *The Journey of a Slave.*

That night I closed my eyes and lay in my bed thinking about my journey. It had brought me so far. As sleep transformed my thoughts into dreams, I saw myself wandering the landscape of my mind. Alone, I walked through the dry deserts of slavery, almost beaten by the hard sandstorm that blew. Blinded I continued before discovering the rich orchards of True Black Consciousness. Famished I picked the ripe fruit from the long flowing vines and supplemented my journey ahead. Lost in the dark mazes of Lynch's

Plantation, I listened to the strange whispers of The Slave Owner as they spoke in foreign tongues. Deciphering the oblique language, I heard the same voices scream at me in anger. Their words warned me to turn back. Hiking on with blistered feet, I now reached a sign that read - Welcome to The City of Modern Containment, population the Black nation.

With caution and doubt I looked towards the black buildings and shining lights. Below me lived a nation of slaves trapped in a metropolis of modern containment. They carried the traits of the Lynch virus and breed amongst each other like a plague.

Standing on the outskirts peering down, I became aware I was no longer alone. As I turned around, they slowly emerged one by one from the black shadows. Their faces were wounded, tired, and exhausted. Some looked as if they had been travelling for years, maybe even centuries. Their clothes ranged from rags to well groomed suits, but were all dusty and worn. Some wore shoes, others none. Around their ankles were the iron chains and shackles that burdened their travels. How had I not heard the noise of the heavy metal clanging together?

Standing together, they formed a sea of heads ranging from every shade of Black skin, dark to light. There were the dark and beautiful Nubians and Ashanti, with skin as rich as the soil, the copper bronze of the Asiatic, and the golden caramel of the mulattos. As they came closer I began to recognise some of the faces within the mass. There was Sam Sharpe from the Jamaican Slave revolts of 1832, Olaudah Equiano author of the life of Olaudah Equiano, Langston Hughes and other members of the Harlem renaissance. Tupac and Huey P. Newton stood fearless as ever with a squadron of Black Panthers. WEB Dubois harboured books under his arm. Ms Mary Seacole gently tended to wounded and blistered feet. Bernie Grant and Stephen Lawrence stood with members of the Brixton riots and Notting hill uprisings. Long dreadlocks flew in the air as Bob Marley passionately strummed away at his guitar. While Marvin Gaye and Ella Fitzgerald accompanied him leading a choir of voices.

There were so many heroes and heroines amongst them, the famous, and the unsung. Even my grandfather and cousin J-J were present, smiling.

Looking majestic in full uniform, was the dominant figure of Marcus Garvey, closely followed by Malcolm X and Dr Martin Luther King. Each bearing a gift, they stepped towards me. My heartbeat raced fast like a formula one car. I felt myself taking a few steps back as they approached.

Marcus Garvey was the first to speak. His voice was deep like thunder breaking the clouds. "Child, I bring you a gift of Strength, Courage, and Vision. May you use them wisely."

I was dwarfed by his powerful stare. With every movement he commanded respect. The moment was his and all remained silent. In his illustrious manner he returned to stand with the other UNIA and Black Star members. He gave me one last head nod and stroked his thick moustache.

Then, tall and slender with light skin and fiery red hair, Malcolm X was the next to approach. " I guess you already know me?" he said resettling his glasses.

"Yes sir, your El Hajji Malik Shabbazz," I said with childish excitement.

"You can call me Malcolm," he grinned. "My brother, I bring you the double edge sword of speech. May it be your form of attack and means to cut down your opponents in times of need."

Gripping my hand with a firm shake and a hug, Malcolm stood back smiling with the famous charismatic grin. "Salaam my brother, salaam."

Then, as he stepped forward to embrace me, Dr Martin Luther King was almost crying. He held me at arms-length and looked over me.

"Mmmm, mmm, mm." He hummed with delight. "Blessed be the lord who has delivered you amongst us, for it is the lord who surely knows what is in store for you. My child I bring to you today, on this blessed day, the light of hope and humanity, so that you may truly see the path that you must walk. May it shine like a torch in your darkest hour, may it reside in your heart and flow through your body with every heartbeat. May it replenish your hunger and quench your thirst, and may you use it to ignite the minds of the young black and poor!"

Dr. King hugged me as the assembly began to applaud. For a moment I stood bewildered in front of these people. Why had they appeared? I stared at the convoy of martyrs, victims, and slaves, before realising that my journey had not only brought me here, but it had brought them here as well.

It was a crossroads a pivotal moment in which every traveller would inevitably arrive at. Many would stray and become lost, others would frequently pass ignoring the sign, and there were those who never reached the crossroad at all. How each individual chooses their right path was why they had gathered here.

Suddenly there was a strange movement at the back. The congregation began to divide making way for a lone figure. He made his way through the centre. Smiling and nodding, he acknowledged each individual as he passed.

He wasn't a tall man, but he seemed taller than he looked. He didn't have the greatest physique, but it didn't make him any weaker. His aura spoke volumes of intrigue, which uneased me.

He looked at Malcolm, who returned his look with a bashful grin. He looked upon Marcus who's stern face looked militant as he nodded twice. He came around to stand directly in front of Martin placing both hands on either shoulder. Smiling at each other, Martin nodded and ushered the figure over to my direction.

Nervously, I waited as the figure peered at me. He was many years old with woolly grey hair, large round watery eyes and frown marks that lay embedded in his forehead. His wrinkled face had no facial hair bar one or two white whiskers that stuck out of his chin. Standing barefoot with blisters on his feet, his ankles were heavily scarred from where he had worn the leg shackles. His strong hands were rough and gnarled as he took my own hand. He gently led me over near the edge and sat down by a bush. The lights from the city below glowed in the night sky and illuminated one side of the man's face like a campfire. He sat in silence peering down at the city almost waiting for something to materialise.

"Are you scared?" he asked in a soft voice. These were the first words he uttered to me.

"No."

"That is good my son, for bravery is just one attribute needed."

"Needed for what?" I asked.

The old man looked at me with quizzing eyes. "Come my child, you have travelled so far and you still ask for what?"

"It's for the journey isn't it?" It was more a statement then a question.

"Correct my child." The old man picked up two stones. He handed one to me and began rubbing his hand in a circular motion.

"Do you like alchemy?" he asked. Noticing my blank expression, he continued encouraging me to rub the stone. "Never mind," he smiled. "My, child you are one of those who understands the journey. You have an insight into what it is. You have been searching for reasons and answers and have found them. Whether you fill your full potential now rests upon your shoulders."

"What do you mean?" I asked imitating the old man's rubbing motion.

"My child," The old man explained. "Every being has a destiny and a role to play in life. You have found reasons why you and your peers have been suppressed within your roles. Now it is your decision how to act upon it."

The old man stopped rubbing his stone to reveal a smooth gold nugget. I too stopped rubbing. In my hand remained the stone as grey and as rough as it started. Laughing, the old man took both nugget and stone burying them in the ground.

"The power of alchemy," he said patting the soil with his feet. "Is not in the transformation of one form to another, but finding the formula to do it again and again." He looked at me with a playful eye. "Do you have a formula?"

"No," I said wiping the dust from my hand "But I got an equation though."

"Ahh," the old man smiled. "Your equation to empowerment. It is good, but its not quite correct," he paused stroking his chin. "Maybe it needs work, what do you think?"

"No," I shook my head. "It makes perfect sense to me."

"Then you must prove me wrong," he said. "For I am only here to help as I did before."

"As you did before?" I looked into his eyes and was met by my own reflection peering back. "I know you don't I?"

"Of course you know me, as do all of your brothers and sisters."

The Old man stood up. I followed him as he stared down at the city once more.

"I've walked this journey with each and every one of you and will continue to walk with those to come. I carried you when you were tired and released those who refused to walk no more. I will walk every step of every journey until the chosen time is upon us, then I will walk no more."

"What will happen when the chosen time is upon us?" I asked.

"We shall return to our rightful seats and be bestowed with the glory of Kings."

Suddenly there was a cracking roar of thunder and the ground rumbled with the sound of pounding hooves. As a trail of lights appeared in the distance, the crowd became agitated and began hustling back. Soon a legion of horseback riders and carriages began to make their way upon the slope. They forged a new army as large as the first, if not bigger. Some people amongst the first became troubled, others restless, as this new force lined up on the opposite side.

Immediately Martin calmed the people as Malcolm and Marcus ordered them into flanks. It was as though a war was to be waged. Following the old man, I took my place standing by three leaders. It was an honour to stand with such heroes, but what were we standing against?

My thoughts jumped from thought to thought - who was this new militia? What did they want? Did they really believe they could defeat us? And why were we about to fight?

I observed what I could only perceive as my enemy. Each and every head was covered in a white hood like members from a Klan rally. They carried whips and nooses as well as other tools used to enslave. They held their torches high and burned books. And as the flames of hatred burnt, I noticed that beneath the masks their skin colours varied as much as ours. Only this time their skin went from ebony black to ivory white. Their jeers and chants were louder than any mob you could imagine. Then in the same fashion as before, the mob began to divide making way for a new arrival.

I looked at the old man and watched as he smiled to himself keeping a keen eye fixed on the centre.

"Who is it?" I said.

The old man said nothing. He put a solitary finger to his lip ushering me to be silent.

"Who is it?" I asked again.

As the horse drawn carriage came closer the old man looked at me and said, "An old friend has come to pay us a visit my child. Say nothing and be on your best behaviour."

The carriage came to a halt and two hooded men ran to open the door. Placing a stepladder in front of the carriage door, the hooded men stepped back waiting for the occupant to exit. As the figure walked slowly down the steps dressed in 18th century aristocratic attire the mob began to cheer. The figure chuckled and lapped up his applause like an actor on stage. He waved his hands high, silencing the crowd.

Unlike his following he was not masked and I recognised him instantly. It was the Slave owner in the carriage. Gloating with a smug grin over his pompous face he stepped forward hands wide and spoke.

"Well, well, well, what do we have here I ask myself?" There was silence as he spoke. "A gathering of some of the greatest minds, scholars and head figures from a worthless nation, or a convoy of lesser fools to insult my intelligence."

His face became full of disgust and contempt as he looked upon the old man.

"Why, oh why have you gathered here once again old friend? To lend your support to what, this," he pointed his fat digit at me. "This worthless wretch that stands beside you?" He laughed. "He's a lost cause, not even amazing grace could save him. Look at him. He's a child amongst us men. He knows nothing of the world and its ways. What could he possibly offer to your cause? He is a street urchin, a peddler of narcotics who thrives on what he does. He knows no better and acts no different than the rest of his generation. He's a beast. A slave to be tamed and proclaimed as mine!"

For the first time the old man spoke up in my defence. "Yes, he is a street peddler as was Malcolm, but he is no beast. He has potential and that is why you are here, as are we. I will guide all those who chose to be guided and know their right place in history, and there is nothing you or your minions can do for his destiny belongs with he only."

"Nothing I can do?" The slave master raged. "Nothing I can do? I who have as far as possible closed every avenue by which light may enter their minds. If I could extinguish their capacity to see the light, my work would be complete; they would then be on a level with the beasts of the field and my people would be safe. Nothing I can do! I told you once before my friend, and I will tell you again. I will whisper in the hearts and minds of all those who will follow."

"But you are losing the battle old friend," The old man grinned. "Each year my children show progress. Each year they will walk further down the path, until the day the journey is complete. You fear this child as much as you feared any other that has been sent before."

"Fear!" The slave master scoffed. "You speak of fear as though I should bare some? Shall I take it that you have chosen yourself a champion, old friend? Perhaps a leader, a saviour, no a messiah for your pathetic cause."

"Take it as you please, and call him what you want. " The old man answered. "It makes no difference to what he is."

"Makes no difference, but it makes all the difference, old friend."

The Slave Master looked at me with a devious glare. If there was truly a serpent in the Garden of Eden, it was with the same grin he led Eve to temptation. Clearing his throat the Slave Master held one hand upon his hip and threw the other in the air as he began to recite.

"So a champion stands before me with no inhibition or fear, gallant may our young noble warrior be. But from the flesh and bones of man come heart's desires and the entrances to their souls. If your champion has, but one soul then your champion have, but one weakness that may bring him to fortune's bleakest. So bring forth what the heart desires and yields, and behold what even the gods could not shield. Behold your champion's Achilles' heels."

The slave master beckoned over to his henchmen. Leaning into the carriage the first henchman led the delicate frame of a woman out by one hand. Her gown was sky blue silk and the bell shape bottom half of the dress made her look as though she floated on air. The corset squeezed her ample bosoms into view for all to admire. A pendant hung motionless from her black choker like a neo light above her breast. Her hair was jet black in contrast to her golden caramel complexion. The hood on her navy blue petticoat rested carefully on her head. Wearing white lace gloves, a white mask covered her eyes.

Her movement was sensual and predatory like a lioness stalking her prey as she slowly approached. Pressing her body against me, she stroked my face. I could feel her heartbeat whilst mine soared out of control.

"I love you," she whispered tenderly in my ear. "I always have, do you love me?" The question went unanswered as our lips brushed together before becoming entwined. Her tongue breached my mouth. Reluctantly I pulled back knowing exactly what was happening. She dropped her mask to the floor. Persistently she pulled my head to her chest. Kissing her neck, my member slowly began to rise. Her hands gripped my back and confessed her excitement. Her voice was slow and inviting.

"I love you, do you love me?"

Squeezing where I wanted to be squeezed, and rubbing where I wanted to be rubbed, I couldn't resist the hypnotic chant, "I love you, do you love me?" Her thighs ran between my own, pressing and pushing. "I love you, do you love me?"

Yes, I could hear myself say inside my head, yes, but my will refused to loosen my lips. Her hand tugged firmly at my lower region in an erotic motion. My desires were aroused and her urge was strong.

"Alicia, stop!" I yelled pushing her away.

I had to. I couldn't be so easily taunted. Standing looking at me, hopelessly in pain a single tear rolled down her cheek. "I love you, Gil, DON'T YOU LOVE ME?" she screamed at the top of her voice. Yet the question continued to go unanswered.

Laughing, the slave master skipped forward to console her. "There, there my, dear," he put an arm around Alicia as she sobbed in his chest like a child. "Don't worry my dear their champion is strong, but for how long? How long old friend?" He asked the old man. "Maybe he's not as useless as I thought, this champion of yours."

The old man looked at me and then at the slave master.

"As I said call him as you please, his destiny lies within his own hands. Strength, courage, vision, hope, and humility, he has been equipped with all. Only he knows whether the correct equation may restore balance."

The slave master chuckled, "You've learnt to give nothing away over time hey, old friend. And what about you, champion, what say you?"

My previous instruction was to say nothing, I understood why now. The slave master could use any action or reaction against you to accomplish his goals, never missing a trick.

"Have you no answer as well, champion?" He urged me to speak. When there was no answer he continued. "Well, champion, remember this and remember it well." Reaching into his pocket he pulled out a handful of small white rocks. He smelt the pieces of crack in his hand like they were fresh coffee beans.

"You are a slave, champion, and you will always be a slave, for I know what your heart desires and I know how to enter your soul. I too travel this journey and will stop at nothing to contain you. I have enslaved your people before you and I will enslave your people after you. You will not be free".

Flashing his teeth he walked casually to his carriage enticing Alicia with the white stones. "Look my dear for you, as precious as any stone, jewel, or gold buried in the ground." He kicked at the dirt the old man laid. Then he dug up the gold nugget and presented both sets of rock too Alicia.

Looking at me Alicia paused. The mixture of eyeliner and tears made black tracks down the sides of her smooth face.

"I really did love you," she said snatching the white rocks.
"NO STOP!!!"

When I awoke my body was covered in sweat. My bed sheets were damp from my clammy skin and from somewhere in the darkness of the room, my phone rang. Jumping out of my bed I searched frantically through a pile of clothes for the phone. As the last ring tone rang I looked at the screen. 1 missed call. Checking my list of missed calls the screen read no number. Someone had called me from a private number. I wondered if it was Alicia. How mad would that be for her to be on the other end?

The politics of my lifestyle and conscious mind were beginning to take their toll. They had manifested themselves in my dreams. I needed to pull myself together. I was a Road Nigga. I had to preserve that frame of mind. I couldn't be conscious of this and that and do my hustle at the same time, or could I?

It was a conflict that I knew wouldn't be resolved in one night. Not tonight anyway.

Pulling on my tracksuit bottoms I went downstairs and fixed a drink. *Damn* I thought, *I'm gonna have to strip and change those sheets.* Just then my phone rang again.

"Hello" I said croakily.

"Nah it's me, Gil. Whassup?"

"Yeah, what's the time now?"

"Boy, its 3 o'clock now. By the time you get there I'm likely too be sleeping."

I was tired. I didn't want to get up, but the person on the other end was persistent.

"You got the right money yeah. No tick, no change, no shorts, Spark's rules. You know that's 120 yeah?"

"Okay, okay give me about twenty minutes and I'll be there, and make sure you're there, I ain't waitin 'round for nuffin."

"Yes, yes I know you do, I love you too okay. I'll see you in twenty minutes."

Hanging up the phone I thought to myself, oh well the bed sheets will have to wait. The air outside was cold as I wheeled my bike to my secret stash. Looking around to see if anybody could see me I quickly moved into positions and retrieved my bounty. Wrapped in a plastic bag and tissues I unravelled my stash. Looking at the collection of wraps in my hand, I picked out six twenty bags of rock and put the rest back into the hiding spot. I shook the remaining six bags in my hand and took a quick smell of the cocaine and cellophane aroma. I imagined it was the smell of money as I put them in my mouth. *Boy, its time to get paid*, I forced myself to believe and began peddling slowly through the cold and barren streets.

*

Fuckin' ignorant bastard Jade thought as she turned the page. *This man's got no morals.*

***

CHAPTER: 10

THE CITY OF MODERN CONTAINMENT

The Journey of a Slave.

"Final call my brother, final call my brother!" The tall man cried at the top of his voice. Smartly dressed in a black suit, white shirt, and red bow tie the distinguished uniform of the Black Muslim was being ignored as he tried to sell his newspapers. He stood out like a buoy on the seacoast, as people hustled passed him oblivious to his cries.

"Final Call, Final call, get your final call here brother!"

I looked at him and laughed. The Nation of Islam didn't have the same presence in England as it did in the United States. I wondered - was that down to the government ban on Louis Farrakhan or were there other factors at play. It didn't seem fair BNP membership was on the increase, the neo-nazi leader had visited Britain to spread his views. Kombat 18 and racist bombers were all things the black community had to deal with. Maybe a couple of speeches from the black leader were well overdue.

Watching the Muslim sell his papers I felt a sense of admiration for him. Here was a man who'd made a conscious decision and wasn't ashamed to have the conviction to carry it through. It would probably be just as easy for him to sell drugs or steal, but here he was trying to do his bit for the better of a community. I pictured myself in the suit and red bow tie. It didn't suit me, besides on the surface the Nation of Islam seemed to have too many contradictions with orthodox Islam. Nevertheless I decided to show my support and purchased a paper.

"How much for a paper bruv?"

"One pound my brother." The man said, handing me copy.

Reaching into my pocket I pulled out a handful of change and handed him a pound coin.

"Alhamdulillah my young brother," he said shaking my hand. "Enjoy your read."

"Inshallah, bro," I returned the pleasantries "You enjoy your day too."

"Salaam!" The man said grabbing my arm. "Are you a Muslim brother?"

"Who me bro?" I replied. "Nah, I just know a few things about Islam and that."

"Mashallah that's good," The man said turning to check his stack of papers. "But have you ever thought of extending your knowledge and awareness by coming to the Mosque, brother?"

"Nah that's not really my thing" I said pulling an awkward face

"Mmm, I understand," The man smiled. "Many of Black Britain's self awareness is so integrated with multiculturalism and integration that the idea of white devils and a black God is blasphemy to you. But you can learn much more if you're interested".

"Nah it's not that, bruv." I said, knowing I'd just been lured into conversation. "If the white devil ting, is your ting, then that's your ting, innit. Like, I done read" I said waving my paper, "That the Nations of Islams ideology has changed from the reunion of Louis Farrakhan and Elijah Muhammad's son and ting, but the whole religion thing. No offence brother, but that's not me innit."

"No offence taken," The man stepped back "It seems as though you know a little more than I credited you, brother."

I laughed politely at the compliment.

"Are you sure you won't join me just once at the mosque." The man asked. "It would really please me to introduce you to some of the brothers."

I looked around dubiously, "Err, I'm not sure, bruv. Like I said it's not really my thing."

Maybe it was the uncertainty in my voice, but the Black Muslim took the paper out my hand and began writing on it.

"Listen brother, this is my phone number. My name is Lennox X. I want you to do me a favour because you seem like a smart guy. I want you to sit down and think about your life and your community and if there's any reason you need help, then I want you to call me. Can you do that for me brother?"

"Yeah, yeah safe," I said automatically. "I'll think about it."

Shaking Lennox's hand, I took my paper and walked over to the wall to wait for Mel. It was another five minutes before he arrived, wearing a grey hooded Nike tracksuit, a Nike hat, and a pair of Nike Air Max trainers. He was even branded in white Nike socks.

"Wha gwan nigga?" He said pulling down the peak off his cap. "I never took long did I?"

"Long enough, blood," I grumbled. "What was you doing up in there anyway?"

"Nothing. Just dealing with a sell."

"What!? In that office block?" I looked at the building. "I hope you checked for cameras?"

"Nah man its safe." Mel said counting some money. "Alicia sorted it out."

"Blood!" I slapped him in the chest. "I thought I said 'llow shottin' to Alicia."

"What you hitting me for, you fool?" Mel pushed me. "I didn't shot Alicia nothin'. She was linking me with one of her work mates." He said screwing up his face. "Anyway what's your problem? She don't even smoke anymore."

"Yeah well," I paused. "I just don't think we should shot her anymore."

Mel looked at me with a smirk on his face. "Wharm, rudeboy, you been dreamin, dream again?"

"Fuck you." I said getting up. "You keep making jokes, you fuckin' clown."

"Easy, bruv, calm down," Mel said throwing his arm round my shoulder. "Look Alicia's got links and as long as that brings us money who cares?"

I didn't reply to his last statement. "Oh yeah," he continued. "She told me to tell you hi. She wanted to know if you were upset with her for something?"

I looked at Mel. "Upset at her for what?"

"I don't know." Mel held his hands up. "She must've clocked that you don't like serving her.

"Nah," I dismissed the idea. "Just tell her we're cool and try not shottin' her. I get a bad vibe about her, like it ain't right or something. We all use to go college together."

"So," Mel said. "That don't make no difference. You shot to Leky innit, and he used to go Hammersmith and West London with us. What's the difference between him and her?"

"Nothing" I said getting annoyed. "Just forget it."

"Okay, nigga, whatever you say." Mel said snatching the paper out my hand. "What you doing reading that Black Muslim shit, you know that ain't nothing but propaganda."

"Firstly, blood, don't call it shit," I said snatching the paper back. "And secondly, whether it's propaganda or not, how does this propaganda hurt you?"

"Well let me see." Mel scratched his head. "Firstly, because when you start reading this shit, you start acting all moody and shit, and start trying to get all philosophical and shit, talking 'bout 'life's a journey' and shit, and 'we're all slaves' and shit, go on and on about and the 'crossroads to life' and shit, and the 'equation to blah, blah, blah' and shit. And on the realz, that shit hurts my ears and shit. Now do you understand my shit, nigga, or do you want me to carry on?"

"You know you're a fool innit? You don't understand do you? Your mind has been polluted with so much propaganda that you can't even identify the truth when it comes along".

"What, and you believe that's the truth? White devils and the prophet Elijah Muhammad."

"No, but"

"But, what?" Mel interrupted "There is no buts, those people are just as bad as the white people. They're the ones who killed Malcolm X"

"Yeah, but why did they kill him? What were their motives? Life ain't always black and white. As a big man," I poked him in his chest. "You need to learn when the wool is being pulled over your eyes by both black and white people if we're going to advance in life. When you do that, then come and talk to me about propaganda."

"Long!" Mel said clapping his hands together and rolling his eyes. "As long as I'm getting paid that's all I care about. Farrakhan, Tony Blair, Paddy Ashdown, and William Hague can keep their shit. And you can keep your speech. You're all long."

"You see, that's what I'm talking about. If they're the major leaders and you don't care what they're up to than you're a slave. You're a give me food, whip me, and send me out into the field slave, and an idiot."

"Whatever, G, I'm a slave," Mel closed the debate "Come let's go."

As we got to the car I had to ask Mel again. "You really don't care do you?"

"No, why should I care? What, you think that them people care about what we're doing? Fuck that, as long as I've got what I want that's all I care about."

Mel was always brutal with the truth. He was the stereotypical proletarian. The way he thought, the way he dressed, even the way he spoke. Sometimes I knew exactly what he would say and only asked to confirm my suspicion. It was like I 'd read the design manual he'd been programmed with. But more frightening was the knowledge that he wasn't unique. Mel was just one amongst millions. I call them Proles and Lynch Slaves and you should know their importance.

You see, it's frustrating to be on a journey with companions who have no sense of directions, but it is destructive when your companions do not care of the direction they are heading. Mel like so many others knew enough to seek knowledge of his journey but refused. He cared little of his destination, but more on how he travelled. He would rather travel in comfort and end up in the gutter, than struggle and return to a throne. Even worse he refused to identify what he was and the people around him. It is a policy of Modern Containment and it has become detrimental to the travelling slaves.

The slave's objective (as in you and me) is to travel upon their journey passing through each city until the journey is over. These cities represent social structures and obstacles designed by *'the Ruling Groups'* to contain and delude. The Ruling group do not reside in these cities and have as little contact as possible with Proles and Slaves. So a policy of *'Modern Containment'* is systematically applied to house, contain, and trap as many slaves as possible to breed with Lynch slaves and Proles.

Identifying the Lynch Slaves and Proles
It is important on your journey to be able to identify Lynch slaves and the Proles as they are not necessarily your enemy and are often your brethren. For the Lynch slave his ultimate objective is the same as your own, but he is unaware and has been corrupted or mis-educated to believe otherwise. A person is usually born a Lynch slave through parentage and has the traits installed on to him by parental and social nurturing. A Lynch slave can be very dangerous, but once educated may also become a great companion upon the journey.

The Proles on the other hand are in my definition: those of different races placed amongst the population of the City of Modern Containment. They maybe of White, Asian, or mixed race origins, and their own objective will depend upon their ethnic background. Traditionally the Proles or Proletarian is described as the lowest class or working class of a community. In George Orwell's novel *1984* he describes the Proles as living in a world within a world of thieves, bandits, prostitutes, drug peddlers and racketeers, (doesn't necessarily mean engaging in such activities) this is the basic habitat for both Prole and Lynch Slave.

Now I speak from experience and knowledge of these two groups. I grew up in the inner city streets of West London. The majority of my friends and family came from working class backgrounds and live in or around council estates. These estates where we played and lived, were and still are the most frequent dwellings for Lynch Slaves and Proles. The bulk of inner city problems, affect Lynch Slaves and Proles and are increased by these dwellings. My father had been a drug dealer and a petty thief with no ambitions. My mother was the dependent figure, a lynch slave, making I myself a Lynch Slave through maternal conditioning.

The Characteristics of the Lynch Slaves and Proles are very much alike and some times the only way to distinguish the two is through culture and colour. The Ruling group considers them as the two elements, which produce the Low. So often despite their differences they are contained by the same methods. Here are some of their characteristics and methods so you may identify the Lynch Slaves and Proles named The Low.

- Their ignorance is the primary weapon used for containment. The Low are too shattered by labour, to be more than irregularly conscious of anything outside their daily lives. They do not read and misunderstand the importance of reading. We live in the age of information. Books are readily available at bookstores, libraries and even the Internet that may provide the blueprints to economic equality, but the Low will ignore them. The act of forbidding reading to acquire knowledge was one of the original forms of containment. The Low will prefer to acquire knowledge from corrupt media and television stations with bias and one-sided views.

- Materialism and greed are also influential forms of containment used to enslave the Low. Each year the Low will spend billions on consumer goods and designer wear. They easily become the target market for any business venture. The Low are primarily consumer people with a strong desire for status symbols. Driven by greed and the attraction of designer brands they have little thought for savings and investment. I have seen cases where some Lynch slaves would rather neglect their children and buy the latest footwear, chain or designer Jacket. The majority of the Low live a paycheck from poverty and believe a flash car is living large.

- They are covered in the branding of others such as Nike, Adidas, Versace, Prada, and often scorn or have little knowledge of their own designers. They spend their money building solid communities for others with no support of their own.

- The Low relies heavily on the government to supply sufficient education for their offspring (especially the Lynch slaves). They do not believe in constantly scrutinising what is being taught and whether it meets the correct standards. They do not achieve great levels of higher learning and the Lynch males show a high percentage of failure in the classroom. The majority of their offspring are more interested in the materialistic wealth of entertainers, sportsmen, and celebrities. Ultimately it is usually the Lynch slave and Proles' poor education that leads to their involvement in crime, drugs, and incarceration.

- It is not the Lows' desire that they should have strong political feelings. The larger evils invariably escaped their notice. If the Low were to realise that everything they did was a political statement, how they dressed, speak and interact with others, then politics would play a deeper role in their society. It is common to hear a Low say "I don't vote because it doesn't make no difference" or "I ain't voting none of their candidates represent what I stand for." Their lack of involvement in politics means the lack of adequate rights, rules, laws, and constitutions that govern their lives. Many Low remain ignorant of political ideology and politics unless it disturbs their lives, for example a tax or restriction. A Low is more likely to vote for the winner of a reality programme than a candidate in general election.

- Their aim, (when they have one) is to abolish all discrimination and create a society in which all men are equal. But they show little value for human life. Lynch slaves are notorious for acts of violence against each other. They are still controlled by distrust and envy, and show lack of self-control and respect. The statistics of black on black crime rises each year, due to the fact that Lynch slaves pride themselves on reputation and credibility.

- A Low male will often disrespect his female by beating and abusing her. Some males have been known to solicit their wives or children into prostitution.

- At least a two third of the Low are from dysfunctional families and broken homes. There is a low level of marriage amongst them and many of the Lynch males have more than one conquest. The Low, contribute to a higher rate of teenage pregnancies and single parent families. Interracial coupling is common among the Low although Asian-Proles are more reserved about interbreeding. There are more interracial relationships between Lynch Slaves and Proles in Britain than any other country with 48% of Lynch males in mixed relationships. You may have even heard a Lynch slave say, "I prefer white girls. They're not as aggressive as black girls." This is created by the role of the male and female being reversed by Willie Lynch himself. The Lynch slave woman has been trained to be independent from her male. Her independence and assertiveness is often mistaken as aggression to weaker males.

- A Lynch male is more likely to live at home with his mother for longer periods. Because of the mothers installed fear, she still nurtures her sons to be physically strong and mentally weak. A Lynch slave living with an absent father is more likely to be dependent on his mother. He may even suffer from an Oedipal complex and when he leaves home he may often look for a woman who will act as a substitute to his mother.

- There is a high level of unemployment amongst the Low. The Low are more likely to have a job that at times they will believe is beneath them. The Low are highly dependent on a welfare state.

- Large numbers of The Low, will have an instant dislike to Police officers and the law. There is a great distrust between the Low and the Law. The Low will see the police officer very much like the overseer of the slave days. He does not like the officers/overseers watching him, he will co-operate with officers/overseers as little as possible. The officer/overseer are known to be corrupt and to abuse their powers. In Britain over a thousand Low have died in police custody in the 30 years between 1970 and 2003. The police force in Britain has been labelled institutionally racist and has problems with recruiting officers of ethnic background. Because the police officer is used as an enforcer to contain, the officer or the overseer is one form of containment used that the Low do recognise.

It was a daunting fact that I lived amongst the Low. I mean just because you were a Lynch slave or Prole didn't make you any less decent than anyone else. The problem I had with the Low or slaves was I could see them everywhere. They verged on every corner, behind the shop tills, schools, colleges, work place, and clubs that I attended. They lived in the same house and ate at the same table. They were my society and they multiplied like a cancer everyday.

Think about it yourself, you can probably name ten people instantly with these characteristics.

Subconsciously, they could ruin lives before they had begun. By passing on their social traits and contaminating the soil or environment their seeds grow within. How does a Lynch slave break the cycle that is inbreed throughout his nation, if he knows nothing of it? Looking towards myself as an example, I knew through True Black Consciousness, I became aware of my own state of mind and containment. Yet the path I'd travelled was no easy path, and the majority of things I've done, I wouldn't prescribe for a person or their child. Many traps and obstacles lay in the path like a roadblock. The journey was not going to be easy. The Lynch slaves were my brethren and the proles our allies. It was only fair that they had the right to become companions on our journey. Ultimately the Low would need to be awoken or rebel against containment. There was a need for the return of revolutionary thinking, which marked the age of the 1960's. I closed my eyes picturing where I had read it before: *"Until they become conscious they will never rebel, and until after they have rebelled they cannot become conscious."*

When Mel and I got back to my house, the smell of curry goat and rice aroused my hunger. Walking out the kitchen with a tray of food, my sister Andrea passed us and walked to the living room.

"Oi!" I yelled looking at her plate. "I hope that's not my food you know."

"Excuse me?" Andrea turned back. "When have you ever put food in the cupboards let alone in the pot?"

I followed her into the living room. She sat at the dining table amidst a pile of books. I was determined to stress my point.

"Andrea, I hope that ain't my food."

"I don't know whether it's your food or not." Andrea said looking up. "I saw food in the pot and decided to eat it." She coughed over the food then pushed the plate forward. "Here you can have it if you want."

"Andrea, you can't do that." I fumed. "You can't just come in the house and take food out the pot, you know that's my food and what about mummy?"

"What about mummy?" she said with her mouth half full.

"What if that was mummy's food? What's she gonna eat?"

"Well, it's a good thing that I spoke to mum then, isn't it." Andrea waved her fork. "She said I could have the food in the pot, and told me to tell you to get a takeaway like you usually do. Okay?"

"That's why I can't stand you. You don't even live here no more. You see what I gotta put up with, bruv." I said to Mel who was standing in the doorway.

"You alright, Mel," Andrea smiled.

"Yeah I'm cool, Dr Drea." Mel replied.

"Don't call her that shit, bruv. Look at her," I said picking up the remote control. "Why you got the MTV on if you're studying? You're gonna fail your exams."

"Oh shut up." Andrea pushed up her face. "Why don't you go to your room and grow up you little baby boy?"

"Baby boy my arse! You better make sure you don't eat my food next time."

I switched off the TV and stomped upstairs. In my room I drew for the shoebox under my bed and started counting my reload money.

"Oi, Mel, how much work we got left in the stash?"

"Boy, about a 'Q and an 8'." Mel said flipping through a magazine.

"What, you think we should reload now or later?"

"You might as well do it now, blood, so we can cut and wrap it before the evening rush."

"Mmmm." I grunted.

I picked up my phone to call Sparks. His phone rang out. As Mel put on some music I began to think. Look at myself, look at me, a Lynch slave who knows the Equation to Empowerment, but what am I doing to empower myself. I hung up the phone watching Mel dance around the room and look at himself in the mirror

"Do y'know how fuckin' gay you look?"

"Shut up you fool," Mel laughed. "What did Sparks say?"

"He never answered."

"Try him again."

Pressing the redial I realised The City of Modern Containment still had me trapped. For all the knowledge I had, I still was no better off. And what about the Low, the Lynch slaves and Proles, they were worst than me. How do you get through to the likes of them? I concluded the old man in my dream was right. My equation wasn't correct. It took a lot more than an equation for empowerment. Empowerment needed to begin with awakening the Low's conscience. Then a revelation came to me from the most unlikely source.

"Oi, listen to this tune, bruv!" Mel shouted. "I love this tune."
Although I'd heard the song a thousand times, I listened carefully finally hearing the message as Mel accompanied the artist karaoke style.

> *I hear Brenda's got a baby, but Brenda's barely gotta brain.*
> *A damn shame the girl can hardly spell her name.*
> *That's not our problem, that's up to Brenda's family.*
> *Well let me show how it affects our whole community.*

"Oi, bruv, you know Tupac's heavy!" Mel said rewinding the track. "You know Biggie can't talk to Pac. Dem boy dere's not real! All they can talk about is Versace ha-she, what's that? Man, wear Versace like nothing over here. That's nothing to me. Tupac spits reality." Mel had finally said something of value.

It was true Tupac was our modern day prophet. He was a shining star amongst so many rap stars. Years after his death his recordings still touched and moved people. He was adored by his people, which were the Low, and educated them on a parallel untouched by any other. In a time of capitalism he was the last of a long line of activists. A self made millionaire that stood for more than just money. Tupac gave hope, where there was desperation. He was a thug, a scholar, a lover, and a fighter. He could not be contained and like many other martyrs was ultimately destroyed by the people around him.

"Gil!" Mel continued. "I'm telling you. Somebody needs to make a film about
 Tupac. Trust me on that one."

That's when it began to dawn on me. To escape from the City Of Modern Containment, the slaves would need leaders that will know how to manipulate the control of the media. This will lead to the partial education of the slaves giving them enough to be aware. These leaders will also need to know how to overcome economical factors. The Low, hold entrepreneurs in high esteem. As I picked up the phone to call Sparks again, the question I asked myself was who will lead us?

*

Jade sighed aloud as she flipped the page once more. She was finding it hard to dislike the author. With every chapter she wanted to shout at him and steer him down the right path, but the more direction Gilyan Gates lost, the more she seemed to understand.

***

CHAPTER: 11

Evening was fast approaching and Jade still hadn't done the majority of her chores. She knew a call from her mother was imminent, saying 'it was time to come and collect Jayvan', but Jade didn't stress. She was fully engrossed in her book. If World War III began and Jade was the only person who could stop it. The world would suffer another holocaust waiting until Jade had finished her book.

DIVIDE AND CONQUER   *The Journey of a Slave.*

The time read two o'clock on the big face clock hanging on the wall of the barbershop. As Springer turned me around in the old style barber chair, I felt totally relaxed. I sat in the metal and leather chair with the cape wrapped around my neck, while Springer crafted away at my hair.

There's something therapeutic about a barber's chair. It's as though you are shedding an old skin to start anew. You would sit back and have a trim, a shave and by the end of your haircut you'd feel like a new man, refreshed and vitalised.

The barbershop also doubled as a communal focal point for friendly banter and chitchat. A person didn't need to buy a newspaper to find out what was going on in the world, the barbershop was much more effective. From the latest football signings to current affairs, it was all discussed in the barbershop, with everyone giving their own unique point of view. The debates that arose in the shop could start from something as minor as the new Chinese shop opening around the corner and end upon terrorism and the Middle East. They could last for hours or even days as every time a new customer entered the shop, a new opinion entered the debate.

Forget the House of Commons and Question time, some of the best debates took place right here in the local barbershop. Customers and barbers could become just as heated and animated defending their favourite football team as any politician or backbencher defending their political party. On this particular Saturday afternoon, the regular debate proved to be no different. I don't really remember how the argument had begun, but at the point that I became interested, Ade and Edina were the head speakers. Ade had been one of the main barbers at the shop over a number of years. Popular with the customers he had cut his hours to study a Masters degree at university. He was a dark skinned Nigerian in his late twenties who fancied himself as one of the new wave of conscious black men. His opponent Edina was a small red- skinned West Indian woman in her mid forties. Her long dreadlocks hanged down her back and she wore an African print scarf. It wasn't unusual to see her in the barbershop. She would come every other week to have her grandson Lemar's hair cut. She was a strong and opinionated woman and it was her comments that made me sit up and take notice.

"Ade," Edina addressed the barber. "If it wasn't for us West Indians you Africans boys wouldn't even be here."

There was a round of *'ow!'* before Ade hushed the crowd to answer.

"Edina are you serious?" He frowned. "Without West Indians, Africans wouldn't be here. Please. Don't you think it's the other way around? West Indians are the descendants of African slaves therefore without us, isn't it impossible for you to even exist."

"Ade, don't get smart with me," Edina waved her finger. She too had to quieten some of the disgruntled backbenchers. "You know that is not what I'm saying. What I'm saying is that without us you wouldn't be here in England like you are now, in terms of status, lifestyle and attitude."

Ade looked at her with an exaggerated look "How?"

"It was West Indians," Edina proudly tapped on her chest. "That paved the way for Africans in England. We were the ones who fought against racism and made noise when no one would. When the majority of you Africans came over, we had already broken a lot of barriers and were establishing our own rights as British citizens. When most of the Africans came they were calling themselves Eddie instead of Ade. They were dropping their African names and replacing them with English names to be more accepted. Am I not right Michael?" Edina turned to the older barber cutting at the head chair "It was us West Indians that taught you Africans to be proud of yourselves, it was us that taught you your history"

"Hold on!" Ade stopped cutting hair. "Are you saying that West Indians taught Africans about their history?"

"Yes! That's exactly what I'm saying. Without West Indians in this country, you Africans wouldn't act like how you do now."

I wasn't sure whether Ade had problems with Edina's argument because she was an older woman or because of the line she had taken but I could see that he wasn't his usual self. He seemed uncomfortable with the subject and reluctant to thoroughly pursue the argument.

It was common for the barbershop to erupt in a West Indian vs. African debate. They were always the most entertaining. They would begin with the comparison of wealth, riches, sports, landscapes, tradition, dishes, and cultures. Then in mid flow the Africans might have an internal dispute, which regularly involved the Nigerians and Ghanaians. The Nigerians were almost always labelled the most arrogant of the African nations much like the Jamaicans for the West Indies. The Jamaicans would label other islands like Barbados, small island countries and say they ate monkey. The Grenadians would be called the most incestuous claiming frequent interbreeding within the island. Grenadians would retaliate by saying the Jamaicans produced a nation of illiterate criminals, and the Jamaicans would call the laughing Nigerians the biggest criminals saying '99.1% of global fraud was committed by Nigerians'. It was a circus of laughs and insults that divided our nations but unified our barbershop.

Today a passionate Edina had Ade up against the ropes.

"See, Ade, the point I'm making," she continued. "Is much more than the silly little arguments you men have in here. It's not about African vs. West Indian, which you think it is."

"What makes you think that?" Ade replied.

"Simply because of the way you took offence."

Springer tapped me on the shoulder. Laughing he pointed at Ade's sour face.

"Ade," Edina continued. "I was there when these original arguments were a real divide amongst black people. When the Africans looked down upon West Indians and called us white men's slaves."

"Yeah, but West Indians aren't exempt." Ade stopped Edina. "Plenty West Indians used to call us, traitors and boob-boos, even spear chuckers."

"Yes, I'm not condoning or denying that." Edina conceded. "But there were many Africans ten, twenty years ago, that denied African's part in our history. The majority of slaves were stolen from Western Africa and transported to America and the West Indies. And there were many West African tribes that had a part in that."

"See!" Springer called to Ade. "There's always some greedy Nigerians in the middle of shit."

"Hold on a minute, sweetie," Edina silenced Springer. "I haven't finished speaking. Reserve your comment until after." She turned back to Ade. "Sorry, Ade, now what I was saying is that, same way black people as a whole made white people look at the role they played in slavery. We West Indians made Africans look at what role they played in our history."

"Okay," Ade nodded his head thinking. "But that doesn't justify you saying that West Indians taught Africans their history. That's just stating historical facts. "

"Aaah, but this is where you need to concentrate." Edina smiled. "Tell me who's history does slavery belong to?"

"Both African and West Indian history. Because it records strong events in both pasts, it naturally becomes history to both African and West Indian history."

"And what about Malcolm X?" Edina asked. "What's his relevance to their history?"

"Well me personally," Ade said. "I would call Malcolm X American history, but seeing as he did visit and lecture in Africa, I could also say that his visits maybe recorded as African history."

"No, Ade," I interrupted. "Don't try to cover yourself, answer the question properly. One or the other."

"What you talking about?" Ade snapped. "I don't need to say one or the other, I've already answered the question. Its American history with relevance to African history."

"Edina!" I complained. "Tell him to answer properly. One or the other."

"Shut up man," Ade cursed. "You're not involved."

"So what," Springer shouted. "Answer the question, nah man."

The crowd started to get excited telling Ade to answer the question properly.

"Hold on hold on." Edina said quieting the all male audience. "Ade I will except that answer, but seeing as you said slavery recorded strong events in both West Indian and African history, I would prefer if you answered on the belief that Malcolm X marked a strong importance to Africans."

"Okay," Ade grinned. "Seeing as I've been backed into a corner by my own words not anybody else's"

"Shut up and answer the question." Springer heckled Ade. There was a ring of laughs.

"Okay, okay," Ade said finally prepared to answer. "I 'm gonna say that Malcolm X is American history."

"Now," Edina clapped her hands together as though she was about to pray. "Do you understand what I mean when I say West Indians taught Africans about their history."

We all looked at her puzzled

"Ade," She smiled "Your first answer was the correct answer, but because we as black people have been taught so much division between us, that you've over looked Malcolm's relevance to Black history."

"No!" Ade protested. "You said to me to choose between the two."

"No I didn't," Edina replied. "Nobody heard me say that. I told you to concentrate. The first thing I asked you was his relevance to history. Then after your reply, I asked you to decide whether he was important to African history. You decided he wasn't."

"Yeah but he's not." Ade argued. "He doesn't hold a strong importance to African history."

"Ade are you a dyam fool?" Mikey said, standing by his chair. "Ade put down your shears because as far as I'm concerned, I don't employ idiots. That is the stupidest thing I have ever heard come out of your mout', and believe me I've heard a lot of shit come out your mout'"

"Oh, Mikey, shut up man." Ade whined.

"No." Mikey insisted. "How can you say that Malcolm X has little importance to African history? Malcolm X has importance whether you're African, West Indian or British. From you're a black man, Malcolm X has importance. Furthermore he's important to world history whether you're white, black, American, Christian, Muslim or Jew."

The barbershop was humbled from the backlash of Mikey's words.

"That is exactly what I'm trying to teach all of you," Edina said "Not just Ade, all of you. I never once said slavery or Malcolm X belonged to any particular history. Ade chose to make that division in histories, automatically setting African against West Indians. The truth is, all history begins in Africa. The fact that the slaves were stolen and enslaved in the Caribbean and America are chapters in Black history. Think about the slave revolts black history, the colonisation of Africa and apartheid black history, the watts riots black history, the black panthers, Nelson Mandela, Steve Biko, Walter Sisulu, the Egyptians, Adam and Eve all of them are black history."

There were at least fifteen black men present in the shop that day, and we all listened to what Edina said like little children listening to a school teacher. We sat on the perch of our seats. Barbers stopped trimming with no complaints from the clients. It was the first time in my life I witnessed the barbershop come to a stand still for anything other than a cup final. Edina had captured our intellects like the pied piper and we listened to her melody of black spirit.

"What you young men must do is stop letting your difference divide you. That is one of the worst things about black people. We as a race are always divided in our struggles. We never want to unify for the better of our race, we never want to work together for the longevity of black people. That is why black empires of the past have all been conquered."

As Edina spoke, Stevie Sinclair a local mixed race boy got up and left the shop. I felt there was an irony in his leaving. I knew Stevie well and he needed to hear Edina speak just as much as anybody else.

"The enslaving of the Africans created a sub race or Semi-African which you boys now recognise as West Indian, Afro-American or mixed race. The slaves were inter-breed, lost their original language and customs, replacing them with new. This is what has caused a divide in our race. You look at each other and don't recognise that you're the same black Africans with the same black history."

"Preach, sister, preach!" Mikey shouted in an American accent.

"Michael, behaviour" Edina smiled "I'm trying to be serious." Again she turned to Ade. "Now, Ade, do you understand where I'm coming from? I don't want to put it all on you, but we West Indians supported the political movements in Africa. We raised money for the ANC and boycotted white companies, as we knew that Africans and their history is where ours began and we fought for the opportunities that your generation has now."

"Edina," Mikey said waving his comb. "What do you think of all these young boys running around with these white girls then?"

There was a slight moan and few laughs, before Springer said, "Yo Mikey what's that got to do with history brudder?"

"What? Don't bother ask me no questions," Mikey said getting flustered. "It's my shop and Edina is my friend, and I want to hear her opinion on all you liccle boys that run around here with white girls and what she thinks as a black woman."

"So wait," Ade interrupted. "Mikey, you never troubled or thought about troubling a white girl."

"I never said that." Mikey grinned. "I said I wanted to hear what Edi's opinion on you little boys and your white girls."

"So what, can she speak about you as well then?" Ade asked.

"No!" Mikey threw his comb at Ade. "You, never hear me jus' tell Springer don't bother ask me no questions. Just cut the man's hair, nah bwoy!"

There was another roar of laughter before Edina quietened the shop once more, turning another page on her book of views.

"Well really, Mikey," she began. "I think that is a whole other subject and depends a lot on the two individuals and their motives. But in the content of black history and these young men in front of me, I think that if one of these boys were my son, I wouldn't be happy if they brought a white girl home."

Edina's answer didn't surprise me, but left me confused. My mum had said things like that in the past, like 'I bet you bring a white girl home' with disapproval. But I always took that as her generation. She wasn't racist she just preferred that I dated black girls. Edina statement was different it was a yes and no answer.

"What exactly do you mean, Ed?" Ade asked. "That's a bit of a politician's answer."

"I mean, you boys have no sense of your own history, as was proven today. All you're concerned about is yourself. Now if you have little knowledge of your own black history, how much do you think these white girls have? If you young men don't learn about your history who will pass on your history to your children?"

Edina threw the question out for anyone to answer. When the question went unanswered she continued, "Look, there's fifteen grown men in here and none of you can answer me. Why? The reason is because you don't know.

You boys are out here killing and robbing each other over foolishness. What happens when you're finished and are left dead or in a prison cell? It is us Black women that have to provide and clothe your children. It is us who have to teach them the lessons they need in life. As a woman that is hard enough, but if you're a white woman trying to bring up black children or mixed race children if you wish to call them, what black history do you pass on? What lessons do you teach them? That is why I don't agree with mixed race relationships at the moment. It is a trend, a fashion statement among your generation to be black. You treat the colour of your skin like a status symbol, and some of these white girls use you as status symbols. 'Oh my boyfriend's black.' If a white girl wants to be with you she should want to learn and know about your history and culture to get a full understanding of you. You boys don't know your history to teach these girls and that is dangerous to black people. If you lose your history, you lose your identity as a race."

There were a lot of nodding heads and I was the first to speak.

"So, Edina, do you think as black men we should only be with black women to preserve our race?"

"No." Edina shook her head. "I think as Black men you need to get up of your arses and stop thinking about yourselves. Get rid off this take, take attitude that you have and educate yourself with practical goals."

"Yeah that's what we're doing." I said foolishly. "Look at Ade he's doing a Master degree."

"Yes," Edina pointed at Ade. "Lets look at Ade he's doing his masters, but lets ask Ade what are his overall goals?"

All head turned to Ade as he thought about the answer.

"Well first," He began listing. "I want my masters, a good job, house, family and then I'll probably start my own business."

"And then what," Edina asked. "What comes after that?"

"How'd you mean?" Ade replied. "Like a family and the full nine yards?"

"No, I mean once you accomplished those goals, your personal goals, what do you plan to give back. What goals do you plan to pass on to your community?"

Ade frowned realising he hadn't planned that far ahead.

"Okay, let me leave Ade." Edina tapped him gently on the arm. "I think he's been under the spotlight too long. What about you, Gil," She pointed at me. "What do you plan to give back. We looked at Ade's goals, now let's look at yours. Where's your goals?"

"I don't know I guess, I'm still defining them." I replied. I hoped it didn't sound as stupid to Edina as it did to me.

Suddenly I felt small and shallow, like a man with no aspirations for his life. Edina looked and frowned

"Hold on, Gil. I watch you run up and down these streets with your liccle friends selling all that you can sell, and you mean to tell me you have no goals in life." Instantly Edina demeanour changed. "You think crack is what you're going to give back to your community?"

Her attack surprised me and came from nowhere.

"Rah, Eddi, I don't sell crack." I tried to defend myself

"Gilyan, don't lie to me." Edina voice boomed with disgust. "I've known you from you was a child. I use to baby-sit you and watch you play in the Wendy house with my daughter. You can't tell me you don't sell crack, you might tell your mother that but you can't tell me that."

"Hol' on!" It was my turn to retaliate. "What, you think that gives you the right to tell me anything? You can't tell me shit!"

The humming of hair clippers accompanied on looking eyes and sniggers.

"So tell me, Gilyan Zachariah Gates, if I don't tell you who gwan tell you. Your mother ain't gonna tell you, she turns a blind eye to everything you do. Your sister is always away studying and your father, well he's worst than you. You think I want to see you standing on some corner pushing crack into one of my grandson's hand? No mister, I don't think so."

Edina was treading on thin ice. I didn't like people talking about my family, and I didn't like people broadcasting my business.

"Gilyan," she continued her rant. "I know your mother is a good woman, she taught you better than that. You should be ashamed of the business you conduct amongst this community."

"Ashamed of what!?" I stood up "You don't know what your talking about you ol' hag. Shut your mouth before I lick you down."

"Oi!" Mikey shouted. "Watch your mouth boy. That's a big woman you're talking to, have some respect!"

"What? After she's talkin' 'bout my family in front of the whole shop! Like it's Saturday's football results. Are you fucking crazy?"

"Oi, Springer," Mikey put down his shear "I don't know what do your bredrin, but you better warn him, before I knock out his teeth."

"Knock out whose teeth, you fucking PUSSY!"

Suddenly the shop erupted into chaos as Mikey flew into a ranting rage. No one was going to disrespect him in his own establishment. Egos and reputation were now on the line and I refused to back down. As Mikey lunged towards me, I tore the cape off my neck and reached for the bora in my back pocket. I wasn't taking any chances. Underneath the cape I flicked the blade, as Edina and other customers tried to restrain Mikey in the far corner.

"Come then, come then!" I shouted as Ade and Springer held me back. I remember thinking - the moment he jumps on me, I'm going to plunge this knife in his stomach. Then in the mist of the whole spectacle, 4 year old, Lemar began crying. Frightened by the drama, tears streamed down his face and he bawled out for his grandmother.

"Granny, Granny!"

The sight of Lemar was like a pause button. Immediately everyone froze becoming aware of the scene which broiled over in front of the child. Edina grabbed her grandson close and squeezed him in a tight hug.

"I'm sorry baby. Granny's here it's alright, it's alright"

I looked at Edina realising my anger had got the better of me. She had touched a truth that I was trying to ignore. Huffing and puffing, I scrutinised her with thoughts of lashing out. But whom did I want to hurt? Was it Edina or was it myself?

"Gil," Edina tried to compose herself. "I'm sorry, I'm sorry son. I had no right speaking of your family like that, but I love you young black boys like I love my own children. I've seen you grow and seen you be corrupted by your father and the fools you call friends. You are one of the smartest boys I know, and you risk it all for fancy clothes and easy money. Una-nah-know drugs are instruments to divide our community. You know that, Gil, all of us know that."

Edina's words singled me out, but they were directed at everyone in the shop, old and young. Still I wanted her to shut up and be quiet. Why did she need to preach to me? She wasn't my mother and I wasn't the only nigga juggling in London.

"You're not listening," I snarled at her. "I don't sell no drugs."

"Listen to the woman," an old man said from the corner "Ah reality she ah talk."

I cut my eye at the man. My face remained firm as I delivered my final word "I don't sell no drugs."

"Okay, Gilyan." Edina conceded. "You don't sell drugs, but listen to me. You are walking a path that so many black boys have walked before honey and it leads nowhere. There are so many of you out here willing to senselessly kill each other over something that you think can bring you resources and financial freedom. The truth is that it only divides you more and places you into the traps of society and the system."

Edina spoke with a passion that came straight from the heart. The build up of water in her eyes was visible and she fought to hold them back. I couldn't remember the last time anyone had taken time to speak passionately to me about my life. Now Edina stood in front of me like a gladiator challenging me to think.

"Do you think your special, Gilyan? No, do you think you can escape the same traps as the others, is what I really want to know? Look and ask yourself do you want to end up like them or do you want to make something of yourself. Do you want to be known as a man with no goals or a man that has accomplished his goals? You can tell me you don't sell drugs if that's what you want child, It makes no difference. The truth is that we both know deep down you're worth more than that, Gil. Please, please, please don't let people fool you into thinking any different, and don't let them divide and conquer us. You black boys are our fathers of the future, we need you to procreate, provide and protect our race not destroy it."

It's been a couple of years since that incident in the barbershop. Yet Edina's words still whisper in the back of my mind. I saw her a good number of times afterwards, but we never spoke again, at most a civil glance was shared. I was younger then and cared little about my ignorance, nor my state of beliefs. Edina never tried to reason with me again and I forever regretted how I spoke to her. Every time I rode to meet a punter in her estate, I imagined she was looking from behind her net curtains, thinking that boy never learns. What I wouldn't do to speak to her now; guidance is a limited resource. Edina had warned me about the journey and attempted to express its traps. Now I saw them in the City of Modern Containment and its inhabitants the Lynch slaves and Proles. Divide and conquer, it was another method that would keep us contained.

Without our correct history, Black history, we are divided as a race and vulnerable. Black history is the one thing that will unify us all in one nation and one race sharing one goal. Edina had endeavoured to pass on this message of unity which I scorned. This morning, before I sat down to write this passage, I attended Edina's funeral. My hands trembled as I lay a handful of carnations by her grave then watched them lower her coffin into the ground. Her black marble tombstone read in gold letters 'Here lies Edina Mary Wallace a teacher and caring mother to all, may she rest in peace.' Kneeling down by her grave I finally confessed my ignorance and whispered, "I understand now. By giving back we can protect our race, not destroy it."

*

As Jade reached the end of the chapter her phone rang, "Hi, mum... Oh you're back, okay. How was it? ... Good, good, good... How's Jayvan?... No, no, no, I'll speak to him later...What time? I'm not sure mum... I'll tell you what to do. Just bathe him and put him in his pyjamas when you're ready. Worst come to worst I'll pick him up in the morning... No I never said that, mum... I said worst come to worst...Yes I know you've been looking after him all day mum...yes I appreciate that...Okay mum! I'll be there when I get there."

Jade finally cut her mum off. She looked at the time thinking, was it still possible to finish her book before collecting Jayvan.

***

CHAPTER: 12
A PHONE CALL AND A DATE FOR 2

It was another quiet evening studying at home for Jade. She enjoyed the rare moments of solitude. After spending all day working, the last thing she wanted to do was try and study around Jayvan. With deadlines looming, she made a vital call to Anita.

"Don't worry about Jayvan," Anita agreed to baby-sit. "I'll bring him home later."

It was exactly what Jade needed to hear. The long essay writing and studying was beginning to take its toll. She wondered whether she would ever make it through university. Sometimes she contemplated giving up. Maybe it would be better if she waited until Jayvan was in school. He was such a mischievous little boy. He was always up to something, drawing on the walls or beating the cat. One evening when Jade returned from work, she found him in the bathroom with her mother's purse. He was standing over the bath running the taps. He'd taken out all the coins, notes, and receipts inside and poured bubble bath over them.

"Jayvan! What are you doing?" Jade had yelled.

Dropping the bottle of bubble bath, Jayvan looked at his mum, "It's dirty money, mummy. Jayvan give it bath-time."

Reflecting, Jade couldn't help laughing. They were constantly telling Jayvan put down the dirty money. She sighed. Jayvan was growing up so fast. She worried about how Ivan's absence would affect Jayvan's early years.

Taking a break, she looked at a picture of Ivan and herself holding Jayvan at three months. It seemed like only yesterday when they'd first met. Jade was 17 and her best friend Tania was seeing Ivan's then friend Joe-Jo. They had all gone to a party together in Ivan's car. During the ride Jade thought Ivan was rude and arrogant. He thought he knew everything and begged anyone to prove him wrong. Ivan thought Jade was frigid and argumentative, while Tania and Joe-Jo just thought Ivan and Jade liked each other.

It was only after a few more staged meets at Tania's house that Ivan shyly asked,

"So what, can I get your number or what?"

"Or what?" Jade replied.

She enjoyed embarrassing him. He was too egotistical and impertinent. However, it was too late for Jade to play like she didn't like him. She remembered asking Mark about her future boyfriend.

"Yeah, I know Ivan," Mark said. "Yeah, I remember him from back in the day. Little Terror from Cumbala estate, he's a little bad boy still. You better watch out for him, sis, he might break your heart."

"Are you crazy?" Jade dismissed the notion. "I know what I'm doing. I ain't stupid."

"Good, I hope so." Mark sparked up a zoot. "I don't wanna 'ave to hurt no one's son. You get me?"

"Whatever," Jade fanned the smoke away. "Why do you call him Terror?"

Squinting his eyes Mark took a long draw on his zoot and said in a deep yardie accent,

"Wharm, rudegirl you nah kno'. The bwoy is a bloodclaart terrorist." He laughed. "Dats why dem ah call him Ivan de Terri'ballllll."

Jade punched her brother in the arm "You're so stupid."

Jade smiled. All that was in the beginning when things were good. Now all Jade and Ivan did was argue. At present they weren't even together, but it made no difference to Ivan.

"Watch, Jade. I'll kill you, if you have any brerz 'round my son." He continually threatened. "I'll come out and lick out you're teet'. Den sit down in jail for another ten months. Trust me on that one."

Putting the picture back, Jade sighed. Ivan's problem was he always wanted things his way, but was never willing to work for what he wanted.

Jade didn't care about Ivan's threats anymore. She was to busy maintaining to worry about men and the 99 problems they bring. Jade had fooled herself before that it was a rough patch they were going through and things would get better. Sometimes they did, but then it would all climax with Ivan ending up in jail. This was the third time he'd been sent to prison since they'd been together. Each time he promised things would be different and each time Jade warned him she would leave. Well this time things were different and Ivan failed to recognise that they had responsibilities as parents.

Reading *'Journey of a Slave,'* Jade began to understand why some Black men were childish and immature. Why they were easily sidetracked and neglected their responsibilities. All alone in the flat with her books Jade concluded it was no excuse.

Suddenly, the buzzer on the intercom interrupted Jade's thoughts. Jade answered "Hello. Who is it?"

"Jade! It's me," the voice on the other end screamed. "Open the door quick!"

A minute later Tania came sprinting into the flat. The plump little brown skin girl hopped around like she was doing the riverdance as she took of her coat and announced,

"Oh, Jade I'm bursting to go pee Move out the way."

Disappearing into the toilet she threw her coat at Jade.

After Tania finished relieving herself, she came strutting into the living room where Jade had made herself comfortable on the leather armchair.

"Where is he then?" Tania said with her hands on her hip.

"Where's who?" Jade said trying not to laugh at her friend.

"That sexy little child you stole and try pass off as yours. Jade you know you're to ugly to have such a beautiful child."

"Excuse me?" Jade sat up. "May I remind you who you're talking to Miss Lil-piece-of-weave-and- glue-will-fix-me."

"See, that's why I never liked you little red skin girls." Tania said fixing her weave. "Just cos you got a little coolie in you, you think your Queen of England."

"In this house," Jade said in a posh accent. "I am the Queen, get it right, darling."

"Err check you though." Tania said holding her chest as if taken back. "Okay, Ms. Queen Godfrey the 1st of Badric estate, where is my Prince Charming, then?"

"He's over at my mum's. Anita should be bringing him back any time now."

Tania sat down on the sofa running her hand on the leather. "What? New leathers, waaahh. Where'd you get these from?"

"Oh, don't bother ask," Jade said waving her hand dismissively.

"What, Jade find new man I see." Tania said teasing.

"I wish. One of Mr Man's friends brought them round."

"Is that how Ivan's going on from jail, Jade?"

"Oh, please," Jade rolled her eyes. "Sofas don't mean nothing, Tan. I need a man, Jayvan needs a dad; not just bloody sofas to sit on. Ivan should be here taking care of us instead of sending people around with all sorts of shit."

"So you need a man now, hey," Tania grinned. "Can I take it the queen, start get lonely and turn lady in waiting hmmm?"

"Oh, shut up and mind your own business." Jade threw a cushion at Tania.

The two started laughing. Then Tania jumped up suddenly.

"Yes, Jade!" she clapped her hands together. "I almost forgot. Guess who I saw today walking past Southside shopping centre, trying to play like they never see me."

"Who?" Jade said leaning forward in the chair.

"Joe-Jo, the dirty crackhead! I saw him with one nasty little white girl. The two of them looked like they hadn't wash in a good two weeks."

"Nooo," Jade held her hand over her mouth. "Don't lie."

"Yes, rudegirl! Liss'en to me," Tania took pleasure in Joe-Jo's downfall. "He was wearing some dusty old Air Max and some rip up old pattern Moschino jeans jacket. I swear, I couldn't believeeee it was him. After he try diss me. The flipping fool! I swear, anyhow he'd said anything to me I would of spat in his eye. The boy done see me you know, Jade; with his dry face and picky head, then he try run clean into McDonalds."

Jade couldn't stop laughing. "Oh, poor Joe-Jo, he use to be so nice."

"That's right!" Tania said vindictively. "He use to be nice. Now he's bruk!"

"Oh shut up!" Jade said defending Joe-Jo. "After you use to love him off."

"Yeah, that was then. When he was flexing," Tania made a money sign with her fingers. "When he use to do his little thing and he looked peng. Now he just looks nasty and wrong. Mmm emm," Tania shook her head in disgust. "It's all about my Glen now. He's got his own car, his own house, a job and he knows how to treat me. No, no, no I've got no time for people like Joe-Jo."

"See, Tan," Jade waved her finger. "I always knew you was a gold digger."

"Please!" Tan put her hands on her hips. "After all the money I use to borrow that fool, I don't think so! Anyway, there's nothing wrong with wanting a man who knows a woman's worth you should try it sometime. Why don't you let me hook you up with one of Glen's friends?"

"No, it's alright," Jade turned down the offer. "The last time I let you hook me up, I ended up with Ivan and look how that's turned out. No, I'd rather be on my own thank you, just me and my son."

"Oh go on, Jade." Tania plead. "Glen's friends are always asking about you. What about Trevor you thought he was nice, and you lot really got on."

Jade thought about it. She did actually think Trevor was quite nice. They'd met when Jade and Tania had gone to a football match to watch Glen play. Sitting in the cold stadium, Jade asked Tania who the tall chocolate thunder in the number seven jersey was.

"Oh that's Glen's friend Trevor. He works in accounts," was the first thing Tania said. "I'll introduce you later if you want."

When later came, Jade thought he looked even better in his suit and tie. His hair was cut low, which gave him a sleek look complemented by his sporting physique. He was a good conversationalist and the two hit it off. Now Jade wondered. It had been a long time since she'd had any good loving.

"No, Tan, I've got to many things to do," She declined. "I haven't got time to go out. Besides, who's gonna look after Jayvan?"

"Stop being silly, Jade you know you can get your mum or Anita to look after him. You're making some weak excuses."

"I'm not, Tan, it's just..."

"It's just that I'm still in love with Ivan," Tania mocked Jade in a pitiful voice. "And he would kill me if he found out. Come on, Jade, you're the best looking girl I know. You can't sit around waiting for Ivan. Ivan gets locked up for the next 5 years and what you're expected to wait? That's a joke ting. Do you think if you were in jail Ivan would wait for you? No. So you might as well start enjoying yourself while you can. Besides you're not even together."

Tania's mouth was like a machine gun rapidly shooting down any thoughts of guilt towards Ivan. She made some good points and Jade was beginning to crumble under the pressure. Then Jade breathed a sigh of relief as the buzzer rang came to her rescue.

It was Anita who came up with Jayvan fast asleep and ready for bed. Taking Jayvan from Anita's arms, Jade ushered her sister into the living room while she put Jayvan to bed. Removing his coat and laying Jayvan in the bed, Jade kissed her son goodnight.

When she came back into the room, Tania sat quietly on the sofa, smiling like a child who had just stolen some cookies from the jar. Anita looked at Jade arms crossed and stern faced.

"What's wrong?" Jade asked.

"Jade, what's this about you don't have anyone to look after Jayvan on Friday night?" Anita asked.

Puzzled Jade looked at her, "What d'you mean?"

"Tania said she's been trying to get you to come out," Anita explained "And you keep telling her you can't go out. Don't you think it's time you went out a little, Jade?"

"I'm not going out, Tania." Jade ignored Anita. She hated when they ganged up on her.

"You see what I mean, Anita?" Tania jumped up. "I've got a nice man for her and all she keep saying is I'm no going out, I'm not going out."

"Come on, Jade," Anita tried to convince her sister. "Tania's got a nice little fancy man for you and you're there acting like some old hermit. Stop being silly."

"That's what I'm saying 'Nita," Tania laughed. "I think we should go and buy her some cats or something."

"No, no!" Anita cackled. "That's it. No sister of mine is turning into no, cat woman at 23. Tan babes, don't watch Jade, I'll look after Jayvan, you just come and pick her up from early ya' hear."

"Thanks Anita."

And there it was. Before Jade could even amount any defence, Tania was already on the phone to Glen sorting out the arrangements. Anita sat next to her little sister.

"Jade, you hav'fe start mek da most of your life. Learn to move on!"

*

Ivan had fallen asleep inside the Securicor van that was used to transfer the prisoners from prison to prison. Locked inside the small-seated cabin, his body began to ache. The sweatbox as everyone called them, had tiny cabins for each prisoner. There was never enough room to stretch your legs, and the plastic seating was hard and uncomfortable. A one-way window brought in the light from the outside, while the window on the cabin doors allowed the guards to check on the prisoners.

Resting his head, Ivan didn't contemplate looking out the one-way window. When he first started going to jail, he would climb on his seat and stare out in case he saw somebody he knew, or perhaps some live girl walking past. He would bang on the window hoping to get their attention. Sometimes the banging would alert a person to his presence, but they would only acknowledge with a glance. It made no difference what he did, they couldn't see inside. The re-enforced windows were a reminder of his exile. Here's one last look of what you could have had before you are punished. Ivan no longer took the symbolic last look. He had no need for symbols of an outside world. He was no longer a freshman, he was entering his senior years. He was well on his way to being a career criminal and realised the best way to get through your bird, was to forget about what you had on the out and deal with what you got.

He chuckled to himself. I got caught, that's what I got. Closing his eyes he thought about his last moments of freedom.

"Flipping Briggy," he muttered to himself. "I told him we should've parked up."

Ivan and his Co-D (co-defendant) Briggy, had been caught literally red handed. They'd been watching the Securicor deliveries at a small bank in Shoreditch. Nana had taken a fifteen-man squad there once to do a 'Fly-it'. Ivan remembered the day well. He made 16K in one grab. Briggy had been nervous and no sooner then the gang of black boys had gathered he was the first to move. Rushing inside the bank in a ball of chaos, Briggy and Nana were the first to scale the large glass screens. The shutters were useless at this stage because it would mean that the cashiers were trapped inside with 10 - 15 desperate criminals trying to get out. There was no organisation. You simply steamed in, grabbed what you could and made sure you weren't the last out. If you got nothing, you got nothing. In the worst-case scenario, you always hoped one of your bredrins got enough to bring you in.

Since then, Ivan and Briggy had been back a number of times, but the layout of the bank had changed. They'd added more security. The screens went straight up to the ceiling now. The 'Fly-it' and 'P.O'. days were now over. To find a decent one you had to go further and further out of London. All that was risky business, trying to get back with out getting shif (arrested).

"Nah, security boxes are the lick now!" Briggy had bragged. "I love tearing down some sloppy old security guard and grabbing that box."

Nana and Briggy use to believe there was a method to selecting the right box. If the guard was going in, then the box was empty or had coins. When he came out that's when they had notes. Ivan thought that was all bullshit. He felt it all depended on what the bank needed to hold or transfer.

The day of their arrest, Briggy's nerves got the better of him again. As soon as he saw the guard he pounced, throwing blows to the man's face. The security guard toppled under the onslaught and Briggy stomped him to the ground. Moving in, Ivan snatched the first heavy grey security box and ran to the car. Turning around to see where Briggy was, he saw his co-d fighting off some have-a-go- hero. Pulling out his gas, Briggy, pepper sprayed the man in his eyes.

"Go, go, go!" he yelled diving into the car.

Frantically Ivan swung the car through the commotion and onlookers. Twenty minutes later they were on their way to Streatham to put the box in the freezer and freeze the colour dye inside. Ivan's heartbeat was falling to a stable rate. His adrenaline rush was just coming down when the security box exploded. Purple dye sprayed all over the car.

Ivan remembered the dye covering the windscreen. Panicking he tried to put the wipers on, forgetting the dye was on the inside. In seconds the toxic dye began to burn their skin. Stopping the car in the middle of traffic, the two jumped out screaming in pain. They were later arrested inside a nearby newsagent's, pouring water over each other.

The police charged them in connection to nine other robberies and assaults, which they denied. In the end it was their mobile phones that brought their downfall. The police used the phone signals to pinpoint their proximity to the crime scenes in comparison to their alibi. The weak witness descriptions only strengthened the cases. On the third day of trial, they both changed their pleas to guilty. Ivan was served with a five and Briggy a seven for robbery and four accounts of ABH and assault to run concurrent. Ivan could still hear the judges hammer banging down. Bang! Bang! Bang!

"Wake up, fella. You're here now."

Ivan opened his eyes to see the scrawny-faced screw looking in. He wore a white shirt and black tie. Again he knocked on the window before unlocking the cabin door.

"Put your left hand out, fella," he said handcuffing Ivan. He balanced a cigarette from his thin pink lips as he spoke.

"Okay, fella, lets get you out of here and booked in. How was the trip?"

Ivan stared coldly at the man. He knew the type. Talk to the inmates; gain their trust by being their friend. Ivan didn't trust any Screw, why should he? He returned the guard's pleasantries with a grunt.

Inside, Ivan sulked. He hated the tedious rituals of reception and booking. First you had to wait for everyone to be led out of the sweatboxes. Then one by one you were called to be booked in. The screws became like rats on a rubbish heap, scouring through inmates belongings bit by bit. Checking for contraband and other items, they were like scavengers.

"Oh you can't have that in here, no, we only allow twelve CDs, oh that stereos got an alarm, its to big, this piece of canteen is open we have to throw it away."

To Ivan, HMP Haughton Hill was no different to the others. It could've been Feltham, Dover, Portland, High point, The Wrer, Wanno or The Mount. They were all the same, same rules, same regimes, just different faces. One of the screws pulled a black pair of corduroy Armani jeans out of Ivan's belongings to be listed.

"What, are they real, Mr. Wilks?" the other screw said speaking in a whiney nasal voice

"Yes, I do believe they are Mr, Jones," the brutish Mr Wilks said in a North Yorkshire voice.

Jones looked at Ivan, "How can you afford to buy a pair of real Armani Jeans? Bit expensive aren't they?"

Ivan couldn't resist he had to say something, "Because my salary ain't 14k a year. I earn that type of money in minutes, nah seconds," he said sniggering to himself.

"Did you hear that, Mr Wilks?" Jones said listing the jeans. "This young man reckons he earns 14 k in seconds."

"I did, Mr Jones," Wilks continued rummaging through Ivan's belongings. "Funny that, isn't it?" he said looking up

"Why's that then, Mr Wilks?"

"Cos' he won't be earning anything like that in the next five years, believe you and me, Mr Jones."

The two screws burst out laughing as they continued to process Ivan's belongings.

After a physical from the doctor, Ivan was put in the holding tank the other side of reception. The holding tank was always Ivan's first insight into how well he'd get on in each prison. As every inmate was processed and placed into the tank. Ivan analysed each inmate from the first glimpse. Everything was taken into consideration, their colour, the length of hair; any scars, their walk, tattoos, weight, height, and eyes. The eyes said a lot. Sometimes you could tell how long a person's sentence was just from their eyes. Over there, in the corner, the slim mixed race dude about late twenties, tall, stubble on his face, gaunt features, long arms, rocking backward and forward. Him Ivan thought, he looked like a burglar or a street robber. He looked like he was a smoker. He might be able to fight, but not for long, no stamina. He'll be hitting the gym regular when his frame starts to fill out. Now him over there, the little white guy, sitting holding his belongings between his feet. He looked like a first timer or just starred up from Y.O.'s. His screw face betrays him, he's taking too much in, too eager to prove himself. In Youth offenders like Feltham and Dover all that's fine, you don't want anyone thinking you're a '*fraggle*'. Now this is big man's jail, different things. People ain't on trying to prove they're hard, they wanna do their bird and go home. Ivan shook his head knowing the lad had too much to prove. He grinned. You gotta knock them ones out quick, no talking.

Then next inmate that walked in was different. He looked straight into Ivan's eyes with out a flinch. Ivan sensed his prowess. The man read Ivan's own profile in the quick glance before seating down. He was in his early thirties and was definitely a contender. He'd definitely been going gym, but hadn't over done it. He strode across the tank with his belongings and sat down neither intimidated nor intimidating anyone. Immediately he ignored everyone and everything around him and opened his book. Dressed in the standard prison uniform of denim blue jeans, a white and blue striped shirt, and a burgundy sweatshirt, Ivan could tell he had a connection in supplies. His clothes were too fresh. A connection meant he'd probably been here a while. The book and the black, red, and green armband he wore on his right arm all pointed to one conclusion - Lifer or long term.

Ivan thought, *yeah I know your story. You got life'd off now you decide you wanna make something of yourself. Re-educate yourself. Too late for that now NIGGA, you're in the belly of the beast for life bro.*

Ivan smirked trying to get the man's attention. Generally he tried not to fuck around with Lifers, they had nothing to lose. They were already there for anything from sixteen years upwards. Extra convictions meant nothing to them, plus you never knew when one of them was about to snap. The world passed them by and they had no way of slowing it down. However, this one irked Ivan with his airs. As Ivan sucked his teeth aloud the man peered up from his book for a second then back to the page. Ignored, Ivan looked over at the hot plate that had just been opened in reception and stood up.

The screws opened the tank so the men could get their food. As they lined up, Ivan picked up a metal food tray and plastic mug and took his place. He analysed the food on offer. Catering always varied from jail to jail. Some were decent and others were like gruel. At Haughton Hill the food was subcontracted and was sent in ready to heat each day. Ivan looked at the sloppy shepherd's pie and overheated veg and thought yeah *I'm glad I'm not eating that shit.* The halal food for Muslims was always the best. Sliding his tray across the counter Ivan asked the prisoner serving,

"Yeah, bro, gimme some halal food, yeah."

"What?"

"I said gimme some halal food," Ivan pointed at the Muslim cuisine. "Halal, halal."

"Oh hello, hello mate," The prisoner waved at Ivan "How are you today? I'm fine." He said laughing with the other inmate serving.

"What! Are you taking the piss, bruv?" Ivan said getting vex.

He looked into the man's beady eyes. *I should've known,* he thought. The Three Lions tattoo, the number one all over, the exaggerated cockney accent;

Ivan guessed the man; was probably some dumb football hooligan or BNP racist, locked up for doing his best football factory impression. *So what* Ivan thought, *this white fuck's never heard of Cass Pennent, no?*

"What, mate?" The prisoner smiled "All I'm doing is saying hello. What's wrong?"

"Hear what, pussy," Ivan put the tray on the counter. "I ain't playing no games. I'm a Muslim, so you better gimme some fucking halal food, before I come round there and."

"And do what you fucking muppet?" The man threw down the spatula "What? You want some do ya? Do ya!" he said giving it large.

Before Ivan could answer, the Lifer stepped in front of him.

"Yo! What's the problem here, Bain?"

"What is he one of your lot, King?" Bain said backing down a bit. "Cos' I'll tell you what, mate, you better put him on a fuckin' leash before I tear his eyes out, son."

"Hear what, Andy," King spoke calmly "Me and you both know you ain't tearing anything out down here. So like I said, what's the problem?"

"Look, King, I ain't got no problem with you." Andy said with respect. "But a little muppet like that!" He pointed at Ivan. "Ain't coming down 'ere and tellin' me what's, what. I don't care if he's a Muslim, he'll eat what I fuckin' giv' 'im."

"Who you calling a muppet? You pussy!" Ivan yelled as King held him back. "Don't touch me!" Ivan pushed King "I don't know you rudeboy!"

"What's going on here?" Mr Jones yelled as he appeared with Mr Wilks and two other screws. "You in trouble already, Little, or is it you King?" he said looking at the two black men. Ivan noticed there was no mention of Bain's involvement.

"No, there's no problem, Mr Jones." King reassured the officer. "I was just asking Bain if it was all right if Little had my halal food. His name's not on the list of Muslims."

Jones looked at Ivan then at Bain, "Well, Bain?" he said.

"Oh yes, Mr Jones," Bain grinned. "That's fine. I did try to tell the young man we have limited food, but he seemed to get very excitable."

"Okay," Mr Jones stopped Bain from bullshitting. "Just give the man his food."

As the screws went back to work, Bain put the piece of lamb on Ivan's tray.

"Mind your mouth next time, son, or you might not be so lucky."

"Go fuck yourself." Ivan said holding up two fingers.

Inside the holding tank Ivan sat down next to King. He didn't want to look like he was begging friend, but thought he should make alliances.

"Yo, blood, sorry for switchin' on you back there. You know how it is innit. Man dem get a lil hot-headed when man's chattin' shit, you get me cuz. But no disrespect fam."

"It's cool," King said picking up his book.

"What you ain't gonna eat nothing." Ivan said trying to smash the broken ice. "I'll cut dis up if you wanna share?" He cut the lamb chop in half.

"No, don't worry," King declined. "I got plenty canteen upstairs."

"Safe, blood, man appreciates that."

"That's cool. What's your name, prince?"

"Ivan," Ivan said chewing on his meat. "But the man dem call me Terror."

"Bless," King offered his hand "The name's, King."

They shook hands and began to chat.

"Listen, Ivan," King said "Don't let man like Bain get you so irritated. Them man are big fools."

"Nah, bruv," Ivan shook his head "The brudder tried it. All that, 'hello, hello,' business, he's trying to make me look like a fool. That's dissin' my religion. You know I can fight over that. That's Jihad."

King looked at Ivan. "That's not Jihad. Jihad is more than fighting over someone mocking your religion. The term describes struggle in the way of Allah, not only over ones enemies, but over one's ego. You got a lot to learn if you're gonna be a Muslim, brother."

"How you reckon?" Ivan said eating his food.

"As a Muslim, you should know that ignorance of one's religion is something that even the prophet blessing be upon him, went through. It even says in the Qūran, 'him onto his religion and I on to mine'. Just cos somebody mocks your religion, doesn't mean you call *Jihad as-sayf*. Secondly, if your intentions are not just, then that's haraam. You ain't fooling me," King smiled. "If Bain tried it with me like that, I wouldn't be having it either."

The men started laughing as their alliance was made. Entering the tank, Mr Wilks called a list of new arrivals heading for house block 1.

"Little!"

Grabbing his gear Ivan bumped fists with King, "Safe, bruv I'll see you around, yeah."

King nodded. "Yeah, bless, my prince. Mind how you walk and ting."

When Ivan got to his wing he looked about. *Beirut* he thought. Beirut was the name given to most induction wings. They were always the worst, because no one stayed on them any longer than 3 days. They looked like a war zone, with paint peeling of the walls, torn seat covers, broken snooker table. The cells were even worse, the toilets stank, and the dust was like a carpet on the floor. No one ever cleaned their cells on Beirut simply because they weren't there long enough.

Ivan looked at his watch. He arrived on the wing with ten minutes of association time left. Digging through his belongings he searched for his phone cards. The phones were empty, he had just enough time to phone Jade and speak to Jayvan. Dialling Jade's number the phone kept ringing out. *Come on, Jade, answer the phone* Ivan thought.

Even though Ivan always phoned to speak to Jayvan, hearing Jade's voice on the other end wasn't too bad either. After the third try he decided to try her mobile.

"The mobile phone you have called is currently unavailable." Stated the automated voice.

"Where the hell is she?" Ivan slammed down the phone. He couldn't understand "She knows I always phone on Friday, she knows that."

*

Finally Jade's big Friday night had come, yet she still harboured mixed feelings about going out. She wasn't comfortable with the scenario. Tania had rushed round to the flat straight after work, not allowing Jade to pick out an outfit. She grabbed a handful of clothes, make up, boots and shoes, and shoved them into the car.

"Tania let me choose an outfit first." Jade tried to complain.

"No." Tania hurried. "We can do that at my house. All you're gonna do is say 'I haven't got nothing to wear' and try and pull out on me. This way you haven't got, no choice."

Maybe it was the fact that she felt she was being forced to go out that made Jade uncomfortable. Jade didn't like to put on too much make up, just some lip gloss, a touch of foundation and a little eyeliner and she was good to go. While Tania fussed about everything

"No, Jade I want to give you the full treatment."

Tania picked out a number of sexy outfits and lay them on the bed for Jade to choose. Jade didn't like all the fuss. She'd been out many times before and didn't see why today was so important.

"Because you're going out with Trevor." Tania repeated like a broken record.

Trevor meant little to Jade, she was her own woman and decided she would dress for herself, not to impress any man. When Glen and Trevor arrived they were dazzled as Jade stepped out wearing a see through Christian Dior halter-top with Swarovski crystals and beads, and a pair of black Karen Millen harem trousers. Slipping on a pair of black straps she announced.

"We're just waiting on Tania. She's only gonna be a minute. Go and sit down."

With a grin on his face Glen looked at Trevor as they walked into the living room. Whispering, he said, "I told you she's live. What do you think?"

Trevor was rubbing his chin in awe. He'd only been in Jade's presence for 30 seconds and he was already enchanted. "Yeah, I'm definitely feelin' her." He said with a dubious look. "But are you sure she's on it?" He felt nervous.

"Of course she is," Glen squeezed Trevor's neck back. "Tania phoned me from Jade's house to arrange all this. Trust me that's you. No long ting. "

The evening started the night at the trendy ION bar in Ladbroke grove. It was all about light drinks and small talk, before they decided to move on to Cirque in the West end. Glen had insisted that they take two cars and Tania drove Glen's BMW compact, while Trevor drove his Audi A3. Tania and Glen used the separate cars to make progress reports.

"So what do you think of him, Jade?" Tania quizzed in the compact.

"Talk to her a bit more, Trev' Glen advised in the A3. "You're acting like you're not interested."

By the time they got to the club, both Jade and Trevor were feeling the pressure to relax, but that soon disappeared after Glen tripped and spilt his drink on the dance floor. After five minutes of hysteric laughter they soon began enjoying each other's company.

Trevor seemed like a nice guy, Jade reasoned. He constantly attended to her needs, getting her drinks, and making sure she was having a good time. Yet she kept thinking about her situation with Ivan. Eventually she told Tania she wanted to go home.

"Why what's wrong?" Tania shouted over the music.

"Nothing, I'm just tired. I wanna go home and rest."

"Alright," Tania sipped her drink. "Give me twenty minutes and I'll sort something out."

Ten minutes later Trevor came over, "Are you alright, Jade? Tania said you wanted me to take you home."

Stupid bitch, Jade thought in her head as Tania stood with Glen by the bar waving.

"Oh I'm fine," Jade said being polite. "I'm just feeling a little tired."

"That's cool," Trevor said. He was still trying to play the gentleman. "Let me get your coat and I'll drop you home."

Jade handed him her ticket for the cloakroom. As he disappeared she shook her head as Tania came over.

"What you shaking your head about?" Tania laughed sipping another Archers and lemonade. "You wanted to go home, so I asked Trevor to drop you."

"Tania," Jade whined. "I don't know the man like that. What if he tries something?"

"Don't be silly," Tania frowned. "Trevor wouldn't do that. Anyway if he did you should be grateful, when last you get some?"

Jade tapped Tania's glass as she tried to drink.

"Ow! You bitch." Tania cried holding her lip. "I can't believe you just did that."

"Yeah, I hope you drink too much and throw up," Jade smiled as Trevor returned.

Saying bye, Tania whispered, "Slag," in Jade's ear.

As they pulled up outside the block Jade played with her bracelet. It was an awkward situation. Jade did like Trevor, but she didn't want to give him the wrong impression. At the same time she didn't want to look like she wasn't interested. Lowering the Usher CD playing on the set, it was Trevor that took the initiative to say something.

"Well I know its late and your tired so I'm not gonna be stupid enough to ask to come upstairs. But I really had a nice time tonight Jade, I'm really glad you came out. You really looked beautiful today."

"Thanks," Jade said blushing. "I really had a nice time too."

"So tell me if I'm making a fool of myself. But what would you say if I suggested that you left your number with me, so we could do something like this again."

"I might ask you what you meant by something like this?"

"Okay," Trevor smiled and stroked his chin thinking. "What if I were to reply simply to enjoy good company?"

"Then I might ask how you intended to enjoy that company?" Jade said playing with Trevor. As he put his arm behind her headrest, Jade smelt the aroma from his aftershave and her heart begun to race. Her chest felt warm and her breathing became heavier. She hadn't noticed how close she had moved towards Trevor, as he leaned forward. His voice became low and inviting.

"What if I were to say as a friend, who may possibly seek more of your female company at a later stage."

"Then I might ask where's your phone?"

Jade moved closer as he leaned forward to kiss her. She closed her eyes as their lips met and brushed her tongue along his. Jade tilted her head and moved back encouraging Trevor to pursue her. Then suddenly there was a bang on the window. Startled Trevor and Jade both jumped looking up. Staring into the car Mark frowned at his little sister.

"Oi, what you doing?"

Putting her hand over her face, Jade looked at Trevor as Rolly pushed his ugly face against the glass.

"Mark, what you doing?" Jade threw her hands up. "Get away from the car!"

"Just hurry up and say goodbye to your little boyfriend." Mark banged on the window again.

Lost, Trevor looked at Jade, "Do you know them?" he said nervously "I mean if you need me to."

"No," Jade stopped him "Don't worry, that's my older brother and his friend. Look I better go, where's your phone?" Storing her number in Trevor's phone Jade gave him a kiss on the cheek and said goodbye.

When Jade got out the car Mark did not look happy. His face was all twisted.

"Jade what you doing gettin' feel up in man's car."

"Who was getting feel up!" Jade slapped Mark on his arm. "I was talking."

"That didn't look like no talking to me." Mark fumed. "I thought you was suppose to be with Ivan?"

"Ivan, Ivan, Ivan!" Jade screamed. "Are you bloody working for Ivan? You're like the flipping FBI, Mark. I told you I broke up with Ivan two months ago, so I don't know why you're round here at this time asking me questions."

"You're not with Ivan anymore?"

"No," Jade snapped.

"Oh, okay then, I never knew that," Mark said calming down. "Next time don't let me catch you kissing up with man like that again."

Roland stood in the background laughing, "What's up Jade?"

"Hi," Jade said with a fake smile.

Jade didn't like Roland. In truth she found him repulsive. He made her cringe. He was always watching her like some old pervert, licking his lips. Jade was forever telling Mark 'you need to get rid of that sweaty bastard'. Every time she saw him she thought he was a filthy little parasite. This time was no different. She crossed her arms stopping him from looking through her top.

"Mark, what you doing here so late anyway?"

"I got a present for you."

Putting his arm round his sister, Mark walked Jade over to the parked up Corsa. "There, it's yours" He said "So I don't wanna hear nuttink about how you can't go here and there, or about Jayvan being cold at night waiting for no bumbaclaart bus."

"Seriously, are you really givin' it to me? Mark!" Jade yelped with excitement.

"Yes, you can have it, what's' wrong with you?"

Jade jumped in the car and felt around to get a feel of the car. Roland leaned in on the open door. "Yeah, we knew you'd like it Jade."

Jade could smell his musk and sweaty body odour looming over her in a cloud of stench. "Thanks, Rolly," she said pulling the door shut.

Speaking through the gap in the window Rolly asked, "Is that your new boyfriend then, Jade?"

Jade looked at him trying to hide her disgust "Yeah, we're in love" she said sarcastically.

Climbing in on the other side, Mark slapped her on the leg and gave her a look that said play nice.

"Rolly, go warm up the Golf," Mark shouted. Waiting till he had left, Mark looked at Jade with disappointment. "Why you so hard on Rolly? He's only trying to be nice."

"Err," Jade said pushing up her face. "He's gross, he makes me sick, Mark. I told you, stop bringing him with you when you come to see me."

"Leave him alone, he's alright." Mark laughed. "How's your book?"

"Mark," Jade kissed her brother on the cheek. "I really love that book. It really made me sit down and think about certain things. I'm gonna send it to Ivan, but first me and you got to sit done and talk."

"Whoa!" Mark joked. "This must really be a serious book if me and you need to sit down and talk. We ain't dun that in a long time, sis."

"I know, Mark, but I really wanna, talk about a few things with you and Ivan."

"Ah, so you do still think of Ivan when you're kissing up next man." Mark teased.

"Fuck you, Mark." Jade stuck up her finger. "I'm trying to tell you something and all you can do is take the piss. I wish everyone would just stay out of my business. I already told you, I'm not with Ivan, but you're still going on. How comes you never say nothing to him when he's running round and going to jail with his friends?"

"Whoa, whoa, calm down sis," Mark held up his hands in submission. "I'm only playing with you."

"Well, I don't find it funny." Jade said glumly.

"Okay, okay," Mark squeezed his sister's hand. "Point taken, Ms, Godfrey's daughter. Don't bother listen to me. You know what I say..."

They both recited it in unison, *"What makes you happy, makes you happy"*.

Mark left Jade with a promise that he would come and see her during the week and bid his sister goodbye. Jade loved her brother. He was always full of stupid anecdotes Before Jade got into bed she thought about it - *what did make her happy?*

***

CHAPTER: 13

Preparing a parcel to be sent to Ivan, Jade folded a blue Nike tracksuit and fresh packs of underwear into a small pile. She gathered 12 CDs he requested, and wrapped them in newspaper, to protect the cases. Smiling she added a few pictures Jayvan had painted, thinking, *that does not look like a dog or a bird*; crazy child. Finally Jade picked up 'The Journey Of A Slave'. Holding her beloved book she was reluctant to pass it on. She had become attached to its by-chance philosophies and sociology. At times, it frustrated her and at other times made her weep. Eventually its essence had come to symbolise a small wishful hope inside. Jade fretted about how Ivan would receive it. She wanted some assurance he'd read it, not overlook it as nonsense. Taking out her fluorescent pen, she highlighted the passage she knew would appeal to Ivan most.

THE INSTITUTE OF THE STREET   *The Journey of a Slave.*

The whole history of civilisation is strewn together with creeds and institutions which were invaluable at first and deadly afterwards.

It was a dark hour when I first realised that I would soon be leaving the institution that I loved and had grown up in. It was an institute that had challenged and pushed me further then any other, an institute that I had made my heart, and home for so many years. It was an institute where I had forged friends and family and my ties towards it were second nature. This institute wasn't a school or a college, a church or a hospital. This institute was the streets and it was the last element containing me within the City of Modern Containment.

The cold and hard concrete slabs that paved our streets, the corner benches where we sat for lectures and debated countless theories, the estates and tower blocks where we performed practical exams. The streets were our institute where we acquired our knowledge and credentials and it was real. The Institute of the streets is so real that it's a worldwide university and you can go to any city on Earth and you'll find a campus at some level. London, Manchester, Harlem, Compton, Hong Kong, Beijing, Kingston, Port Of Spain, Delta or Lagos. Each city produced graduates and students from the

Institute of the Streets. Sometimes its possible to recognise students from the colours of their frat houses like the Bloods and Crips, other times their one man alone.

Formerly known as The School of Hard Knocks, the Institute of The Streets is fundamentally a school of sociology, economics and business. However students are now offered the chance to study in other diverse areas such as chemistry, psychology, politics, and criminology. Popular courses range from: Narcotics, Robbery, Thuggery, Burglary, Fraud, Prostitution and Pimping, Extortion, Bribery, Blackmail, Kidnap, Rape, and Murder. Each year countries introduce bills and laws to deter students and each year millions more enrol.

The Street is the greatest institute in the world because it can take an innocent boy with nothing and turn him into a ruthless and successful businessman. With a history of racial equality and self-employment, the Institute of The Streets' is a young boys ticket to a world of social inclusion and financial wealth. Some of our earnest scholars and fraternities have shaped the course of history, business and politics worldwide. Mobsters, gangsters, thugs, hoodlums, pimps, con artists, convicts, hit men, pushers, thieves, crooks and hoes. Whatever your chosen profession, The Institute Of The Streets guarantees students a sturdy and unique education matched by no other. The Institutes motto ***Platea est verus*** translated from Latin means, 'The Street is Real.' It is a global phrase you will hear used by institutes, students and scholars.

Right now as my words are being read, there will be those of you who immediately know and recognise the power of the Institute, and those of you who will feel I'm exaggerating. If you're from the first group, maybe you've been a student or are still studying. Maybe you've had a friend, brother, sister, father or even mother that attended the institute. Ultimately you are aware. For the benefit of the second group and in the hope that you may learn something, I will demonstrate how real The Institute of the Streets is.

The Oxford dictionary definition of Institute is: *'1. an organised body for the promotion of an educational, scientific or similar object.'*

With this definition, a person may instantly argue that the streets is not an organised body. In defence I would ask what are the gangs and hoodlums that control the streets? They are organised fraternities. To add to my argument, if you can point out drug dealers, pushers, and crooks, then you can give a structure to a group of people working together. The streets' has its way of organising people into different categories pending on their strengths and weakness. Finally what really makes the Streets an institute is it's promotion of education.

The Streets will educate a person on how to dress, how to walk, how to talk, who to talk to, who to be seen with, and who not to be seen with; how to react, when to react, what music to react to, what movies to watch, what car to drive, where and when to drive it, how to hide, when to hide, when to fight, how hard to fight, when to watch, and when to listen. Eventually the education a student receives becomes instinctive. It becomes their way of life and sometimes the end of their life. Most importantly the streets teaches a person how to provide or how to survive. ***Platea est verus: The Street is Real.***

The most common age for students to enrol in developed countries is usually aged between 13 and 25. This may also be the most prolific and dangerous period of learning. Often students become disillusioned with education and conventional areas of society and enrol looking for an alternative to life.

To a young boy who is showered with media images of materialism, glamorising fast cars, easy money, drugs, and women. The Institute of the Streets becomes his chosen choice of academy. Early enrolment may also be down to family upbringing. Past students may pass on ethics taught at the institute to younger siblings or children from an early age. Home study kits may include, Scarface, Goodfellas, The Godfather trilogy, Menace II Society, Carlito's Way and most good gangster movies.

Tutors at the Institute are generally past students and seniors who are essential to the recruitment and enlisting of new students. They are mentors guiding freshmen into the correct use of codes and conduct at the Institute. To Freshmen students, our mentors are huge influences, often setting new levels of obtainment for students to meet. Together they will find new solutions to solve obstacles and trends that affect their chosen courses. In the Narcotics foundation course, a mentor may choose a student and teach him the following criteria:

- How to traffic narcotics as a runner
- How to chop and wrap narcotics
- How to evade suspicion from general public and police.
- How to wash and cut for quality control.
- Customer service and credit control.
- Occupational Hazards (How to avoid being robbed, arrested, or substance abuse)

Foundation Narcotic courses are also accompanied by intermediate and advanced courses. Extra units may include:
- Weaponry and Ammunition.
- Strategic defence and hostile take-overs.
- Import and export.
- Money laundering.

The incentives of this course are high profit margins and the ability to maintain a steady income opposed to other courses like Street Robbery. Also a student majoring in narcotics has many other options to minor in fencing. At the End of the course a student may join our alumni and be credited with a new title like 'Top Shotter', 'Baller', or 'Baron'.

You see, the one thing people won't tell you about the streets, is that it's an institution. It's an institute just like any school, university, police force, or prison and they won't tell you how easy it is to become institutionalised.

If you feel abandoned by family the streets are there. If you feel let down by the education system the streets are there. If you lose your jobs and need to eat the streets are there. People say 'that won't happen to my children or me', but if you don't provide the right type of education and community it will.

The institute of the Streets produces it's own community and education, like a society within society. If a community fails to curtail the Institutes enrolment then that community slowly becomes consumed by The Streets.

QUESTION: What happens when your children idolise and relate to the local hustlers and drug dealers, driving the latest BMW or Mercs you can't afford? What happens when that hustler begins educating your children with their own opinions and propaganda? What happens when that hustler teaches your child to turn a stolen TV or Video into a £100? When that £100 turns into an eighth of crack and an eighth to an ounce, and an ounce to a kilo. Even worse what happens when he teaches your child to smoke that eighth to gain profit for himself?

ANSWER: Your child and your growing community becomes gradually institutionalised to the streets. You find erosion in moral standards, respect, and the value of life. Why because each generation of students is all about business and money. Armed with a warped desire and understanding of the Institutes motto "***Platea est verus***" they know *"The Street is Real."*

And now with that understood, let me detail the next part of my journey. It begins with a phone call. Some might say it was destiny that Sparks phoned me that night, but I never really knew the real reason why he had summoned me. He had called from a phone box, screaming an address to a council flat in South Harrow. He told me to get a minicab to the top of the road, get out and meet him at the address. Sparks said that Mel and Kooba would be waiting there. I wasn't to phone him again, and I was to leave my mobile at home. It seemed like something serious so I didn't ask any questions; I knew all would be answered when I got there. When I arrived the cab driver pulled up at the top of the road as told.

"That will be eighteen pounds please," said the Nigerian driver.

His number was two-four, and he drove a Ford Mondeo. I hated travelling in his car. It always smelt rank and swamped with body odour. I handed him a crisp twenty-pound note and told him to keep the change. Following the numbers of the street, I came to a small block of flats at the bottom of the road. The intercom to the block was broken. Somebody had tampered with the emergency override to gain entrance. It was easy enough. All someone had to do was give the fire control a sufficient whack and they were usually in. It was something Sparks had taught us to access the blocks in the estates.

I pulled my hood up covering my face as I entered the block. It was a small block with one stairwell that was stained with dried spit and urine. I hopped and skipped my way up to the fourth floor and opened the glass door to the landing. There were four doors; two on either side. I was looking for number 12. As I approached the faded sky blue door I could hear loud music beating from the other side. I banged on the door with my fist. I was sure someone would hear me over the music. There was no answer. Of course not. Sparks' last instruction was to buy a Snickers bar. When you get to the door, put it through the letterbox we'll know it's you.

I reached into my pocket and pushed the chocolate bar through the letterbox. 30 seconds later the music lowered and Kooba opened the door munching on the Snickers. Kooba was 6'5 and weighed about 20 stone. He was a mean bastard and was Sparks' right hand man.

"Wha blow, Double G you cool?"

"Yeah," I said trying to look pass him. "Where's Sparks?"

"Inside." Kooba indicated. "Come"

I followed him into the flat. The light in the passage had been smashed and there was glass on the floor. Light came from the bathroom and bedroom either side of the passageway. I wondered how Kooba had managed to see the

Snickers drop in such dim light. As I passed the bathroom I noticed that the bath was running. Then we entered the front room. Inside was a mess. It had been ransacked. There were tapes, CDs, photos, and sofa cushions scattered everywhere. At the far end of the room Mel and Sparks stood over a battered Stevie Sinclair. Holding a bike chain in his hand, Sparks vindictively lashed it across Stevie's shoulder blade. Stevie screamed out in pain from his twisted mouth. I could already see that it was broke or fractured at the least.

Mel was the first to turn round and nodded at me. He looked exhausted and wiped the sweat from his brow with his t-shirt.

"Wha gwan, G."

"Cool, blood, you tell me." I answered.

Sparks turned around with the chain still in his hand. He looked like a boy in a candy store who couldn't stop smiling. Hands wide open, he greeted me with a Cheshire cat grin.

"Gilly the Kid! Wha gwan nigga? Look which little pussy hole we found."

I smiled nervously as Sparks pointed at Stevie.

"Trust me, blood, its along time!" Sparks yelled as he beat Stevie again. He began to lash Stevie to the rhythm of his voice. "I've - been - looking - for – this - liccle – fucker - yoot - 'ere. Along time! And - now - I - fin' - him, - Jah - know - I'm - gonna - do - more – than - just - hurt - him! But first I want to know, where's my work, where's my work?!"

The last blow hit Stevie in the face splitting his cheek. Sparks began laughing. His adrenaline was running on a power trip. His ego was inflating and it made me nervous. I had a feeling he wasn't the only one tripping as we all gathered around.

"Oi, Mel go and turn off the bath," Sparks ordered.

He crouched down to look Stevie in the face. Stevie's eyes were black and closed from the swelling. His nose was broken and thick red blood poured over his top lip to join the river from his mouth. He was dressed in a blood stained t-shirt and boxer shorts. Whether they caught him or stripped him like that I couldn't be sure. His hands were tied behind his back and legs tied together. They'd used plastic cable ties like the type police sometimes used to restrain suspects. Once applied properly there was no escape.

Sparks was chillingly calm as he spoke to Stevie.

"Yo, pussyhole," he grabbed Stevie by the collar "I want you too know. I'm gonna teach you a lesson tonight, if it's the last thing I do. Nobody steals from me you unnerstan'? Nobody!"

It was a bitter subject for Sparks. I don't think any of his workers had ever stole from him before. See Sparks was one of the 'olderz' from the manner. He was one of the first real shottaz that I ever knew. In the days when shottaz were still called drug dealers, he was one of the original *'Kisser Kash Krew'*.

In West London *'Kisser Kash Krew'* were legendary. They set a new standard. They were the first to rob Rollies and Cartz, then the first to wear Rollies and Cartz. They were the first to drive big whips, and rock designers, and the first to pack heat. They'd walk into clubs and kiss a handful of money then throw it up in the air. They had everything a nigga wanted. To some of us growing up then, they were like kings in this world we called underground. Everybody knew them.

They established crack dens in Fulham, Ladbroke Grove, Shepherds Bush, Acton and West Kensington. They stuck up whoever for whatever. They could've been unstoppable, but after internal beefs, surveillance, police raids, and a high profile case most of *'Kisser Kash Krew'* were arrested and sent to jail.

In the aftermath, Sparks set up his own operation putting some of us youngaz into business. He gave us mobile phones with punters on the lines and gave us weekly salaries. After a while he gave us commission on whatever we sold and split the profits. Eventually he sold the lines to us with the promise that any work we brought, had to come from him. Most of us were happy with the deal, because it meant that we earned more and were loyal to Sparks anyway. Sparks had other man's like Kooba and Stevie who dropped of the reload and collect money. They acted like lieutenants. Often Sparks never had any contact with any drugs at all. This made it harder for the police to arrest him. He trusted both Stevie and Kooba until Stevie went missing on a pick up with Sparks' money. He just disappeared. No one had seen or heard from him until now. Over a year later, Sparks had found him and sought repentance from his ex- courier.

He stamped furiously on Stevie's mid section as though he was crushing grapes at a vineyard. As he did, Stevie began coughing up blood. His body was forced to release his bowels as a result of the heavy blows. The air quickly became rife with the smell of excrement. There was a chorus of disgust as Stevie lay moaning in his own mess.

"Urr that's fucking foul." Mel said returning into the room

"Well what did you expect?" Kooba slapped Mel on his neck back. "That's what man mean, when they say there gonna kick the shit out of someone. Not that schoolyard shit you do."

"I beg you tell him again, Kooba." Sparks held his hand out.

"I swear, Sparks," Kooba said slapping Sparks hand. "These little niggas give me joke. Next thing you know they'll be throwing up, I lie?"

"Fuck that!" Mel cussed. "I ain't throwing up, I'm just saying that's fucking foul."

While they stood around laughing, I couldn't stop looking at Stevie lying on the floor peering up. His eyes were gone. Pain controlled his every movement.

"Gil, G-man, you alright, yeah?" asked Sparks.

"Yeah, yeah man I'm cool."

"Okay then, G, help us get him into the bath." Sparks said

"Get him into the bath for what?" Mel asked.

"Because we want to wash and shampoo his hair," Kooba said sarcastically. He grabbed Stevie underneath his armpit. "Grab his legs, and stop asking stupid questions."

"Err I ain't touching him." Mel stepped back

"Grab his fucking legs and stop going on like a bitch!" Sparks shouted

" I ain't touching him." Mel refused.

"Don't worry," I said helping Kooba. "I'll do it."

"Watch," Sparks warned Mel. "I'm gonna make you take his clothes off you little pussy!"

Together we dragged Stevie to the bathroom. There was a thud as Stevie splashed in the water and hit the tub. The water was ice cold and he tried jumping out. Immediately Kooba hit him in the throat with his heavy hand and Stevie fell back into the tub. Holding his neck, Kooba pinned Stevie down until the water began to dilute with blood and shit. Stevie kicked and splashed, drowning beneath Kooba's grip. When Kooba finally did let go, Stevie came up gasping for air. Sparks called Mel.

"Oi, Mel, get in here you effin idiot and take off this niggas clothes"

"Yeah one minute." Mel called back from the other room.

"Get in here now!!"

Mel came strutting in wearing a cooking apron and a pair of yellow washing up gloves.

"Sparks what's wrong with this brer?" Kooba laughed as Mel danced around the small room.

"He's sick." Sparks grinned. "Don't laugh. It only encourages him."

"What," Mel began jesting about. "I done said, I ain't touching him, and I ain't touching him."

"Just take his clothes off," Sparks pushed Mel forward.

Mel tore Stevie's wet t-shirt off in one great heave. His yellow skin was tainted with bruises and open cuts.

"Go on, take off his shorts as well." Sparks ordered.

Mel followed the command. Tearing the elastic band and the rest of the shorts, Mel slipped them over Stevie's bound legs. Laughing, he tossed the shit filled underwear over to where I was standing.

"Stop fucking about you, dick head!" I snarled at him

"What! Shut up you fool." He tried flicking water at me. "You ain't done nothing since you got 'ere."

It was true. I hadn't done anything. I didn't feel comfortable with the situation. This wasn't what I was expecting, but sometimes when you're in for a penny, you're in for a pound. Not wanting to lose face I grabbed Stevie's head and slammed it against the taps. The impact created a gash in the top of his head. Instantly blood showered his face and he screamed out.

"Yo what you doing?" Mel said jumping back.

"What'd you mean?" I brushed him out my way. "I'm doing something innit you dickhead!"

"How's that helping you pleb?"

"It's doing more than you flicking shit about."

"I'll flick it in your face in a minute."

"Go on then!" I pushed Mel. He stumbled back into Kooba

He was thinking about lunging for me when Sparks stepped between us. "Alright, alright that's enough! Stop bickering and act proper. We're not here to prove who's the hardest."

"I put my money on Gil," Kooba tried instigating. "I reckon he'll knock you out, Mel."

"Stop fucking about, Kooba," Sparks said pushing both Mel and me into separate corners. "I'll bust all your heads if I don't get what I want tonight. Is that clear?"

"Yeah," we all agreed. No one argued with Sparks.

"Good." Sparks said. "Now lets all go into the other room, tidy up a little and chill."

As we were about to leave Stevie tried to speak. "Please, Sparks" he muttered. "Get me out of here, please."

It was the first words I had heard him speak since I had entered the flat. We all looked at him shivering in the cold water. I could hear it in his voice. He had reserved all his energy to beg for mercy.

"Please Sparks, please, don't hurt me no more."

Looking at my three companions I knew his plea had fallen on deaf ears. He would be beaten to death if Sparks desired and no one would save him. We waited as Sparks stood over him thinking. Sparks reached for the light string and pushed us all out.

"Fuck that, nigga," he said turning the light out. "Everyone next door,"

So that was exactly what we did, we all went into the front room and chilled while Stevie lay dying in the cold bathtub. It was surreal, everyone was so unruffled, like it was an everyday occurrence. Mel found Stevie's Playstation and began hooking it up to the TV. Kooba and Sparks began billin' up from a bag of weed. I remember clearly because they used some blue Rizla I had in my pocket from wrapping up earlier, and for some reason I objected to Sparks tearing the box for a roach. I don't now why, but I just did. Weird. For the next half an hour I sat motionless on the sofa staring at the computer. As the high-grade weed and control pads were being passed back and forth. In my mind I kept telling myself I had to do something, but what?

Before I knew it a whole hour had gone. Kooba had made a cheese sandwich and was wholeheartedly devouring it, while Sparks and Mel where engrossed in a game of Gran Turismo.

"Oi, Sparks," Kooba said with his mouth full. "How long you gonna leave that nigga in the bath for? It's been about an hour now."

"For real," Sparks looked around. "G-man, I beg you go with Kooba and get that piece of shit out the tub."

"Fuck that." Kooba mumbled. "I'm eating. Let Mel go."

"For real," Sparks kicked Mel. "You go."

Mel threw down the control pad. "How comes it's always bloody me. I'm like the bloody dog's body round 'ere, while all this fat fuck does is bloody eat."

"Carry on you little dickhead," Kooba warned as he caught food falling out of his mouth. "See if I don't bust your head."

Mel followed me into the bathroom. I searched for the string-pull to turn the light on. Stevie lay unconscious. I would've thought he was dead, but his body still shivered in the cold water. Mel retrieved his rubber gloves off the floor, and positioned himself between the sink and the bath.

"Oi, Gil, I'll grab him under the arms and you pull him out yeah."

As we bent down to lift Stevie up, he opened his eyes and peered right up at us. Instantly we both dropped the heavy half-dead carcass and jumped back out of fright. Mel started laughing.

"Shit, blood, he fucking frightened me."

The image of Mel standing over Stevie's body with rubber gloves and an apron did more to me. Pinned against the wall I had a flashing image of myself lying in the tub. Mel called to me "Gil, Gil"

I was in a trance. I saw myself in Stevie. In a micro second it flashed from me to the old slave and then to Alicia. She looked right at me shivering in the water. Her body was bruised and ruined. Her breasts were covered in goose pimples, as her erect nipples floated like icebergs in the murky water. Her face was contort with pain and bludgeoned with agony. Her voice spoke in tiny broken whispers, "Gil, I need your help. I need your help." Again the voice repeated itself as I stood still. "Gil, Gil, I need your help."

It all came rushing back to me. Mel stood in front of me with his hands on my shoulders. "Gil, are you alright, bruv?"

"Yeah, yeah I'm fine."

"Alright then, help me out bro. On three pull"

Mel gave the count and we dragged Stevie out and placed him on the floor.

"He's bloody heavy." Mel puffed.

Stevie lay on the floor like a wet fish. "Please, pppplease," he murmured from between our feet. I looked at Mel.

"I ain't feelin this shit at all. Why didn't you tell me what was goin on, on the phone?"

"How?" Mel protested. "How was I suppose to know what man was on. Dem man just told me to follow dem, next thing I know everyone's runnin' up in the crib and Sparks is saying to phone you. What could I say? I never had no say in it."

"Well we gotta do something."

"Like what?"

"I don't know. Get him out of here or something."

"Are you mad," Mel's eyes widened. "For what reason, so Sparks can switch on us? Nahhh bredrin I don't think so. Just let Sparks handle his business. This shit ain't got shit to do with us."

"Says the man with a half dead naked guy between his legs"

"Look, G, I never put him in this position."

"What are you talking about? You were beatin' 'im half to death when I came in."

"Yeah only cos Sparks told me too."

"Oh my days!" I raised my hands in disbelief.

"Okay, okay, okay, just shut up." Mel quieted me. "Look let's just take him back in the front-room and let Sparks deal with him."

"Blood, have you seen how Sparks is acting. You know they're gonna kill him right?"

"Look, so long as Sparks does it, I don't bloody care. That's not my business, that's not your business. He fucked with the wrong person, now he's gotta pay. It's between him and Sparks. This ain't got nothing to do with us."

"So you're happy to be an accessory to murder?" I asked.

"G," Mel pulled his face whining. "What's wrong with you? Why you always got to be so dramatic?"

"Because if this ain't drama," I pointed to Stevie. "What is?"

There was silence as we looked at the tortured body.

"What you lot doing?" Kooba said entering the room. He startled us. "Don't just look at him," he huffed, "Bring 'im thru."

Kooba helped us drag Stevie to the far side of the front room. He cut Stevie's bonds loose and handed the knife to Sparks. We stood around in a semicircle. The curtains were drawn and the music was placed up two notches as the proceedings began.

It was Sparks' court and he played judge and jury. He played with the kitchen knife prodding it at Stevie's chest. The quick jabs pierced the skin and tiny red beads began to appear. Sparks jabbed the blade again. This time slowly he twisted the knife opening up a wound. Stevie's screams were drowned by the music. When Sparks stopped, he signalled for Kooba to lower the volume.

"Lessons, lessons, lessons," He sighed. "I don't know why so many blackheads have to learn the hard way."

Sparks wiped the knife across Stevie's face leaving a trail of smeared blood. He paused for a second in deep thought, then smiled to himself.

"Ha, let this be a lesson to you man," he waved the knife at Mel and I. "I got this saying that goes, stealing is bad, but stealing from the devil is just plain stupid. No one's gonna cry for you when you a get pitch fork stuck up you're arse."

Walking over to the stereo he put the music up again. He took out his Zippo lighter and sparked up a joint he had wrapped earlier. He took a hard pull.

"You see something, Stevie, I always liked you," he said shouting over the music "You ain't the smartest brother, but I got to give it to you. You really got balls."

As Sparks spoke, Kooba walked over and gripped Stevie in a headlock.

"I know that now. We all know that. I mean you're just sitting there with your balls hanging out bredrin. You see the problem with having balls and I mean big balls." He said drawing on the spliff. "Is that certain niggas start acting like dogs, and they think they can run wild and fuck everybody in sight."

He chuckled to himself playing with the lighter.

"You know what happens to dogs and niggas like that, bredrin?" Sparks placed the lighter between Stevie's legs "They get neutered."

Aaaaaaahhhhhh!!!!! There was a gut-curdling scream as Sparks lit the lighter and set Stevie's testicles on fire. Within seconds his pubic hair disintegrated and melted into his skin. He kicked out and struggled under Kooba's grip, but Sparks stood on his leg and continued to hold the lighter smiling.

The smell of burnt skin and hairs was as perverse as the sight of Stevie's scrotum burning raw red. Pieces fell off as he tried to protect his sack. I looked at Mel. We both cringed, but couldn't bear to turn away. It was gruesome (In later days I would pray to God, if I ever met a violent death, let it not be by burning), however I continued to watch.

When Stevie looked ready to pass out, Sparks ordered Kooba to let go. Stevie slumped to the floor, but a kick from Sparks saw that he stayed conscious. He rolled over crying in pain. His hands covered in blood, from rubbing his burnt skin.

"Now," Sparks crouched down grabbing Stevie's throat. "We know what type of nigga you are, now let me tell you what kind I am."

Once again the music was lowered. Sparks inhaled on his spliff before blowing it in Stevie's face. "You see, Stevie, I'm one of those niggas who's like a dog too. One of those dogs who's always loyal and lovin' to the man dem. But I'm not one of these dogs if you kick dem or hit dem, that lowers it's head and cowers in the corner."

Menacingly Sparks held what was left of his zoot next to Stevie's eye. All the time Stevie was panting in pain.

"No, if you hit me, I'm the type of dog that's got to bite back. It's in my nature. I'm vicious like that, I need blood." Spark's grinned as the hot ash fell on Stevie's face. "You see if you steal a bone from a dog like me. I haven't got the time to sniff it out, I smell the last person near my bowl and I bite them. I gnaw at them, I tear down on them until there's nothing left. That's why they brought out the dangerous dogs act. For dogs like me!"

Sparks pushed the spliff in Stevie's cheek. "We're dangerous, Stevie! Dangerous! if provoked we can kill!"

He thrust Stevie to the floor and pulled out a Colt M1911. It was a faded black pistol and looked aged. He titled it to the side, playing. He lined Stevie up in his sight. Mouthing the word *pow*, over and over again. "POW! That's you gon' jus like dat," he said, finally placing the weapon on the side. He smiled.

"Now, Stevie," he said. "I'm gonna ask you once. And let me be clear from now. If you lie to me, or send me on any wild goose chase, the next thing you hear bark won't be my mouth, it'll be the sound of my machine. Now where's my money?"

Defeated Stevie mumbled an address.

"What?" Sparks gun butt him in the face. "Speak up you pussy."

"Cmon, Sparks, ease the man up ah bit."

"What?"

I didn't realise I had spoken aloud until Sparks glared at me.

"I don't mean no disrespect," I held up my hands. "But give the man a break, his jaw's fucking broken. At least let him write it down or something."

"What do you know how much p's this pussy stole from me?"

"No."

"Exactly! So shut the fuck up and sit down. Mel," He called. "Find some paper for this pussy to write on."

Retrieving an old envelope Mel placed it in front of Stevie. His hands were deformed and crippled with pain. "Sparks, lemme write it," I said taking the pen from Stevie. "It's easier."

Sparks sucked his teeth and told Stevie to hurry up. I wrote down an address to a lock-up in Stanmore and Stevie told Kooba where he hid the set of keys and explained how to get in. Sparks smiled. He'd been smiling all night.

"This better be it, Stevie." He said passing the envelope to Kooba. They whispered to each other then Kooba said. "You lot are gonna hav'ta stay 'ere till we get back,"

"What, I ain't staying here," Mel argued.

"Yes you fucking are!" Sparks snapped. "There's no way this piece of shit's giving me a boog address and disappearing the first minute we're out of here. You and Gil are gonna wait here till we get back, do you understand?"

"Whatever," Mel sulked. "Do what you like, just don't take all night."

"Sparks, what happens if it's not there?" I asked

"Don't worry about that." Sparks said tucking his gun behind his back. "We'll deal wid that if it's not there. Just tie him up and keep an eye on him till we get back."

Sparks gave me a wink as he and Kooba left the room. Mel followed them to the door leaving me alone. I looked at Stevie. Defeated he seemed to just lie there as though it was the end. His body looked repulsive, with all the infliction it had suffered. Curled into the foetal position, his body involuntary twitched and trembled, from shock. His injuries were an assortment of red and purple, cast against a yellow canvass of mulatto skin. It was sad. Stevie had once played semi-pro. There was talk of him kicking ball for a premiership team. Now he looked like life and Sparks had kicked him one too many times. Torn and burnt flesh hung grotesquely from his body. I couldn't imagine the pain he was in. If Sparks didn't kill him tonight I was sure that the shock would. Things weren't looking good. The night had spiralled out of control and all I kept thinking about was *'if this brer dies tonight what the fuck happens next?'* It was something I wasn't willing to find out. I ran into the bathroom and grabbed a t-shirt hanging on the radiator. Tearing it into strips I began to run it under cold water. I said to myself over and over

"*Got to help Stevie, can't let him die.*"

I came running back in the room to find Mel. He'd already started tying Stevie up with a fresh set of cable ties. I grabbed him by the collar and pulled him away.

"What the fuck you doing?" Mel yelled. I ignored him tending to Stevie wounds.

"G! What you doin'? We're suppose to be tying him up." Mel tried to stop me.

"Get off me!" I pushed him away. "The man's just had his balls burnt off and all you wanna do is tie him up. What's wrong with you?"

"Me!" Mel grabbed piece of the T-shirt. "Rudeboy you're losing your mind. Sparks left orders to tie him up and that's what I'm doing. You need to calm yourself down and stop acting like a pussy.

"Pussy!" I yelled. "What the fuck you know 'bout pussy? You're the one waitin around for Sparks to fuck you.

"What?"

"You heard me. You're the one who hangs on to Sparks' every word like a bitch. At least I got my own mind. I swear you're not even thinkin'! This shit is fucked. Fucked!" I pointed to Stevie. "Look at 'im he's half dead and you still wanna tie 'im up. For what? Where the fuck is he running to? Use your brain, think."

"Ah stop acting all high and mighty." Mel threw the piece of rag at Stevie "If you don't tie him up what you gonna do?"

"I don't know, but I ain't tying him up and watchin' him die."

"So like I said, what you gonna do?" Mel waited for an answer. "Look, G, don't think I wanna be in here doing this anymore than you? But Sparks is right. It's a dog eat dog world out here and we gotta move like dogs. The man stole Spark's work. What do you really expect Sparks to do? Shake his hand and say ah forget about it. It's nothing. Nahh, G," Mel shook his head. "That's not how we live. Man and man hav' to let people know not to fuck wid man; otherwise everybody's gonna try a ting. You know that shit. So stop playing like you need to help him anymore than me, and let's tie him up."

Mel was right, but that didn't change the fact that Spark's had drafted me into this shit. This had nothing to do with me. I didn't like being manipulated. My instincts made me suspicious. I always said, if a man needs you're help, for right or wrong, they should always give you the choice whether to help or not first. If you accept, then you accept the consequences too. That's what friends do. Sparks had denied me that choice.

"Fuck Sparks." I knelt back down to help Stevie. "I never signed up for this."

"Okay, G," Mel gave up reasoning. "You do you yeah. But If Sparks says anything and I mean anything. That's between you and him. 'member I told you that, yeah."

I ignored Mel as he sat back and sulked. I turned to Stevie, he was shaking more than ever. He kept mumbling sorry over and over. I feared he was going into shock. He was disorientated. I rushed to the bedroom to find some clothes.

Kicking through the mess I found an Adidas tracksuit top and bottoms. I grabbed them and the duvet cover and returned to the front room. Mel was busy wiping down the Playstation and control pads

"What's that for?" he fumed.

"I need to put some clothes on him. I think he's going into what-u-call-it. Hypothermia."

"Blood, Sparks ain't gonna like that. Not tying him is one thing, but puttin' clothes on him's another."

"Don't worry about Sparks. I'll deal with Sparks."

I lent down and struggled to put the clothes on Stevie. I tried to be as gentle as possible, but he cried as I pulled his arm into to the sleeve. I tried my best to keep him conscious.

"Cmon, Stevie man. Keep talking to me, bruv. It's Gil. I need you to keep talking."

"Gil," His words were slow and faint. "It's cold."

"I know man, but I'm trying to warm you up, bruv. I'm trying."

"Why?" Stevie asked. It was a valid question. "Leave me, let me die"

"I can't do that, bruv. That ain't part of the plan." I reassured him.

"He's gonna kill me anyway," Stevie mumbled. "Leave me. Don't let him see me die."

"C'mon, Stevie man, you ain't gonna die." There was little conviction in my voice.

Stevie smiled as I lay the duvet over him and a cushion under his head. Mel stood over my shoulder observing.

"He's gonna die."

"Shut up!" I yelled. "No one ain't dying to tonight, okay." I turned back to Stevie. "Stevie, you're gonna be alright mate, don't worry." But I could feel him growing weaker and weaker. I had to keep his mind active. "Stevie wake up man. Don't go sleep. Talk to me. How's your mum nowadays?"

"It was her," he said "It was her who did it, not me."

I didn't understand what he was saying. "She did what, bruv?"

"She stole the work. She stole it off me."

Lorraine was Stevie's mother. A white woman in her early forties who loved reminding me, "I'm one of Sparks' original punters." She seemed to pride herself on it. "I gave him all his punters 'round 'ere. I'm the one who started him off."

People had often teased Stevie about his mother when we were young. It wasn't hard to see she was a crackhead and a junkie. When you're young you don't understand why some adults have erratic behaviour. But as you get older the pieces begin to fit. By the time we found out Stevie's mum was a prostitute, his life was already ruined. He'd been in and out of care most his life while people preyed on his mum. When Lorraine was younger she didn't look that bad, she could definitely pull the Johns in. But after Stevie's baby sister died, she really hit the brown hard. Sparks once told us when he was coming up she used to suck his dick for a bag. He always denied fucking her, but I found that hard to believe.

"What do you mean she stole it?"

"She stole it off me, Gil," Stevie struggled to speak. "I left her in the house that day...when I came back she was gone with half the parcel."

I couldn't believe it. It warranted Stevie's actions. No one knew why he'd just taken off with Sparks' drugs like he did.

"Why didn't you tell Sparks?"

Stevie tried to chuckle, but ended with a heavy cough. His face winced in pain. "He's crazy. He'll kill her. She's a crackhead to him, Gil."

"But, Stevie he might have."

Stevie grabbed my hand. "Don't be stupid. She means nothing to him, but she's my mum." He tried to sit up.

"Stevie, lay down man."

"Gil I've never had no dad or any other family. My granddad died years ago. She's all I got. Do you know what it's like not to have anyone, and the only person you love is on yeng."

For some reason I randomly thought about Alicia. "No, I don't know." I replied.

"I swear, Gil, it hurts." Stevie coughed. His voice was getting fainter. Tears rolled down what was left of Stevie's face. "It hurts so much, Gil, and all you want is a hug or a kiss. Someone to just say its gonna be alright. I swear," he cried. "She loved that shit more than she loved me."

"C'mon man, that ain't true."

"You think so. Ask Sparks who told him where I live. That bitch chose an eigth-ball of crack over me. She fuckin' killed me, Gil. Years ago. She killed me before I even a had chance."

Stevie closed his eyes and I felt his body slump in my arms. He didn't move. He lay still. Mel came closer and sat beside me. We both expected the worst.

"Is he dead now?" Mel asked.

"Not yet." I said picking up Stevie's fragile arm. There was still a feeble pulse. I wasn't sure how long it would last. We let him rest and waited for Sparks and Kooba to return.

*

The wait was long and morning was fast approaching. The first break of light began to shine through gaps in the curtain. The sky was a twilight tint of violet and blue, which shone upon the outside world. In the early hours those who would soon be up and heading to their regular 9-5 were oblivious to the going-ons of the number twelve flat. It had been hours since Sparks and Kooba had left and Mel was beginning to panic. The weight of the situation was beginning to dawn on him. Paranoia set in and he was convinced that something had happened to them. He ran numerous scenarios aloud, while I kept a vigil on Stevie's condition. We were running out of time. He needed medical attention.

"Gil, we need to get out of here man. It's morning, people are gonna be around soon."

"We ain't leaving yet,"

"What's the use of staying man? Sparks and Kooba done ducked out hours ago. They ain't coming back. Somethings happened to them. They must've got shiff or something. We gotta leave." Mel said eager to go.

"What about Stevie? We can't just leave him like that."

"Okay, but we can't afford to be seen leaving this flat. If he dies"

"He ain't gonna die."

"Okay, but if he dies. I don't want no one I.D.-ing me as no murder suspect."

"So what do you wanna do, Mel?"

"Listen I think we should wipe down everything and leave before it gets to late. When we get a little further down the road, we can stop at a phone box and call an ambulance. They'll come find Stevie and take him to the hospital, he'll be okay there."

I held my head debating. Before I could reply there was a sound at the door. Somebody had a set of keys and was beginning to come in. The sound of the key being pushed in the door sent shivers down my back. It was one of the most explosive moments in my life. My heart stopped as I saw Mel pick up the bike chain.

"Hide" he mouthed as the footsteps came creeping slowly down the passage.

Mel stood behind the door ready to pounce. I was sure it couldn't be Sparks and Kooba, they knew the signal was to drop a Snickers bar through the letterbox. I ran and stood beside Mel as the footsteps drew closer. I looked at Mel ready to strike. As the large frame stepped around the door, I managed to push Mel off balance as the chain lashed in Kooba's back.

"Aaaahh! What the fuck you lot doing?" Kooba held his shoulder. He snatched the chain from Mel. "You could've fuckin' killed me."

"Good," Mel retort. "Where the fuck you been? Where's Sparks?"

"I'm right here," Sparks stepped in the room. "Wha gwan? You lot look shook."

"Where the hell you been?" I asked on edge.

"Pardon?" Sparks replied.

"I said, where you been?"

Immediately Sparks frowned. "Firstly, rudeboy, slow your row and mine your tone when you're speaking to me yeah, cos I ain't in the mood. You're getting ahead of yourself." He sucked his tooth picking at a piece of meat stuck in his back teeth. "Know when to address me properly."

"Sorry," I said humouring Sparks.

"Hmm," Sparks sat down on the arm of the settee. "We went down to the lock up, then we went to sort out some other shit." He finally pulled out the piece of meat and wiped it in the sofa. "Why?" he asked. "Have you got a problem?"

"No," I answered. "But how comes it took you so long to come back?"

A smile bordered his face from cheek to cheek once more. "Cos we had to count up."

"How much you find?" Mel jumped in.

"Enough." Sparks reached into his pocket. He tossed a bundle of money at both me and Mel. "There's two gib each. You boys done well tonight, but I'm not sure about all this," he pointed to the corner where Stevie lay in the duvet.

Kooba gave Stevie a kicking nudge and he groaned. "He's still alive, Sparks what you wanna do with him?"

Sparks didn't look pleased. "Who put the clothes and duvet on him?"

"I did."

"Did I tell you to do that?"

"You didn't tell us not too." I said. There was defiance in my voice. "You didn't want us to let him die did you? How was you gonna question him if the drugs weren't there?"

"Hmm" Sparks screwed up his face. He got up scanning the room. "It looks pretty tidy in here you lot wipe down or what?"

"Not yet," Mel was quick to answer. He didn't want Sparks to know we had considered leaving. "We was waiting till you got back"

"What about talking." Sparks asked. "Did any of you talk to him?"

"Nah," Mel looked at me. "There was nothing to talk about."
"What about you, Gil."
"Nah." I lied. "You told us not to. Besides his jaw looks broken"
"Good," Sparks said. He walked over and examined Stevie.

When Sparks back was turned I gestured to Mel to tell him we wanted to leave. He shook his head and mouthed, *"You."* I grit my teeth and mouthed back *"pussy."* He pulled a face and gave me the finger.

"Yo, Sparks" I asked nervously "You got your money. Can we get out of here now?"

"Yeah in a minute start wiping the place down and get rid of any prints first."

We did as Sparks said and pretended to wipe down while he and Kooba stood over Stevie whispering. Together they were plotting. Heads nodded and shook from side to side and they kept looking over their shoulder at Mel and I. I gave them five more minutes and the game was up. The sun had finally risen and I'd run out of time and patience. I looked at Mel as we wiped "Screw this, you got your car outside?"

"Yeah it's parked two roads away why?"

"Sparks ain't playing me no more. I'm outta here. You comin'?"

"Yeah" Mel nodded his head enthusiastically.

"Cool," I cleared my throat to get the two plotters attention. "Yo, Sparks what you man on? Cos we're finished, blood, so we're gonna be out of here, if that's cool wid you?"

"No its not cool wid me," Sparks stood with arms crossed. " You ain't finished until I say you're finished, so get back to work."

"Nah trust me, blood" I threw down the rag I was using. "We're finished."

Sparks did not look pleased. "Liss'en, Gil don't piss me off. We got a lot work to do and we're running out of time. So if you know what's good for you do as I say and get back to work."

"What you mean, if I know what's good for me? Me and Mel been 'ere long enough. If you came back when you were suppose to then things would be different, but right 'bout now we wanna go. So we're going."

"Mel, is that what you want too?" Sparks turned to Mel.

"Yeah kinda," Mel petted to say. "We've been here ages, but I'll stay if I have to."

"No Mel," I switched "Tell him we're dus'ing. There's nothing left for us to do here Sparks. You got your money, Stevie's almost dead, we've cleaned up, what the hell are we still doing here lets go!"

"They got a point, Sparks," Kooba agreed. "It doesn't make any sense staying, unless."

"Look! Everybody shut up," Sparks ordered "Nobody's going anywhere 'till I say so."

"What's the point in that?" I quizzed

"The fucking point is that I'm in charge and nobody leaves until I say so. If I say we ain't finished here, we ain't finished."

"And what if I say we are finished"

The argument quickly became a stand off between Sparks and me. The line of command was slowly fading with every unexplained act Sparks committed. He began to get frustrated. His mind was going into overload trying to stay four steps a head of us. From nowhere he drew his gun and pounced on me. He pinned me to the wall.

"What, you fucking pussy. What, do you think you bout it?"

Sparks rammed his forearm underneath my chin pushing pressure on my throat. He held the gun under my right eye gently pushing the barrel into the socket.

"Well, tell me den?" He snapped. "I swear I'll fucking bury you. Tell me your 'bout it."

Edging away from the gun I wanted to say something, but fear gripped my tongue. I could see Kooba grinning from the corner of my eye. He came closer and stood beside Sparks. "Sparks, wharm to you man. Let my man go. He's not the one you're vex with."

"Yes I am!" Sparks shouted. "I'm vex with all of dem. Who do they think I am?" He spat saliva all over me as his spoke. His breath was warm and stale.

"I bring all dese lickle pussies in and now all of you wanna do is get smart wid me. Me! I swear down how many of you niggaz have I gotta teach a lesson before you get the idea?" I tried to struggle under Sparks grip, but he clapped me in the face with the side of his gun. "What! Stand still what's the matter with you?"

Sparks kneed me swiftly to my midsection. I staggered forward, winded. He kicked me to the floor then dragged me on all fours over to where Stevie lay. He held my face towards Stevie's, and our three heads faced each other in a triangle. He grabbed me by the scruff of the neck and pushed the gun to my throat.

"Look! If you haven't noticed, this is what I do to people that upset me, bredrin. Now if you think you're a bad-man! Lemme see you grow some balls and say you goin' home. Go on!" Sparks roughed me up. "I dare you to upset me."

I said nothing studying Stevie's face. The blood had started to dry and tighten his skin. He looked up at me and gave a pleading gesture. *Don't upset him Gil.*

"C'mon, G." Sparks goad me. "Be a bad-man, show me you're 'bout it. Show me you got some balls. "

"Take the gun out my face and I will."

"What?" Sparks said. He looked at the others in disbelief. "Say that again."

"I said take the gun out my face and I will. Anyone can be a bad-man wid a gun in their hand."

"Is that so?" Sparks smirked. "Okay, show me." He stepped back and laid the gun on the floor. "If you're bad-man pick up that gun and show me what you can do."

He grinned calling my bluff. "Go on, pick it up."

I looked at the old Colt as it lay on the carpet. I wondered could I get to it before him. If I could, I'd stick it in his face and make him beg me. I'd show him what being on the other end was like. I'd smash the butt in his face and ruin his nose. Who did he think he was? I was sick off being his lackey. Fretting about how Sparks was going to react about this and that. I'd teach him a lesson for once. All I had to do was get the gun. But I cowardly dare not move. "Sparks, I don't want no trouble." I held my bruised face. "I just wanna go home."

"Den pick up the gun you pussy, cos I ain't playin'. Either you pick it up or I do. One or the other."

Looking into Sparks' eyes I could tell he was serious. I'd over stepped the line and he wanted to teach me a lesson. I decided to make my move. Quickly I side-stepped and dived at the weapon, but Kooba grabbed me and threw me into the corner. Sparks swiftly swooped up the weapon, but Mel held him back.

"Sparks! You're going too far now." Kooba fumed. "You can't play wid da yoot like dat."

"Why not?" Sparks raged. "Move," he pushed Mel out the way. "You just saw what he did. He was gonna shoot me."

"No he wasn't," Kooba stood like a human wall between us. "He was just tryna get da gun, like you told him. Stop tryna push buttons out here. All my man wants to do is go home, so let him go."

"Fine." Sparks barged Kooba out the way. He stepped towards me. "You wanna leave pussy, leave. But gimme my money back." He reached into my pocket and took the two grand. "This is for niggas with balls not shook ones like you. Here Mel," He tossed the money to Mel. "Take this little girl home, I don't wanna see his face round da man dem again." He turned back to me. "And hear what bredrin. I don't wanna hear no talk about you start up your own phone or any of that shit. You're over on road. And if I hear any talk, about wha gwan tonight; believe me, I won't hesitate to run up in your yard. Do you overstand me?" I nodded my head. "No don't nod your head" Sparks slapped me across the face "Say it."

"I overstand."

"Good, fuck off" Sparks said heaving with anger. He was so disgusted he spat in my face. "Get the fuck out of here, before I change my mind."

Walking away I wiped my face. There were tears in my eyes. I'd been humiliated by someone I'd once called my friend. I'd shown a weakness and challenged my capo's authority for the wrong reasons. In my mind I knew I'd broken institute rules - *You never go against your crew*, which meant I had therefore warranted the scolding I received. It was inevitable. I'd made a mistake. I hadn't stayed true to my crew. Now I was expelled. Instantly I regretted my actions. I wanted to say sorry. I wanted to say I was wrong. I didn't want to leave, but I realised I had too. I had moved on. The goals of my firm were no longer sufficient. I wanted more. I had matured and developed along my journey. I had outgrown my companions and their ideology.

Before I would have thrived over beating a man to death, thrived on making drug money, thrived on taking orders from Sparks, now I saw it for what it was - part of the process of containment. So, maybe I wasn't being expelled. Maybe I was graduating. Maybe I'd learnt all I would learn in my chosen course? Perhaps this was my final test – whether I could kill someone or not? Had I passed or had I failed? I wasn't sure. All I knew stepping out into that first morning light was that I was leaving the institute forever. If this was my chance to get out then I was going to take it. And if the *'Institute Of The Streets'* scared me, being left with the unknown journey petrified me tenfold.

"Oi, come we go." Mel said leading the way to the car.

As we sat in the BMW the silence was morbid. Something had died. Mel kept staring at me every two minutes. I could feel his look burning at the side of my face. Why didn't he just speak or open his mouth. Was he ashamed of me too?

"What Mel, what is it?"

"Nothing."

"No, don't say that, Mel, talk the truth. You think I'm weak innit? You think I should've fought back."

"Blood, don't be stupid. You did what you needed to do, to get us out of there. Fuck the rest. Sparks was on some mad power trip. You did the right thing." He handed me a tissue from off the dashboard. "Wipe your mouth."

I hadn't noticed my lip was bleeding. My whole face stung from the scuffle with Sparks. Mel turned off the A40 on to Askew Road. "Look, G, if it weren't for you I wouldn't've said nothing and Sparks wud probably have us chopping up Stevie's body right now."

He beeped his horn as he as an Audi RS5 cut across him at the roundabout by Ravenscourt. He took the second left and turned down the back of Hammersmith.

"Mel, what you think they're gonna do to Stevie?" I asked.

"I don't know. To tell you the truth I don't care."

As Mel drove through the morning traffic of commuters and mothers on the school run I began to fall asleep. When I awoke he'd parked outside my block.

"You cool, G?" he asked.

"Yeah I'm fine. What about you?"

"I'm not sure." Mel shifted in his seat. "I was just thinking, is our lives like a movie or what. I mean some of the things that happen to us, it ain't meant to be like that. You know what I mean?"

"Yeah I know," I sat up. "It's like you ask yourself '*did that really happen?*' You even tell yourself that shit belongs in a movie or book or something anywhere, but our life."

"Yeah, yeah that's what I mean." Mel started laughing. We both laughed. It was a laugh of relief. The night's events were over and today was a new day.

"Yo, G, if your life was a movie what would you call it?" Mel asked.

"I don't know," I said. "I'd probably keep it simple something like *The Best laid plans.*"

"Yeah that sounds cool. If my life was a movie, I'd call it *'No Tick, No Change, No Shorts"*

"Why?" I looked at him knowing that was originally Sparks' phrase.

"Cos I swear God's some shotta. He never gives niggaz like me and you a squeeze."

"You're mad." I laughed getting out the car. "What squeezes do you need? You still got 4 gee in your pocket and a beemer. Life can't be that bad."

"I don't know," Mel smiled. "It ain't good, it at ain't bad, it just is. What am I gonna do cry?"

***

CHAPTER: 14
POLITICS OF THE YARD

Ivan couldn't concentrate with his cellmate watching him. He lay on the top bunk trying to read *Black Girl Lost*, a novel written by Donald Goines. Donald Goines' books were like gold bars in jail. Ivan hadn't met a nigger in jail or who'd been jail that hadn't read a Donald Goines book. To have a Goines in your collection was an important asset. You could bargain and haggle, extra batteries, food, and music all on the strength of a promised period with a Goines book.

Goines was like the Black Mario Puzo. Instead of Italians and the Mafia, Goines wrote about that ghetto shit. About the pain and grief of black and ethnic characters that Ivan could relate to. Like other writers Iceberg Slim, Chester Himes, and Herbert Simmons, Goines' books were set in the backdrop of the American ghetto. He held no punches, the violence was real, and the characters mirrored the prison reader. There was never a happy ending just an end. Goines was Ivan's favourite writer. He wished that the UK had their own Goines, the closest they'd had produced was Courttia Newland and Alex Wheatle both incredible writers, but neither could tell it like Goines.

Ivan watched his cellmate closely as he paced around the room and stopped at the foot of Ivan's bed. He looked like he was ready to burst. He was agitated and stared frowning at Ivan. Slamming the book down, Ivan sat up.

"What, what's wrong with you?" he said watching the young black man in his face.

The man was brown skin and about 5'6 with a wiry frame. At first glance he looked harmless, but something about his mannerisms screamed troublesome. His afro was wild and uncombed. Whiskers shot from his face and chin, which he liked to call a beard. He was young, but his face looked hard and restless.

"Terror, you're taking forever with that book man." The man complained "You're not suppose to take so long with Donald Goines books. Three days max. Lemme read it now."

"Dorian what's wrong with you?" Ivan hung his feet over the side of the top bunk. "How you expect to read my book before me? I just got it. Look, read one of the others till I'm finished." He passed a next book over. "Try this one *Journey of a Slave*."

"That's long, I've read that." Dorian tried grabbing the Donald Goines.

"Move!" Ivan drew back. He kicked the air near Dorian's head. "I ain't playing with you. You're gonna rip my book."

"Ahhh!" Dorian yelled, "Come on, Terror, man! I beg you, let me read it. Wharm to you?"

Frustrated, Dorian stepped back to rethink his strategy. "Hear what I'm saying. Play me at Dead Card Black Jack, and if I lose I'll read another book, and! I'll give you a pack of custard creams."

Ivan smiled at his cellmate. Dogman aka Dorian Gustav or DDG as he liked to call himself, did not take no for an answer. It wasn't hard to see why he was in jail. Short tempered, hyper active, impatient and quick tongued, Dorian wasn't the type to play the game by any rules; he made up his own. He kept Ivan entertained and on his toes. Everyday they spent hours, debating and arguing because neither would allow the other to have the last word. Even in his sleep, Dorian argued. The only time he was quiet was when he was reading or writing. Ivan enjoyed his company and competitive spirit. They'd even invented a new card game called, '*Dead Card Black Jack*' just to prove who was the better player.

The rules were virtually the same as standard Black Jack played in English jails; only your opponent would choose a card from your hand. The chosen card would be placed on the side and unless it was a queen, eight or king, it had to be your finishing card. Otherwise it would have to be in your last three for example: in a two-man game the king reverses back to a player. If your chosen card was a king, you will need to lie something on top of the king in order to finish. Dorian picked up the cards off the side.

"So what you saying, Terror? One game."

"Okay, get the table."

Jumping down, Ivan helped Dorian move the table into the middle of the cell. Together they'd tried to personalise their cell as much as possible. They'd torn a bed sheet for a tablecloth and used the left over rags to wipe up messes. They neatly displayed their canteen like products on a shop shelf and covered their pin board with cut outs of the best female flesh Club magazine and Men's Only had to offer. They both had stereos, but used Ivan's for the most, until the weekend. Weekends meant Westwood and Goldfinger on Radio 1. That's when the two inmates would play both stereos for that surround sound effect.

Dealing the cards out, Dorian and Ivan began playing when they heard Bait-man shouting from a couple cells down, "Oi DDG, DDG, come to the window!"

Dorian looked at Ivan "What's he want now?"

Douglas Rodigan aka Bait-man was titled so because everything he did was bait. If you ever asked anyone about him, the person would answer, "he's bait, don't do nothing with that brer."

Bait-Man was the only person Ivan knew, who could get caught stealing coffee from the prison workshop.

"Oi, Gustav," He yelled. "Come to the window, man!"

Knowing he would call all night Dorian went over to see what Bait-man wanted. Leaning on the windowsill, Dorian shouted through the bars. "WHAT!"

"Oi, Gustav, I'm ready for you, now!" Bait-man yelled "Come we battle on the yard tomorrow. What you saying?"

"That's bait!" Dorian yelled back. "I done told you I ain't battling for free no more!"

"Don't be shook!"

"Who's you calling shook, you waste-man!"

Ivan called over to Dorian "Oi, he just got his canteen. Tell him to put something up if he wants to battle"

"Oi, Bait-man," Dorian called "Hear what, big son. True you sound eager, I'll tell you what I'm gonna do for you. I'll battle you for three snicker bars. What you saying?"

There was a short pause, then Bait-man shouted "Okay, but if I win, I want two packs of pawn cocktail crisp and a Ribena!"

"Yeah that's cool," Dorian laughed "But you ain't gonna win." Dorian began to call King. "Number ten on the 2's, number ten on the 2's! King, come to the window!"

"What's up, D?" King called back.

"Yo, King, be the judge tomorrow, yeah."

"What do I get for judging?"

"Nothing!" Dorian yelled. "You get to be judge. But if you're lucky Bait-man, might get his girl to suck your dick. Dem man need to give out as many bribes as possible wid their weak rhymes."

"Fuck you!" Bait-man shouted. "I don't need to bribe no judge. I'm gonna murder you tomorrow wid bare lyrics! Watch!"

Getting excited Bait-man started spitting lyrics from his window. There was a choir of mixed abuse and heckling. Dorian looked at Ivan shaking his head.

"Who does this nigga think he is, Jay-z?" he laughed. "Oi, Bait-man, Bait-man," Dorian shouted. He waited for Bait-man to reply.

"What!"

"GET YOUR HEAD DOWN MATE!" Dorian shouted slamming his window shut.

*

At Haugthon Hill, inmates were required to have at least one hour exercise every day and were permitted to go outside to the yard. The object of exercise was for inmates to walk laps around the yard. However, once in the yard the prisoners would scatter off into their own little groups to talk. Ivan and Dorian gave each group it's own name. There was the *Fake Firm*, which consisted mostly of white inmates. Dorian said they all looked like wannabe football hooligan's who sat around drinking in some pub after the big match. It was no surprise that this was the corner run by Bain and his mates. Then there was the Taliban Squad because it was made up of mostly Asian and Arab Muslims. Then there was Trench Town, which consisted of a few Yardies and a couple Ja-Fakins. Istanbul & The East Block, was where the Turks, Albanians, and Eastern European inmates congregated and the last group was theirs, Haughton Hill's finest The Noir Syndicate. Ivan told Dorian to stop calling them that. It made them sound like a gang.

"What, Terror you don't know 'bout The Aggy Noir." Yet what Ivan had witnessed amongst the gathering was nothing like any gang he knew.

Ivan remembered the first time he floated into the corner. King was the master of ceremony holding everyone's attention as he spoke of black history and self-identity. Looking around, he noticed some of the men wearing black, red, and gold armbands or badges, similar to King's. Each day they discussed black politics and how they affected them. Each inmate, added their own personal opinions, solutions, and stories. In youth offenders, Ivan had never heard men speak so openly about anything other than offences, and he was drawn to listen. As time went on he noticed how the men acted as a collective. They supported each other frequently sharing phone cards, canteen, and literature with no squabbles or debts. They'd even produced a petition that was being signed all over the prison. The petition spearheaded by King, argued that the black inmates should be supplied Black history and self-awareness programs, and also requested the subjects be added to the prison curriculum.

Ivan admired King. When they met he didn't realise the influence one prisoner could have over a group of people. Sometimes when King spoke it sent shivers down Ivan's spine. He had a charisma that made the most hardened criminal listen. His appeal came from the fact, he never sounded like he was preaching more reasoning with you. The irony was, in another lifetime he could have been a great leader. Now he was just another black man in jail that made up the statistics on some official report.

Standing in their assembly, the Noir syndicate were joined by some of the other members of the house block as Dorian and Bait-man faced off, ready to battle. The crowd was excited and one dark skinned Yardie shouted, "Murder dat bloodclaat, DDG!"

King stood between them like a boxing referee keeping the opponents apart.

"Okay, each man get to spit twice," He said "Two spits and that's it. At the end I call the winner. Judges decision is final, who wants to go first?"

"Let him go first," Dorian said. "I'm the champion."

Bait-man began rocking to an unheard beat, looking for his flow. A frown appeared once he had finished searching his mental archive, and he unleashed a verbal flurry.

Bait-Man spit 1
Gimme a fist full of pounds and watch me beat this boy to the ground/ Hear when the Bait-man breaks bones crushing a pussy to the ground/ I bust shots so you know I get around/ that's the Bait man when you hear the gunshot sound/ Boom there's nothing left when I enter the room/ like Indiana Jones in the temple of doom / like Tony standing in frank's room/ Why don't you take a one way trip to the resurrection/ because when I'm finish with you there'll be no body for inspection/no body for collection/ because I'm as murderous as needles for a lethal injection/ so DDG mind your mouth before I fill it with a weapon/blow you're your head off for nothing but simply correction/ I'm like the drug squad so you better start confessing/ cos' know you're like the little piss sample I be testing.

Deadly Dorian Gustav spit 1
Baitman you and your boys could never shake man/ break man/ yo I take man/ I bust shots on a gay man/ heard you and boys got charged with rape gang/ in Wanno where you tried to rape man/ now that a different type of train man/ you talk about guns/ but you can't aim man/ you should never try shame man/ I wrote the game man/ running with a new game plan/ I 'm something like Damon (Dash)/ and that's a vain man/ so somebody give me a chain man/ cos' its all about the

money and fame man/ flying to the Caribbean or Cayman / in a private plane man/ fuck a couple of girls while I'm sipping on champagne man/ I leave a mental stain on your brain man/ because I'm like Malcolm X and that's a great man/ what I do here you could never maintain man/ cos you're like a pink poodle/ you're to tame man/ please don't ever try battle me again man/ lyrically your a lame man/ I'm, like Maximus, so ARE YOU entertained MAN/ now ask the crowd what happened and they'll tell you that DDG just ate man, WHAT!

The crowd started to go wild from Dorian's reply. Things were heating up and there was a lot of pushing as the inmates formed a circle around them. The screws looked on nervously. They weren't quite sure whether a fight was about to break out or not. Stepping away Ivan recognised a familiar face walking over from the other side of the yard as Bait started his second spit

Bait-man spit 2
Yo the man dem know I'm a bad man/ so easy seckle my yoot before you catch a backhand/ you know I kick off heads like Jackie Chan/ that's my provocative/ I'm a angry black man/ and you don't really want to see how angry I can get/ I'll blow your legs off like a Vietnam vet/ have you hopping with no chance to step/ So come on if you really wanna take a bet/ you know you ain't ready yet/ you don't get money/ you get giro checks/ so show some respect like De Niro in casino/ cos we know/ I'll slap the colour out your skin leaving you whiter than an albino/ my hands move more brown than Bobby or Nino/ I know you ain't never seen dough/ so toe 2 toe ...uh uh uh hold on hold on

Just as Bait man had the crowd behind him he fumbled his lines. Dorian started jumping around laughing and hyping the crowd "What, hold on written lyrics let me show you about battling raw freestyles."

Deadly Dorian Gustav spit 2
Listen son even with your written shit you're still weak/ I have pussies like you scared to speak/ I rhyme heavy like my name was Jayz/ and in comparison your just Bleek/ we can battle all day or we can battle all week/but with that last verse I guess you just hit your peak/ run out of steam so now you just dream/ your better off getting your pipe you little cracked out fiend/ I got a magnum and a m16/ that will rinse off in your spleen/ cos every time I rhyme I do nothing but gleam/ in my DNA there's a musical gene/ mutated with knowledge I show how to make cream/ I'm revolutionary like my man Huey P/ check it the power of a panther resides inside me/ a warrior till the day they murder me/ with my rhyme style I give you the third degree/ leaving you in hell or in purgatory/ willing to stand in front of your maker and commit perjury /I got more stripes than Burberry/ instead of

trying to battle me/ you should sit down and learn from me /Bait-man don't ever try to punk me/ I told you before you fucking monkey/I 've seen your style and I definitely know ya/ if your Tony Montana then I'm a Alex Sosa.

That was the end as every one started jumping up, roaring loud as the screws came and dispersed the crowd. Dorian came over laughing with King holding his Snicker bars. Offering one to Ivan he said, "Who's your friend?"

Ivan introduced the dark skinned, yellow-eyed man, "Yeah this is my bredrin Rolly. He moves with my babymother's brother. Rolly dis is Dorian and King."

Dorian and King with no nasal problems greeted Roland, and decided they would leave Ivan and his friend to talk while they joined the others. Breaking the Snickers in half, Ivan handed one half to Roland who began to explain that he had been sentenced to 7 years for an 'aggy'. He told Ivan that the police had caught him from bite marks and saliva from a sandwich he'd been eating. Ivan tried not to laugh, but wondered why the hell Roland was eating a sandwich while committing a burglary.

"They produced my D.N.A. from blood samples found inside the house." Roland continued. "The woman had this cat innit. It scratched me up in my face. Some traces of my blood were on the carpet. So after that I was bang to rights and pleaded guilty.

"You pleaded guilty and they still gave you a seven" Ivan said surprised "That's harsh. What court was you in?"

"Blackfriars, I got Colville."

"Uhh, he's fuckery. I heard he gave Tiny and Dogzbody 16 last year."

"I know," Roland wiped the sweat under his armpit with his jumper. "I'm fumin', I'm gonna hav'ta try appeal."

"So what happened to Mark?" Ivan asked

"Nuthin," Roland said "Mark's cool. They don't even know he was in there. They only had the DNA on me. I think that's why they give me so much, cos they knew there was two off us involved. I swear down I'm fuming. If I ever hold one of those judges," Roland made a strangling motion with his hands. "I'll squeeze their neck. Anyway," He changed the subject. "How's tings with you and Jade, you must be vex?"

"Vex about what?" Ivan said bewildered

"About Jade and her new man?"

New man? Ivan's first reaction was to explode, but instead he listened as Roland filled him in.

"Yeah, me and Mark caught her outside the flat one night, lipz-in' up with some brudder in a A3. Mark had to drag her out the car and brush her."

"Is it?" Ivan faked a grin "Seen. What happened next?"

"You know," Roland shrugged his shoulders. " Me and Mark musta chase off the boy and that, then Jade started cussin'. You know how she goes on. Making up bare noise about she's in love and ting. Dats gal dem innit?" Roland curled his lip. "It didn't look like anything serious though. Then again she did say she's in love, so who knows. Why? That don't bother you, does it, Terror?"

"Nahhh," Ivan played like he wasn't concerned. "Don't be silly that's a minor. Jade can do what she wants, that don't bother me."

Ivan smiled because his words and thoughts did not share the same bed. Ivan felt like smashing Roland's face in the ground as he gave an account of Jade's antics, but why kill the messenger. It wasn't Roland who had offended or betrayed him; it was Jade. She was running around with some guy, had some guy near his son, and had the audacity to believe he wouldn't find out. Slowly Ivan's face twisted into a mask of anger and jealously as he thought of Jade sharing herself with another man. Kissing, touching, stroking another man all the time believing he wouldn't find out. Over the last few months Ivan had detected a change in Jade's attitude. She had become slightly cold and unsympathetic to his incarceration. Ivan knew the signs when a new influence beset upon Jade. He had convinced himself that she was reading some new book or another, only this time he was wrong. If Jade had found herself a new man and was in love he'd soon find out. *We'll see how much she's in love he thought.*

*

Jade couldn't understand Ivan's attitude. He phoned the house moaning and complaining that he couldn't see Jayvan and how Jade's family tried to make the boy forget who his dad was. Yet when he told Jade to book the visiting order, he said not to bring Jayvan. Jade worried about Ivan sometimes. This had been the longest time he'd ever been sentenced. She wondered whether the time away was finally playing on his mind. Even though they had their arguments, Jade knew Ivan was the only man she really wanted. She didn't want to be one of those girls with baby-fathers here and there. She didn't like the idea of children from different fathers. Anita had a different father from Mark and Jade. Jade remembered one Christmas when they were opening there presents, when Mark began teasing Anita about her father. The tag on Anita's present read from Daddy to Anita.

"That present's not from your dad," Mark said. "That's from our dad. He felt sorry for you so he wrote daddy on it. You ain't got no dad, Anita."

Jade remembered Mark jumping up ready to run. Normally Anita would have chased and beat him, but this time she ran to the bathroom and locked herself in. It took their mother two hours to coax a tearful Anita out. It also took five minutes of belt lashing for Mark to realise he'd ruined Christmas. Jade knew she never wanted any reason for her children to be divided, especially on who their father was. No, Ivan would be her only babyfather she thought even if it meant no more kids.

At the prison entrance, Jade waited in line with all the other wives, girlfriends, mothers, sisters, bredrins, and spars that made the fortnightly pilgrimage to the appropriate jails. She watched as children pulled and yanked impatiently at arms, and prison officers checked V.O.s and ID. She was so glad she hadn't needed to bring Jayvan. Standing with her arms up while the female guard patted her down and asked her to take off her shoes, Jade wondered what was on Ivan's mind. He seemed so agitated on the phone.

Jade stepped back as the sniffer dog passed by the visitors, then stopped in front of a shaven headed, white man with tattoos.

"What's it stopping in front of me for? I ain't got nuffin," the man grumbled as the prison officer asked him to step out the line.

Jade knew that procedure meant a strip search, or leave the premises. Buying a few sandwiches, crisps, and drinks from the canteen, Jade sat down on the middle chair for visitors opposite the single chair for prisoners and waited. Ivan was one of the last inmates to come out. Wearing a fluorescent yellow bib over his neatly pressed prison uniform he sat down on the chair opposite Jade.

"Where's Jayvan?" he said picking up a sandwich.

Jade looked at him, "You told me not to bring him."

"Yeah, yeah I forgot." Ivan said brooding.

"Are you alright, Ivan?" Jade asked at the sight of his miserable face.

Ivan ignored her noticing Dorian. He sat slumped in the chair with his arms crossed knowing his visitors hadn't turned up again. It was his fifth consecutive ghost-visit. Dorian always said he didn't care, but Ivan always felt sorry for him. He sat alone while everyone hugged and chatted with family. Eventually the screws would tap him on the shoulder and remove him. Each time Dorian walked the mile of shame back to the wing as eyes looked on knowing his people ghosted him.

Oh well, Ivan thought, *soon I won't even be getting any visits either.* He looked Jade in the eye trying to hide his anger. Seeing her face didn't make it any easier. She smiled innocently and fixed her coolie black hair. Ivan wished he had dealt with the matter over the phone like he originally intended.

"So what's been happening then, Jade?" he said gulping some cola.

"Nothing much, I'm fine." Jade smiled. "I handed in another module the other day and got a distinction. My tutor really thinks I'm one of the strongest in my finishing year. I think I might get a 2:1"

"Okay that sounds good, yeah pretty good, but what else has been going on, Jade?"

"Well, I've been looking at new nurseries and pre-schools for Jayvan, and I."

"Yeah, yeah, yeah," Ivan said cutting her off. "But what else has been going on, Jade?"

Jade was confused. "What'd you mean?"

"Well," Ivan sat back in his chair. "Obviously I know you're not stupid, Jade, because you're going Uni, you just got a distinction on your last paper, your tutor says your one of the strongest in your year, now the question is do you think I'm stupid?" Ivan leaned forward putting down his cola. "I'm going to ask you again, Jade, and if you don't answer me correctly I'm gonna get vex. What else has been going on?"

"Listen, Ivan," Jade said baffled. "I don't know what you're trying to imply, but if you got something to say, I think it better you say it now before I get up and leave. I didn't come here for no argument."

"Who's arguing?" Ivan snapped. "No one's arguing yet. As far as I'm concerned, I'm asking you what have you been up to."

"So why you acting so aggressive. You're acting like I done you something, I haven't done you nothing, Ivan."

"That's right!" Ivan raised his voice. "You haven't done me nothing have you, Jade?" He dashed his half eaten sandwich on the table. "Okay seeing as you can't be honest with me. Let me tell you about what you haven't done, yeah.

You ain't showed me no respect when I phone, you talk to me like if I'm an idiot, when I send my friend around with things you act like they're not needed."

"They're not needed," Jade interrupted. "I can look after my son, Ivan."

"Hol' on a minute!" Ivan held up his hand. "Don't loud talk me, Jade. I gave you a chance to speak and you didn't want it, so now I'm speaking."

"Well speak then!" Jade refrained from cursing.

"Don't speak to me like that or I swear I'll embarrass you up in here," Ivan warned.

"Fine." Jade said trying to avoid a scene. "Just say what you have to say."

"Good," Ivan continued. "First off let me explain, Jayvan is our son, not your son, our son. Jay for Jade, and van for Ivan, that makes Jayvan, that makes him our son. If I send things for our son, through my friends, you don't make them feel like some bastard when they come to the door. Do you unnerstann' me, Jade?"

Jade wasn't an idiot. She looked at Ivan knowing he had been planning to have an argument. Telling her not to bring Jayvan, the little arguments on the phone, it was all clear. He'd been sitting in his cell rehearsing exactly what he was going to say for days. The only thing Jade didn't understand was why. What had she done or not done to provoke him now. Whatever it was Jade decided two can play at that game. Ivan wasn't the only person who had been planning things they wanted to say. She waited and listened to him moan. She could feel her emotions getting the better of her.

"Are you listening to me, Jade? Because I swear you're taking the utmost liberties."

"How, Ivan" Jade said getting upset. "What have I done?"

"Look at you," Ivan said grinding his teeth. He could see she was holding back the tears but he wanted her to cry. He wanted her to feel like an idiot in front of everyone in the room as he felt like an idiot to the outside world. "You think you're so smart, but you can't even listen properly when I'm speaking."

"Well speak then and stop playing games."

"Who's playing games, Jade, me or you?" Ivan frowned, "Let me ask you a question. What do I do every Friday night?"

"Phone the house." Jade answered.

"Why, Jade?"

"To speak to Jayvan."

"Yes, Jade, that's right. I phone the house every Friday. Every Friday I phone the house to speak to our son, okay so you remember that. Good. Now I want you to remember that Friday I phoned a couple moons back and you weren't in. You know that Friday when I couldn't speak to our son Jayvan? Where were you, Jade?"

Jade gave Ivan a puzzled look. "I told you, Ivan. I went out with my friends. That's one silly little Friday ages ago and now you want to make a big thing out of it. Why is it so important now?"

"Because you're a lying bitch!!" Ivan said raising his voice.

"Excuse me!" Jade said as one screw tapped Ivan's shoulder. He told Ivan to lower his voice.

"You heard me, Jade." Ivan pointed his finger "You're a nasty little ho'. You never went out with Tania that night did you?"

"Fuck you," Jade slapped Ivan's finger out of her face. "Who do you think you're talking to? I'm not one of those stupid jezzies you write letters to. I told you I went out with Tania and her boyfriend. If you want to think anything else that's your fucking business, I don't care. So don't dare think you can talk to me like that."

"Oh I know you don't care" Ivan said curling his lip. "That's why you're there fucking next man in dere car like a liccle ho'."

"What!" Jade mouth gaped open.

"What, you think I don't know?" Ivan said smugly "I heard about you. Up in some A3 getting dig out like any old ho'. Is that how you're going on, Jade? Anyone can fuck you if they got a nice ride. You're a ho', rudegirl, a ho!'"

Ivan watched as the tears began to run down her face. That's what he wanted to see. From the other side of the room he could see King and his wife watching with concern. Bain sat with some bald headed friend laughing. *Cry* Ivan thought. *Cry in front of my friends and enemies. Make yourself look stupid, like you made me look.*

"What, you're gonna cry now? Cmon, Jade," Ivan sniggered. "I thought you was better than that. It's too late to cry me a river now. When you was out there with other man, depriving me of speaking to my son, did you cry me a river then, did you?"

Jade kept shaking her head. Taking a tissue out her purse she wiped her eyes trying to stop her make-up from running. "You're a fool, Ivan, you're an idiot."

"Yeah, I know," Ivan said smiling to himself. "Because I trusted you. I thought if you wanted to get fucked you'd at least have the decency to do it inside a yard. Not let man come off road and tell me that they caught you fucking in a car."

Immediately Jade stopped crying and looked up. "Who told you that?"

"It doesn't matter. It's the truth innit? I beg you tell me different."

"Pardon!" Jade said in disgust. Her whole demeanour changed. "You call me a ho,' accuse me of slackness, and then you wanna ask me about the truth?"

"Yeah." Ivan said casual like.

"Fuck you, Ivan! I want to know who told you that now!" Jade had, had, enough. She wasn't about to be embarrassed in front of the whole jail just because Ivan and his friends wanted to talk about her. "You tell me who told you that now, Ivan or I swear to god I'll get up and walk out that door and never come back. You decided!"

Ivan scoffed at her bluff. "You ain't going nowhere until I say so, you unnerstan'"

"Oh you think so," Jade said standing up. "Try me."

Ivan grabbed her arm. "Don't touch me!" Jade yelled pulling her arm away.

Embarrassed, Ivan quickly sat back in his chair trying to blend. "Alright, alright," he said. "Sit down, before you get dashed out."

"No." Jade said. At that precise moment she hated Ivan, and she didn't see why she should stay. "Tell me who said that or I'm leaving."

"Okay," Ivan conceded. "I'll tell you, but afterwards you bettah promise to tell the truth, Jade. Promise."

Jade sat down. "Fine. You want the truth, Ivan, have it your way. I'll promise to tell you the truth, after you tell me."

Ivan hesitated for a moment, then Jade moved to get up.

"It was Rolly." Ivan confessed "He said, him and Mark caught you lipsin' some guy in an A3. He said Mark chased the guy off and you started cussing your brother. Telling everyone how you were so in love. What are you in love, Jade?"

At first Jade said nothing. She thought about something her mother use to say. A truth told with bad intent will always beat all the lies you can invent. Then she looked at Ivan with hurt and disbelief.

"Rolly told you that and you believed him, Ivan?"

Again Ivan hesitated. "Yeah," he said hanging his head. A part of him was scared to admit that he was frightened of losing Jade. "Everything made sense. Your change in attitude, you not being home, it all made sense. Everything. What's not to believe?"

Jade remained quiet for a second, she was still in shock. "Wait let me get this right. Roland Bonsu told you that and you believed him?"

"Yeah."

"Wait, Roland Bonsu told you that, and rather than confront him you sat around listening to that filthy rat talk shit about me?" Jade had heard enough. "Are you dumb?!"

"Yo!" Ivan pepped up "Mind your mouth, before I..."

"Before you do what?" Jade snapped. "Slap me. Go on then. That's what you want to do, slap me in front of all these people isn't it. Because I'm a whore, that's what you think of me isn't, Ivan? Roland told you I was a whore and you believed him. Well, didn't you?"

Ivan was beginning to lose control of the situation and didn't like it. "Listen just calm down Jade."

"No!" Jade refused. "According to you and your little rapist friend, I'm a whore."

"What you mean rapist friend?" Ivan said confused.

"What, your little friend Roland didn't tell you he was in for rape?"

"Nah, nah, nah," Ivan tried to defend Roland. "Rolly ain't in for no..."

"Don't bother tell me he's not in for rape," Jade shut Ivan up. "Because my brother dun told me he is. He told me he came in and heard your dirty friend upstairs raping that woman."

Ivan sat in denial. He didn't say anything; he just crossed his arms and looked around the room.

"Ohhhh." Jade clapped her hands mocking Ivan. "He didn't tell you that did he? But he can tell you that I'm fuckin next man. Well let me tell you something about this so-called ho', Ivan. You want the truth I'll give you the truth. The truth is, I was tired, Ivan. Tired of always being on my own, tired of not having someone to hold me, tired of lying to Jayvan telling him his daddy's working at the big building with the gates. I was tired of you acting like a little Lynch slave, tired of having to be the only person responsible for our son, not my son, Ivan, our son. To be honest, Ivan, I was tired of Uni, tired of work, tired of isolation, tired of my sister telling me to leave you, and tired of people pointing there fingers and whispering that's Terror's babymother. Are you listenin' to me, Ivan? I'm tired of smiling and looking like I'm coping. I'm not."

Jade's hand was on her chest. She gripped her top as if she were ready to tear her heart out.

"For one night, Ivan, just one night. I wanted to forget all that and have some fun. I wanted someone to look upon me as an attractive young woman for once. So I went out with Tania and her boyfriend, and his friend and had fun. And yes, when the night was over, yes I kissed him goodnight, Ivan. And now suddenly that makes me a ho' because Mark and his rapist friend caught me kissing a guy goodnight. Look at me, Ivan! We're not even together."

Ivan sat playing with the thread on his bib, avoiding all eye contact.

"So you didn't fuck him then?" he said.

"Ivan," Jade cried. "Is that all you care about? You don't care about anything else except how you look do you? You don't even care about how I feel do you?"

Ivan remained quiet.

"What about Jayvan?" Jade asked. "Do you even care about how you being in jail affects him?"

"Course I do," Ivan barked "But he's young, he don't know no different."

"That's right," Jade said "He doesn't know different, but neither do you. Look at you. You're constantly in out of jail. Do you think I want Jayvan around that? Him growing up thinking its okay to go in and out of jail because that's what his dad did? Wake up, Ivan. You're not no big man, you're a boy, a silly little boy, running around aimlessly. Tell me, Ivan, when's it going to stop? When am I going to get the man I need?"

Jade's words cut deep like a jagged knife, but all Ivan allowed himself to focus on was that she had been in that car with another guy. Eventually his pride got the better of him.

"So what, you're not happy with me den? If you wanna a new dude, go on den. See if I care. But trust me, if you do I'll make sure you regret it, Jade. Believe me on dat one."

"See what I mean, Ivan!" Jade yelled. "You're not listening! I don't want any one else. I wanted you. But you're so foolish that you can't be the man I want."

There were tears in Jade eyes. "I never asked you to rob or steal anything for me, or come home with bundles of cash. I never asked for any of that. All I wanted was you. Now I'm not even sure if I want that."

"So what you tryna to say?"

"It's over, Ivan!"

The statement rolled of Jade's tongue before she had even realised. The conviction in her voice shocked her. It was final. Ivan and Jade were no more.

"I've had enough," Jade continued. "It's time to grow up and realise what you are."

"What am I, Jade?" Ivan snarled. "You tell me what I am, seeing as I am too stupid to realise. What am I? An animal, a fool, a bastard, not good enough for you, what! Go on, Jade, you tell me, before you go running off."

Jade sat for a moment pitying Ivan. He couldn't function without conflict and Jade yearned peace. Emotionally drained she felt like Ali in *The Rumble in the Jungle*. Ivan had mentally pounded at her for years. Bullying his way through their relationship. He imitated Foreman constantly shoving and pushing Ali against the ropes, but now Jade Ali was ready to fight back.

"You're a slave, Ivan," Jade said. As she spoke she envisioned her words like a mighty blow that would send Ivan to the floor. "A slave, Ivan, because you don't know how to fight the real issues oppressing you. You don't know how to break the chains that hold you captive."

Jade's heart was racing. Standing up, she could feel her legs trembling, but the clarity and conviction in her voice remained strong.

"Greed, jealousy, and pride, you brought them into this relationship, Ivan, not me. You and your friends, you're all slaves. You were born slaves, live like slaves and if you don't change your ways, you're going to die like slaves."

Jade was on a roll and the whole visiting room turned to watch her.

"You can't contain me no more, Ivan. I need a man not a slave. I love you, but I 'm not doing this anymore."

"Well don't then!" Ivan yelled as the screws came running over. Mr Hewitt stepped between the couple to defuse the situation.

"Ms." He addressed Jade. "I'm sorry, but I have to ask you to calm down now or leave."

"There's no need to be sorry." Jade said gathering her things. "I'm leaving now anyway."

"Good, fuck off!" Ivan said spraying spit. He was now surrounded by three prison officers who tried to keep him seated. "Just make sure you send, MY SON up here with my mother, and don't friggin' come up here again! You fucking ho! Fuck off!"

"Fine," Jade said. "If that's what you want, Ivan. I'll sort it out with your mother."

"Yeah that's what I want." Ivan shouted as people watched in horror. "I don't wanna see your face again you ho'."

There was silence as Jade prepared to leave. She didn't want to end things like this, but knew Ivan wouldn't have it any other way.

"Goodbye, Ivan."

"No, Jade this is bad-bye, don't think I'm gonna be locked up in here forever. I'll see you and your lil boyfriend on road. Trust me I'll see you."

"I know you will, Ivan. I know you will."

"Good! Good!" Ivan pushed the screws before taking his seat. He sat grinning as though he had gained some victory over Jade. "Wait, before you go, Jade I want you to tell me something," Ivan's grin seemed to increase. "If you're not a slave and you're not a ho', then what are you?"

Jade had never been so sure of an answer in her life as she was with this one.

"I'm a queen, Ivan. A beautiful black queen."

"Ah queen," Ivan scoffed "Ah queen, yeah?!"

"Yes, Ivan." Jade said. "A queen. The next time one comes into your life, maybe you'll know how to treat her."

*

After Jade left, Ivan was removed from the visiting hall. Agitated the officers suggested he had to wait before he could return to his block. Ivan didn't argue. He pounded his fist in his hand and paced up and down until he eventually simmered down.

When he got back, association had just ended and everyone was getting ready for bang-up. Wank-magz, CDs and cassettes were quickly being traded for the last time before everyone was locked behind doors. Marching to his cell, Ivan grabbed his flask and joined the queue for hot water, when Dorian came running up. He pushed in front of Ivan filling up his flask.

"Yo, Terror," He said excitedly. "You know I'm so glad I got ghosted today, innit"

"Why?" Ivan grunted

"Brutha man, lissen to me." Dorian raved. "See when I come back to da wing, Mr Harris must of let me go gym. See when I got down there, I must of seen your bredrin. What's his name? You know the frowzy one."

"Rolly Bonsu?"

"Yeah Bonsu that's it. Well lissen to this anyway, I must have been doing my reps with Ewing," Dorian stopped to act out the weightlifting action. "When two-two's I turned round an' see your bredrin get knocked!"

"What? Don't lie by who?"

"Rhodes. You know that white dude from house block 3. Looks like a tonk version of Rodney from Only Fools and Horses. My man musta come and knocked your bredrin out cold. Sparked him one punch."

"Nah you're lying. What for?"

"That's da next piece I hav'ta show you." Dorian frowned. "Rhodes musta said when he was on House block 3, him and Bonsu were banged up together. He said he read my man's papers innit. He said Bonsu ain't just in for aggy."

"He's in for rape." Ivan interrupted.

"Yeah." Dorian said getting peeved. "How comes you never told me that before?"

"I never knew," Ivan said as a dread came over him. "My girl just told me on the visit."

"Gwan, blood," Dorian held up his fist to touch Ivan. "What you and Jade back together again. What, I must get a bring in on one of her bredrins now?"

But Ivan wasn't listening, "Where's Rolly now?"

"Stinky went straight to nounce-ville, blood! They took his stuff to protection unit about ten minutes ago. Why?"

Ivan walked away leaving Dorian standing at the water urn. The reality of his actions was beginning to dawn on him. How could he of been so foolish to trust Rolly's word over Jade's. When he got to his cell, he was overcome with anger. He needed to hit something, how stupid had he been to ever doubt Jade. He started to see red. Suddenly the whole block heard a horrifying roar of anger as Ivan began to tear the cell apart. Dorian came running to the cell.

"Terror!" He shouted "What the fuck you doing? That's my stuff too."

Ivan didn't care as he threw Dorian's stereo crashing against the wall. He tore the pictures and calendar up and started breaking the furniture.

"Ivan, Ivan!" Dorian shouted grabbing hold of his friend. "Calm down."

Snapping out of his rage, Ivan stopped. Breathing heavily he looked at Dorian before lowering his fist. By now a crowd had gathered outside on the landing. King pushed his way through. "Ivan what's wrong?"

Ivan said nothing and pushed past the crowd. At the end of the landing Bain stood laughing with a couple of his cronies.

"What's wrong, Little, mate?" He jested. "Did'ya girlfriend find a new rood-bwoy to keep her company at night?"

That's all Ivan needed to hear. His blow came fast and solid, connecting smack on Bain's jaw. It dazed Bain and he staggered forward trying to put Ivan in a headlock. The rest of his gang were quick to join in as the screws' whistles were blown. Defending Ivan, King and Dorian readily joined the fight with Ewing and Gooden following.

It was no holds bar, with fist and kicks flying everywhere. There were cries of "Bang up!" and the thunder of boots running onto the block as the men fought.

Bain yelled at the top his voice, "I 'm gonna fucking kill you, Little!" as the group of men were dragged away to the segregation block, but Ivan wasn't listening as the officers tried to restrain him. An hour later in a cold dark cell Ivan's belongings were finally brought to him. "That better be all my stuff," he snapped at the officer.

The man ignored him and slammed the door shut. Feeling angry and alone Ivan sat on the floor fuming. He played with the bite marks in his arm and rubbed his aching face. He looked at his swollen knuckle thinking, *'watch, when my hand gets better I'm gonna whack up Bain again.'* He thought about whacking up Rolly, the screws, everyone that did him wrong, the whole world if necessary. But deep down he knew that wasn't what was eating away at him. His mind was restless. Getting up, he forged through his belongs and found the book Jade had sent him. He was disgusted by the title *'Journey of a Slave'*, but would read anything if it stopped him from thinking about Jade.

***

CHAPTER: 15

It was Ivan's fourth day in the segregation unit. He gathered most of the others had been sent back to the wing, especially Dorian, because his constant shouting and yelling, out the window had stopped after day two.

He figured he'd probably be up in front of the governor later or tomorrow for adjudication, where he'd get a couple days and loss of earnings for fighting. He didn't care. A stint in solitude always comforted Ivan. What the screws didn't realize was he never had any qualms about being isolated for short periods. It gave him a getaway from the ongoing pressure of prison bravados. Yet what Ivan was beginning to realize, was he was falling into a regular pattern.

The same way the block removed the everyday pressure of jail; Ivan was slowly using the isolation of jail to remove the pressures of life. Each time he came back the sentences became a little longer, the charges a little stronger, the prisons a little further.

Ivan would have never have seen the signs had he not started to read 'Journey Of A Slave'. At first he had his reservations about the book. Originally because it had come from Jade and the way he felt about her continually angered him. Then later he found the book patronizing and preachy. He thought that the author was confused about the reader he was writing for. He continually felt the need to explain himself to an audience who didn't know 'road', but to the real man dem like Ivan, it sounded as though he was trying to preach. That was a big mistake in Ivan's books. *'You can't preach to the real man dem'* he would kiss his teeth from chapter to chapter.

Ivan believed in simplicity. A thief couldn't tell a murderer that he was wrong for killing without being a hypocrite, but he could reason why murder was worse then stealing. That was the problem with society as a whole, Ivan concluded. There were too many preachy hypocrites. Better they sort out themselves before they came to talk to him.

Ivan had thought the same of the author until he read a passage Jade had highlighted in fluorescent ink. The chapter was absent of preaching and made Ivan question some of his own philosophies. With bitterness, Ivan had began to accept the truth. He was slowly becoming institutionalized to both the streets and prison. Surprisingly the thought hadn't yet disturbed him. Ivan had found more annoyance in the tone of the author, who undoubtedly inspired Jade's outburst a few days ago. But as Ivan creased the spine of the book turning the page something resonated with him. He scratched the side of his nose, continuing to deny the insight he was receiving, clarifying in his own mind.

'*The only reason I'm sill reading this book is because I wanna know what happens to my man, otherwise I woulda dash this ting long time.*'

THE QUEEN RETURNS WITH THE TALENTED TENTH

The Journey of a Slave.

What do you call a cook that doesn't cook, a baker that doesn't bake and a hustler that doesn't hustle? Nothing. You don't call them anything because you don't recognise them for what they are. This was how I felt in the aftermath of the Stevie episode. I felt like nothing.

The most destructive thing I can think of for a person, must be lack of self-esteem. It had been almost three weeks since the incident at Stevie's flat and I found myself moping aimlessly around the house. The days passed slowly. Now officially, legally, and illegally unemployed, I became tortured with boredom. I'd lie on my bed for hours looking at the ceiling thinking about shottin'. I was used to the fast grinding rituals and routine it brought, the mobile phone always ringing, the constant moving from place to place, the exchange of money and the weight of money in my pocket, the awareness of every person on the street, who was watching, and the positions of CCTV. I even missed the danger of a possible police chase and the time consumed cutting, weighing, wrapping, and reloading of work, the chit-chat and banter of the punters, the disciplining of cats; the bargaining, and fencing of goods. The constant rush and barrage of calls, it all made me feel as though I was always needed; as though I played a major part in the order of society. It was like a roller coaster ride of adrenaline everyday, and each day I returned once more. It was my own addiction, like the punters I was accustomed to serving. It was strong and I knew the hazards, I couldn't deny I was addicted to the chaos.

Now that chaotic lifestyle had gone over night and I was left with the repulsive craving of my addiction. In my head someone had said 'you can't ride the roller coaster anymore.' Someone said 'your addiction has to stop'. It was the same voice that sort to show me my journey. It was the same voice, the same voice that said slave or king, gutter or kingdom. The same voice. It was warm and nurturing, a voice of guidance that asked me to slow down and see reality. Yet I was used to moving at the blurring speed of a hustler. Now everything moved too slow, allowing fear and regret, to besiege my mind. Now a second voice spoke loud and clear, challenging the first. Creating a new confusion it was ruthless, angry, and bitter. Spurred on by my ambition, it screamed from the darkness.

"You fool, what are you doing?" It would say. "You know we need to hustle, you know we need dough. You know that's what we do best!"

"But I want more."

"What is more? This is all you need, don't be stupid. The streets are our home, the man dem, our family, the drugs, our food. "

"But people live without, why must I always be the worst?"

"Because that's what you are, the best of the worst. Learn to embrace who you are."

"Who am I?"

"You are us, we are you, we are the streets. Return to us, return to what you know best."

"I'm scared"

"Scared because they tell you, you belong elsewhere. You belong with us, making money."

I closed my eyes as the conflicting voices created pandemonium inside my mind. I pictured a great war being waged upon my soul by two armies. On one side stood the warriors of Consciousness brave and strong. They had been the underdogs for many years, living in an occupied land. Their oppressor was the ruling empire of Practicality and Desire. Practicality and desire had ruled with an iron fist for a long time, now the tide was changing. They had conquered the mind, by producing illusions of strong desires and showing the most practical ways of achieving such goals. They had seized all riches of knowledge and corrupted the thoughts. They had slaughtered and raped the morals, and enslaved clear judgement with the hankering of wealth and an appetite for desire. While their tyranny had plagued my mind, consciousness had begun an underground resistance. Now the armies of consciousness were rebelling against their oppressors. In return the empire was destroying consciousness' propaganda by destroying my self-esteem and identity. All my achievements and identity were measured and defined by the streets. If I removed everything I accomplished in the streets, then what had I accomplished? It was a mental battle that would be one day named *"The Great War of Principals"*.

If I returned to selling drugs the status quo would be restored forever. If I chose otherwise then consciousness would win their first major victory. The battle continued as I fought the torment of depression, which perpetually played on my wits. In truth if I was an addict to the street hustle, then this was my version of cold turkey complete with withdrawal symptoms.

I knew that the streets kept me contained within the City of Modern containment. I knew that through my actions and thought process I exemplified the Lynch slave. I knew that the ruling group had need to maintain power by nominating successors. I knew of the downfalls, traps, and hereditary programming that had been indoctrinated into my people to keep us down. I had looked towards the ancient kings and civilisations. I had even produced my own equation to empowerment. But if I had acquired all this knowledge why did I still feel I needed the streets? Why had I not been empowered? Why was I still questioning my abilities? Why had I found myself lost on my journey?

The signs were clear, as were the directions - Containment or Freedom. But what did freedom mean and what lay beyond the city? My mind was pecking around for guidance like a lost chicken in the yard. Once again I had reached another crossroad. Ahead of me stood the unknown and every other direction lead straight back to the city. I felt like the moth and the flame with the city being the fire. Only the difference was, I was a moth born in the fire. The question I asked myself was how does such a moth escape doom? Everyday I tried to solve that riddle.

Eventually the constant flicking of cable channels and daytime TV had worn thin. I looked around the walls of the council flat I called home. There was a damp patch in one of the top corners. The wallpaper had started to peel. Mum had talked about decorating soon. I knew if I didn't become active before long, she would rope me into decorate for her. I didn't mind the decorating, it was the idea of having to shift furniture and pack things up beforehand that deterred me. Then everything would be piled between my room and the passageway. All that was too much hassle. The flat already felt claustrophobic.

It was weird. In past times the flat had been my sanctuary from the madness outside, now it felt like a prison. Each moment the walls seemed to close in and the room became tighter. I had started going on endless walks to clear my head and today was no different.

I grabbed my jeans jacket and stepped out the door. Everyday it was the same thing as I walked the streets with my hands stuffed in my pocket. I felt like I was suppose to be somewhere in life but hadn't reached there yet. Everyday I mentally marked off the calendar, and everyday I noted I hadn't reached my destiny. I was beginning to hate my journey, beginning to wish I would simply forget all I had sort after. *Why couldn't I just be content* I thought to myself?

On this particular day I'd walked up towards Baron's Court and near Hammersmith and West London College. I turned down the Talgarth Road and finally ended up near Hammersmith Broadway. I crossed the road outside the office blocks and looked around. He wasn't there.

"I'm always here," he'd said. But Lennox X, with his suit and red bow tie of the Nation of Islam was nowhere to be seen. I cursed myself as I sat down on the wall. Why had I thrown away the paper he had given me?

The thought of one day using his number was foreign to me. Finding guidance through religion was for others. I couldn't see myself, following the preaching and interpretation of God by another man. Yet now more than ever I wished I'd stored Lennox's number somewhere amongst the others I called, friends.

Sitting on the wall outside the office block I let out a deep sigh. The dark grey sky broke and pellets of rain fell upon my brow. Motionless I sat watching the flurry of people rush out of work and head off to their home life. The rain began to soak my denim jacket changing the stone wash blue from light to dark. It's always me I thought. It's always me that has to struggle. It's always me that goes through life alone. Where's my guiding hand, where's my guardian angel, who's gonna help me when I'm flat on my face? Where's my companions on this journey? Where?

My questions were filled with angst. Then a familiar voice spoke, shattering my thoughts like a china plate. The feeling of wet raindrops seemed to stop as I looked up and saw the smiling face. "What's up, stranger? You look like you're lost."

"Nah I'm fine," I said. "I was just looking for someone. What you saying?"

"I 'm fine. I haven't seen you around in a while what's going on?"

"Nothing," I shrugged my shoulders. "I was just looking for the Muslim brudder that does be out here selling the papers."

"Oh I haven't seen him around here in a while, G babe."

Everything seem to slow down as Alicia stood in front of me wrapped up in a short black trench coat. Holding an umbrella to shelter us, she wiped a strand of hair from her face as the harsh winds blew. It was a complete transformation from the summer long gone when she first resurfaced. Her smile was radiant and her skin glowed. She stood out like a lighthouse beacon in the rain. We looked at each other in silence. I couldn't believe how different she looked. I said nothing, but my heart rejoiced for a moment.

The queen had found her throne again. Alicia managed to take me back to that feeling of boyhood innocence once more. As her lips formed words, my eyes unknown to her celebrated and cheered, *'Long live the queen, my gracious queen.'*

> Ivan stopped reading and began laughing out loud. He lay the book down and he shook his head in disbelief. "Nah, nah, nah, she couldn't have." He mused to himself.
>
> He looked through his canteen for a chocolate. Tearing open the wrapper he began chomping on a *Mars* bar. Again he shook his head in disbelief.
>
> "That's ridiculous." He read the words again – *my gracious queen*.
>
> It was there in black text, but he still couldn't fathom how absurd women could be. For all Jade's big talk about being a queen, she had stolen the idea from how this writer dude saw some old skool crackhead he wanted to fuck. What a load of bullshit, Ivan thought. Is that who Jade wanted to emulate? A crackhead. Arrogantly he chuckled, "I would never see no crackhead as a queen," he laughed and read on.

"You sure you're alright, G babe?" Alicia asked. "Your clothes are soaking wet."

"Nah I'm fine." I said climbing to my feet "I'm gonna dus' now anyway before I catch a cold."

"Might be too late for that." Alicia said. She reached into her handbag and pulled out a handkerchief. Wiping my face she squeezed my nose. "You probably gonna need this. Your nose is running."

Turning my back I quickly wiped my nose and shoved the handkerchief in my pocket. "Thanks." I blushed

"Its okay, G babe." Alicia laughed. She paused for a second then said bye.

I nodded, "Yeah cool, I'll see you later." and walked off in the opposite direction. There was nothing else to say. I felt the damp cotton handkerchief in my pocket and shook my head. Alicia amazed me. She looked like a totally different person. She looked content.

"Gil!" Looking over my shoulder, I saw Alicia still standing in the same spot. She ran towards me trying to fight off the wind and rain. She linked her arm under mine. Handing me her umbrella she said, "Look, I don't care what you say, you look like you need a friend. Come to my house and chill out for a while."

After all the drugs I'd sold her, I was surprised she held no bitterness or malice towards me. I wondered why she was being so cool? I looked at her, "Do I have a choice?"

Squeezing close to keep warm she looked at me and said "NO!" and led the way.

You know when they say don't judge a book by its cover, so you turn it over and read the passage on the back. After that you open it up in the middle and read a couple of paragraphs to get a feel for the book. Or perhaps you see the trailer of a film and feel that film isn't for you. You probably judge people the same way too. You look at a person and maybe you know just a little bit about them. Oh that's so and so, he did that, and she slept with him. You hear a little and think and you know all about that person. That's ignorance getting the better of you.

When I got back to Alicia's flat I realised how little I knew about her. She had been placed in a one bedroom flat in the West Kensington estate in W14. I expected it to be a hollow shell with very little, clothes to be thrown on the floor and dishes to be piled up in the sink. When I entered Alicia rushed me out of the corridor and straight into the living room. The room shocked me with its pine wooden floors, leather sofa suite and wide screen TV.

The walls were painted in a fusion of natural terracotta and roasted red, giving it a warm feeling. Posted around the room were large green plants and African carvings. A framed picture of a young Alicia in a Chippie top and a teenage boy in a corduroy Click suit sat on the mantle piece. He wore a red bandanna and his hair was in twists with patterns on the side. Large scented candles everywhere and a dinning table rested in the back of the room.

"Put on the TV or some music if you want G." Alicia shouted from the other room. "I'll be one minute!"

I walked over to an alcove of shelves where her hi-fi sat. Alicia's CD collection consisted of mostly mid 90's R'n'B and soul. I began scanning through the list, R Kelly, Jodeci, Mary J Blige, Zhane, Intro, SWV, Silk, Shai, Boyz II Men and so on. Finally I found 2Pac *'All Eyes On Me'* album hidden under *'The Best Of Aretha Franklin'*. I put it on.

As the west coast beats of Deathrow floated through the airwaves, I analysed Alicia's bookshelves. There must have been over a hundred books. At first all I could see was the usual suspects Terry McMillian, Toni Morrison, Maya Angelou, and Alice Walker. A couple of *Babyfather* books and *The Yardie Trilogy* by Victor Headley sat between Jilly Cooper novels and Jackie Collins. Then I saw a book called The Nigger Factory. It was the author's name that stood out to me - Gil Scott Heron. I picked it up and started fingering through the pages.

"What's that you got there?" Alicia said holding a Nike tracksuit in her hands. "Here try this on it's too big for me so it should fit you."

"You sure?"

"Yeah, take your clothes off and I'll put them on the radiator to dry."

"You sure this ain't just some trick to get my clothes off"

"Oh shut up you big head," Alicia took the book from my hand. "This is a good book, G have you ever read it?"

"Nah I was just looking at it cause the author got the same name."

"Oh yeah, Gil Scott Heron. You know who he is right?"

"Nah," I said taking off my top. "I thought he was some musician and shit"

"Yeah he is. He's also a poet and an author. The same guy that wrote *The Revolution will not be televised.*"

"What's that?" I asked.

"What do you mean what's that?" Alicia frowned. "You've never heard of *The Revolution will not be televised?*"

"No"

"Come on, Gil," Alicia looked as me as though something was suppose to click in my head. She began to recite the song. "The revolution will not be televised, you will not be able to stay home brother. You will not be able to plug in, turn on and drop out. You will not be able to lose yourself on crack and weed, skip out for beer during commercials, because the revolution will not be televised. The revolution will be no re-run brothers; the revolution will be live."

"Oh that song. Yeah I know that song"

Alicia looked at me smiling with a giggle "What you laughing at?"

"You don't know it, do you?"

"Yeah, course I know it."

"Okay what else does he say?"

"Err the revolution will not be sold at the record store or on CDs by Jayz or Biggie Smalls the revolution will not be televised."

"No he doesn't say that you fool. Admit it you don't know."

"Okay so I don't know it, but you can teach me innit."

"Yeah I suppose I can do that for you." She said looking into my eyes.

Her stare was intense as we stood there for a second. It was almost as though she was waiting for me to say something or she was trying to read my thoughts. I wasn't sure whether she was flirting with me or not and began to blush.

"What should I do with these" I picked up my wet clothes.

"Give them to me." Alicia smiled. Taking them I thought she stroked my hand. It was a brief stroke. "I'll hang them to dry and then come back and teach you something."

Smiling again she left the room.

That night I sat listening to Alicia talk about life. She taught me what she knew and I taught her what I knew. She taught me about her struggles as a black woman and I taught her about mine as man. We spoke of love, friends, and the future. For the first time in weeks all my problems seem to be gone. Alicia had opened up a forum where we could speak openly about our truest thoughts. For a moment we forgot our past. I'd never been her dealer and she'd never been my punter. We were never slaves we were something much more. I taught her about the kings and queens, and the journey of a slave. In return Alicia taught me the next step in my journey, she taught me about the Talented Tenth.

THE TALENTED TENTH

The Talented Tenth was written by the black sociologist and author W.E.B DuBois in September 1903. DuBois was one of the most influential black scholars of the 20th century. He was also the first black person to receive a P.H.D. from Harvard University in 1896 and in 1909 was a founding member of the National Association for the Advancement of Coloured People (NAACP).

Between 1897 and 1914 he pioneered a number of extensive sociological studies on the black society of North America. In these studies, he investigated the belief of social science being used as a valuable tool in analysing and solving race problems faced by blacks. At the turn of the century, sociology was still a growing field of study. There was not one institution of higher learning across the globe that had adopted its capabilities as a catalyst to answer the problems of a minority group.

From these studies DuBois produced 16 research papers that were published as an important historical series by Harvard. The papers included *'The Suppression Of the African Slave Trade,' 'The Philadelphia Negro'* and *'The Talented tenth.'*

In the *Talented Tenth* essay, DuBois manifests the idea of racial leadership and the responsibility of a race to produce leaders from its own people. He stated:

"The Negro race, like all races, is going to be saved by its exceptional men. The problem of education, then, among Negroes must first of all deal with the Talented Tenth; it is the problem of developing the Best of this race that they may guide the Mass away from the contamination and death of the worst, in their own race and others."

In this paper, DuBois called for the creation of a Black aristocracy or elite that could influence the race into practices, which would combat racism and white bigotry. The Talented Tenth would primarily consist of a foundation of scholars, professionals, and businessmen. This elite group goal was to set examples for good citizenship for the whole community. He also deemed it the responsibility of the talented tenth to guide the other 90 percent. In his essay, DuBois argued that the validity of the Talented Tenth would not only benefit the Black race, but the American nation.

"If it be true – and who can deny it – three tasks lay before me first to show from the past that the Talented Tenth as they have risen among American Negroes have been worthy of leadership; secondly to show how these men lay be educated and developed; and thirdly to show their relation to the Negro problem."

Selecting a number of leaders from the past, DuBois illustrated the achievement of talented so called Negroes. Demonstrating how the likes of Frederick Douglass, Alexander Crummel, and Sojourner Truth, had not only worked shoulder to shoulder with white men, but without them would have made abolition in the United States and the *Emancipation Proclamation* impossible. Hailing a group of his peers, the next group of gifted leaders he highlighted the regeneration, these individuals strived to uplift people.

Describing the Black political status he warned: *"Unless he (The Negroes) have political rights and righteously guarded civic stays, he will remain the poverty-stricken and ignorant plaything of rascals."*

Throughout his essay, DuBois focused on the training and the aim of this group The Talented Tenth. *"Can the masses of the Negro people be in any possible way more quickly raised than by the effort and example of this aristocracy of talent and character?"* DuBois greatest concern was that it should be The Talented Tenth that should become the teachers and the teachers of teachers of Black people.

"How then shall the leaders of a struggling people be trained and the hands of the risen strengthened? There can only be but one answer: the best most capable of youth must be schooled."

DuBois didn't debate about what the schools should teach rather the effects of the person teaching. He states: *"that each soul and each race-soul needs its own peculiar curriculum."* This identifies the fact that at some points a white teacher will be inadequate to teach black students vital lessons and vice versa.

Later analysing DuBois' thesis, I realized his research almost a hundred years ago was still relevant today in the 21st century. It supported my earlier conclusions (see How to make a slave) on the problems of the government education for ethnic groups in the UK. The question I now asked, was how realistic is it now to create a talented tenth.

Being a man of education, DuBois also looked at the practical side of producing such a group. *"All men cannot go to college but some men must; every isolated group ... must have for the talented the few centres of training where men are not so mystified and befuddled by the hard and necessary toil of earning a living, as to have no aims higher than their bellies."* In this quote I believed DuBois was highlighting the need for scholarships. In today's climates there are larger financial fees placed upon students. In Britain grants have been removed and replaced with student loans. This means a person graduates with debts of excess amount. With the added cost of living, the option of higher learning becomes even more illusive to those from poorer backgrounds. In basic terms a man cannot concentrate a 100% on studies if he must pay the bills.

Described in his own words as the crucial question, DuBois raised the matter of the success rate of employment to this Talented Tenth. *"Do they earn a living? It has been more than once the higher training of Negroes has resulted in sending into the world of work, men who could find nothing to do suitable to their talents."* At the time DuBois quoted from the Atlanta conference that nearly sixty per cent of the total number of educated blacks then found in employment, occupations included 53% teachers, 17% clergymen, 6.3%

physicians and 4.7% lawyers. DuBois concluded that the men and women in these roles already formed the basis of a Talented Tenth.

"He is, as ought to be, the group leader." He sought to challenge these people and underlined the fact that *"it need hardly be argued that the Negro people need social leadership more than most groups; that they have no traditions to fall back upon, no long established customs, no strong family ties, no well defined social classes."*

DuBois then called for the talented tenth to be furnished with the opportunities to deliver such social needs. His reasoning was to have, *"...placed before the eyes of almost every Negro child an attainable ideal."*

Defining The Talented Tenth value as role models for aspiring black children. Those from the group were to be benchmarks or, to have a standard which would be designed to epitomise achievement in the Black community.

In DuBois' attempts to evaluate the Talented Tenth, as a racial leadership, he identified two key points that the Talented Tenth must challenge.

ONE: *" It must strengthen the Negro's character, increase his knowledge and teach him to earn a living."*

TWO: Recognise the mind set of the students *"we could give black boys trades, but that alone will not civilise a race of ex-slaves; we might simply increase their knowledge of the world, but this would not necessarily make them wish to use this knowledge honestly."*

To tackle these obstacles DuBois advocated the strengthening of an education system through culture and community. He argued *"Education is that whole system of human training within and without the school house walls, which moulds and develops men. If we then start out to train an ignorant and unskilled people with heritage of bad habits, our system of training must set before itself two great aims - the one dealing with knowledge and character, the other part seeking to give the child the technical knowledge necessary for him to earn a living under the present circumstances."*

DuBois made a clear clarification that some of his contemporaries were drunk with the vision of success, if they believed their work at the time had been accomplished.

"Without providing for the training of broadly cultured men and women to teach its own teachers."

Instead he defines that *"human education is not a matter of schools"* and depicts an idea of education through sociology; *"the training of one's home, of one's daily companions, of one's social class. Now the black boy of the South moves in* *a black world – a world with its own leaders, its own thoughts its own ideals. In this world he gets by far larger part of his training, and through the eyes of this dark world he peers into the veiled world beyond. <u>Who guides and determines the education which he receives.</u>"*

Finally in the essay, DuBois gave two clear warnings to the ruling group and other societies of the consequences of not helping the Black race produce a Talented Tenth.

"You have no choice; either you must help furnish this race from within its own ranks with thoughtful men of trained leadership, or you must suffer the evil consequences of a headless misguided rabble." DuBois points a finger of responsibility that is owed to the Black race *"Here is a race transplanted through the criminal foolishness of your fathers. Whether you like it or not the millions are here, and here they will remain. If you do not lift them up, they will pull you down. Education and work are levers to uplift a people."* DuBois was right. In my own evaluation the ruling group had yet to respond.

DuBois ended 'The Talented Tenth' essay with the defined thought that, unless inspired by the right ideas and guided by intelligence. Education is insufficient to the needs of a black race. He urges for the emergence of The Talented Tenth as "leaders of thought and missionaries of culture among their people."

Like DuBois, I was not born a slave of physical bondage, but have walked in the timeless shadow of slavery. With the sins of the world before us, the application of a Talented Tenth is still vital to the survival of the black race. With Lynch Slaves to the left of me, Proles to the right of me, and the Ruling group in front of me, I wondered can such cultural training of leaders be neglected? A great inventory of the Talented Tenth, lay in the pages of history. Some we can immediately identify by face and name: Malcolm, Martin, Marcus, Mandela, Marley, Harriet Tubman, DuBois, Steve Biko, Newton, Seale, Angela Davis, and Rosa Parks. Others will remain unsung.

As I sat in Alicia's flat, I realised that I had a lot to learn. It was clear the Talented Tenth were my guides on my Journey. They were the characters and individual that showed the strength to lead. Similar to DuBois, I recognised that *"The Black race like all other races is going to be saved by its exceptional Men & Women."*

Then a dark question arose. Was I exceptional? Did I have any other skill other than turning wraps into ten pounds?

*

As Ivan reached the end of the chapter he closed the book and laid back. He played with his bruised knuckle pondering the same question as Gil. What was his unique talent? He thought criminality, but was that really a talent? If it was, it wasn't something he wanted Jayvan to inherit. He knew if the day ever came where he had to visit his son in prison he'd cry.

"Fuck!" He thought aloud. Criminality wasn't a talent at all; it was a means to an end. Leaning back on his bed, Ivan reached for a picture of Jayvan. The little boy smiled at the camera with his bottle in one hand, Ivan's Platinum chain around his neck, and a mobile pressed against his ear. Ivan loved the picture. He always hung it high and whenever someone saw it they'd always say "Is that your boy? ... He looks like a little bad man," or "Your boy looks like he's gonna be hectic when he's older."

"Yeah," Ivan would smile proudly. "That's Younga Terror right there."
Ashamed, Ivan put the picture down. The reality of a future visiting order with his name on it was too much. He didn't even want to think about the possibility of one day being on the same wing as his son. Ivan felt confused.

Reaching for the book again he flipped back a few pages and began reading the text Jade had highlighted. He studied the word institutionalized and cross-examined it with his dictionary.

***

CHAPTER: 16

Ivan was in the middle of Asr prayers when the screws came to his cell to take him to adjudication with the governor. Ignoring them he continued his salah and did an extra 8 rak'ahs and then gave du'a. During his prayers he prostrated for longer and recited the longest verses from Quran he could remember, as the guard grew impatient.

"Come on, Little," Mr Carroll said in his northern accent. "The guv'nor's waitin."

Ivan glanced at the guard with his shabby uniform and beer belly and said nothing. All the time he smiled knowing, the one area that most screws feared meddling in was religion. As soon as they were deemed to have stopped an inmate from practicing his religion they could be accused of breach of human rights, a serious charge. Ivan relished this fact and so kept them waiting.

When he'd finished he looked at the officer and said, "Allahu-akbar, I'm ready now you kafir. Take me to your Shaytan. On the day of judgement you will be with those sent to the hellfire for your bad deeds. 'member I told you dat yeah."

"Shut up you flippin terrorist and hurry up," Mr Carroll sneered. "You wanna pray I don't mix some pork in your lunch this afternoon."

"Then they'll arrest you for choppin' up your wife." Ivan sniggered as he was led away.

The adjudication was just as Ivan predicted. He was charged with fighting and causing harm to another inmate. Under the circumstance he pleaded guilty claiming he was under extreme emotional pressure from splitting up with his girlfriend. In light of the earlier incident in the visiting hall, the governor Mr Whyte was lenient with him.

"Okay, Little," Mr Whyte looked up from Ivan's file. "I'm not usually this generous, but I'm feeling in an extremely good mood today."

Playing with his *Mont Blanc* pen he eyed Ivan with a stern look. He was a gaunt looking man with sharp features and silver hair. His gold rim spectacles sat on his hawk like nose as he twisted his mouth. "You seem to have an exceptional talent for getting into trouble, don't you?" Mr Whyte raised an eyebrow waiting for Ivan to answer.

"Yes, sir," Ivan responded. "I know, but I'm trying to avoid getting into anymore. I'm trying to learn to turn the other cheek, count to ten and walk away. Those type of things."

"Hmm, I hope so," Mr Whyte grimaced. "Otherwise I'll come down very hard on you the next time you appear before me young man."

"Yes, sir."

"Good. As for now I'm putting you on governor's report. You will be placed on basic regime and docked two weeks pay. In addition you will also complete another two days in solitary confinement, where you will have time to think about your transgressions. Is that understood?"

"Yes, sir."

"Good. And, Little,"

"Sir?"

"Consider yourself very lucky that you never received extra days for causing such a ruckus in my prison. Fighting will not be tolerated. Is that also understood?"

"Yes, sir."

"Good," Mr Whyte scowled. "Mr Carroll, please escort the prisoner back to segregation."

Mr Carroll signalled for Ivan to get up and follow him. Heading towards the block Mr Carroll looked at Ivan with a smug grin.

"What you smiling at?" Ivan snarled

"You," Mr Carroll smirked. "What happened to all your shaytan and Muslim talk? Did Mr Whyte scare it outta you or what?"

"Shut up you fool!" Ivan stopped in his tracks. "Mr Whyte didn't scare nothing out of me."

"No?" Mr Carroll smiled. He gestured to Ivan to keep walking "Well you didn't half sound like a knobhead in there. All that yes sir, no sir, I thought you was one of us for a minute son."

"I ain't your son."

"No, but I'm very fond of you," Mr Carroll teased Ivan. "So I'll tell you what, lad, if you behave I'll put in a good word with the S.O. on y'ur houseblock, and we'll see if we can get you a tea-boy job, hey. "

"Later!" Ivan said as they reached the Seg-Unit. "I'd rather eat shit before I become any tea-boy for you man."

"That can be arranged too, if ye like, lad?"

Ivan kissed his teeth as Mr Carroll opened his cell door. "Oi, Mr Carroll you know you're a fassie innit. You know if I ever saw you on road, I wouldn't pet to lick you down."

"Oh don't be like that now, lad. You were so well behaved upstairs."

"That's upstairs," Ivan spat in the toilet. "Don't think I'm any idiot, I done read the 48 laws of Power. Rule number 1 says, never outshine the master."

"Oh that's good." Mr Carroll clapped. "You can read and you know your place. Well done."

"Errrn, shut up you fool!" Ivan said with disgust "Don't get it twisted, I know who's the ruling group in this shit hole, and I also know who wields the power, and it ain't you, with your liccle cell key." He laughed mocking Mr Carroll. "Oi, you see man like you. You know why you fear man like me? Because I know, outside this pussyhole institution, you're nothing. The only talent you got is turning that key. Even a monkey can do that."

"Yeah?" Mr Carroll said turning red in the face.

"Yeah." Ivan stepped forward trying to antagonise the prison guard.

"Well, you know what I think?" Mr Carroll pushed Ivan back. "I think you're full of shit, with an exceptionally big mouth and no talent at all."

Ivan cracked his knuckles and clinched his fist "Put your hand on me again and see if I don't show you how much talent I got."

Mr Carroll stepped out the cell with a scornful look. "It's no wonder your ol' lady left you, mate. You truly are a knob-head."

"Better than being a screw," Ivan shot back. "Go turn your fuckin' key, you pussyhole!"

As Mr Carroll slammed the door and the heavy lock sounded, Ivan sat down and reached for his book. He smiled knowing he had riled Mr Carroll. He considered if he didn't know any other talent, at least he knew how to get under people's skin, and began to read.

KINGS AND QUEENS II   *The Journey of a Slave.*

Alicia brought two drinks in and we sat on the floor surround by books. The light from the muted TV blurred away while the low sounds of Jodeci played in the background. Alicia glared at me with a smirk on her face.

"What you laughing at?" I asked.

"You." she replied, "You're quite studious aren't you? You're a lot different then I thought."

"I'm different, what about you?" I gestured to the room. "You're the one with all the books and the African carvings. I mean I didn't expect that from you."

"Oh," Alicia frowned. "So what did you expect?"

She put me on the spot, and for the first time I felt a bit awkward. I hadn't a clue what to say. "I don't know I kinda pictured you... like something different" I hesitated.

"Like what?"

"I don't know, Li. Something different, innit." I was struggling to find my words and Alicia could see it. "I mean you surprised me. You're different to what I was expecting. In a good way though."

"Hmmm," Alicia gave me a suspicious look. "That's not answering the question, but I'll let you off the hook."

"Good." I wiped my forehead.

"So is this what you wanna do in life?"

"What?"

"You wanna be a leader of something like a Malcolm X or Marcus Garvey?"

"Me, a Malcom X?" I laughed dismissively. "I don't think so?"

"No you know what I mean." Alicia smacked my arm. "You wanna be like a leader, a teacher, one of the talented tenth. Someone who could speak to the youngsters and tell them what it's like."

"Don't be stupid," I sipped my drink. "What could I teach the youngaz? The youngaz ain't gonna wanna listen to me. I don't even wanna listen to me. I mean what the eff wud I say. 'Oh stay in school and get a good education blah, blah, blah.' They got enuff people spouting that crap to dem. They don't need me chattin shit as well. Black yoots need more than someone to chat to dem, they need a person who is gonna revolutionise the way we black people think. Someone who's gonna say it's time for change and this is how we're gonna achieve it."

"Hmm, okay right I see." Alicia murmured unconvinced. "So can I ask you a question?"

"Yeah"

"Do you always talk so much shit?"

"Huh? What you talking about?" I scowled.

"You." Alicia pointed her finger. "You talk about what people need, but when someone asks you if you're that person you turnaround and say nah that's not me."

I looked at her like she was crazy.

"You know what, Gil, you're right." She continued. "The youngaz don't need to hear you chattin shit and neither do I? You don't even sound like the same person I've spent the evening talking with. You know what you sound like? Like a Lynch slave." Alicia leered. "Yeah, you're scared of the journey. You're scared of what the other people might say."

"I ain't scared."

"Yes you are. You're scared of failing, so you'd rather make excuses and run around on the streets. Go on, tell me if I'm lying. Tell me if that ain't the truth. You're scared."

I was pissed. Who did this girl think she was? Trying to use my own philosophies as a weapon against me.

"You don't know what you're talking about."

"No? Okay then tell me this. If I don't know what I'm talking about, why do you feel your journey's stopped? Why do you feel you're lost? Why were you so desperate that you were loitering outside my office block looking for some Muslim guy, in the rain?"

"Hold on, hold on!" I cut her off. "Don't try and make me sound like some madman standing in the rain okay. Cos you're blatantly missing the point. I wasn't saying that right about now, I ain't lost. I was saying I ain't scared. If there was a revolution I'd be right there on the frontline doing my ting, but I just ain't no leader. There's a difference."

"Bullshit! The only difference is you'd rather be a follower than a leader, because you're frightened of the burden of leadership. You don't want fingers pointing and eyes judging you, saying him, is that your leader?"

As Alicia spoke she reminded me of my dream. The slave master had looked upon me and doubted my ability. He questioned me until I now questioned myself.

"Listen to me, Gil. If you sit around doing nothing, you're worst than all the man dem out there selling drugs, shooting each other, and robbing each other. You know why? Because you have the knowledge to do something and you refuse to use it. You also refuse to share that knowledge, which is worst than ignorance. It's what the ruling group did to hold us back."

I became speechless as her message hit home. How could I argue with her? She was right. Whenever I was challenged to admit the truth I always opted to remain silent and now was no different. My jaw clenched tight and my tongue pressed against the roof of my mouth. My heartbeat bounded like a heavy drum and I could feel the pent up anger inside. I felt vexed. I tried to control myself. Other than Edina, Alicia was the first person to ever confront me with the truth. She had stripped me and left me feeling naked and for a moment I hated her.

"How as a race are we suppose to empower ourselves if those with the knowledge refuse to empower themselves? The reason your equation doesn't work is because there is no action on the intention, why, because you're scared."

"Maybe I am scared," I snapped. "Maybe your right, but that doesn't change anything! I'm still stuck here ain't I. I'm still stuck in this bullshit area, with these bullshit people looking at me like I ain't worth shit. It's all fuckin bullshit! I'm arguing with my bredrins and losing my mind over bullshit! And you know the wickedest thing about it?" I gulped down my drink and looked at her. It was Alicia's turn to be quiet as I nearly lost it.

"I don't care no more! The world can do with me as it pleases, as long as no one don't ask me for shit! And they can put that on my grave!"

I slammed down the glass. My hand was trembling. Alicia could see my anguish. I was like a wounded animal, in pain and in need of help. My mask had fallen and the act was over. It was a moment of clarity. There was no big gangster, no thug, no bad man, there was just me, a lonely soul looking for help. My eyes began to well up and I hung my head to hide my grief. Alicia moved closer and held my hand. Lightly she stroked the back of my neck.

"It's okay to be scared, Gil," she said in a soft voice. "It's okay to be angry and sad, but at some point you've got to find yourself. My granny always used to say, the reason misery loves company is because self-pity is always crying about herself."

"What's that meant to mean?" I looked up.

"It means I know what you're going through."

Alicia began to undo the buttons on her blouse as she came closer. The blouse smoothly rolled over her shoulder, revealing a navy lace bra against her caramel skin. Her cleavage sat in the bra cups like two golden orbs.

"I know what its like to doubt yourself." Alicia pointed to a small burn scar about an inch long above her left breast. I hadn't noticed it before. To me Alicia's body was perfect with no imperfection or blemishes. She twisted herself lifting up her arm to point to another small scar by her ribs. "Look."

"What happened?"

"Life." Alicia said nonchalantly. For a moment there was indifference in her face and her mind wondered for a second. "Things happen to you when you lose your self value. You do things and you let people do things and before you know it misery's got company." She tried to smile. "Try not to doubt yourself, Gil. You're better than that."

"Li," I stroked my finger on her scar "Can I ask you a question?"

"Mmm, hmm."

"Why'd you start smoking work?"

"I suppose it was after my brother died." She pointed to the photo on the mantle piece "I guess I never coped with it well. We did everything together and one day he was just gone. It left a void in me that nothing could fill. Then one day I met a guy I thought I was in love with." Alicia paused looking into an empty space as though she could see a kaleidoscope of her life. "At first he was nice and sweet. That's' how you all are at the beginning. Then he began to twist things. He used to abuse me, beat me, tell me I wasn't worth anything. He just liked to hurt me." Anger swept over Alicia face as she continued to speak. "And all the time I kept loving him like a fool. I never knew he was an under cover smoker, but one night he came and held me down. He pushed himself inside me. I told him no, but he slapped me and carried on. When he finished he lit a cigarette and started burning me. All the time he kept laughing and telling me, look at you, who's ever gonna love you, who's ever gonna want you?" Tears began to roll down her cheeks and she nervously played with the bottom button on her blouse. "I remember laying there, thinking it's true. Who's ever gonna want me now?"

"That ain't true, Alicia," I said wiping her face "You're beautiful anybody would want you."

Alicia held my hand trying not to cry. She kissed me on the cheek accommodating my naïve attempts to comfort her. She continued her story.

"After that night. I lost myself. I began to bun. I thought it would relieve the pain, it never, it just caused more drama; people watching, looking, pointing their fingers, and talking behind my back. Gil, I know what it's like from first hand. I know what it's like to be in hell, and nobody wants to help you. Nobody. You learn not to care. The problem is if you don't care, then how do you ever expect things to change?"

Alicia drew her legs up to her chest and buried her head in her knees. I put my arm around her shoulder to comfort her. I rubbed her back. Her skin was smooth and velvet soft. I stroked the back of her neck as she looked up at me wiping the tears from her eyes.

"It's all cool now, Li," I said. "Things have changed now."

"How?" Alicia asked.

Slowly she let down her legs and started to raise her skirt. Her legs were beautifully toned. Her hands seemed to glide upwards forever as I watched her unveil the tops of her thighs. She wore a navy lace thong that matched her bra. I could feel the pressure my member created against my boxer shorts as I gradually began to rise. I don't know whether it was deliberate on Alicia's behalf, but she couldn't be aware of how much I wanted to hold her at that moment. As she opened her legs slightly, she pointed to a cigarette burn on the inside of her thigh.

"I'm marked all over with these scars, Gil."

"So," I gently stroked the scar on her thigh. "They don't mean nothing. They're scars of life, like you said. They're what make you who you are."

Slowly I leaned forward and kissed Alicia. As our lips pressed she opened her mouth and I glided my tongue in caressing hers. Methodically my hand moved up and down her thigh until I decided to pull her legs around my waist. She sat on my lap and reached down into my boxers. Face to face we looked into each others eyes. She said nothing as my hand ran the length of her back and gripped her firm buttocks. I squeezed each cheek firmly, as she began to move in a slow grinding motion. She closed her eyes and bit my lip. She rubbed up and down against my rod, the friction felt nice. My dick was hard. It was a moment that I had dreamed about for years. I didn't care about the past. I was gonna fuck Alicia. I wanted her. I placed my face against her chest as she tenderly stroked me. Her hands reached down and cupped my face. She lent forward to whisper in my ear. "Thank you, Gil. You know it was you, don't you?"

I lay her down on the floor spreading the books. "What was me?" I said pulling down my sweat suit bottoms. Alicia wiggled as I snatched away her underwear. Her fingers tickled my back like spider legs, as I readied myself between her. Supporting my weight with one hand, the other ran the coast of her outer thigh then came inward. Gently I pushed my fingers deep. Her walls were warm and moist as I began to fondle and stroke. I took my time making sure I was attentive. Caressing her breast I suckled and kissed her scar. I blew on the side of her neck. I pulled my hand away replacing my fingers and filling her chasm. She let out a slight groan. Grabbing the back of my neck she breathed hard and bit my lip again. "It was you," she whispered in my ear.

"It was me that did what?" I whispered back. I felt her nails claw my back as I ground down with my hip. I gyrated slowly, pushing and pulling back teasingly.

"It was you," she said as I thrust deep. "It was you. I changed for you. I could see it in your eyes." I felt her legs wrap around mine and she clung to my torso. "It was you. I changed for you."

Stopping, I looked at her. "What are you talking about?" I said sitting up.

"It was you, Gil." She said trying to draw me back in "I stopped smoking because of you."

Instantly the mood was lost. "What's wrong?" Alicia asked as my face changed.

"What did you jus' say?"

She looked at me bewildered "I said I stopped smoking because of you. Why, what's wrong?"

"What'd you mean what's wrong?" I frowned.

Alicia sat up unsure what was happening. "I'm talking about you. I've know for ages that you used to like me, Gil. I could tell from the way you use to look at me when we was at college"

"We hardly ever talked at college."

"That's cos' you were shy, but I knew you liked me."

"So! What's that got to do with smoking?"

I didn't like where the conversation was going. I thought Alicia was playing with me. Why did she wait to bring this up now?

"It's because of the way you looked at me," she explained. "I remember how you looked at me when I first saw you again. The first time I called Mel, and you were sitting in the car. I saw you as I went by. You looked at me and I saw it in your eyes."

"You saw what?"

"What you were thinking."

"You saw what I was thinking? What bullshit are you talking?" I said pulling my bottoms up "You can't tell what the fuck I was thinking"

"Yes I can!" Alicia snapped. "You were thinking, is that her? Is that what she turned out to be?"

"That ain't what I was thinking."

"What were you thinking then?"

The question came fast and I didn't have time to think. "I don't know. I knew I recognised you, I was trying to remember from where."

"You're lying." Alicia said "I can see it in your eyes. What about all the other times?"

"What times?"

"The times when you sent Mel to deal with me. The times when you didn't want to come? Go on tell me what you were thinking then?"

"I don't know."

"You told him to stop shottin to me, why?"

"I don't know." I turned away from her, looking around the room for my clothes. I couldn't take her interrogation. I wanted to get out. Why was she asking me this now? I felt she was trying to manipulate me but for what? I never tried to hurt her. What did she want? I was confused.

"Gil, I'm talking to you look at me."

"What?!"

"Why did you tell him that?"

"I don't know, Alicia! What do you want me to say?"

"The truth!"

"Because I didn't want you to smoke! There I've said it. I didn't want you to smoke. There, are you happy now!" I said jumping to my feet.

The music had stopped playing and Alicia stood in front of me. She still wouldn't let the subject die. "Why?" she tried to stroke my face.

"Don't touch me." I slapped her hand away. "I've answered enough of your questions, I ain't answering no more. Whatever little game you're playing I ain't interested. Can you go get my clothes?

"Gil," Alicia stepped forward. I kept her at arms length. "I'm not playing games with you. I jus' wanna tell you how I feel."

"And I said can you get my clothes? I'm not interested in how you feel. All I wanna know is, can you go get my clothes?"

Alicia stared at me in disbelief. With her arms wrapped around herself and her blouse still hanging off her shoulders, she couldn't comprehend what I was thinking. Tears began to roll from her chinky eyes. "So you're gonna leave? Jus' like that?"

"Yeah. Why not?" I screwed up my face "This shits long."

"Fine." Alicia rushed out of the room.

She gathered my clothes next door and she shoved them in my arms. They were still a touch damp, but I weren't complaining. We stood in silence as I changed. Then Alicia followed me to the front door. I unlatched the lock.

"Wait," Alicia stopped me. "This is silly, don't go."

"Nah" I shook my head "I can't deal with this shit. I think it's bes' I go, don't you?"

"I don't want you to go," Alicia tried to convince me. We began fighting over the door latch. "I want you to stay. I want you to listen to me. I want you to know when I look into your eyes, I see something different. I see someone who looks at me differently to anyone else, somebody that looks at me for who I am, the real me. That's why I want you to stay. That's why I want you to look at me. So I can look into your eyes. I love looking in your eyes."

"Alicia stop with this eyes bullshit!"

"No!" Alicia said defiantly. "No. When all other eyes looked down upon me and loathed me, and said I was dirt and made me feel like nothing. It was your eyes that made me believe. It was your eyes that said 'what are you doing to yourself?' It was your eyes that said 'you're better than this.' Your eyes were the only eyes that refused to watch me destroy myself. Do you understand that?"

She ran her hands along the contour of my face stroking my eyebrows. As I looked down at the floor Alicia softly kissed each eyelid. I held her wrists shaking her. I needed her to understand

"Look at me Alicia. Forget my eyes. I'm the same brer that sold you crack. The same brer that sold you tens and twenty, I'm the same brer that did that to you, so let's not sugar-coat shit. I did that to you with these hands." I held my hands up for her to see.

Gently Alicia took my hand and kissed it "And I forgave your hands." She said. "I forgive them because I love your eyes. They're beautiful. They opened my eyes, Gil. They let me see what I needed to see." She tried to close the door again. "Don't leave, Gil. Let me open your eyes and blind the others you're frightened of. Let me be the one to do that for you Gil. Don't go, stay."

It was like a movie, the end scene in Casablanca. She was the heroine and I was the hero. It seemed only right to kiss her. I wanted to kiss her. Stroking Alicia's face she smiled. I needed to be honest with her.

"I'm sorry, Alicia I can't. This is real life, it's not no fairy tale." I was being honest. Life didn't end happily ever after for people like us. Not out here.

"I can't be your knight in shining armour," I said. "I can't save you, and give you the fairy tale ending you want. If you changed and stopped smoking, whatever you want to call it. You did that for you, not me. Now I got to do the same for myself."

I stepped out into the hallway. I couldn't look Alicia in the eye. It was time to say goodbye. I had desired her for so long, sought after her, and now I was leaving her, why? It was an unnecessary sacrifice. I kept telling myself, Alicia was a queen how could a queen share her throne with a slave?

Maybe that was the problem with my race. A Black queen should never have to share her throne with anything less than a King. I was still a slave on my journey, how would I affect Alicia. What would happen if I got lost again; where would I lead her? No, I decided as I turned to walk away, Alicia would not be a companion on my journey. Our paths would cross, but we would not travel together.

Then from behind me she threw the most frightening and chilling question I had ever heard. Each word was like a knife being twisted in my heart, like somebody scraping their nails on a chalkboard. She said *"I love you, Gil don't you love me?"*

*

As Ivan finished the page he realised he was gritting his teeth, but he didn't know why? Agitated, he threw the book down and started pacing his cell. After a few strides he dropped down and started doing press-ups. He needed to release some off his frustration. He couldn't understand why the last passage troubled him so much.

"Why didn't Gil just fuck her?" He asked himself. That's what he would have done, that's what any man would've done. "He's some off-key brer." Ivan concluded, but that still didn't explain why he was so annoyed with the chapter.

When he'd finished three sets of 50 press-ups, Ivan pulled the mattress of his bed and stood the bed frame up. "He's a dickhead," He reasoned laying the mattress at the base of the upturned frame to steady it so he could do some pull-ups.

"He's dumb," Ivan told himself once more. "He's stupid." He continued to think as he pulled himself up and down. "This is suppose to be the girl that he wanted for so long, and now she wants him, what does he do? Pushes her away. Why?"

Ivan couldn't get it out of his mind. Why would any man do that to the girl they loved, even if she did use to smoke crack?

"Nah, nah, nah, I ain't buying it" Ivan said as he put the bed back.

Sweating he opened his barred window, grabbed his flannel and soap, and began to wash his underarms in the sink. Rinsing his face, Ivan looked at himself in the mirror.

"If that was me and that was my girl, I would..."

Suddenly he stopped mid sentence. Wiping his face he finally realized why the chapter jarred him. He didn't have a girl. He'd pushed Jade away just like

Gil did Alicia. Stunned, Ivan moved to the bed. He sat for a moment fondling his book. The story had a different circumstance and different characters, but continually Ivan found Gil's thoughts and actions kept mirroring his own. This latest parallel was a stark eye-opener. Glumly, Ivan sat trying to straighten a dog-ear on the book cover. He was beginning to accept the truth. Perhaps if he really did love Jade, he might have to let her live her life without him. Perhaps she deserved more than he could give her. Looking at his barred window Ivan smelled the pages of his book. It smelt like Jade.

***

CHAPTER: 17

It was a Monday afternoon when Ivan was finally brought back to the wing. Most of the inmates were either at work or education, so he slipped back unnoticed. Fortunately, he was allowed to return to sharing his cell with Dorian. Quickly unpacking his things, he looked around the cell he had demolished over a week earlier. Dorian had done his best to restore it, repositioning his meagre canteen display, replacing furniture and sellotaping torn posters. In the corner of the windowsill he rested his broken stereo.

Ivan could see Dorian had tried to fix the damages with no avail. The CD compartment had been cracked in to two, the antenna snapped and the cassette gate taped up. It was officially useless. Ivan knew Dorian must have been struggling without any music. On previous occasions Dorian would go stir crazy if he went 72 hours without some form of melody. He'd sit rapping and tapping on the table to amuse himself, which usually sent Ivan mad after a few hours. Taking his own ghetto blaster, Ivan laid it on Dorian's bed as a good will gesture and apology. Ivan grinned. He'd been in a rueful mood all morning. Taking out a piece of prison paper he thought about writing a letter to Jade.

Looking at the 24 blue lines on the white sheet, he sat twiddling his pen and chewing the lid. He hadn't a clue how to start. If he were honest, he wasn't even sure Jade would read it. He pictured her seeing his handwriting and tearing it up instantly. Then he dismissed the notion knowing Jade wasn't that petty. He surmised that a simple apology was never going to be enough, and pretending to take the high road, appealing for Jade to settle the bad blood between them would only vex her more. The dilemma Ivan had was what could he write to provoke Jade to correspond in the manner he desired. He didn't want to sound needy and he didn't want her to shun him. Putting the pen down Ivan sighed. He thought, *how would Gilyan Gates go about dealing with this*. Looking for inspiration he picked up his book finding his page...

THE TENTH TRIBE   *The Journey of a Slave.*
OF CULTURALISM

The affect of a woman's love is a strange thing. I will not pretend to understand it nor will I ever wish to fully comprehend it. It has been known to drive men to insanity, and it has been known to be their salvation. From the love of a woman, a child may be conceived. From the same love of a woman a child may become a man. Finally from one woman's love to another, a man may learn to love a woman and love himself. That night at Alicia's flat had changed my life forever. My travels upon the journey had been in great jeopardy of me regressing. I had been lost in a foreign territory and had contemplated settling down to a life in The City of Modern Containment. To live amongst the Lynch Slave and Proles in ignorance was one thing, but to live trying to ignore them was a tragedy of madness. I can only imagine a sickening fate, where my thoughts convicted me to a life of living hell. Where my soul ate away at me everyday like rats feasting in the gutters of life.

Hearing Alicia utter those dreaded words "I love you, Gil don't you love me?" Was like an enchantment in one hand and a curse on the other. Knowing that a black queen could love me with all my shortcomings had spurred me on. I had picked up the little belongings of knowledge I possessed, and recovered my feet for the journey. Yet embarking on the journey again took me away from the very love that healed my aching feet, a love that soothed my empty belly and lightened my burdened back. Alicia had been the unknown catalyst so many times upon my journey, now we were destined to be apart. I cursed the fortunes of love's fool as a cruel fate.

I knew for me to complete my journey, the likes of Alicia, Sparks, Kooba, Mel, and the world they inhabited I needed to escape. Alicia had provided me with the beginning of a blueprint, a map, a compass point or star I could follow. She had unmasked a trail, a set of footprints that disappeared off into the distance. These footprints belonged to Abolitionists, Revolutionists, Activists, Warriors, Princes, Kings and Queens. The talented tenth. Now I chased those footprints. The absence of Alicia's love would only become like wind is to a flame. Either it would extinguish the small or ignite an inferno. I had to look closer at the talented tenth. They seemed to be the answer to the leadership and guidance upon my journey.

I began my research by looking for the exceptional one in ten throughout black history. I was soon able to identify a list of crusaders that had fought for the social and economic rights of black people. Plentiful to begin with, I noticed this list of crusaders slowly began to diminish through the decades. As I looked upon today's talented tenth I begin to recognise a distinctive pattern was apparent.

The talented tenth of the late 20th and early 21st century were no longer activists for their race, but were instead capitalists. They no longer desired the greater goals of the black race, but preferred the individual goals of capitalism. In the 21st century, there is a sufficient number of well-qualified and successful blacks that are in the positions to fit into a so-called 'Black elite'. The problem that now arose was whether this Aristocracy had missed its true purpose to elevate its people. Like true aristocrats many of today's talented tenth had allowed elitism to segregate them. Only a handful of these elite still maintained strong ties in their communities. When I thought about my own community I couldn't name one black doctor that I knew personally. Nor could I ever say that a black business tycoon ever visited our youth centre or school. The only real black professionals I saw outside sports and media were in criminal law, barristers and solicitors.

Examining my generation and our leaders I realised that the presence of a true talented tenth was absent. The idea of a group of leaders that promoted strong characteristics among our community was either missing or being ignored. Our group leaders were no longer doctors and preachers. The majority of my community didn't even attend church.

Perhaps this was a reason why some of the leaders we currently did have, weren't effective. It became obvious. The majority of people within our communities were not looking for leaders who were attached to some sort of religious organisation. Leaders who tend to force-feed religion and spiritual healing as a means to solve our immediate and financial problems. They were looking for leaders that would deal with the social and economic problems of the community. They were looking for leaders who could give them real solutions, to real problems, and not tell them to kneel down and pray. They did not want the attachment to a religious organisation which could be perceived as hypocritical, contradictory or redundant. It seemed to me that in the UK, this type of leader may be respected or at worst tolerated, but lacked the non-secular, economic political clout warranted for leadership and mass appeal.

Quickly it became evident to me why for many of us, third and fourth generation black youth and *Proles*, our role models are now created from images that we see on television and in the media. They are entertainers, athletes, musicians, and celebrities. These are people who are not necessarily always educated. They are people who possess raw talents and have harnessed its full potential. Growing up, we quickly learn not everyone is born with the potential to run fast or to sing beautifully. There must be a balance of achievable goals for the black children and *Proles* to aspire to. This is why the new talented tenth must strive to use their influence in the correct manner. Inspiring the people into the right social practices and education.

The irony of today is that with all the facilities to educate and raise ourselves, we are failing. Instead, opting to use the same facilities to entertain each other and complain about our woes. Thinking of my own education, I wondered was this because of the lack of positive role models left in the community. If there were some black mentor schemes that had pushed me, would I have been a scholar or a doctor now? The answer to that question will go unknown. The question that is now relevant is: without the correct role model, who does the youth substitute The Talented Tenth with?

I've already stated the celebrities, athletes, and entertainers but there is one other group that lies in the community. With goals that are more realistic and attainable we return to the hustlers. These are the ghetto celebrities with the lifestyle that the media are helping to glorify in movies and TV. If the segment of the black aristocracy does not take responsibility to aid the non-talented tenth, the gap between the two becomes bigger.

The talented tenth must not allow themselves to be segmented away from the other ninety per cent. They must not create a black aristocracy that looks down on their brethren. They should interact and play their desired roles in the community. If not this will recreate the greed, selfishness, jealous and envy that slave masters used to contain. I thought to myself that WEB DuBois's theory of an educated black elite would have to be redefined. A person, who is truly exceptional and worthy of the title Talented tenth, would not miss the fullness of his/her talent by the selfish goals of capitalism. And a person who refuses to share their talent cannot be considered exceptional. No, there must be a clarification of the meaning Talented Tenth. In its truest essence

> *'The Talented tenth will only be the exceptional few, educated or uneducated that will gainfully seek to save their race.'*

I looked at it like this - if we are the Lynch slaves that live in the City of Modern Containment, who were the black elite? Where did they live? If they segregated themselves, and looked down at us, scorning their brethren for being uneducated, then those black elite, black capitalist or Buppies were no more than Modern day 'House Slaves' because it is 'The True Talented Tenth's' purpose to bring about change and reform.

*

"Brap!" Ivan made a gun salute with his two fingers as inspiration hit him. Immediately he grabbed his pen and started jotting down words before he lost his train of thought.

"Dear Jade" he recited as he wrote. "As I write this letter I want very much to apologize to you, but I'm sure my words will fall on deaf ears. So before I attempt to, I want to tell you about two words I have seriously been thinking about for the last few days. They are CHANGE and REFORM.

***

CHAPTER: 18

There weren't many people Ivan trusted and even less that he could confide in, especially when it came to personal matters. So he wasn't sure how to react to King's prolonged silence after he finished reading the letter he wrote for Jade.

"Well, what'd you think?" he asked.

King frowned, scratching the back of his head. "You want me to be real with you?"

"Course," Ivan said.

"Where did you get the idea for change and reform from?"

"What?" Ivan looked at King. He wondered how the man knew he'd stolen his focal point. "How'd you mean? I just thought it up."

"Ivan," King stood up. He looked Ivan in the eye. "Talk to me man. You just said you want me to be real with you, be real with me. Where'd you get the idea from?"

Ivan smiled mischievously. "One book I'm reading called *Journey of a slave*." He handed the book to King. "It's about this brer. He's a shotta and he talks about all these different things, like how history and politics affected black people over centuries, and that slavery is one of the reasons why nuff man either shot or smoke today. All things like that. It's heavy still."

"Okay" King smirked at the book.

"Oi, King trust me, blood," Ivan prodded the book. "Dis book is deep. I'll borrow you it when I'm finished."

"Cool," King scanned the pages. "So how's the book relate to your letter?"

"Well," Ivan thought hard. "In the book, the brer's going through this transitional phase and he kinda disses this girl he likes."

"Why's he diss her?"

"Because he used to shot *ting* to her. But true she's cleaned up her act; I think the real reason is that he thinks that he'll keep bringing her down. So he kinda jus' ducks her."

"Hmm" King murmured. "He pushes her away? Similar to you and Jade?"

"Yeah, kinda." Ivan said slightly embarrassed. He remembered King was in the visiting hall the day he kicked off with Jade.

"So what happens in the end?" King asked as he picked up an orange and started to peel the skin.

"I don't know," Ivan shrugged his shoulders. "I ain't finished reading it yet."

Shaking his head King dropped the orange peel in his plastic bowl and sat down at his table. He had a chessboard set out in mid game and studied his next move.

"Ivan sit down," King gestured to the empty chair. "I wanna talk to you seriously."

Ivan took the seat and positioned himself opposite King. He too studied the board.

"Ivan," King said in a laden voice "You know I've read that book. To be honest I've read it a few times and I know the story back to back."

Ivan looked at King puzzled. "So why you makin' me explain it to you then?"

"Because I wanted to know your understanding of the character," King munched on a segment of orange. He spat out a pip and threw it in the bin. "Lemme explain something to you." He said turning the chessboard 180 so he could see it from the opposition's view. "You see, the problem with your letter, it lacks sincerity. You need to see it the same way I see this board, from both sides." King spun the board back.

"If you send that letter to Jade, what do you think she will think?"

"I'm not sure," Ivan frowned. "That's why I came to you."

"Well I know Jade less than you." King stated. "So how relevant is my opinion?"

"Cos you know how people think, blood. I wanna know if you think she'll believe what I'm saying. You know me, cuz. Just tell me if you think it sounds good."

"Yes Ivan," King sighed. "It sounds good, but I don't think Jade will believe it."

"So what you saying then? You reckon I should write it again?"

"No. I'm telling you to be more sincere. Don't try and dupe your girl with big notions of change and reform when you don't believe in them yourself. Be real with her. Otherwise it will only be a matter of time before you expose yourself as a fraud if you go 'bout things that way."

"How'd you mean?"

"Look at the guy in this book. Do you know the real reason he ducks the girl? It's because after talkin' all that fraff about his journey, the girl exposes him as a fraud. He's got all this big talk, but he lacks sincerity and his actions show no intention."

"Yeah" Ivan said enthusiastically. "That why his equation don't work innit."

"Exactly. The reason why the guy in this book knows that he can't be with that girl, is because he knows he needs to change. Think about it." King spun the board back round to it's original position and made his move. Ivan leaned to examine the play and nodded in silent agreement.

"Oi, blood you're heavy you know. That's why I came to you." Ivan said standing up. "I'm gonna rewrite dis ting and come back and show you. That's cool yeah?"

"Mmm, cool," King sucked on another orange segment. "But do me a favour first. Finish reading the book."

"Ah c'mon, blood. Course I will." Ivan grinned. "That's standard innit."

Ivan bopped out of King's cell and back to his own. He jumped on his bunk thinking 'I like King, he keeps it thorough.'

Ivan had King down as a real nigga, no bullshit. He always said there was a shortage of those type of niggaz in life, and anytime he bucked one he wanted to stay in touch. Friendship meant a lot to Ivan and he valued the man's advice. Smiling, he propped himself up ready to read ...

LIKE THEY DO IN SOUTHALL   *Journey Of A Slave*

Mel wove through the traffic along the Uxbridge road as we made our way to Southall. With one hand pulling and dragging on the steering wheel and the other quick shifting on the gear stick, he was in his element. There was something about the idea of controlling the mechanical beast that excited him. Today was no different and he slipped in and out of lanes cheekily cutting people up.

"Rah, did you see that, bro? That chick try, not let me in," he said indicating to a blonde in a silver Peugeot. "The cheeky bitch, I should put my high beams on in her bloody face"

" 'llow that, what's wrong with you?" I stopped him from flicking his lights.

"Cool man," Mel pushed my hand away. "You're like an old woman."

"Bruv, I'm thinking 'bout you, you know." I warned. "You've got food on you, and you're driving like a mad man. If feds draw you down, what you gonna say when your ridin' it."

"Nothing," Mel slowed his speed. "I'm gonna say I told you not to pick up the soap when you come to the cell crying."

"Shut up you fool!" I slapped Mel around the head.

"Oi!" Mel yelled. "Can't you see I'm driving?"

"Well drive properly den." I laughed.

It had been a little while since I'd been on a run with Mel. He understood that I wanted to distance myself from the hustling and he didn't lay any pressure on me. However I still followed him on little missions here and there. That evening he'd asked me to follow him to Southall to meet Rabbi. Rabbi was our little Asian link. He usually brought a couple ozs of brown each week. We'd first met him back in college when he was looking for a draw of weed.

Back in the day all the smokers at college used to hang out under the stairs. You could go there at any lunch, break, or free period and find heads there. Amongst the clouds and rabble, everyone would be trying to shot their little bits and pieces. Shunk, mersh, poxs, sess, grade, stolen phones, bikes, laptops, whatever. If you needed something for a price you let people in that spot know. That was the early stage of my career. Mel and I were still selling mainly green. Mel's older cousin Brown was our main supplier. He recently made a link in Dam that was bringing in some potent skunk. The skunk was so strong you could smell the buds from our pockets. That's how we met Rabbi.

Rabbi wasn't one of our usual customers. He usually brought from another Asian dude called Khan. But by chance Khan happened to be A.W.O.L. that day and as they say one man's misfortune is another man's gain. I remember that first morning when Rabbi first strutted up looking for a quarter. I was tired with sleep and heavy bags still around my eyes. I thought to myself *'why's this little rat face inspecting the bags so hard?'* I almost snatched it back out of his hand and sent him on his way. It was a good thing I didn't though cause Rabbi was back by lunch looking another 3 cockles and another eighth by the end of the day. Immediately we took a shine to Rabbi. He was good people, but most of all he networked beautifully amongst the Asian kids in and out of college.

Because Mel and I worked as a team there was rarely a period when one of us wasn't under those stairs and Rabbi brought punters left, right, and centre. He was so good that we'd give him ounces on consign and let him run with it. He began to shot in his local area in Southall and built up a nice base of clientele. Soon he had his own little shottaz stretching out to Harrow and Northolt. There was no stopping Rabbi. As he got larger, the natural progression to stronger drugs was a simple transition for him. So initially we played middlemen getting supplies from Sparks and skimming off the top. We solidified a good working relationship with Rabbi, so he preferred to use us as one of his regular suppliers to begin with. Eventually Rabbi got a direct link to some brothers in Pakistan. He never went into too much detail. The way Rabbi was rollin' now he didn't need us, but he was smart. He never brought all his work from the same supplier in case it got lumbered with some bad gear. The last thing anybody wants is to be stuck with a couple boxes of crap gear (Sparks taught me that, he taught me a lot). So Rabbi always brought a couple oz or a bar or two from us to see what other stuff was out there. It was crazy seeing him blow up and we loved reminding him about who first put him on.

As we entered Southall it was like entering another country. For anybody who has never been to Southall it is like an Asian capital in West London. Everything along the high streets embodies the Asian community and culture. The roads are thriving with Asians in traditional dress and head garments. The shops stock and sell clothes, food, and jewellery all marketed for the Asian community. Posters of blockbuster movies are replaced with those of Bollywood stars. The radios in each shop are tuned to play the vibrant sounds of Punjabi music. The streets are filled with Indian, Bengali, Pakistani, and Bangladeshi people going about their business. You could play a game of spot the black as well as spot the white in Southall.

As we drove through little Bombay as it was sometimes referred to, I looked around. There was one thing that struck me about the community. It was the fact that no matter what anybody argued they were actually a successful community. The majority of shops and stores along the street were Asian owned. Not only were they Asian owned, but also they were designed to cater for the Asian need. The money being spent and reinvested into the shops was Asian money. The employees behind the counters and on shop floors were Asian. In a country that was not their own, the Asian population had established a number of communities and thrived. Their influence on British culture was so great that Vindaloo curries were the favourite dish throughout the land. Most importantly, it was the unity and culture of their communities that empowered them.

Mel pulled up in the car park of the McDonald's. It was opposite a local restaurant Rabbi had once taken us to called TKC. On the other side of the car park a group of Asian boys gathered around a kitted out Ford RS turbo and a Suburu Imperza. A mixture of hip hop and drum and bass blared from their car amps, base tubes, and subwoofers. They seemed to just be loathing about. Mel picked up his phone and called Rabbi.

"Where is he?" I asked when Mel finished.

"He says he's about five, ten minutes away, he ain't gonna be long."

"You should've phoned him before we got here." I searched in the glove compartment for something to listen to. "You know how Rabz likes to take his time."

"For real," Mel fixed the weight of drugs he had under his balls. "I don't wanna be sittin' round too long." He pulled out the parcel and tucked it under his seat.

"You wanna go inside and get something to eat so it's not too bait," I asked.

"Nah, fuck it," Mel scanned the area. "We'll wait here ten minutes."

We sat in silence watching the guys by the car messing around. One of them threw a gherkin at the another and ended up dropping his burger as he ran away.

"So, G," Mel turned to me. "Have you been thinking about what I said the other day?"

"What's that?" I watched the Asian boys play fighting.

"You know what I'm talkin' 'bout." Mel rolled his eyes hoping he wouldn't have to say. "Have you thought about what Sparks said and that?"

"Nah, man," I turned to look at the car park entrance. "I ain't getting involved in no shit, no more. Especially not with Sparks anyway."

"Ah c'mon, G." Mel plea. "You know Sparks done said to tell you he's sorry and shit. You know for Sparks that's a big thing. He wants you back on board."

"No way." I said adamantly "I ain't feeling him. He's the type of brer that looks out for himself and only himself. Fuck Sparks, he's a snake."

"Come man he ain't no snake," Mel pretended he didn't know better. "He's a hot head, yeah, but he's not a snake. Look he's gonna give us more responsibilities, more dough if you come back on board."

"No way," I shook my head. "Trust me, Mel, I'm not getting involved with that brer and you should 'llow him to. I don't care what he says, he can't be trusted. Nah that's me finished."

"Come on, blood think about it."

"Nah there's nothing to think about." I waved a dismissive hand. "Forget about it."

"Rah, listen to you, with all dat forget about it shit," Mel joked. "Who you think are Tony Soprano?"

"Fuck Tony Soprano," I laughed. "Dem boys only run Jersey. They can't even talk to the Corleones."

"Yeah, you keep going on like Corleone, and see if you don't get shot up like Sonny."

Mel and I both started laughing. It was good to be rollin' again even if it was for a little while.

"Oi, G!" Mel noticed two Asian girls leaving the McDonalds. "Look at the breast on that Punjab, rudeboy."

The girl was about 5'7 with long black hair. She wore denim blue jeans and a dark tan leather jacket that matched her shoes. The low cut body top stretched tightly across her bosom, advertising her cleavage and Dolce & Gabbana.

"Oi, she's heavy." Mel licked his lips. "Oi, G, I gotta move that up."

"You ain't getting thru on no punjab rudeboy, trust me on that one." I laughed.

"Why not?"

"Nah man," I tried to persuade Mel. "Dem girls there don't get down like that. Dem Asian gal don't go out with blackheads. Their family would kill them. String dem up. It's a disgrace on their family to go out with black man."

"Shut up, man! Don't be stupid."

"Ask Rabbi when he gets here, if you don't believe me. Some of dem Indian bodz are the biggest racists, even to their own kind."

"So, I don't care." Mel ignored me. "I ain't trying to fuck her family. I'm trying to fuck her. It's all about the forbidden fruit nowadays my brudder and she looks ripe."

Before I knew it Mel pulled up the blue beamer right in front of the girls cutting off their route of exit. Winding down the window he introduced himself. "Excuse me miss, sorry to bother you. My name is Melrick and yours is?"

The girl looked at Mel then at her friend. She seemed slightly hesitant at first then smiled after an encouraging nudge from her friend.

"Tasha. My name's Tasha."

"Hello Tasha." Mel grinned. "I was just wondering if you could spare a moment to settle a little dispute between me and my friend."

"Go on," the girl said.

"You see I noticed you from over there," Mel pointed to the McDonalds. "And was instantly attracted to you. I told my friend that I would like to acquire your number so I may court such a beautiful young lady. He then told me it would never happen because Asian girls don't mix wid black guys."

"No, I never said that," I protested.

"Shut up man," Mel tried showing off. "That's what he said, but I said you looked way too beautiful and intelligent for that"

Tasha looked at Mel. "Are you serious?"

"About what?" Mel licked his lip. "The Asian and the Black ting or about me being attracted to a beautiful and intelligent looking woman."

Tasha laughed. "You really think you're a player innit?"

"I try." Mel grinned. He thought he was in there. "What's your friend's name? Tell her to come round the other side and talk to my friend, he's shy."

The friend came round to my side and introduced herself as Reetu. She was a slim petite girl with a pretty face, long hair and dove eyes. She had a cute smile.

"So what d'you say 'bout that number?" Mel asked.

"Well, Melrick." Tasha leaned forward. I couldn't help stealing a look at her chest and comparing it with Reetu's. "First of all, if I didn't give my number to you, it wouldn't be because you're black. It would be because I wasn't attracted to you. And secondly, I don't give my number out to strange boys in flash cars."

"Okay" Mel nodded his head. "What if I gave you my number would you phone it?"

"Yeah, I might." Tasha flirted.

Mel reached into the glove compartment and retrieved a pen. Dipping into his pocket he pulled out a brown note from a roll of money and began writing on it.

"Sorry Tasha," He smiled handing her the ten pound with his number on. "I didn't have anything else to write on. But hear what, why don't you take that and call me. You can buy me a drink sometime."

Tasha grinned. As we spoke to the girls I gave Mel a sly punch noticing the gang of Asian boys coming over. They slowly surrounded the car.

"Yo, Tash, what's going on here?" One of the boys shouted.

He was about 6ft with a slim build, gelled hair, and a thin goatee beard. His eyes were sunk into his head which gave him a hawk like appearance against his narrow nose. His thick eyebrows seemed to join together on his face like a caterpillar, creating a frown. His presence appeared to irritate Tasha.

"Nothing. Why don't you mind your own business?"

"What if I decided to make it my business?" The guy said grabbing Tasha's arm. "Who's your little friend?" He motioned to Mel and I.

"Why you don't just ask me the question, bredrin?" Mel said getting out of the car. "And let go of the girl while your doing it."

The guy eyed Mel sizing him up. "What?" he snarled.

"You heard me." Mel replied.

The guy let go of Tasha and Reetu quickly pulled her out the way. Seeing the gang was ready to pounce at any moment. I reached down into the door compartment and picked up Mel's metal cosh. I climbed out the car and swung the cosh in the general direction. "Move away from the fucking car!" I shouted.

They were slow to react, but took one step back. They were waiting for the first guys lead. He glanced at me then locked eyes with Mel smiling. I didn't like the situation at all. We were two black boys outnumbered 3 to 1 in the middle of Southall, with a car filled with heroin. We were supposed to be blending and trouble was something we should've been avoiding. Instead, Mel squared up to the Asian boy.

"What, have we got a problem here?"

"Yeah, we got a problem." The boy spat on the ground. "We don't like your type coming in our manner and talking to our girls. This ain't Stonebridge or Brixton you know rudeboy." He finished talking in a mock West Indian accent for the benefit of his entourage. Moronically they began cackling like a bunch of hyenas.

Mel stood his ground. "Whatever, Rupesh, Prattesh or whatever your name is. This ain't Bradford or Burnley either. I'll knock your fuckin' teeth out if you talk to me like that again."

"I'd like to see you try," The boy held his hands wide offering Mel out. "You fucking blackie!"

"What!" Mel lunged forward.

Immediately Tasha jumped in front of Mel trying to hold him back. "Leave it Melrick. He's not worth it."

The boy began to call Mel out as the crowd became restless. As they pushed forward I swung the cosh, keeping a distance between. I knew I wouldn't be able to hold them off for much longer.

"What, come on then! Come on then!" The tall boy started shouting as another tried a lunging kick.

Just then a light metallic purple Mercedes CLK Kompressor, roared through into the middle of the crowd. The small Asian driver wearing Armani sunglasses jumped out of the car. The mob quieted down as he looked at us and walked over to the tall boy.

"Yo, Jinesh what's going on here?" he asked.

"Yo man, what's good my nigga." Jinesh greeted the man. "These nig-nogz came down here and started troubling the gal dem."

The driver looked at us scrutinising the cosh in my hand. He looked vex. Stepping towards Jinesh, he drew back his hand and slapped Jinesh across the face. The crowd was shocked. The smack was awesome. Jinesh held his face bamboozled. The man started cursing in broken Asian and English.

"Do they look like they're harassing those girls?" He grabbed hold of Jinesh by the scruff of the neck and slapped him again "You fucking idiot! Dese are my people, don't ever let me catch you disrespecting my people! Fucking say sorry right now!"

Holding the side of his face Jinesh looked down at the floor. There was a big red handprint slapped across his mug. He felt like a fool.

"Sorry," he mumbled. "I didn't know you was Rabbi's friends."

"So you should be, you little pussy." Mel spat at Jinesh. I pulled him away and touched fists with Rabbi.

"What's gwanin, Rabz?"

"I'm cool," Rabbi hugged Mel and I smiling.

He turned to the rest of the Asian boys. "Yo all of you look at these two brudders right here. If I ever catch any of you messin' with them, you're in trouble. Do you understand?"

There was a few disgruntled yeses and nods to their disappoint.

"Okay then, well get lost! Rabbi ordered the gang off the car park.

Laughing, I greeted him properly "I'm glad you come when you did, man. What's happening man?"

"I'm cool," Rabbi smiled "I just brought another house down North Harrow this time."

"What, that must be three houses now?"

"Nah, two houses and a maisonette." Rabbi grinned.

Relaxing, I handed the cosh to Mel. He was still fuming as Tasha tried to calm him down.

"Yo, Mel," Rabbi called "Come lets get something to eat. Ask the girls if they want to come."

"Yeah hold on one minute." Mel said playing with the cosh in his hand.

He didn't say anything, but I could tell from his face he was going to do something stupid. Before we had a chance to stop him he was already on his heels after Jinesh,

"Yo, yo, Jinesh hol' up bredrin!" he called.

As he ran towards Jinesh, his hand went up. I watched on as one of Jinesh's friends tried to push his friend out the way, but it was too late. Jinesh didn't have a chance. As he turned around, Mel swung the cosh with all his weight in Jinesh's face. There was a cracking noise of bone as Jinesh fell to the floor screaming. Mel stood over him and kicked him in the face as the other Asian boys came running.

"Don't you ever call me a nigger again, you pussy!"

"What the fuck?" One of the boys said pushing Mel out the way.

Short and fat with a ponytail and goatee he looked at Rabbi with disappointment. "Rabbi, this ain't right, man." he ordered the others to help Jinesh to the car.

"Well what you want me to do?" Rabbi smirked "He shouldn't of called da man a nigger."

"Yeah, but there's no need for that." The man pointed to Jinesh. He was all limp and his face was pouring with blood. "They're suppose to be your people. Fuckin' control them."

"Control who?" Mel tried to push past me and Tasha. "Man ain't no fuckin dog."

"Okay, okay," Rabbi said stepping in. "Cool I'll sort it, AJ. Take Jinesh to the hospital and phone me later, we'll speak."

Rabbi put his arm round Mel pulling him away. "You're a fucking mad man, you. Gil call the girls and let's go get something to eat."

That incident remains vivid in my mind for two reasons. The first was that cracking sound of Jinesh's cheekbone made caving in. Watching Mel deliver that blow I thought it might have been uncalled for, but still who am I to judge. The second reason was because of the level and structure of unity amongst the Southall community I witnessed.

Regardless of what anybody has to say about the Asian community in Britain. Those who speak out against their arranged marriages, religions, and their caste system; no one can deny the cultural frameworks they do have in place are effective.

The Asians in Britain have installed at home and abroad a defined social framework of long established, traditions, customs, strong family ties, history, and religions they use to fall back upon time and time again. This cultural safety net, if you wish to call it, exists throughout their community and is used to direct those inside. In many instances it is the same framework or community that is used to deter or punish people. You may often hear an Asian person say, 'Oh that's against my religion,' or 'my family wouldn't like that.'

This act demonstrates the individual's responsibility to uphold their cultural framework. The consequences of not doing so may result in, scolding from the family or being frowned upon by the community.

Because of the slavery factor, the same evolution of our own black or original African customs was either destroyed or tampered with. Our history was removed and rewritten, customs banned forbidden and divided, and our religions replaced. Our safety net had been sabotaged with holes. It is now up to us to restore the correct cultural framework in all of our Black communities.

Now my praise doesn't only fall on the Asians, I praise oriental, Italians, the Irish, Jews, and Muslims. I even praise the customs that we do have in the Black community. But most of all, I applaud those who stand to protect and maintain them, which brings me to my second point. Culturalism.

At this point it is imperative that I state from early that I'm not a racist. Nor am I a segregationist. Yet what I've learned from the journey is, that one has to preserve the needs of his culture or nation. Whether Jinesh realised it or not, he was sending out a clear message, or a warning to ward off people. His message was -This is our race, our nation, and our culture and I will do what I feel is right to protect it.

Now imagine you had a house and a happy family life governed by your rules. Would you allow a person to come in and disturb this household? Would you allow them to influence what happened in that household or direct your children into choices you opposed? Would you allow that person to move in his own family and say "lets share this household?" Would you let them also make decisions that affect your household? No you wouldn't. You would fight as much as possible to keep them out. You might even advise your children not to mix with these people.

This is what many of the other races do. They try to guard their cultural framework and ward off any undesirables. But in the context of the world and society things do not work like that. Especially if you have stolen a person, or invited that said person to stay. Your home is now their home. To harbour the above attitude and belief, now makes you a racist, not a nationalist.

All these so called white supremacist and segregational groups like the British Nationalist party, the National front, Combat 18 and the Klu Klux Klan are not nationalist they're racists or extreme culturalists. They don't wish to promote or preserve their nation because their nation (like it or not) consists of ethnic groups. A bona-fide nationalist preserves his nation by, accepting each element of its nation and providing the sufficient framework to sustain patriotism to that nation. Britain is now a diverse country with many multi-cultures. The nation no longer mirrors the 1950's and the British Nationalist should be as much a Black or Asian man as a White man.

How Jinesh and I differ in thinking, is that Jinesh was being a racist or extreme culturalist, because he chose to completely exclude the mingling of races to protect his culture. Culturalism is the latest disguise used to hide racism. Here is Jinesh like the racist he wishes to protect his culture by excluding others from it. He believes his culture is superior, or maybe it will be eroded by outside influences. How should us as a Black community respond to this type of attitude? Simple, leave them.

The reason why other cultures and races find us undesirable is because they look at our culture and see nothing they desire. Yet as soon as we produce something that interests them, like a music or a style of dress, what do they do? They exploit it. They want to make it apart of their culture. The undesirable is now desirable.

So once again I want you to imagine the house. This time, imagine it is a house of culture on a street and each race has its own house of culture. The street may represent your country or the larger world. The White House would be the biggest on the street with the Black house being the smallest. Instead of standing at the gates of the White House and other households begging to come in, we must reconstruct the cultural foundation of our own household. If every individual and their actions were a brick, how would our house look? Painted with negative images of black on black violence, sexual promiscuity, lack of unity, gun crime, broken families, absent fathers and poor academic achievements? I ask again, how would our house look?

Perhaps it may look derelict, and in need of restoration. Conceivably the house may even be condemned unfit. If you lived in one of the other households on the street, would you let your children play in a condemned house? Or would you even want it on your street or in neighbourhood?

The problem we have here, is that some Black people are so busy trying to be accepted by other races and cultures that we neglect our own. We need to concentrate on building businesses to provide materials for our household. We need to politically furnish our household, so the other households will learn to respect what we have built. Once we have achieved what is necessary, the other households will not fear the influence we bring. They will invite us as respected guests to their homes and seek our children to play with theirs. The Buppies would not run off trying to be something there not. Lead by The Talented Tenth, The Lynch slaves will be aware of their ignorance and their effects on the community.

Unknown to me at the time, but the incident in Southall became another pivotal event. It re-energised my thirst for knowledge, and reasoning had broken the floodgates of the reservoir of my conscious thoughts. Any battle between consciousness and greed had concluded with the obvious victor. Upon The Journey I had now found a cart and a mule to travel on. Although it wasn't a horse and carriage or a V6 engine with a 280- brake horsepower, it was transport. Culturalism would be the Vehicle that would transport the Slave and his companions along our journey. The speed in which we travelled depended upon the strength of our unity and will to succeed. I mentally pictured myself finding this abandoned mule and cart. Climbing aboard the cart, I picked up the leather reins and held them in my hands. Engraved on each rein read the name of many organisations and black parties, the first name painted in gold was ***Marcus Mosiah Garvey.***

*

Ivan smiled turning the page. King was right. Gil hadn't changed, he was still there shottin' bits here and there with his bredrin to get by. Maybe that was why Ivan had grown to like the author. He did what he needed to get by, and dropped a few jewels of knowledge at the same time. Ivan couldn't fault Gil for that. Like King, he labelled Gil a thorough nigga.

***

CHAPTER: 19

Ivan stood outside his cell waiting for Dorian to find his wash kit. As King approached, he stared over the tier at Bain and his gang, congregating round the pool table. Bain looked up and smiled trying to provoke him. He mouthed the words "Soon, boy soon."

Ivan held his hands out wide and mouthed back "When ever you're ready."

He knew eventually Bain would make his move, he just wanted to know when. They'd been gearing up for a fight ever since they first bucked heads in reception. The score now lay at one nil to Ivan after their last confrontation and he expected some sort of ambush at some stage. He wasn't stupid. He knew Bain's ego would force him to retaliate so Ivan evaluated with King and Dorian all the opportunities Bain had to attack. Because Bain was Church of England and Ivan a Muslim it wouldn't be on the way to church or mosque. Because Bain worked in the reception area and Ivan went to education, it wouldn't be on the way to work neither. There would only be three more places Bain could strike. One was the waiting room before visits. Ivan was going to rule that out, because he wasn't expecting anymore, but King warned that would be foolish. The second area was the gym, but Dorian reckoned there would always be enough people around to make sure it was a one-on-one. The only other place Bain could choose was on the Houseblock, most likely the showers or Hot Plate. For this reason King forbade Ivan from going to the shower area without him and Dorian. They each took turns to shower while the other two guarded.

By the end of association, Ivan was wound up after spending all evening trading looks with Bain. He was almost happy to return to his cell and hear the door slam. Frustrated, Ivan jumped on his bed and punched the pillow.

"What's wrong with you?" Dorian said turning on the radio. "You letting my man wind you up?"

"I can't help it," Ivan fumed. "Some days that fassie gets to me, fam. I just wanna knock him out."

"I know," Dorian grinned. Then he frowned thinking. "But do you really think you can take him again, though?"

"Course!" Ivan sat up. "I'll spark him standard. No long ting."

"I don't know, Terror?" Dorian teased. "Andy's kinda big, and the first time you got a lucky punch in."

"What!" Ivan said in disbelief. "Blood, I'd weigh him anyday."

"Boy, I'm not sure about that."

Ivan looked at Dorian smiling "D, I don't know why you're trying to wind me up, but don't make me jump off this bed and beat you up."

"Shut up you fool!" Dorian kissed his teeth. He picked up *'Journey of A Slave'* and pelted it at Ivan. "Go and read your book. You're not ready for me yet."

Ivan caught the book laughing, "Oi, D, you know you're lucky you're my boy, cuzzy. Otherwise I woulda hadta hurt you." He smiled making a crease in his page.

BLUEPRINTS & PROTOTYPES *Journey Of A Slave*

The rain beat down on our face as we walked the full extent of the North End Road. We passed through the busy market and up past the frontline on the West Kensington Estate. Outside the Grapevine off license stood the usual suspects. Huddling under the stairs and by the bus stop they gathered idly about discussing everything and nothing. It seemed like some of the faces had spent their whole life outside that blasted shop and were still there. They'd been stopped, searched, arrested, charged, tried, jailed, released, and were still in the same spot.

I remembered back in the day, when the line had been alive with the authentic activities of a frontline. The Older crew would set up shop and the cats would flock to them like disciples to the messiah. Girls in short skirts and tight tops would roll past in the summer, displaying what they had to offer to the young hustlers out there doing their thing. It was a different time. Nobody worried about Jakes and surveillance cameras. Richie Sniper ran around terrorising everyone in sight with permission from the older man. Bully and his gang of drunks staggered about getting high and trying to chase us youngaz for any goods we had. We would park stolen mopeds round the back of the Chesesemen Terrace and just chill waiting for our opportunity to run the frontline.

Yet things had changed now. The cameras on top of the Lickey House tower block looked down on the line like the eye of Big Brother, while the cameras on Desborough House covered the back of the estate and Thaxton Road. No one stood outside the Grapevine hustling anymore. The real hustlers had deserted the frontline. It was a barren corpse of past glory and nostalgia. Only the drunks, bums and the young teenagers with no youth clubs stood out there now. Occasionally in summer you may see a small gathering, but never business and never for too long. The notorious West Ken frontline was dead.

As the cold wind blew across the grey wet skies, we forged on in the rain. I felt the weight of the book tucked safely inside my pocket. It was a present from Alicia. At first I refused to open it. Gift wrapped neatly, the parcel lay on the top of my bedside cabinet for weeks. My mother, Andrea, and Mel had all pestered me to open it.

"What's in that present?"

"Why don't you open it?"

I had often picked it up and played with it. Contemplating to myself what it was and what it meant. I hadn't spoken to Alicia since that night and I had no intention of doing so. Why she sent me a gift was no concern of mine. Finally it was Mel's irritating persistence that forced me to open the present.

"What's wrong with you?" He whined. "Hurry up and open that present man, you got it there jus' catchin' dust. Open it up"

"What for?" I said tidying my collection of Source Magazines. "It's not hurting no one where it is. Leave it."

"It's not going to hurt no one if you open it." Mel moaned dusting off the present. "I swear you're going on like some my yoot. Com'man tell me the truth. Something happened between you and Alicia, innit?"

"No." I scowled. "Why?"

"You tell me. Why's she givin' me presents to give to you, and why you so shook to open them that you got to leave it sittin' here for months?"

"It ain't months."

"Months, weeks, what's the difference? You're still shook to open it."

"I ain't shook to open it. What's there to be shook about?"

"Well open the present then," Mel said tossing the gift over.

I sat up on my bed and held the parcel. Pausing, I caressed the neatly wrapped object looking for the best way to open it without completely shredding the paper.

"Open the present nah man. Wharm to you?" Mel hurried me.

Tearing the paper, I looked at the black and tan cover of the book.

"It's a book," Mel said in disappointment.

"Durr," I said mocking him. "What, couldn't you tell that?"

"Obviously," Mel lied. "What is it?"

It was *'The Nigger Factory'* by Gil Scott Heron. The book I'd first troubled at Alicia's flat. I guessed she'd sent it as a reminder of that night. I flicked through the pages from the back of the book until I got to the front. Hand written in blue biro was a message from Alicia. I shut the book quickly. Paranoid of Mel's watchful eye, I placed the book on the bedside cabinet and moved away before he noticed. I picked up my signing on book.

"Oi, what you on, bruv? Follow me to the jobcentre."

"Yeah, we'll go in a minute." Mel said grabbing the book off the bedside cabinet.

"Put that down." I tried to snatch the book back. He dived over my bed and rolled onto the other side.

"Rah, can't I see the book, blood?" he darted out of reach. "What you hiding?"

"Nothing!" I snapped. "Jus put the book down."

"Rah, hold on!" Mel smirked. "There's a message in here, bro."

"Don't read that," I managed to snatch the book out of his hand. "That's private! What's your problem you idiot? Why don't you grow up and stop acting like a fool. You get on my nerves sometimes."

I wasn't in the playing mood. Mel could tell he'd hit a touchy subject. He didn't retaliate or cuss back as usual. He casually stroked his chin then calmly said.

"Cool, I hear that, bruv. You're right. Sometimes I do act like a fool. It's your private business, I should respect that." He held his hands up. "That's my bad, I won't do it again."

"Safe," I said knowing that was the closest Mel and I went to doing apologies.

"Cool, but now I know something happened with you and Alicia." He grinned. "I ain't gonna tease you or say nothing. Like you said it's time to start acting my age, but I'm telling you. You need to stop lying! You banged Alicia."

"I never banged Alicia, she's a crack head."

"Correction, bruv, she's a former crackhead." He said smugly. "And that don't mean shit. We know plenty people that smoke undercover. Why don't you just admit it man. You banged her."

"No."

"Why not? I would. Alicia's looking kinda live nowadays."

"Look, man," I stopped Mel pestering me. "I never banged Alicia. If I did I would've told you."

"No you wouldn't you liar. You're a sneaky bastard. What happened?"

"Nothing, never happened?" I smiled.

"So what you smiling for? I wanna know what you're hiding in that book."

"Okay, okay, okay," I walked over to my hi-fi and put on some music. "If I let you read the message will you shut up?"

"Yeah, show me the message and I won't ask nothin'. My mouth will be sealed." Mel pulled a zip across his mouth.

I flung the book over to him. Looking out of my curtains I spied two kids kicking ball down stairs as Mel read the message out loud.

'Dear Gil, this is for he who dares to use his eyes and follows in the footsteps of the Brave. For he who knows that he walks the same street, and in the same shoes as the Great. To he who believes that he can open the mind and heart of his Race. To he who will finally open his eyes and see, his Destiny. To he may I open his beautiful eyes in a perfect moment of Clarity only so that he may see what I see,

with all my love Alicia.

"Emm, mmmm. What's that all about, bruv?" Mel said getting excited.

"I don't know, she's crazy." I took the book from Mel so I could read the message myself. "She's smoked to much yeng."

"Later, I'm telling you. You banged Alicia! I don't care what you say, there's something blatantly gwanin between you lot. Some different ghetto romance."

"Shut up man and stop being stupid."

"Wooooo!" Mel began prancing around the room pretending to rabbit fuck every piece of furniture in sight. "I done know, G, I done know. You banged it, you banged it, you banged it and didn't even show meeeee!"

Mel was acting so dumb, that I couldn't help laughing. "Hold on!" He stopped looking at the book again. "There's a P.S. at the bottom. Look, it says walk to this address."

Peering at the address, I looked at Mel "That's at the top of North End Road."

"Come we go then." Mel said throwing his car keys in the air and catching them.

"What about the jobcentre?" I need to sign on."

"Fuck the Jobcentre." Mel said "I'll speak to D's mum when we get dere, she'll sort you out."

Half an hour later as we walked to the address, Mel's eagerness had turned into a mumbling whinge. "I don't know why we got to walk in this rain. I got a perfectly good car. It don't make no sense to me."

Lately nothing I did made sense to Mel. He cursed and complained frequently, "You need to fix up blood, you got man walking in the rain for some..."

"For some what?" I said cutting him off sharply. "This was your stupid idea."

"Easy, calm down,' Mel checked himself "What you getting all touchy, touchy for. All I was going to say is there's no need for us to walk."

"Look, Mel," I explained. "The message said to walk so I'm walkin'. If you don't like it, you can dus', no big ting."

As we passed the frontline, Bully's doltish frame called from the doorway of the Grapevine. "Yo M's, G, wha gwanin? Any work about?"

Huffing, I ignored Mel signalling over to the gorilla like simpleton to follow behind.

"Easy, Mel what's happenin'?" Bully greeted Mel with his fist out.

"Nothin much," Mel replied. "What's good?"

"You tell me, you know I had court earlier today innit. They're trying to do me for aggravated."

Disinterested in Bully's bull, as we called it I walked ahead. Looking over my shoulder I noticed a black Mercedes E-class trailing behind us. Both Bully and Mel had noticed it too, as they seemed to delay their transaction. The car drove about 12 ft in front of me and pulled up. My thought was beef and I slowed my pace to a cautious walk. As the window wound down a familiar voice shout "Wha'am Zulu!"

There was only one person who called me Zulu - my dad.

Callum 'Cally G' Gates, or Callous Cal, as my granny use to call him, was the original part time parent; there when he wanted something, there when he needed something, missing any other time. I looked at the car thinking *where'd he get that?* Then I realized I didn't care. He'd probably borrowed it from a friend, or taken it from the latest consort that put him up. Either way, I figured he wouldn't have it for too long.

I leaned down to say hello and noticed the tall dark middle aged man sitting on the passenger side. In the driver's seat my father grinned expecting me to be impressed with the luxury car. "What's happenin' son?"

"Nothin'," I shrugged my shoulders. "I'm cool."

"You remember your Uncle Alfie, innit son." My dad gestured to the man.

"Yeah, course," I said nodding to Alfie. "He brought me my first pair of football boots."

The man looked over me in amazement, then at my father. "Cally, no. That's not Zulu is it?"

"Yeah, man."

"The same little Zulu that used to run about the house mashin up everyting in sight?"

"Yes man ai de same Zulu nah, Alfie." My dad said changing his voice into a Jamaican accent.

"Cally, he looks just like you." Uncle Alfie smiled back at me. "You look just like your dad you know, Gil. How's your mum and Andrea?"

"They're fine. Andrea's in medical school now."

"Yeah!" Alfie said genuinely surprise. "So she's gonna be a doctor den. Gwan."

"Yo trust me Alfie!" My dad started boasting. "I and I pickney dem have plenty brains I-drin. Dem get that from me. Jah know me na lie."

Watching my father brag I thought to myself, *I don't ever want to be like that.* He never provided, never helped and never supported his children. Yet he was always ready to claim sole responsibility for my sister's achievements (mine were never plentiful). He epitomised the worst of the Lynch slaves. He would never achieve anything in his life. When he died he would leave nothing behind. No property, no empire, no knowledge, no legacy, nothing just an old headstone. If there were a prototype for the Lynch slave it was surely he. Wearing a gold chaps bracelet, chain and sovereign rings, in his late forties, my father was still up to the same stupid scams and hustles he'd been on in his twenties. Selling a little weed, benefit fraud, gambling, and anything else that wasn't classified as hard work. It was this man who was meant to be my original companion on the *Journey*, a person responsible for supplying me with guidance along the way. Embarrassed, I reckoned I'd long surpassed any knowledge he had to supply.

"What's happenin', Cally?" Mel said running up to the Car.

"Yo what's happenin, star? You cool? My dad reached across Alfie to touch fists with Mel. "Where the car dere?"

"Err, I left it at home. We're only going down the road."

"Wha'am you and Zulu want a lift?"

"No we're safe, dad," I stopped Mel from answering.

"Okay, son." My dad said not caring any unless. "Me and your Uncle gonna go on some runnings and ting, yeah. You cool? You need some money?"

My dad knew I didn't need money. He just wanted to look good in front of Alfie.

"Nah, I'm cool, dad. It was nice to see you again Uncle Alfie." I shaked Aflie's hand.

"Yes, yes, Gil," he smiled warmly. "You walk safe now and be careful."

"What you talking about Alfie?" My dad roared. "That's my Zulu warrior yah'nah. I teach 'im everyting 'im know. Watch he's gonna follow in my footsteps. A warrior that Alfie, remember me tell you that seen." My dad turned to me. "Listen Zu-Zu, I'm gonna call you later okay."

"Yeah. I'll speak to you later dad."

Later never came. The next time I saw my dad was five months later. The car was gone and he was looking to borrow 30 pounds to put on a horse. A sure bet he assured me, and I assured him, I wanted my money back or he better not come around me again. Sometimes it was better to deal with him that way.

As I watched the black Mercedes pull off into the traffic, I thought to myself - If I had the power to do anything I would eradicate the Lynch slaves and their prototypes from existence. I would re-educate them and place them back as positive members to our society. The dilemma was how. For over a century, leaders and scholars had been fitting pieces to the jigsaw puzzle of equality. Now I wanted to add a piece to the puzzle. With the importance of a corner piece, I wanted to place Culturalism in the puzzle.

Roots of Culturalism

If I begin by defining Culturalism as *'The promotion and preservation of one's culture, through the communal and cultural framework,'* then the basis of Black Culturalism would find its roots deeply embedded in the soil of Black Nationalism and Garveyism. For those who know little about these principles, many say they begin with Marcus Garvey.

After the First World War, there was an era of Global Black awakening and an insurgent wave of Black Nationalism, especially amongst Black soliders who had served their countries. Amongst this time of unrest the philosophies and career of Marcus Garvey had made him the pre-eminent symbol of Black Nationalism. His teachings of Black pride and racial independence caused him to be the predecessor to many black leaders and organisations such as *The Nation of Islam* and *The Black Panther Party*. Malcolm X's own father was murdered for being a devoted follower of Marcus Garvey. So who is Marcus Garvey?

Born in St Ann's Bay Jamaica in 1887 Marcus Mosiah Garvey with his ideas of *'Black is Beautiful'* and *'Back to Africa'* is now remembered as the Black Moses and a champion of our race. In 1911 Garvey moved to England where he attended the Birbeck College. While studying in London, he became involved with other blacks struggling for independence from the British Empire. This period would give the young Garvey a new outlook on Black Nationalism. On returning to Jamaica, he founded the Universal Negro Improvement Association, an organisation dedicated to the uplifting of people from African ancestry.

An adherent believer of self-help, self-reliance and self-determination Garvey toured the United States in 1916 promoting the activities of the UNIA and his message of 'One God! One Aim! One Destiny. On meeting Garvey in 1916, fellow black activist Philip Randolph and founder of *The Brotherhood Of Sleeping Car Porters* described Garvey as **one of the greatest propagandists of his time.** Garvey impressed a number of his peers against the backlash of critics and organised the first U.S. branch of the UNIA a year later and published a newspaper for Blacks called The Negro World.

Unlike DuBois, Garvey was an advocate for segregation. He openly doubted whether the Ruling groups of the United States, European colonies, and British Empire would agree to treat Blacks as equals and Garvey became no stranger to controversy and radical thinking. On a number of occasions Garvey met with the Grand wizard of the Klu Klux Klan about reparation. Writing in The Negro World

"I regard The Klan, the Anglo Saxon clubs and White American societies, as far as the Negro is concerned, as better friends of the race than all other groups of hypocritical whites put together. I like honesty and fair play. You may call me a Klansman if you will, but potentially, every white man is a Klansman as far as the Negro in competition with white socially, economically, and politically is concerned and there is no use lying."

Garvey's open and strong overviews on the black struggle, resonated with Post WWI Africans, West Indians, Black Brits and Americans ready for change. Unhappy over fighting for countries and not having equal rights, Garvey's message was spread worldwide by sailors, migrant labourers and travellers. His message gave a new hope and spirit to black people and his movement based upon a Black global experience, was something fresh, Blacks could relate to. These factors created a diverse following of millions, who adapted his larger framework to fit their own needs. When he intended to tour Africa and the Caribbean in 1923, many nervous colonial governors of Europe labelled him a troublemaker. Joining together, they recommended he be banned from entering their territories. The significance of Garveyism became imperative to the decolonization in Africa and his philosophies can be found in early manifestos of parties such as the African National Congress.

Garveyism and Black Nationalism spread and within time, the UNIA had hundreds of Chapters worldwide. It was a phenomenon that would've had Willie Lynch turning in his grave. At its height, Garvey formed a number of businesses from investments. One of these ventures was The Black Cross Navigation Trading Company.

Maintaining his belief of Europe for the European, Asia for the Asian and Africa for the African, Garvey made a bold move buying two steamships for his Back to Africa program. Unfortunately this would be his downfall. Although the ships made a number of journeys to the motherland, the companies became involved in corruption and fraud. Being a poor businessman Garvey was unaware of the dishonesty and was arrested and charged with fraud. For this reason, Garvey and the UNIA received much criticism from the government and other black Critics. WEB Dubois, who originally opposed Garvey's race segregation, scrutinised his manhandling of business and investments. The U.S. government later deported Garvey back to Jamaica. After his release in September 1929, Garvey founded the People's Political Party in Jamaica, but he never returned to the United States and the heart of his movement struggled without him. Sadly, Marcus Mosiah Garvey died on June 10th 1940 not realising his full dream.

Post Garvey Culturalism.

After Garvey's success and failure, many other organisations have emerged across the globe, each preaching their own version of Black Nationalism. Yet none since Garvey have been as prolific as the Nation of Islam and the Black Panthers.

The Nation of Islam

Much has been written about the Nation of Islam and its history, from the relationship between Elijah Mohammed and Malcolm X, to being dubbed 'The hate that hate produced.' They've had media backlash, from the profile of new converts like Mohammed Ali, the distortion of Islamic beliefs, corruption, assassinations, and conspiracies. However, regardless of their negative media image and the fact they once promoted black segregation in the strongest sense, what has constantly been over shadowed by the N.O.I.'s ongoing politics, is the positive effect they have had on the majority of their converts. Buried abstractly amongst their religious philosophies is a unique template for the equality and the ascent of the Black race. Not to be mocked or overlooked, the N.O.I. have produced a number of valid blueprints for any would-be organisation to consider.

- Similar to other Extreme Culturalists their framework maintains the preservation of their culture through internal moral codes and practices. These moral laws are policed by the Fruit of Islam, dedicated and trained members. Breaking the codes may result in expulsion and suspension for offenders.

- The N.O.I. have many courses for their members on how to act like responsible, respectable and civilised individuals. Both young men and women are taught current events, the importance of strong households, imagery of father figures, business principles and home economics and hygiene. Scheduled every day of the week these activities create a unity and fellowship among students and their community.

- One of the most important factors in the N.O.I. policy is their recruitment regime. The Nation have been under praised for their rehabilitating of criminals and drug abusers. The Nation's successful recruitment regime depends on reforming the once negative character to positive. Using a six-step plan, which includes the education and support of new recruits, the N.O.I. use reformed members as role models to other undesirables. The transformation of Malcolm X is still held as a testimony to the success of such programs. This style of recruitment does two things directly to our community. One: it tackles crime and drugs, and Two: it promotes the efforts of redemption through support and unity within the culture.

- The Nation like the UNIA promoted the idea of Black owned and run business. In each city the Nation of Islam has built mosques and businesses that promote the spending and investing of money into black owned enterprises.

- The Nation of Islam also produces a number of publications and newspapers. *'The Final Call'* and 'Mohammed Speaks' both focus on reporting black issues.

The Black Panther Party

Equally relevant to the struggle is the legacy of the Black Panther Party. Proclaimed in 1968 by the Head of the FBI J. Edgar Hoover, as "the greatest threat to internal security of the U.S." the Black panthers were formed in 1966 Oakland, California, by a group of black students. Headed by Huey P Newton and Bobby Seale, the panthers promoted a radical revolution and a political message of "Power to the People." Born out of oppression and frustration, like the Nation of Islam, the Black Panthers did not tolerate violence against the oppressed. Yet in comparison, they fought for the rights of not only the Black but also poor and oppressed. The Black Panthers with their militant and politically aggressive stance, have become a symbol of the rebellious sixties. The persecution and tragedy of their fallen members by the US government has not been forgotten. Today through studying Culturalism and empowerment, their revolutionary framework is a valuable prototype.

- Like the Nation and the UNIA, the Panthers also held an infrastructure based on rules and a central committee. Violations also conclude in suspension or being expelled.

- The Panthers also developed a series of social programs, which catered to the needs of the Black and poor. Creating over 35 formulas which came to be called Survival Programs. Including free breakfast for kids, schooling and education, senior transport, free bussing to prisons, legal aid and manufacturing and distributing free shoes. These programs provided a model for humane social schemes.

- Because of theses activities, the Panthers' profile was raised in the communities. While the government denounced them as communists the communities saw them as a political vehicle voicing the interests of the people. The Panther recognised the power of the American political machine and the needs and conditions of their communities' motivated organised structure.

- The Panthers produced a fundamental Ten Point Plan similar to the UNIA allowing their framework to be adapted worldwide. Like the Nation of Islam the panthers had headquarters in over 40 states, which created positive imagery of Blacks in the ghettos of America.

- When The U.S. declared war on Vietnam, the panthers (who did not preach segregation) received support not only from the poor youth being drafted, but also the middle class white youth too.

- In 1974 The Black Panther Party achieved Garvey's message of black power determining the destiny of black communities after supporting Glen Wilson's campaign in Oakland and making him the first black Mayor in American history.

Having analysed these blueprints and prototypes, we can now look at which elements would be necessary to create a new Culturalist movement. With huge advancements in civil and human rights we are in a prime position to achieve the socionomic goals, that our predecessor fought so passionately for. Unfortunately, if we do not apply the adequate cultural framework, all our efforts will be in vain. We will constantly miss our opportunities to be on a level peg with the ruling groups. If all our so-called Black leaders and scholars truly want to find a solution to our problem. Maybe they should sit down and study these prototypes to produce the accurate formula.

- If Garvey said, *"every community where the Negro lives should be developed by him in his own section, so that he may control that section or part of the community. He should segregate himself residentially in that community so as to have political power, economic and social power in that community."* Does that not make him a Culturalist?

- If those same sentiments are echoed in the action of the Nation of Islam. Does this not make them Culturalists? If the Black Panther Party produced 35 Survival programs to tackle socionomic problems of their community? Does this not make them Culturalists?

- If the 1944 manifesto of ANC Youth league which Nelson Mandela was a member states: *"Africans must struggle for development, progress and national liberation so as to occupy their rightful and honourable place among nations of the world."* Would Mandela and the ANC not be classed as Culturalists?

- If WEB DuBois said, *"The Negro race, like all races, is going to be saved by its exceptional men."* Shouldn't his Talented Tenth be dubbed Culturalists?

If Culturalism is *"The promotion and preservation of one's culture, through the communal and cultural framework."* Wouldn't all the above comprise some element to produce the needed formula? If Culturalism is applied in some form or another, by the other races (i.e. religion, politics) etc, does our race not desire a structured organisation that administrates the cultural and political matrix of Culturalism?

I looked at the address on the book once more. "This is it"
"What, this," Mel peered around "Why she tell you to come here?"
I had no idea. Alicia's address had led us to a small park just behind the Burn Jones and Avonmore estate.
"Nah it must be somewhere else." Mel ranted "I can't believe Alicia got us out here to come to some stupid park."
As I took in the surroundings, his voice became distant squawks as he flapped his arms about. I blocked out his complaints as the wind whistled in my ears. I was searching for something. My eye panned the scenery. An old bench with green paint peeling off, litter blowing in the wind like the urban tumbleweeds, graffiti on the stone walls where crews had tagged their names, names that testified to the late night bunnin session in the park. Why did Alicia want me to come here? What could she see that I couldn't?
I watched as Mel threw a ball back over the fence of the Avonmore primary school at the request of a little boy. On the far side of the park was the Burn Jones estate and behind me stood the old catering studies block of Hammersmith and West London College. Looking up at the orange brick building I could see my old classroom. Most of my classes were at the Barons Court site. It's the site where most things happened, but every Thursday we had a personnel class in the catering block. The building was usually empty just the catering students downstairs and some performing arts students upstairs. I used to wonder upstairs every so often pretending to look for Kwame. He was always a big mouth, he was probably the one to tell Alicia

that I liked her. I never trusted brers that moved around with too many girls. They usually turn into girlie-mouth brers talking everyone's business.

"Gil what you doing?" Mel shouted. "Come, blood, this is long. Lets go home"

"Wait, man!" I hushed him.

I knew Alicia had a reason for me being here, one that only I would understand. But what was it? I watched Mel as he began to walk out the park.

"This is long bredrin. I'm dussin. You can stand out here in this park if you want."

I didn't answer him. I looked up at my classroom again. I remembered one afternoon I'd seen Alicia outside with some of her dance class. They had been mucking around and practising dance routines. I remembered they'd stopped to read something on the far wall of the back. Then it became clear to me. *Of Course* I thought running to the other side of the park. I used to look at it every Thursday from the window in my class. On the far side of the park on the wall that separated the estate from the park, was a plaque.

"Mel!" I screamed, "Mel! Come! I think I found it!"

Pulling away some overgrown shrubbery, it was still there. The plaque was made from heavy duty iron and painted black with faded gold lettering. Somebody named Kenny West had tagged over it not knowing its value. I ran my fingers along the raised letters.

"Is this it?" Mel asked over my shoulder.

"Yeah, this is it." I smiled. "This is what she wanted me to see."

I stood in amazement. I'd walked through the park so many times and never once read the plaque. I never once realised its significance. I looked at the message in my book it made perfect sense.

For he who dares to use his eyes and follows in the footsteps of the Brave. For he who knows that he walks the same streets, and in the same shoes as the Great.

"Don't you understand?"

"No," Mel shook his head in confusion. "I swear, both you and Alicia are mad. You got your own little thing going on."

"Look man," I grabbed his arm. "Open your eyes, what's wrong with you? What does the plaque say?"

Mel read the plaque aloud. "This park is dedicated to the late Marcus Garvey founder of The Universal Negro Improvement Association who died in Fulham on June 10th 1940."

The expression on his face changed from shallow ignorance to puzzled astonishment.

"I never knew Marcus Garvey lived in Fulham."

"Exactly." I grinned. "Do you understand what she means now? Look." I pointed to her message. "He who knows that he walks the same streets as the great."

"So what she sayin', G. Marcus Garvey used to bop 'round 'ere?"

"Yes."

The light bulb finally went on in Mel's head "Rah, that's deep."

I looked at the plaque again. How did Alicia know I would find it? It was as though she knew me inside out. I wondered why she refused to give up on me? Did she really see something in me that I couldn't? Did she know the destiny which lay ahead? All the time I had been seeking to follow in the footsteps of our great leaders, not knowing that I already walked the same streets. I looked down at the ground around me. I pictured West London in the late 1930s, horses and carts, old red buses, trams and cars, the infamous fog and mist that surround the city and men in bowler hats and black suits. Through it all I could see Marcus Garvey walking upright, sturdy and proud, as his Nubian skin turned heads in amazement and disgust.

"Look at the state of this park though." Mel said. "Is this how they respect Marcus Garvey? There's rubbish everywhere, graffiti, there's not even a statue, just a little plaque, hidden at the back of the park. Furthermore, the bloody park is hidden at the back of nowhere. That's wrong."

He was right, but what were we doing to respect and acknowledge Marcus Garvey's legacy? Together Mel and I tore away some of the heavy shrubbery covering the plaque and vowed to come back and clean the graffiti off. He reckoned Marcus Garvey deserved more of a memorial, but he would have to wait. As the skies began to open again, we left.

The walk home was a lot different than the walk to the park. We talked about being blessed to walk the same streets as one of great black thinkers. We always talked about what it would be like to go to Harlem and walk the same streets as Malcolm. Or go to Egypt and walk the same earth as the pharaohs. Yet here we had our own chance everyday to walk with the spirit of Marcus Garvey. I wondered what he'd think about us selling brown and crack. What would he say to stop us walking down the road of degradation and despair?

At home I sat looking at all the posters I had recently pinned on the wall. Malcolm at the window with the gun; Marcus dark skin, thick moustache and uniform; Dr King glazing towards the sky, Chuck D and Public Enemy; Huey in the straw chair; Pam Grier with the Cleopatra afro and Tupac all eyes on me poster. They were all watching over me waiting. Seeing as they were I decided to put on my "*All eyes on me*" CD. Placing it straight on '*I ain't mad cha*' I pressed the repeat button. Sitting down at my desk I held the pen over the paper and thought about my Journey. As I began to write I thought of the last part of Alicia's message. *To he who believes that he can open the mind and heart of his Race. To he who will finally open his eyes and see his Destiny. To he may I open his beautiful eyes in a perfect moment of Clarity only so that he may see what I see.*

And with those words in mind I began to write the first pages of the book you are now reading. I began with, THE FORMULA...

***

CHAPTER: 20

"Oi, Ivan, are you listenin'?"

Ivan looked up from his book. He hadn't noticed the screws open the door for the last hot water run. Two inmates stood with the large steel urn guarded by an officer, while Dorian filled up his mug and flask. "Where's your flask?"

"In there," Ivan pointed to cupboard.

Quickly Dorian retrieved the flask before the screw had time to remind him it was suppose to be one full flask per cell. Dorian grinned as the officer closed the door. Grabbing a tea bag he dashed it into his mug.

"Oi, Terror, you want tea or coffee?"

"Huh?" Ivan grunted, still trying to concentrate on his book. "I'll have tea."

Dorian shook his head knowing that the tea was only going to go cold. He sat down and switched on the radio informing Ivan his tea was ready.

"Yeah, yeah, bless," Ivan said fully engrossed in his book...

THE FORMULA

The lone man with a vision is a rebel, but a hundred men with the same vision begin a revolution. This formula is written in honour of the revolutionaries of the Past, Present, and Future, and for the ideology of Culturalism.

A) This revolutionary movement or organisation will need a clear and defined aim. *To achieve through the science of Culturalism: the local, national, and global restoration of racial determination, unity, and independence amongst people of African and Pan African descent.*

B) The Movement should be one of a secular nature. This means *The Movement* must be free of any religious leadership or motivation for two valid reasons. The first: the movement's aim is to create inclusion. Any structure based around religion may alienate or exclude core target groups. The second reason, the movement's basic framework will need to be adapted to various groups dependent on demographics. This means that the same framework may be applied regardless of religion or social trends with the same effects.

C) ***The Movement*** will need to be divided into three main working bodies. These bodies should cover the following divisions.
- Economics & Business Division
- Culture & Education Division
- Politics & Current Affairs

It will be the three bodies' responsibilities to address the needs of their communities.

D) The activities and policies of ***The Movement*** should become likened to that of an institute of Black Culturalism and Empowerment. Throughout this institute there should be a set of fundamental principles established. These principles should act like guidelines with the objective of creating strength and character amongst members and recipients.

Role of the Politics & Current Affairs Division
I) At The forefront of ***The Movement*** should be those we call the True Talented Tenth. The Talented Tenth ought to use their success to pioneer and (not manipulate) the ideology of ***The Movement.*** With the blueprint of the Panthers in mind the movement will need to become the political voice of its members and their community. The political division should always seek to inform members of their voting right and its power. In countries where blacks are minorities, the party should look to act as a political watchdog. Whether we are a minority group or not Blacks, pay taxes as well. This entitles our communities to be supplied with the resources and facilities we deserve.

II) ***The Movement*** will need to be one with a visibly strong presence in the public eye. This doesn't necessarily mean in the media eye, but in the eye of the community. It should be in ***The Movement's*** policy to create positive role models that outweigh negative influences. By the simple wearing of an armband, pin, button, or badge, a member can identify their association. This will also give the public an idea of support and growth of the movement. When you think of other movements you can immediately recognise them by some symbol or uniform. Communist use the colour red, The Nation of Islam red bow ties and black suits, the Jews incorporate the Star of David, Christians the cross, and The Black Panthers their black berets. Even the

Nazi had the Swastika. The correct Imagery will become a large part of *The Movement's* branding.

III) The Movement will not be a Black separatist group. It should not seek reparation from white governments. Many members will have no wish to leave the countries that they have been brought up in. These countries are as much our homes as anyone else. Blacks have invested in these countries wealth and economies whether through slavery, apartheid, or slave labour. *The Movement* should seek subsidiaries from governments and corporate companies that have been proven to have exploited Blacks in the past. These subsidiaries will pay for scholarships, education and funding of cultural centres and enterprises. The subsidiaries should not be accepted under conditions where the governments or companies have any influence over policies and structure of *The Movement*.

Role of the Culture & Education Division

I) The Movement should have chapters or centres in each community they represent. Like the UNIA, N.O.I. and Panthers these centres should become a focal point to the community. The centre should aim to re-establish the idea of a whole village bringing up a child. In this aspect the centre will supply activities for both adults and children. It will allow adults to socialise while youth attend activities and courses. The centre will promote a sense of unity and community spirit between the old and the young. Facilities available should include recreational, educational programs, restaurants, lectures, and business seminars. These centres objective will be to promote the culture amongst the community. Although centres should be integrated, they must be orientated towards supplying black cultural food, music, education, entertainment, and awareness.

II) The Movement will need to provide youth incentives. These incentives will take place at the centres and will aim to remove the youth from the negative influence of the streets. The movement will need to understand which incentives will attract the youth. To accomplish this, the movement should have a council or committee that has junior members to represent the needs of the youth.

III) The Movement will need to present a number of social programs to re educate the community, like those of the Nation of Islam and the Panthers.

They should be designed to create better practices in culture, studies, family life, and business. Within these programs should be a Sponsorship and Mentor scheme for prisoners. This program should aim to re educate the prisoner. Supported by an outside member, he/she should become involved in tasks to transform their life, and understanding their past downfalls. On return to the community the ex-prisoner should become an exemplary and valuable member of the community. Like the Nation of Islam, the new member will be encouraged to recruit and support other prisoners.

Role of the Business & Economy Division
I) Strong business links and investment in the community will be vital to the success of ***The Movement***. Initially, the movement should construct a consortium from all the members and ethnic owned businesses within each community. Once compiled this Consortium should be used as a form of networking suppliers and buyers, investors with creditors and employers with employees. Members may be given the chance to present business ideas at a conference type situation. The Consortiums primary goal will be to produce a number of Black owned businesses, operating independently in various markets. These businesses would be part of a conglomerate, and carry the brand name or be associated under the company umbrella. Members will be given the chance to invest in building black businesses within their own and other communities. These businesses should be used as vehicles to supply work experience and incentives to the youth and the unemployed.

II) ***The Movement*** should also aim to target any anti social behaviour and unlawful activities within the community, by supplying security and Community support officers trained to deter drug abuse and criminality. The Support group will need to be formed and seek to win private contracts from local government for the supply of adequate security. In cases where the Police forces have a poor relation with ethnic communities, Support Officers will need to act as a mediator between the two. If arrest warrants or a search of premises is issued by police an independent support officer should be present to certify the correct procedures are met by police. If a suspect is detained a Support officer should be notified to inspect the condition of the suspect at the police station.

III) The media will be a great tool in aiding ***The Movement*** if used precisely. ***The Movement*** will need to create its own forms of media to relay information to its members and communities. In the age of technology it is not enough for a movement to have just a newspaper. We should now seek to add a community radio station, website, and a satellite channel where possible. Programming, journalism, reports, features, and articles should all be marketed from a Black perspective. These mediums should be used as new incentives to the youth. It will be important to promote the youth into areas of the media that Blacks haven't always prospered. The experience gained will be valuable when searching for employment.

IV) The Movement will need to implement a number of businesses and housing that act as halfway houses. These halfway houses will supply boarding to newly released convicts. Those selected will be given jobs in the community businesses. The objective of these schemes will be to introduce the ex convict into new working environments, and away from criminal circles. The major problem a reformed person has once released from custody is they are placed back into the areas of society that turned them into criminals. Attached to the housing, employment and the centres, the ex prisoner should now be in the position to abstain from criminal activities. Similar schemes should be developed for drug abusers.

The work suggested in this formula will not be achieved overnight. It will take a number of years planning and implementing. It is for the oppressed to realise that a revolution will never come to you, you must come together to produce the revolution.

*

Absorbed in the book Ivan jumped down from his bunk and took a gulp of his cold tea. He scowled at the brown fluid and knocked it back before returning to his perch. He turned the page.

THE FINAL EQUATION *The Journey of a Slave.*

As the sunrises in the morning and sets at dusk, marking the beginning and end of each day; out amongst the inhabitants of the world somebody will embark on a journey. No matter if they are Black, White, Asian, Oriental, King, Queen, Slave, or Fool, each person will become a traveller on a journey. Through each individual the trails of life are threshed upon the roads of history and society. The footsteps of one, may be covered until they no longer exist. Or the footsteps of one may be followed until they become a trail for millions. As you commence upon your journey you must now decide how you will endeavour to make your mark. What will be the signs and guidelines you follow? Who will be your companions and how will your footsteps guide future generations? Your actions, your decisions your conduct and your life should signify a complete purpose. For those who have riches and wealth, it is not to be squandered or hoarded. For those who are educated, it is not to call yourself wise. For those who live and suffer in oppression, it should not be in vain. For to live is to suffer, but to survive is to find meaning in that suffering. Each gift of life, wealth, wisdom, friendship, love, and experience are for a purpose. Your task over the journey is to discover that purpose.

The journey you take in life and the position you start will always depend on those who have travelled before you. In my case it was the Old slave, the Lynch slaves, Buppies, and Proles that had voyaged before me. Lack of knowledge and mis-education of their heritage and culture has stunted and contained their progress along the journey. It will be the footsteps of the Talented Tenth that will now guide more. And it will be Culturalism that will mark our return. But it shall be my equation that will be a template for any slave to empower himself or herself.

For the companions of the slave, the equation begins with the awakening of True Black Consciousness. With this new knowledge, the slave must now aim to understand the reason and methods of containment. Once the understanding has been met, the slave must then apply the knowledge. This means he or she must not ignore what they have learnt, but seek to apply this knowledge to their way of life. How does a slave do such a thing? By re-educating themselves and the companions around them. These three things must be multiplied by the teaching of the True Talented Tenth. These are the organisations and heroic leaders of the past that have pushed for acceptance and racial elevation. Each of these blueprints will contain elements of social and economic growth and education. Multiply the number of blueprints used by the number of members and unification of a Culturalist movement and a person will have the key to empowerment. Ultimately we must learn that only through knowledge and unity, will the Companions of the Slave reach the promised Kingdoms of Empowerment.

Throughout this book I have illustrated points when I myself have been met at a crossroad. Now I would like you, the reader, to find yourself at a crossroad. I would like for you to decipher the information you have received. Regardless of your race or origin, I want you to ask yourself: are the arguments I have presented valid? Can a whole generation or race be mislead or guided? If so, where does the responsibility lay? Who was more the fool - Adam and Eve who bit the apple or the snake that mislead them?

Most importantly, I would like the Companions of the Slaves to find themselves at a crossroad and realise their purpose. If you can identify the Ruling group, the Lynch slave, the Buppie, and the Proles, where do you fit in? What will you do to leave your footprint in the road of history? How will that effect your own and the next generation?

When I was a child I thought, talked and reasoned as a child. When I became a man I put aside my childish ways. For the first time in my life I will walk the Journey as a man. From the institute of the streets I learnt my trade, homed an instinct to go against society and took risks. Now I challenge all my peers to take a risk. Those in jail, those on the street hustling, those in college, those who say "what can I do I'm only one person." Yeah me too I'm only one person on the journey. Yet a journey of a thousand miles begins with one step. Learn to take risks, learn to take that first step, learn to plant the seeds of education, so the future generation may taste its fruit, because those who try are destined to become Kings and Queens.

To you I leave a final message. Plato once said *'Every King springs from a race of slaves, and every slave has had Kings among his ancestors.'* From my race of slaves I await the coming of the Kings and Queens that will unite us with our ancestral thrones.

From Slave, to Man, from Man to King, upon the journey with open eyes I sing. When the Old Slave smiles and new days bloom, change will come to every man and to every man that is due

The End

***

CHAPTER: 21
COMPANIONS

Finishing his book, Ivan stared at the last page. He lay still for a moment trying to take it all in. Taking a deep breath and breathing out, he held the book to his chest thinking, *fuck!*

Never before had a book given him a sense of who he was and why. It was a moment of clarity and a chance for redemption. Laying on his bunk, Ivan felt like his soul had been drowning in a sea of myriad sins. For years the tides of mis-education, slavery, and containment had carried him deeper and deeper into trouble, but now he'd finally been thrown a lifeline. The work of Gilyan Gates forced Ivan's mind to swim to the surface and breath again. He envisioned his psyche emerging upon the shores of knowledge naked and bare. He felt he had been baptised with his awakening of True Black Consciousness expressed in the book. And all at once everything seemed to be clear. He understood his unexplained feelings of worthlessness, his desire for money, and his disinterest in education. He understood Jade had been right all along. Ivan was a slave, and now he wanted to set himself free.

Sitting up his mind buzzed with ideas. If *'The Journey Of A Slave'* were a religion Ivan could have claimed to have received the calling. And like most converts, Ivan was eager to spread the word. He wanted to share his found knowledge and he wanted to share it with his close friend and cellmate.

Dorian was listening to the Shortie Blitz and Big Ted Hip-Hop show on Kiss fm. Continually fiddling with the dial to get a sharper signal, he sat at the table scribbling lyrics as the beats floated and crackled through the air.

"Yo, D," Ivan hung his feet off the side of the top bunk. "Turn that down, man, I wanna talk to you."

"One minute," Dorian said engulfed by the emcee on the radio. "I know this brudder. His name's Alaye. He's my bredrin from Grove. He runs this record label, called Sugakane, 'member that mixtape I had the other day? That's dem man dere."

"Yeah, that's good," Ivan ignored Dorian's glee. "But lower the radio, I wanna tell you about this book. You need to read it, its deep." Ivan jumped down from his bunk to show Dorian. "It tells you all about life and why black people go through so much strife."

"Hmm" Dorian ignored Ivan's glee. "That's good."

"Dorian!" Ivan became annoyed. "Are you listening?"

"Yeah man," Dorian tried to fob Ivan off. He was more interested in Alaye's wordplay and delivery. Hypnotized, he rocked his head back and forth. Hanging onto the musical beat Dorian was taken away. He closed his eyes concentrating.

Vexed Ivan switched off the radio snapping Dorian out of his trance.

"What's wrong with you," Dorian jumped up. "Why you switching off the set for?"

"What's wrong with me? What's wrong with you?" Ivan said. "I'm tryna show you something that might benefit you and give you some knowledge and all you can do is listen to that shit."

"Whatever," Dorian sucked his teeth. "Tell me later." He said switching the radio back on.

"Wharm to you rudeboy? Turn it off!" Ivan insisted. "Look at you." He poked Dorian in the chest. "Man's tryna show you knowledge and all you're interested in is next man rapping. This book here can give you some insight, blood. Help you to change yourself and stop being so flipping ignorant!"

Dorian switched off the radio and stood up watching Ivan.

"Who you calling ignorant?"

"You." Ivan squared up. "I'm talking to you, and all you can do is play music over me. Don't you think that's ignorant blood?"

"Come out my face," Dorian brushed Ivan to side. Defiantly he switched the radio on again. Vexed Ivan slapped his hand away

"Oi, don't touch my hand like dat." Dorian warned.

"Don't touch my radio den," Ivan switched the machine off.

Dorian looked at Ivan, "Oh, so it's your radio now yeah."

"Yes." Ivan stood in front of the radio. "It's on my prop list, that means it's mine."

"Okay den, fuck you, you pussy. Keep ur fuckin radio." Dorian fumed. "You better jus' make sure you replace mine, or trus'me there will be drama's in here. I don't care how big man is. About man wanna try call me ignorant. You wanna take a look in the mirror, bredrin."

"Hold on, blood," Ivan sniggered "How you gonna try switch it on me? When I was the one tryna talk to you."

"But who are you to talk to me?!" Dorian yelled. "What the fuck you know about me? You don't know me rudeboy! You don't give a fuck about anyone 'round ere 'cept yourself?"

"Shut up!" Ivan spat back. "What you talking about? You idiot!"

"I'm talking about you. You walk 'round ere like you know man. You don't know me. What, because you see me acting the fool, you think I'm an idiot, yeah? Trus'me, I ain't no idiot, Ivan." Dorian was starting to get flustered "I ain't no joker either. So don't think you can walk around calling me ignorant. You don't even know whether I've read that book or not."

Ivan smirked at the thought, "You ain't read this book?"

"See, that's why you're a dumb brer!" Dorian barked. "I read that book, long time ago. There's nuthin' in there you can show me. I read about the Journey, the Lynch slaves and what not. That's why I didn't say nothing, when you told me what Jade said. I knew what she was talking bout, but you didn't."

"So?"

"So, me and you've been on this house block for over six months together and you don't know shit about me! You don't know shit about King! Furthermore you don't know shit about yourself, and you definitely don't know shit about that book! Lemme show you something." Dorian snatched the book flicking through the pages.

"Look here, here," He pointed to a passage. "It says a Lynch slave can be very dangerous, but may also become a great companion upon the journey. Do you know what that means Ivan?" Dorian tossed the book back. "It means know your companions. Know the people around you. You've been here over eight months and you still don't know the people around you. There's man in this jail that know that book inside out, you dickhead. What, you think you're the only man in here that reads?

"No."

"Good cos dere's niggaz in here that know the brer that wrote that book."

"What!" Ivan said in astonishment. "Who?"

"What you don't know?" Dorian sniggered.

"No."

"Well then I don't think it's my business to say." Dorian smirked and sat down at the table. He picked up his notepad and started jotting down some rhymes. "If you weren't so 'ignorant' I might've shown you, but now I guess you'll have to find out for yourself?"

"Ahh fuck you, you gower," Ivan said feeling defeated. "I try share some knowledge and this how you go on? It's no wonder why black people are so fucked. Fuck you man, you get on my nerves"

"Fuck you. You get on *my* nerves."

Ivan and Dorian both sat in silence for the next 15 minutes pondering their own thoughts. Ivan knew he'd dealt with the situation wrong. He'd definitely misjudged Dorian. He thought all D cared about was rhyming and having a laugh. He was wrong. Perhaps he had only scratched at the surface of his cellmate. He decided to break the unease.

"Yo, D, what you writing?"

"A rhyme."

"Seen. What's it about? Lemme hear it.

"Okay," Dorian smiled. Clearing his throat, he began rocking with his usual freestyle swagger and held his pad up so he could read his lyrics.

"I'm a regular scholar/ a reader of books/ I transfer knowledge onto beats and hooks/ I once had beef wid dis stinky mook/ he tried to feed me second hand knowledge that he got from a book/ I was like no blood/ no G/ look you read a couple pages and you think you can show me/ sit me down and school me like an old G/ Oh Please/ you don't know nuthin 'bout ur Co-D/ you talk a lot shit/ but yeah ur phony/ if this was Africa then you would've sold me/ that's why ur girl left you inna jail cell lonely/ smashing up cells and breaking my Sony/ now you wanna shot me knowledge like it was O.Zs/ Ha!/ the cheek of these south London cronies/ if knowledge was work/ then I'd hold ki's/ and you know me/ nuff man on road say dat they know D,/ hothead yoot know to go OT/," Dorian picked up the toilet roll and tossed it at Ivan. **"or tella man bare face straight up/ go fuck yourself slowly."**

With that Dorian switched back on the radio and jumped on his bed. Disgusted Ivan decided to leave him alone thinking *ignorant brer*.

*

The next morning Dorian completely ignored Ivan. By the time everyone walked out to the yard for exercise the most he had said was "Lemme have some sugar," having already sprinkled some on his cornflakes. Fortunately their discontent for each hadn't gone unnoticed. Observant as always, King detected the tension between the two. He watched as Dorian entered the yard and called over to Bait-man. The two went off to discuss lyrics, while a subdued Ivan also entered and found a corner to himself. King mingled with a few other inmates before joining Ivan.

"Do I detect disharmony amongst the ranks?" He greeted Ivan. "What's going on with you and Dorian?"

"What'd you mean?" Ivan grumbled.

"Normally you two are like batty and bench. Now he's over there with Baitman and you're over here sulking."

"There's nothing wrong with me," Ivan kicked at a cigarette butt on the floor. "You should talk to my man, he's an idiot innit."

"Seen," King nodded. "So, that's got nothing to do with you lot arguing last night?"

"How you know we was arguing?"

"Ivan," King laughed. "You two come like husband and wife. The whole block heard you arguing."

"Well trust me," Ivan smiled. "At least I know I ain't the one that goes on like a chick. My man started goin' on stupid over nonsense. 'member that book I was reading. I try to show him about it, and he started gettin' all hype."

"What book?" King asked. "Journey of A Slave?"

"Yeah."

"So what'd he get vex about?"

As Ivan began to explain how the argument started, King suggested they walked laps around the yard. Amused King listened to what Ivan had to say about the argument and the book.

"King, I ain't doubting no one yeah, but if your bredrin tries to drop some knowledge on you, shouldn't you give them a second to listen?"

"Boy, that's a hard one," King avoided taking sides. "Understandably you were excited about relaying the information you'd learnt, but I think the way you went about it, is where the argument lies."

"So what you sayin'?" Ivan asked. "I'm in the wrong?"

"No not exactly," King grinned. "Things aren't always so black and white, Ivan.
I think you need to remember that sometimes. Remember what I said about the chessboard."

"Yeah, yeah, for real." Ivan contemplated his actions. "Real talk, blood."

King looked over to Dorian who seemed to be watching him and Ivan. He tried to wave him over. Dorian shook his head shouting "Dats long! Don't even bother wid it!"

"You see what I mean about that brer?" Ivan said. "Ignorant."

"He ain't ignorant," King chuckled. "Jus' a bit stubborn."

"A bit." Ivan raised his eyebrows.

"Okay, not a bit," King laughed again. "But forget that for a minute. Tell me what you learnt from the book."

"King," Ivan's face became serious. "Reading that book really opened my eyes. For the first time in my life it made me wanna do something more than road. I mean, sometimes I look at man like you. You're in here talking to bare man, about all different tings and I respect that. You're like what my man calls the talented tenth."

Ivan quickly became animated now he had an audience to listen to him. "But no disrespect, cuz, but when I look at you, I say, I don't wanna be the brer in jail doin' a *L-Plate* and teaching the younga manz about history, politics, and all that, when I got a chance to do something else. Ya get me?"

"I do." King nodded proudly at Ivan's blunt honesty.

"Real talk, blood. I think this book come at the right time for me innit. I mean, I'm kinda using it to reflect on a lot of negative shit in my life dat I wanna cut out."

"Mmm," King murmured in deep thought. "So what do you plan to do now?"

"I don't know," Ivan confessed. "I mean, I ain't really done nothing in my life except steal and hustle. So where I go from here, your guess is as good as mine."

"So you're looking for help?"

"I suppose," Ivan blushed. He knew he wanted to say yes, but he held back.

"Well, you know I got connections with certain organisations and mentoring schemes. You want me to find out what I can do for you?"

"Yeah, that would be bless,' if you could." Ivan said humbly. "I'd really appreciate that, King. I really would."

"Okay." King said fixing his red, black and green armband. "I'll see what I can do."

For a moment the two stood in silence contemplating their own thoughts. Then Ivan remembered something he had to ask. "Oh, yeah, King, there's something I was suppose to ask you."

"Go on."

"Dorian said something about one of the man dem knowing Gilyan Gates. I was wondering..."

"You was wondering if it was me right?"

"Yeah."

"Yeah, I do know Gil." King paused. Ivan noticed King squint his eyes in the sunlight, then realised he wasn't squinting he was frowning. "Gilyan Gates got a lot to do with why I'm here." King finished.

"Rah, did you man have beef?" Ivan asked sensing some bad blood.

"Depends what you call beef," King said. His face became solemn. "I knew Gil along time ago before he wrote that book and set up The BBCP. He was a different guy then, I was a different guy. Our lives kinda collided at a crossroad."

"Are you serious?" Ivan said knowing the severity of King's sentence. "What happened?"

"It's a long story." King stopped staring at the high fenced wall that surrounded the prison. "Let's just say one man's journey begins where another man's ends."

The men fell silent again. Ivan studied King. He'd never seen his friend look so sombre. His jaw tightened and his eyes were absent. For a brief moment his mind seemed to be on the other side of the wall. Ivan wanted to ask him more, but decided to leave him be. King already looked in pain. He turned to Ivan with a woeful look.

"You know sometimes I think no matter how hard some of us try we're always destined to come here."

"I know," Ivan agreed. "Shit only falls one way, and that's down. What you gonna do about it?"

"For real," King smiled. "Listen, I know you wanna know more about me and Gil."

"Nah, blood that's private innit," Ivan protested. "You don't have to show me nutt'ink. That's your private business."

King put up his hands to stop Ivan. "Look, don't worry about it. I'm here to help. Just come to my cell later. I'll tell you then, if you still wanna know."

*

King sat by his table staring at his chessboard. Emptying his flask, he poured hot water into his pot noodles stirring. When King first came to prison he disliked the watery taste of pot noodles. Over time he had acquired the skill of finding the right consistence of flavour and texture to adequately enjoy. Happily, he slurped on a mouthful, with no one to reprimand his slobbery. King had a single cell and was gladdened by the depth of solitude it brought him. Many a time he felt it was more a sanctuary rather than a prison.

Between the stone walls and barred windows he'd received lectures from, philosophers, politicians, scholars, scientists, and strategists. He learned from Nietzsche, Marx, Garvey, Plato, Socrates, Aristotle, Machiavelli, Sun Tzu, Napoleon and Solomon. Here in this prison he travelled the world as his books came to life. And on his black and white chessboard he played countless games, strategizing and calculating his moves. He'd never been into chess before jail, but now he often played against family and friends in corresponding letters. It was one of the few pleasures he had between the monotonous routine of jail. Eating another spoonful of noodles, he nodded to himself writing down a sequence of moves. He then spun the board round and rearranged the pieces. Hearing the first of the cell doors opening, he looked at his watch. He knew it was soon time to tell his story. Ivan would be upstairs in a minute and there would be so many things to explain. The who's, what's, when's, how's? King wondered whether he'd have enough time. Wolfing down the rest of his noodles, King thought at least that would be one less thing to finish before the end of association.

Ivan knocked on the metal door. "Yo, King, what's happening man. I came up as soon as they opened my door."

King told him to come in and sit down. Sitting at the end of the bed, Ivan was excited. He'd always respected King from the moment they first met. Their friendship had really grown. Ivan had met many men in jail, friend and foe, but none as intriguing as King. He always managed to captivate Ivan's attention, and Ivan couldn't wait to hear what he had to say about Gil. King washed his fork in the sink and placed it with his other cutlery as Dorian came strolling into the cell.

"Have you told him yet?" he addressed King.

"I was just about to do it," King replied. You might as well sit down as well."

"Tell me what?" Ivan said not wanting to be left out.

King went into his cupboard and drew out an envelope. He handed it to Ivan. It was from a solicitor's firm. "Read it," he said.

Pulling out the letter, Ivan unfolded the sheet and took his time scanning the page.

"He's a flipping slow reader," Dorian said as they waited for Ivan.

"Be quiet." King said. He wanted to make sure Ivan wasn't distracted.

Ivan looked at the page frowning. The words were clear, but they didn't make sense. He read the page again scrutinizing the document. He strained his eyes with the print, as though it were a puzzle. Looking at Dorian then at King he held the paper out and said, "I don't understand."

"It ain't that hard, to understand." Dorian sniggered.

King gave Dorian a reprimanding look that told him to behave. He turned to Ivan "Try reading it out loud, maybe that will help."

Ivan cleared his throat and read the words for the six ears in the gloomy cell.

"It says - The Individual known as *'Gilyan Gates'* will no longer be registered and identified as such. As of the signed and dated notification, the person formerly known as *'Gilyan Gates'* will hereby be legally known, registered, identified and referred to as *'King'*."

King. The revelation stunned Ivan and left him speechless. He looked up at his friend. His face made still. He looked back up at the page then over to Dorian who had a smug look on his face. "See I told you, you don't know the man dem prop'lee."

"Nah, nah," Ivan shook his head. "You man are joking wid me innit? You're having a bubble, right? Are you seriously tellin' me you're Gilyan Gates?"

King nodded.

"Yeah, but, but," Ivan stuttered. "You said he was dead. You said that's why you come jail. Because of Gilyan Gates."

"I never said that." King smiled. "I said, one man's journey begins where another man's ends. I never said my journey ended."

"Yeah, but that means, that means, you're my man!" Ivan jumped up. "You wrote *'Journey Of A Slave'*. Do you know how nutz that is cuzzy?" Ivan turned to Dorian. "Blood, why didn't you tell me King wrote the book."

"Tell you what?" Dorian dismissed Ivan. "It's not my business. I thought I'd let you find out for yourself."

"Shit!" Ivan hugged King. "Feel like I proper know you and shit, but I don't even know what to call you. What do I call you, King or Gil?"

"Keep it nice and simple," King tried to settle Ivan down. "Call me King."

"Okay, King" Ivan said in amazement. He sat back on the bed staring at King with a smile. King took a seat by his table. He knew what was going to happen next and prepared for the army of questions.

"So, King, talk to me man." Ivan started trying to take it all in. "I mean, what the fuck? If you're Gilyan Gates and you wrote that book, what does this mean? What happened to all the things you wrote? The blue prints, the final equation, the footsteps of the Talented Tenth? I mean, you set that all up right? You was on a movement, positive tings yeah? How comes you ended up here? How come you changed your name?"

"Easy, Ivan, man," Dorian butted in. "Let the man answer one question first."

"Nah, sorry, King. No disrespect. There's jus' so many things I wanna know. Like what happened to Mel and dem man? Are you lot still cool and ting? And what about Alicia? You never linked her after that day did you? Cos in the book you must say.."

"Ivan!" Dorian stopped him again.

"Sorry, sorry, blood." Ivan apologized. "I don't mean to keep butting in. Sorry. I'm jus' excited. I'm gonna shut up. I ain't gonna say nutthin,' the floor's yours cuz."

Silenced, Ivan looked to King. He didn't say anything at first. He just peered at the doorway like it led off to a distant land. Then a slight smirk appeared on his face.

"You two are gonna learn one day, that the past is a foreign country; we do things different there."

"What's that mean?" Dorian asked.

"It means the things you do when you're young, become alien to you as you mature. The things you held valuable become insignificant in comparison to the truth."

"So what's the truth?" Ivan asked King.

King smiled knowing the answer. "The truth is, Gilyan Gates was a Slave and I am a King." He took the book from Ivan's hand. "Gilyan Gates' downfall was that he couldn't stop being a slave no matter what he wrote. By the time I became the King I always wanted to be, I was already incarcerated. I was already here. This is where Gil's journey ended."

Ivan and Dorian looked at King studying the book. They both knew he was serving a life for murder. As he spoke, his tone didn't sound bitter, more remorseful. He played with the book in his hand, trying to straighten the dog-ears.

"Here," King passed the book back. "I really hope it helped you understand a few things before it's too late.

"It did." Ivan said with great sadness. He felt sorry for King. He wondered why some one with such a mind should end up in prison? Reading Ivan's thoughts King got up and handed Ivan a photo from off his pin board. Ivan held it carefully studying the red skin woman with the slit eyes. She looked beautiful. He recognised her from the visiting hall. She was there faithfully every fortnight waiting for King. From the ring on King's finger he knew it was his wife.

"That's my queen, Ivan." King said proudly. She's the ruler of my Kingdom and throne. I love her and it's every King's job to protect his Kingdom, Throne and Queen."

Then it dawned on Ivan as he looked at the picture. She was just as he'd imagined. She was a little older, but the beauty described was captured timelessly in the photo. Her eyes invited you to sit down like a child at her feet. He knew exactly who she was from how King spoke of her. He knew because he felt the same about Jade.

"Its Alicia isn't it? The chick from the book. What happened?"

Dorian looked at King, "Hey, King you know you don't need to tell us anything if you don't want to."

King shook his head. "No, it's cool. I wanna tell you two. We're family."
King sat them both down and made them promise not to repeat a word to anybody. Closing the door. He passed a packet of custard creams around and began to tell them the final chapter in Gilyan Gates story.

"The evening sun blazed across the sky as I sat on the wall waiting outside Alicia's office block. I hadn't a clue whether she still worked there. It'd been months since I last saw her. How would she react to seeing me? Would she be happy or not? I didn't know what to think. I convinced myself, this was ridiculous. I'm sitting outside, waiting on a wall, for a girl, who weren't interested. She'd probably moved on and found somebody new. What was the point?

I looked down at the brown parcel beside me. Inside was the first draft of my book. It still had no title. Looking at the time on my watch I decided to give up. I picked up my parcel and prepared to bop. Then she came out. She was deeply engrossed in chatter with her friend, when I approached. She didn't even notice me until I was right beside her. "Alicia," I said catching her attention.

The moment was awkward. She stopped and looked at me. What was I doing? Instantly I began to panic with doubt. I had let her believe I wasn't interested. I had rejected her when she had opened her heart to me. Now I was convinced she was going to embarrass me. Her sharp stare penetrated my soul, as her eyes looked me up and down. There was a silence. Her friend noticed the friction.

"Alicia, I'm going to walk on and let you two talk." She excused herself politely. "Catch me up. If not I'll see you tomorrow."

"Okay," Alicia hugged her friend and said goodbye.

She turned back to me. Even in anger she looked beautiful, as she crossed her arms and looked at me defiantly. I tried to break the ice.

"You know, they say crossing your arms is a sign of defence or protection." I played.

"Well maybe I need some." She said harshly. "What is it you want, Gil?"

"Nothing," I cleared my throat to speak. I looked everywhere except at her trying to avoid eye contact. "I don't know. I wanted to talk to you. Say I'm sorry for what happened between us and the way I handled the situation. I could've handled it better, I thought maybe..."

"You thought what, Gil? You thought maybe you'd say sorry, we'd go for walk and everything would be okay?"

"No."

"Well what then? This isn't a movie, Gil. I told you I loved you and you left me standing on the doorstep. That was months ago, now you turn up outside my workplace looking for what? Forgiveness? Love? What, Gilyan, what?"

"I don't know," I shrugged my shoulders. I felt like a fool. What was I truly expecting from her. "You know what you're right. I shouldn't of come. I should of come months ago, but I didn't know what I wanted. What I needed."

"Pardon" Alicia scoffed "And now you think you know what you want?"

"Yeah," I said "Here." I placed the parcel in her arms. She didn't say anything. "Alicia I want you to have this. Do whatever you like with it, but I want you to have it."

And that was it. There was no kiss, no goodbye, no dying confession of love. I simply put my hands in my pocket and ran across the road. I didn't even look back. I realised I was always out of my depth with Alicia. If I wanted her love that was the weakest ever attempt at trying to earn it. No this was just me, trying to say goodbye one last time. It was me letting Alicia know what she meant to me.

It was two weeks before the book was due to go to print and I had still no concrete title. My editor warned me, the book would be under scrutiny and would receive mixed reviews. I didn't care, it was being published, that was all I cared about.

I lay on my bed watching a DVD. The clock on my stereo read two thirty am. I had just finished speaking to Mel. After reading the first drafts, he had decided he wanted to be apart of anything that helped us get off the streets. He had this idea about opening a chain of sandwich bars and catering vans. He kept saying "Food, that's where the money is. Cats can always give drugs up, but people always got to eat."

He kept going on about how much people spent at *Starbucks* and *Pret A Manger*. He loved the idea of going around shottin' food to people on their lunch break. He was so keen he carved out a route of office blocks we could hit. He said it would be just like road '*Bitesize... at the right price*'. And instantly that became the plan.

We'd already started gathering all our money together to buy our first van. I used some of my advance from the book to pay a deposit and Mel was outsourcing the companies to provide our food and packaging. He thought he was a big shot businessman and phoned me every night to give me an update. After our conversation I put on a DVD and lay on the bed playing with the handkerchief that Alicia had wiped my nose with that rainy day.

Thinking of Alicia hurt, but I thought to myself, at least she could never deny that she loved me. My mobile phone rang breaking my thoughts. What the hell did Mel want this time? I picked the phone up and saw private number.

"Hello, Hello."

There was no answer, just the sound of somebody breathing down the phone, and the faint sound of a television in the background. *Which dickhead was this now?* I thought. It was late. I wasn't entertaining any prank calls.

"Oi, pussy, if you're not going to say nothing I'm hanging up the phone."

"Wait don't hang up." The voice on the other end said.

It was her, "Alicia is that you?" She sounded like she'd been crying. "Are you alright?" I asked. I imagined her on the other side of the phone

"I'm fine," she said blowing her nose. "I read the book. Did you really mean what you said? You said I was a queen."

"I meant every word, you are a queen." I could tell she was smiling.

"So what you going to call it, there's no title?"

"I know. I was waiting for you to title it."

"How did you know I was going to call?" she asked.

"I didn't," I chuckled "My publisher's been going crazy."

I closed my eyes and listened to her giggle down the phone "You're such a big head"

"I know, but what you sayin' bout dis title? Lemme know so I can put this man out of his misery."

"I don't know, Gil. It's not for me to name it. It's your book."

"No, it's our book." I said smelling the hankerchief. "I wrote it for us, and people like us. Remember that night at your house. You told me that knowledge is something to be shared. I'm just trying to share our story, tell about our Journey. I want you to name it for me, Alicia"

"I don't know, Gil" she said in a bashful manner. "Why don't you come round and we can discuss it."

"What now?" I said.

"No. Three weeks tomorrow." She said sarcastically "Yes now, G. Don't you think we've been apart for long enough. If you really mean what you say then I don't want to be apart anymore."

There's an old saying that goes that 'every wise man ends his journey with a lovers meeting.' That night Alicia confirmed her love for me and I the same. Holding Alicia tighter than ever, I watched over her until morning came. She was peaceful and free, and we were together. The next morning when I woke she sat above looking down. "Did you know you snore, babe," she said kissing me on the lips and stroking my head.

"I don't snore," I yawned and sat up.

"Whatever," Alicia smiled "You better move the bears from your nose at night then if you're planning to stay 'round here more often."

I pulled her down and kissed her again. "Did you think of a title?"

"Yeah, I did,"Alicia pulled away holding her nose and laughing. "But don't say anything else with you're nasty morning breath." She leaned down and whispered, "*The Journey Of A Slave by Gilyan Gates.*"

> Getting up, Dorian searched through King's canteen and opened a carton of Ribena. Sitting back down he said, "So what happened next? You got the girl and ting, but how'd you end up in jail?"
>
> King picked up two more Ribenas and handed Ivan one. Sitting back down, he continued the story.

"Now Mel always said, our lives were like movies. Motion pictures captured on film. He used to say God was one big movie geek, who sits in heaven writing and directing films for his own amusement. If that was true, then I guess all our lives would have to fit into some type of movie genre. Black comedy, crime, thriller, or gangster flick; you choose. In my film, my life, '*The*

Journey' was a story about a young black man finding his way in life, the characters, the script, were all real, and all filmed live. There was no time for mistakes.

After the book was released, there was a lot of interest in what I planned to do next. I did a small book tour and was introduced to many black professionals. It was a significant period as I began developing and networking support for a black culturalist movement. My sister and Alicia encouraged me to write a business plan, and manifesto for such an organisation detailed in my book. I wrote a five-year plan that began with networking the Black businesses and community. Our first venture would be the sandwich business that would offer jobs and work experience to unemployed youth and ex-offenders. We used our network to win catering contracts with local businesses. Then we created a points card that linked and promoted local businesses in the community and gave discounts to members when spending. Eventually our goal was to deliver the cultural, economic, and political vehicle for a social revolution. To return to the thinking of our forefathers and the True Talented Tenth. To promote and preserve our culture through the communal and cultural framework. This was the beginning of our movement and we befittingly named the organisation *'The Black British Culturalist Party'* or the *BBCP*. It was the most exciting time of my life. Everything was fresh and new.

However, if Mel's movie analogy was correct. Well, when was the last time you saw a gangster film where something bad doesn't happen to the lead character? *NEVER*. At the basis of every gangster film is a moral issue, the battle between right and wrong. You *NEVER* see the guy get the girl, the money, and live happily ever after. It *NEVER* happens. Carlito, Tony, O-dog and Kaine, Frank White, even the Corleone family. All these anti-heroes have to deal with their past sooner or later and I was no different. I remember it so clearly. The events remain as vivid as yesterday.

I'd finally moved out of the nest of my mother's council flat and was living with Alicia. I'd been out networking with Andrea amongst some of the medical students at her university, when we decided to visit mum and raid her cupboards. As we entered the flat I could hear mum on the phone. She seemed in a panic.

"Hold on darling," she said. "He's just came through the door, let me get him."

Mum ran towards me with the cordless phone.

"What's wrong?"

"I don't know!" Mum rushed me. "Its Alicia. She's been looking for you."

I grabbed the phone. "Alicia, what's wrong?" there was no answer she'd already hung up. "What did she say mum?"

My mother sat down on the sofa in her housecoat. She was in a frenzy. "I don't know son, she just kept asking for you. Quickly go around there, sumting's wrong I can feel it. Sumtings wrong. "

"What do you mean something's wrong?"

"I don't know!" Mum yelled. "I spoke to Alicia, but she won't tell me what's goin' on. She sounds upset. She keeps phoning here, but she won't talk to anyone but you. I tried to phone you, but all I get is that stupid answering machine. Where's your phone? Why don't you switch the dam thing on?"

I searched my pocket. Pulling out my phone I remembered, my battery had died and I forgot to charge it in the car.

"Shit! Okay what did she say, mum?"

"Gilyan you're not listening!" mum cried at the top of her voice. She started to get hysterical. "She didn't say anything. All she said is she wants you. Please child! Stop wasting time and go and see what's wrong with her!"

"Gil, go, go" Andrea said pushing me out of the room and into the corridor "Go and find out what' s going on, and phone us when you get home. Hurry."

Rushing home I thought what the hell could be wrong with Alicia? Why did she have my mum so worked up? I parked up and ran into the block. When I got to the outside landing, my body froze. My mouth became dry and heart pounded so hard it felt like someone was beating the inside of my chest with a baseball bat. My mind went blank. I looked around at the wooden splinters scattered over the floor. Then I gaped at the doorframe. Somebody had kicked off my door. *My door.* Hold on, somebody had invaded my home, my sanctuary, my territory, my castle. Why?

My first instinct was to phone the police. Then I thought against it. No not the police, I'll phone Mel. Then I remembered my phone was dead. Then a dread overcame me when I realised, Alicia could still be inside or worse. Then the fear over took me – the person might still be inside waiting for me to arrive.

I called out "Alicia" there was no answer. *Damn this,* I thought *Alicia might be in there hurt I got to protect her.* I pushed the door open. Everything was a maze of black silhouettes and shadows. Feeling for the light switch, I flicked it. Once, twice, a third time, the light stayed off. A dim light illuminated the entrance of the living room.

I called out again, there was still no answer. Then I sniffed. The flat smelt strange. I knew that aroma. It was strong, sweet, and seductive. It remained fresh in the air. That's crack. Who da fuck was smoking crack?

Cautiously I made my way to the living room. As I moved I felt glass crushing under my feet. Inside the room was in a mess, plants everywhere, books torn and on the floor. I'd been here before. My heart sank. I stood knowing somewhere along the way I'd fucked up. Worst nightmares, terror, pain, anger, confusion how can I describe the numbing feeling I felt seeing Alicia laid out on the floor. Blood stained her night robe and torn nightgown. The side of her face was swollen and her mouth was bleeding. Blood sipped from a gash in her head. Instantly I crumpled. I dropped to my knees. I didn't even no whether she was dead or alive. I looked around for help, then realizing I was alone I rushed to her side. I was scared. I didn't want to touch or move her. Instead, I straightened the short silk gown covering her modesty. Her thighs were bruised and she was bleeding down below. I couldn't look. I tasted the salty tears as they ran down my face and into my mouth. I cupped her limp body in my arms. Rocking backward and forward, I gazed down at her battered face and black eye, thinking, "Why God? Why would you let somebody do this to her? What has she done?"

As I held Alicia, I noticed something in her hand. It was a small porcelain pipe. Furious I smashed it on the floor. What the hell was she doing with a crack pipe? I felt a surge of anger tear through my lungs and screamed aloud, "Aaaarrrghhh!"

Suddenly Alicia opened her eyes "Gil" she said trying to sit up.

"No don't move," I said stroking her face. "Stay still babe. Stay still. I'm here now, no one's gonna hurt you. Just tell me what happened?"

Alicia said nothing pointing over my shoulder. Before I could turn my head I felt cold metal pushed against the back of my neck. "Don't move." The voice said. It was dark and morbid, but I knew the voice. It was one that plagued my past and wished to destroy my future. "Wha gwan, Gilly the kid?"

In the darkness, Sparks stood above me holding his gun to my face. He drew on a yeng zoot takin' one long pull. His eye's were charged and almost popped out his head. Smiling, he came closer and blew a cloud of smoke in my face. "Put dat bitch down and get ur bloodclaat hands against that wall."

I hesitated. Sparks sensed it. "I ain't playing," he jabbed me in the face with the barrel "Move."

I stumbled back and Alicia grabbed my arm. I could feel her shaking. She squeezed my hand. "Do as he says."

Sparks hoisted me up against the wall. "Yeah, do as I say," He said patting me down looking for weapons. "Liss'en to your girl."

"Sparks, what's goin on? Why you doing this? I haven't got no beef wid you."

"Shut up." He said finding my phone. He threw it across the room. "You don't know what you got wid me. You never do. That's why I got to teach you. You unnerstan'?" He kept the gun pointed at my head. "C'mon talk. Say something. Wharm to you star? You ain't got no mouth no? No? Look at you," Sparks started taunting. "Look at you, and you're lickle cracked out whore. What, do you think you're better than me! Do you?"

He was like a crazed man, pushing and shoving, and spitting all over me. He was so close I could smell the crack on his breath. He grabbed my belt and began undoing my jeans. "Wharm pussyhole, you still ain't got no mout' no? Okay then, lets see if you got some balls?"

He began pulling down my trouser and boxer shorts until they were around my ankles. Grabbing the back of my neck he pressed my face against the wall, and held the cold barrel to my testicles. He shouted in my ear while his body pressed against me. It was like he wanted to rub up on me. "You keep your fucking hands against that wall!" He screamed. "I warned you didn't I. What did I tell you?" He began rambling. "Who's got big balls, Gil? You? You? What did I say about big balls? I said I break dem, didn't I. Is that what you want me to do you? Break some balls for you!"

I said nothing. Trying to think of a way out of this madness. I was shit scared, thinking he was liable to pull the trigger at anytime. Again Sparks smacked the gun across the back of my head. I faltered under the blow. Sparks laughed as he pinned me against the wall again. Using his free hand he groped my balls. The nasty bastard held them in his hand and squeezed them.

"Get the fuck off me, you faggot!" I turned and pushed him off me. He still had me covered with the gun.

"Wooo, fucking hell G-man." He laughed. "Dem some real big balls you got there. Real big balls." He backed away slowly and grabbed Alicia by her hair.

"Owww!" Alicia cried struggling.

"Leave her alone!"

"Shut the fuck up," Sparks ordered. "And sit down, wid your big balls."

Dragging Alicia to the other side of the room, Sparks sat down on the far sofa. He placed Alicia between his feet. "Take that chair dere," he pointed.

I sat down attempting to pull my trousers up.

"No, no you don't." Sparks waved the gun. "You sit on that couch with your hands on your knees, so I can see them, and your boxers around your ankles. I don't want you making no smart moves. I want you to sit like a big pussy ready to get fucked. Cos dat's exactly what I'm gonna do," Sparks smiled. "Fuck you up. No long ting."

There was silence as we sat across the room staring at each other. He smiled with a evil grin, knowing he had the upper hand. "So wha gwan, G?" he said playing with Alicia's hair. "What's going through your brain right about now?"

I didn't answer. "Don't worry," he continued. "I can read minds. Right now, you're thinking you wan' kill me. Yeah that's what you're thinking. Well lemme tell you something. It ain't gonna happen. You know why?" Sparks smelt his hand. "Cos I felt your balls, dawggy, and they're not bigger than mine."

"You think so?" I became drawn into his game.

Sparks shook his head. "You still don't learn do you, G? It's not I think so, I know so. See that's your problem. You think too much. That's why we're here now."

"Because I think too much?"

"Yes." Sparks clapped his hands. "Cos you think too much. You're the only man I know who thinks he can write a book about man and think there ain't gonna be no repercussion. Even Donald Goines couldn't get away with that shit nigga."

"What are you talking about, you're mad. You mean this is all about my book?"

"Yes it's about your book nigga. What else?" Sparks got angry "I don't giv' a fuck about you. It's that fucking book I care about. You should've never wrote that shit. You fucked everything up when you wrote that shit."

"What the fuck you talking about, Sparks?" I said feeling the back of my head bleeding. "You've smoked too much shit. The yeng's got you all paranoid. Put the fucking gun down and let's talk. There's no need for all this shit. All we gotta do is talk." Talk. That was my plan. I knew Sparks loved to talk. He loved to be heard. I thought, let him run his mouth and I'll get my chance when he drops his guard.

"No it's too late for that." Sparks seethed. He wiped his brow. Sweat was pouring over his face. He was hot probably from the crack.

"You were my solider, G," he waved the gun around in the air. "You and Mel were my next in line. I was gonna hand everything over to you and let you run the show. But no, you had to go weak on me. Talking about you don't wanna shot no more, you don't wanna be apart of it all. And you know what? You know what?"

"No, man, I don't. Talk to me."

"I could've lived with that, G. I could've found somebody else. But you had to try and fuck me over."

"Nah, Sparks, I didn't fuck you over man. I'd never do that to you."

"Yes you did, you snitch! You dry snitched on me, you snitch. You told everyone my business in your fucking book. I got Five-O questioning about all types of shit because of you. I can feel them crawling over me, watching my every move. All because you wanna write some stupid book."

"Nah, Sparks man you're paranoid." I tried to reason. "If it had anything to do with shit in the book, why didn't they come to me? Why ain't they questioning me?"

"I don't know!" Sparks shouted. "Maybe you made a deal with them. Yeah, yeah you made a deal wid dem. That's why they ain't shif you yet."

"No way." I protested. "I ain't no snitch."

"Yes you are. I brought you in and you betrayed me. Now I can't function properly. Police are everywhere. They stop my runners and ask them if they're shottin' for me. They follow them to see who they re-up from. Mel, he don't want work no more. He keeps talking about running some sandwich van. What stupidness. Even Kooba wants to lay low for a minute. All of this while my shit goes to pot. Why, Gilyan, why? All because you thought you had the balls to write some fucking book."

"C'mon Sparks, you can't blame that shit on me"

"Yes I can." Sparks' voice became low and his eyes narrowed. "I blame it all on you, then I started thinking. What really makes, Gilly think that he can fuck me over like dat. What really makes you think that those two monkey nuts that hang between your legs are bigger than mine. Then it hit me." Sparks jumped up and slapped Alicia in the face. I leaped to defend her, but Sparks kept the gun in my direction.

"Don't be silly. Sit" I did as I was told and he continued. "Like I was saying. Then it really did hit me when I found out that the bitch you've been fucking is my ex whore. And I get this strange feeling, you know; I start imagining that the two of you are walking around, in this shit hole laughing at me. And you, G start planning to fuck me over all because some ho' that I used to bang, is telling you that your balls are bigger than mine." He leaned over Alicia groping her breast and kissing her neck.

"Is that what it is babe? Are his balls bigger than mine Alicia?"

"Get the fuck off me, Darren!" Alicia pulled away.

"Don't move you lickle ho'," he said pointing the barrel to her nose. He looked at me smiling. "Yeah see, I always liked that about Alicia, Gil. She's one of those feisty bitches. You know the ones you gotta tame. Gotta break them in like a fucking yard animal." I turned my head as he lightly slapped Alicia in the face playing. "What talk to me, babe, you want me to break you, in front of your lil boyfriend? Giv' him a lil show and ting, huh?"

Sparks tore her nightie. Again I jumped to my feet.

"No, Gil sit down!" Alicia screamed

"Yeah that's right, G, get angry." Sparks said rubbing the scar above Alicia's breast. "Show me you got some fucking balls, or sit the fuck down!"

I looked at Alicia. She shook her head. "No, Gil sit down. Please sit down."

"See, that's what I'm talking about star, fucking power. Sit your arse down." Sitting down it became clear as Spark's began laughing. "I guess Alicia never told you, we were once in love." He said trying to kiss her.

"You don't know the meaning of love," Alicia struggled. "Get off me you fucking bastard."

"You see what I mean, Gil?" Sparks let her go. "She's always so rude, always so insolent. That's why I had to teach her a lesson or two. Teach her how to act right towards her man. You still haven't learnt, have you bitch. Tell him, tell him about the scars."

"He knows already," Alicia spat at him "There's nothing he doesn't know"

"Oh is it, good cos' I want him to know everything!"

"Leave her alone Sparks. I thought this was about you and me. About who's got balls?" I said trying to get him to concentrate on me. I had to get that gun.

"It is, but there's one thing I want to know first. Did she ever suck your dick G-man?" He looked at me waiting for an answer "You know she would never suck mine." He shook her face like a rag doll as he spoke, squeezing her cheeks. "The bitch would never suck my tings, not even a lick. I couldn't teach her that, but there's one thing I did teach her to suck. Love taking a lick, ain't that right, Alicia."

Holding the gun to Alicia, Sparks reached into his pocket. In that moment, his whole motion came like a reoccurring nightmare. It was like scene I played out in my dreams many a night. We stood on opposite sides, he held Alicia as a hostage over me. As the dim light shone on Sparks' face, he produced a handful of white rocks. For the first time I recognised him for what he was. A nemesis sent to thwart me like the Slave Master from my dream.

"You see, these rocks here, Double G, they give me power. Power over you, power over her, power over Mel, Kooba, all of you fucks that want to escape your miserable lives. I owned you. Why? Because you all did as I ordered, just to get your hands on it. It makes no difference whether it was to smoke or to sell, I owned you pussies. You were mine to fuck wid." Sparks' eyes where like firing infernos, ignited with pernicious delight. "But every so often, one of you gets smart and I have to teach you a lesson. You see, G-man; I know all your weaknesses. See these," he gestured to the rocks. "They're Alicia's weakness, and she's your weakness. It was the same thing with Stevie, only his weakness was his mum." Sparks grinned. "You 'member what I did to Stevie, innit? You wrote enough about it."

I hung my head ashamed that I hadn't done enough to help Stevie.

"Well it's the same thing I'm gonna do to you. I'm gonna test your weaknesses." He threw the rocks at me and reached into his pocket. "I noticed you broke the last pipe. Don't break this one." He tossed over a small pipe and a piece of cigarette. "Pick them up," he ordered.

"Now what?" I asked.

"Wharm, to you star? What, you never blaze before? Fucking light that shit up."

"No," Alicia began crying. "Don't do it."

"Be quiet," Sparks covered her mouth. "Let him do his own thing. C'mon, G, light that shit up, or I'll blow a hole in you and her."

I had no choice. I prepared the pipe. I lit the cigarette and drew on the cancer stick till the end burnt bright. I flicked the tip of the ash into the pipe and fixed the first rock on top of the ash. Putting the pipe to my lips, I lit the rock and sucked. I closed my eyes and in inhaled. I heard the first crickle, crackle of the yeng as as the smoke filled my lungs.

"That's it, G-man! Smoke that shit till your lung clapse!" Sparks cheered.

I opened my eyes and looked at him. He lent down and gave Alicia a victory kiss as she sobbed between his legs. He was right. He knew my weakness and now I knew hers. I drew the pipe again. The yeng was strong. It didn't take long for me to feel the effects. I smoked more feeling charged, energised, and alert. I watched Sparks rubbing his hands all over Alicia's body, touching and molesting her.

I'm gonna kill you I thought as the crack took over. It was potent. It was what I needed. *I'm gonna kill you.* I drew again.

"Easy, G," Sparks revelled. "You're feeling the lick already. Good, now pass it to Alicia"

I glanced at her. Sparks still had his gun arm round her neck. "Hold on, one more." I said. Sparks laughed. Gloating, he looked down at Alicia.

"You see that bitch. That's power. The man wants another lick."

As he looked up I stepped over to pass him the pipe and grabbed his outstretched arm. I pulled him towards me. At the same time Alicia bit his hand, making him drop the gun. It was time. The fight had begun. I leapt on him, but Spark's was fast, He was vicious in his attack as we wrestled on the floor. I struggled. My underwear was still wrapped around my legs. It left me exposed. I tried to put Sparks in a headlock, but he threw a punch to my face that dazed me. He climbed on top of me, pinning me to the floor. Throwing quick combinations of blows to my head he shouted. "C'mon then bredrin!"

Screaming, Alicia tried to pull him off me, but he flung her aside. I needed another advantage I was taking blows. Luckily the yeng had me rushing. I tried pulling his jumper over his head. He was too fast and resisted. He swung at me again. Then a blow hit me between the eyes and the pain shot to my nose. I felt blinded, as Sparks tried to knock me down and get up. I held on to his legs. I couldn't let him get up. My legs were still trapped in my trousers. I needed to keep him grounded. I bit his leg like a dog gnawing on a bone. He screamed out and kicked me in the face with his other foot. This time the force was too much. I was heading out of the fight. I couldn't see. Then suddenly I heard a bang. I felt liquid and fragments of bone splashed over my face. Then BANG! BANG BANG! It came again in rapid succession.

Three more shots had been fired and the smell of gunpowder filled the room. I lay still thinking, *have I been shot*. Sparks body lay on top of me like a shield. I was frightened to move. "Alicia, don't shoot!" I screamed from beneath Sparks.

The handgun made a heavy thud as it hit the floor. Pushing Spark's body off me, I looked up at Alicia with my blood covered face. I pulled my trousers up and kicked the lifeless lump away. Alicia dropped to my side. Hugging me she started frantically checking for bullet wounds. Her body was shaking all over.

"I'm alright" I said. Her hands kept searching. I grabbed her wrist, "Alicia look at me I'm alright."

Alicia's mind was somewhere else as she stared ghostly into my eyes. She looked at Sparks' body. Blood poured out of his ears and the hole in his head. The exit wounds looked nothing like those of an action film. The gun was still smoking from the barrel. Alicia buried her face in my chest and started wailing. I held her rocking backwards and forwards trying to calm her down. "Sshhhussh, its over now, it's over." I said as she thumped on my chest. "It's over."

An hour later the flat was sealed off and crawling with police and forensics. The blue lights of the police cars flashed across the faces of the onlooking crowd as Spark's body was brought out and declared deceased. Less than a mile away, I sat in the Chelsea and Westminster hospital waiting with my mother and Andrea when Mel arrived. "G. I came as soon as possible. I did everything you said. It's all sorted. How's Alicia?"

"The doctor said she's fine." I replied.

Mel looked at me sensing there was more. I couldn't speak to him. My mouth opened, but only a bunch of stutters, and foreign sounds protruded. Dropping to the chair I broke down and cried like a baby in my mother's arms. Andrea took Mel to the side.

"Drea, what's going on?" He asked. "Alicia gone be alright innit?"

"She's fine, but they're not sure about the baby."

"Baby! Gil never said they were having a baby."

"He never knew. We're not sure whether Alicia knew either." Andrea explained, as two police officers came on the ward.

"Hold on ah minute!" Mel shouted to the two policemen. They ignored him and handcuffed me. I remember my mother burst into hysterics as they arrested me.

"Una hav' no respect. That's my son, leave him alone" She shouted. "He's done noting wrong, leave him alone!"

Andrea tried to restrain her. They were just trying to do their job. I remember one of them said sorry as the other read me my rights. "Gilyan Gates you are being arrested for the murder of Darren Sparkton. You do not have to say anything, but anything you do say will be recorded and given as evidence."

"Sorry Madame, if you could just move out the way"

"What nick you taking him to?"

"You bastards, you white bastards! He hasn't done anything."

"Mum stop it, they're only doing their job."

"If you don't calm down madame, I'll be forced to arrest you."

"Don't say anything, G, I'm calling the solicitors now bro. Don't say nothing."

I could hear all their voices, Mum, Andrea, Mel, and the police officers as they lead me away. All those voices, but none of them the voice I wanted to hear. I was so scared I closed my eyes and pictured Alicia speaking to me "It's okay to be scared, Gil, I'm here with you. I love you, Gil, don't you love me?"

"Yes, yes I do."

*

As King finished the story there was uncomfortable silence. Neither Ivan nor Dorian knew what to say, so they remained quiet. They both fidgeted and stared down at the floor. Finally Dorian was the first to speak.

"Wow," he puffed. "That's mad, I'm sorry to hear that shit."

"It's not your business to feel sorry, D." King replied.

"Yeah, but you were only trying to protect your girl. That's fucked up."

"For real," Ivan found his mouth. "How comes they didn't try you for manslaughter, why murder?"

"After my initial interview, the charges were swaying towards manslaughter, but the police weren't stupid. On investigation they found none of the forensic evidence matched up with the witness reports. The investigating detective knew something was wrong. Alicia and my statements were identical. Almost word for word he said and they too didn't match the witness reports either."

King peered at his chessboard, then beckoned Ivan and Dorian. "Which move should I make?" He pointed at two pieces. "That one or that one."

"Move that one," Dorian said "Loose the knight and save you're queen,"

Ivan disagreed. He spun the board for a moment then spun it back. He looked hard at the pieces, then knocked over King's black king. "You need to start a new game. You've already lost this game in three or four moves, whichever choice you make."

"Hmm, I'm glad you noticed." King began resetting the board.

"Fuck that, what happened next?" Dorian urged King to continue his story.

"In the aftermath I'd panicked. I'd made a phone call before phoning the police then took a gamble. I started throwing blood on Alicia's clothes. I knew that the forensic team would analyse the blood splatters on our clothes and in the flat. This way they wouldn't be able to tell where we were standing, or who fired the shots. I moved the body to confuse them even more. I tried wiping down some of the floor as well. It seemed okay at first, but one witness said he remembered hearing a fifth shot fired roughly ten minutes after the first four."

"How comes?" Dorian asked.

"I fired an extra shot so the gunpowder was on both our hands. The police couldn't prove who fired the gun. But that wasn't the problem. When Alicia had fallen unconscious at the hospital they had to examine her for the baby's sake. Everything had happened so fast that Alicia hadn't told me Sparks had raped her. The torn tissue on her vagina wall was consistent to rape. The autopsy on Sparks' body noted that he had sexual intercourse before the time of death. It had also indicted that he had been intoxicated with narcotics. Blood samples also taken from Alicia, indicated the intoxication of drugs. So the Crown prosecution felt they had enough to amount to conspiracy charges between Alicia and I. They conducted an elaborate story that at some point Alicia had been raped by Sparks' earlier in the night. After I returned the three of us had been at one point been smoking together and I had shot Spark's in a jealous rage after hearing of the rape."

"What!" Dorian said in disgust. "What kinda e-dyat story is that? They can't prove that."

"Apparently the fifth shot can," King continued. "Because it was fired so long after the first four, added to fact Sparks was shot from behind, it was suggested I executed Sparks, equalling murder and conspiracy. They said I had coached Alicia on what to say as to make it look like self-defence, then broken the doorframe and tampered with evidence to add weight to the story and confusion."

"That's ridiculous." Dorian seethed. "Fucking, CPS."

"I know, but my barrister warned, supported with the tampering of evidence, told to a jury of 12 TV soap addicts, it might be strong enough to convince guilt of conspiracy rather than murder."

"It's true," Ivan said. "Conspiracy's a deeper charge. Both you and Alicia woulda been missin'."

"That's right," King nodded. "So, against advice, I agreed to plead guilty to murder if there were no charges brought against Alicia."

"Why?" Dorian asked confused. "You could have probably bust case or got done for manslaughter. There was still enough evidence to prove reasonable doubt."

"No, he couldn't." Ivan interrupting. Had he not been thinking about Jade so much, he might not been able to fully understand. "He had to protect his queen and his baby." Looking, at King Ivan comprehended the meaning in his name change. "It's a king's job to protect his queen. Going to trial woulda meant risking Alicia going down as well. A king doesn't do that. It's better to start a new game."

Ivan looked at the chessboard. "You set up that board like that on purpose, didn't you? It was a test."

"No it wasn't a test." King smiled "It was an example to help you understand. Sometimes life's about starting a new game."

"Is that why you changed your name?" Ivan asked as the wiry frame of Mr Jones opened the cell door. "Bang up in five minutes gentlemen get your hot water now or go without."

Irritated at the intrusion, the three men gave Jones a look that told him, his presence wasn't welcome. King waited for Jones to disappear before he continued.

"Partly," He said. "It was Alicia's idea. She told me I was her king and that everyone should recognise the King in me. Especially people like that." He pointed to the empty space where Mr Jones had just stood. "I guess that's the beauty of it."

King grinned. He stood up collecting his mug and flask. "The day I was sentenced for the murder of Darren Sparkton, was the same day the slave in Gilyan Gates was exiled and crowned King. The moment I stepped inside this prison I began a new game, a new start, but that's another story hey?" King said escorting the men to the door. "Go and get your water. We'll talk more tomorrow."

As Dorian and Ivan left the cell, King paused and looked at himself in the mirror. He barely recognised the man that looked back. He rubbed the hard follicles on his neck remembering when he first entered jail he could hardly grow a beard. Now he had to scrape his face everyday. He sighed feeling aged, especially now he had placed his whole life in front of the two men. His wishes, hopes, dreams, and fears. It was a lot to fathom for his companions. He hoped the information had been digested. He hoped he had done the right thing.

"What'd you think?" he asked the ghost of Gilyan Gates. "Soon, give them time." His reflection said back. Looking around, King visualised the Old Slave somewhere in the cell smiling with approval. Shutting the door, he went downstairs and joined the other prisoners by the hot water urn.

EPILOGUE:
A NEW JOURNEY

King looked around at the number of men that now mingled in the newly renamed BBCP corner of the yard. Their number had risen and more of the men in the jail were beginning to show their alliance by wearing armbands. Standing away from the gathering he observed as Ivan and Dorian led the noisy debate over the murder of a black trainee barrister in police custody and whether the criminal reputation of his brother had anything to do with it. King was proud of the two young men. Together they brought a new energy to inmates old and young. They were beginning to establish a new discipline among the younger inmates that earned their peers respect. Every time a new inmate entered, they were bound, within three days, to ask about the men in the black, green and red armbands. With the support they were receiving from the outside members of the BBCP. They were able to spread the message and supply leaflets and knowledge. And as members were shipped out to new prisons, so the message was cast upon new ears. It still bothered King that Haughton Hill frequently refused to supply a Black history course and self-development program. He thought it would be something their group had to work harder on.

As the debate simmered into general chat, Ivan came over to his mentor.

"What's happening with you today? No words of wisdom from the good old King?"

"Hey less of the old," King said putting Ivan in a headlock. They carried on play fighting until King was out of breath. "Stop, stop sit down for a minute."

Sitting down, Ivan laughed at King "Oi, cuzzy, you're getting old."

"You think I'm the only one? Look at you and him," King pointed over to Dorian. "You man are getting old too. You're maturing. I like that." he said trying to catch his breath. "I noticed how people listen to you. You both speak with passion. That's a special gift. You gotta use it properly."

"How'd you mean?" Ivan asked.

"You gotta learn to channel your passion for something positive," King looked up toward the sky. The warm sun beamed down on his face.

"You know I never had a little brother. It's funny, now I feel like I got two. Both you and Dorian got so much potential and so much ahead of you, that sometimes I fear for you. Look at him." King gestured over to Dorian, who was now freestyling for the gathering.

"He's going home in two weeks. When he leaves here things are gonna be so different. There gonna be worse than you can imagine. All the things he's learnt here, there going to be challenged and put on the line. I keep telling him it's easy in here. In jail all the temptations are stripped from us. We've made it even easier for ourselves,"

"How?" Ivan asked.

King tugged on Ivan's armband. "We can see our allies. Out there you don't know who's who. That's when people see how strong you are. That's when we're gonna be tested."

"Don't worry about Dorian," Ivan looked over at his friend. "He's a madman. He loves his music too much to comeback here. They'll have to kill him first or build a recording studio."

"I hope not," King smiled "I keep telling that boy he's not only gonna be the voice of a generation, but the voice of the revolution."

"Oh it's you that keeps filling his head wid dat shit." Ivan joked. "King, you got him running around the cell, like some mad wannabe Tupac. Always talking 'bout exceptional rhymes, exceptional beats. What's all that?"

"Ivan, have you forgotten already?" King laughed. "The black race will be saved by its exceptional people. Hence the exceptional rhymes, exceptional beats."

Ivan shook his head and rolled his eyes "Like I said, madman."

They both started laughing. When they finished, Ivan caught King gazing at the high fenced wall that surrounded the prison.

"You ever think about going home?" Ivan asked.

"Not yet." King replied. "I got a long way to go before home, so I keep my eye on the journey."

"I hear that," Ivan picked up a stone and tossed it. "King lemme ask you a question?"

"Go on."

"Remember that night Alicia shot Sparks, how'd you feel?"

King took his time to answer. "Honestly, unsatisfied."

"Why?"

"Sparks wanted to die. I don't know why, but he wanted to die. Usually he would've had someone with him like Kooba or Mel with him. That night he was alone. I don't know, maybe he wasn't thinking straight, but he must've realized given the opportunity I'd kill him." King picked up a stone and tossed it as well.

"I still wonder to this day what went through his mind that night. The man was a control freak. I mean, Sparks was so destructive and psychotic he'd do anything to prove he was in control, that he still had power. So I guess maybe in his mind whether he killed me, or I killed him, didn't matter, everyone's lives would be destroyed by his doing."

"So you saying Sparks won. He managed to destroy your life."

"Ivan, people like Sparks never win. Destiny is a force that no power can contain. Its preordained, destined to happen."

Ivan looked at King confused. "I'm lost. You're saying you were destined to come jail."

"Not exactly." King tried to explain. "You remember after Alicia shot Sparks I made a phone call, but to who?"

Ivan thought about it. "I don't know. Me and Dorian always thought you made a call to Mel that's why he turned up at the hospital."

"I did. And what did he say when he arrived, 'everything is sorted'."

"Why'd he say that?"

King chuckled to himself "Sparks thought he had power over people, but he was wrong. He didn't understand we'd worked for him for how many years. We knew everything about his operation, including where he hid his money. Destiny proclaimed that Sparks' money would finance the dreams of The BBCP to be realised and my family would be looked after. Now can you understand destiny? Everybody has their role to play and everyone controls his or her own destiny. Jail was just a by-product. I still got a lot of shit to smile about."

"For real," Ivan touch fist with King as Dorian came jogging over. He pushed Ivan in the head before sitting down.

"What's going on?" he said.

"Nothing" King put his arms around his two companions. "I was just telling Ivan how proud I am to see how much progress you lot have made. You're the future voice and generals of the BBCP." King squeezed both arms trying to put them in headlocks.

"Wharm to you man!" Ivan pushed King off. "Something excite you today or what?"

"Something excite me? What about you?" King nudged Dorian "Oi, D you saw your bredrin here, run out the cell quick time when the mail come today, yeah."

"Oh yeah!" Dorian grinned. "I almost forgot ta bumba!! He never even said who the letter was from?"

"Don't watch dat. That's my business." Ivan grinned.

"Shut up and tell us," King said. "What you tryna hide? It must be from one of your man-bitches, you faggot."

Dorian started cracking up laughing, and he and King started ribbing Ivan on the content of the letter.

"Hol'on, hol' on." Ivan buckled under the pressure "Okay I'll tell you, you flipping parasites. It was from Jade."

"Easyyy!" Dorian said getting excited. "What'd she say?"

"You know the usual, this and that." Ivan played aloof. King punched him in the leg "Aahh 'llow that, blood."

"Speak up den." King ordered. "What she say?"

"Nah, she says that she realises that I'm sorry" Ivan said coyly "And believes that I truly do love her. She said she might consider another chance if I can prove that I'm gonna change. She said that she's coming with Jayvan on Sunday to see me."

"Heavy!" Dorian said hugging Ivan.

"Okay it's only a maybe," Ivan pushed him away "We're not back together yet."

King shook Ivan's hand "It's a start, bruv, that what's important, a new start. That's what we all need."

Ivan nodded his head in agreement. "I know man, that's what I really want." He paused looking for more words. "I kinda wanna thank you mans as well. I mean without you's, I was really slippin', falling. I feel like both you man put your hand out and caught me. If I never get the chance to show you, I want you man to know I really appreciate that shit."

"That's what we're here for brother." King smiled.

"Yeah," Dorian added. "It's nothing. Just make sure you catch me if I fall."

"Of course!" Ivan beamed.

As the screw rang the bell signalling the end of exercise, they got up and walked towards the building. Looking at Ivan and Dorian play fighting, King knew that one-day they would both leave the prison. Haughton Hill was just a resting-place for lost travellers. However, he thought to himself *as long as they stop here as slaves, I'll teach them how to leave as soldiers, warriors, and Kings.* Today two slaves had been selected for a new start. Today heralded a new dawn for the journey of a King.

THE END

SPECIAL PREVIEW

CATCH ME IF I FALL

by D.D. Armstrong

The following extract is from *'Catch Me If I Fall'* the stunning sequel to D.D. Armstrong's first book *'Lynch's Road.'* The story picks up almost twelve months after Dorian has been released from jail. While Ivan and King continue to fight the Haughton Hill regime and old prison rivalries, Dorian has been struggling to rebuild his life. Determined to concentrate on music, things seem to be running smoothly, until Dorian meets up with old associates. Soon the allure of easy money and Shottin' begin to tempt Dorian and things heighten when family issues arise. To overcome new enemies and stay out of jail, Dorian will need his wits about him to identify friend from foe in a deadly game of survival.

In this thrilling follow-up D.D. Armstrong delves deep into the psyche of a young ex-con and the prison experience to construct another multifaceted instalment from London's inner-city underworld.

PROLOGUE:

The pitter-patter of rain bounced against, Ivan's window. Lying on his bunk he stared at the half moon that peered through the murky clouds and barred windows of Haughton Hill. His heavy eyelids bared the burden of anxiety for all was not well. *What have you gotten yourself into D you promised me you'd stay out of trouble.* Ivan couldn't stop thinking where his former cellmate was. How'd he get himself in so much trouble? Climbing from his bed he walked over to the window. Opening it, he reached through the bars to feel the rain gently soak his hand. Watching the water slip through his fingertips and into the darkness, he made a tight fist. He banged his head against the bars in frustration. Each droplet represented his companion falling from his grasp. Looking up towards the sky, Ivan prayed for the safe Journey of his friend. *Don't worry D, King promised me he's gonna sort everything out he promised me. You hold tight wherever you are.*

The sound of Jay-z *'You Must Love Me'* played repeatedly on the ghetto blaster. The night was cold and wet. A chilling breeze blew through the open window, blowing the scent of shame and fear. The street lamp from outside cast shadows and silhouettes of passing figures on the wall like an Indian puppet show. Dorian sat cradling himself in the corner of the room. Rocking back and forth he knew the end was near. Reaching into the pocket of his tracksuit bottoms, he pulled out three notes. Looking at the face of Isaac Newton, the Duke of Wellington and Florence Nightingale printed on the outdated money he cursed them one by one. *You all lied; you all played your part in this. You conspired, you all plotted to deceive me why?* There was no reply. Dorian's words had fallen on deaf ears. The eyes printed on the three pieces of the bank of England sterling, stared back at him with empty expressions.
From somewhere outside Dorian could hear the piercing cries of a cat. Covering his ears he shuffled in the dark trying to hide. Knocking over the table the room became silent as the hi-fi crashed to the floor. Panicking Dorian rushed over to close the window. Fastening the lock he watched as the slender bodied feline scaled its way up the building. Moving like a phantom the black beast paused to stare at him. The yellow eyes, which had haunted his soul, now stared at him seeking vengeance. Fleeing behind the tall wardrobe his heart raced out of control. *Please don't let him get me please I*

promise I'll be good I swear I'll be good. In a deep sweat, Dorian had already stripped down to his bare chest. Quickly reaching for his t-shirt he wiped his brow. Sitting motionless he tried to convince himself *if I'm quiet it will go away, yeah that's right it will go away.* But tonight none of Dorian's problems were going to go away. He had backed himself into a corner and the gods did not favor him. Tears began to swell in his eyes as he mumbled words of repentance. The water began to cloud his vision as his nostrils burnt with a numb sensation. He could feel the warm substance that ran out his nose and into his mouth. Wiping the thick blood with his t-shirt. He attempted to stop the bleeding. A nosebleed was the last of his worries. For a moment everything in the room was quiet. Only the sound of Dorian's breath could be heard and the passing of traffic outside. *I know you're out there you can't fool me and I know you've come for me.* Then the creature at the window as though it could read his thoughts answered. Scratching its long claws against the glass creating a gut wrenching sound. Holding the money and the T-shirt tight in his hand Dorian shivered with fear. He began to panic wrapping the T-shirt round his arm as the scratching increased. The fiendish cries of the cat became aggressive. Bellowing at Dorian to let it inside. Scared stiff Dorian dare not move. Yet the cat kept scratching and clawing. Peering around the wardrobe, Dorian saw his nemesis extended body clawing away at the window frame like the goddess of retribution. The velvet black fur was soaked in patches of blood. While a shoelace hung round its neck like a noose. The cat's high-pitch cry, wailed through the air like the call of a banshee. Petrified Dorian screamed from his hiding place

"WHERE ARE YOU HELP ME!! HELP MAKE IT GO AWAY."

But no one came to his rescue. The cavalry had been dispatched elsewhere.

"Sing a song, please just one song. I promise I'll be good," he whispered trying to compose himself; but nothing came to mind. His mind was blank a wilderness baron. No song or lyric would enter.

"COME ON THEN WHERE ARE YOU? YOU'RE ALWAYS SINGING IN MY HEAD, ALWAYS GOT SOMETHING TO SING ABOUT WHERE ARE YOU NOW!" Shrieking at the top of his voice Dorian's emotions consumed his mind leaving him with one train of thought *I hate you I hate you all.*

Ignited with anger. Dorian's hatred forced him to his feet. Enraged he jumped out of his hiding place finally ready to face his tormentor. The cat was gone.

Spinning around in a circle. Dorian frantically checked the room to see if the animal had somehow magically gained entrance. *He's gone, he's gone.*
Relief came quick and Dorian broke out in a fit of hysteric laughter before flaking out on the bed. Reaching under the pillow he pulled out the bulky form of a Smith & Wesson pistol. Holding the heavy weapon close to his chest, he thought to himself. *Yeah it'll all be over soon and I won't owe anybody shit.* Closing his eyes Dorian listened to the rain that began to beat against the window.

I hear the rain beating against my window/ carrying the lost tears of my kinfolk/ my childhood fears sway on a swing rope/ now the only fears I have are those of a thin hope/ my journey was like walking on a thin rope/ so guess who's dreams went up in a big smoke/ I never really checked the big scope/ Asking King why maintaining was such a big joke/ maybe cos' cause my forefathers were brought over in a big boat/ or maybe there's no god/ there's no big bloke/ so who's gonna stop me from shottin' dese drugs/ and feeling like a big bloke/ Believe I ain't got no one to give hope/ so I wash away my opportunities like raindrops on my window...

Smiling as lyrics began to flood his brain. Dorian sat waiting for his phone call.

***

SMASH & GRAB

LOOK OUT FOR FORTHCOMING TITLES @
WWW.SMASHANDGRABBOOKS.COM